Tenacious Love

RAMONA FLIGHTNER

Grizzly Damsel Publishing
MISSOULA, MONTANA

Ramona Flightner/ Grizzly Damsel Publishing
P.O. Box 624
East Boston, MA 02128
www.ramonaflightner.com

Publisher's Note: This is a work of fiction. Names, characters, places, and incidents are a product of the author's imagination. Locales and public names are sometimes used for atmospheric purposes. Any resemblance to actual people, living or dead, or to businesses, companies, events, institutions, or locales is completely coincidental.

Book Layout ©2013 BookDesignTemplates.com

Cover Design: Jennifer Quinlan

Ordering Information:
Quantity sales. Special discounts are available on quantity purchases by corporations, associations, and others. For details, contact the "Special Sales Department" at the address above.

Tenacious Love / Ramona Flightner -- 1st ed.
ISBN Print: 978-1-945609-01-5
ISBN ebook:978-1-945609-00-8

To My Grandparents:
Grandpa Joe, Grandma Kay and Grandma Ruth,
You were my first storytellers and fostered in me a love of family.
You encouraged me to excel and cultivated my natural curiosity.
You inspired me with your strong social justice values
and dedication to those not as blessed as you.
I will miss you. Always

CAST OF CHARACTERS

BOSTON:

Richard McLeod- brother to Gabriel, married to Florence, blacksmith
Florence Butler – married to Richard, used to teach with Clarissa
Sophronia Chickering- suffragist, mentor to the McLeod women
Aidan McLeod-uncle to the McLeod boys, married to Delia, father to Zylphia, excellent businessman.
Delia McLeod- married to Aidan, mother to Zylphia, still aids the orphanage
Zylphia McLeod- daughter to Delia and Aidan, suffragist and painter,
Owen Hubbard: successful Boston businessman, interested in Zylphia
Theodore Goff- social misfit, inventor, from England, Zylphia's friend.
Parthena Tyler- Zylphia's friend; excellent pianist
Rowena Clement- Zylphia's friend, helps teach her social norms.
Morgan Wheeler- Parthena's nemesis, successful Boston businessman.

MONTANA:

<u>Missoula</u>:
Gabriel McLeod- cabinetmaker, married to Clarissa
Clarissa Sullivan McLeod- married to Gabriel, used to work as a teacher and a librarian, suffragist
Jeremy McLeod- cabinetmaker, works with his brother Gabriel at his shop, married to Savannah
Savannah Russell McLeod- suffragist, married to Jeremy,
Melinda Sullivan McLeod- Savannah and Jeremy's adopted daughter, Colin/ Clarissa/ Patrick's much younger sister
Colin Sullivan-Clarissa and Patrick's brother, blacksmith
Ronan O'Bara- a McLeod friend, a cobbler, injured in mine in Butte, uses wheelchair
Lucas Russell- Savannah's brother, a famous pianist, travels the world performing.
Mr. A.J. Pickens- close friend and mentor to Clarissa, used to work at the Book Depository and Library with her
Araminta- friend to the McLeods, helps care for their children and clean their homes
Hester Loken- new librarian in town, championed by Mr. Pickens
Mrs. Bouchard- sister to Mrs. Vaughan, busybody in Missoula

Mrs. Vaughan- sister to Mrs. Bouchard, busybody in Missoula, blames Clarissa for her family's misfortunes

Butte:
Patrick Sullivan- Clarissa and Colin's brother, accountant
Samuel Sanders – Patrick's boss and friend, lives in Butte
Fiona O'Leary- Samuel Sander's secretary, and Patrick's friend
Elias Laine- miner from Finntown, Patrick's friend

Darby:
Sebastian Carling- runs the sawmill in Darby, married to Amelia, great friend to the McLeod's
Amelia Egan Carling- close friend to the McLeod's – lives in Darby

CHAPTER ONE

The day before President-Elect Woodrow Wilson's inauguration, Clarissa McLeod gathered with other female marchers, all clad in white dresses with purple capes. Alice Paul, the parade's organizer and a leading suffragist, had designed the day's official uniform. A boisterous crowd had burgeoned to watch women march to demand the right to vote. Police stood alongside Pennsylvania Avenue, alternately pushing men behind the low metal chain off the parade route, chatting with onlookers and bemoaning the need to patrol two marches in two consecutive days. Red, white and blue patriotic bunting hung from the balconies and banisters of the buildings lining the avenue in readiness for the next day's inaugural parade, and lent a festive air. A group from a local women's club hawked sandwiches, doughnuts and pies.

However, the most popular item sold this day—by the newspaperwomen in their purple, white and green sashes—was the parade's program. Its cover depicted a woman herald on a white steed proclaiming, "Votes for Women," as she blew her trumpet. Inside, a detailed map showed Inez Milholland, a suffragist and labor lawyer, would lead the parade, riding a white steed, followed by National American Woman Suffrage Association officers. Four sections of marchers would come next: representatives from countries already granting women the right to vote, the pioneers of the US suffrage movement, professional women in favor of the vote and then male supporters of suffrage.

Along the side streets of Pennsylvania Avenue, the marchers, numerous bands and floats awaited their signal to move. The white horse shifted from side to side, its hostler rubbing its nose to calm it. Miss Milholland, dressed in white, mingled with dignitaries at the front of the parade. Clarissa smiled, wishing for a moment she could be a spectator to watch Miss Milholland as she led the parade down Pennsylvania Avenue. As Clarissa made her way past floats and bands, she passed a large double-sided placard, the length of a wagon, which proclaimed *We Demand an Amendment to the Constitution of the United States Enfranchising the Women of this Country.*

Clarissa approached her designated area, choosing to stand in the professional group, as she had recently resigned as a librarian in Montana and had been a teacher before her marriage. She mingled with doctors, businesswomen, lawyers and nurses. Plus she could walk beside her close friend and sister-in-law Florence Butler McLeod. Florence had taught with her at the immigrant school in Boston before she married Richard McLeod. The group of women who had walked all the way from New York City to Washington, DC, would march directly in front of their group, while elaborate floats would bring a decorative and festive end to the parade.

"Clarissa!"

She spun, attempting to locate the caller of her name. Clarissa stood on her tiptoes for a moment and then raced forward, pushing through the crowd. "Flo," she gasped a second before she threw herself in Florence's arms.

Florence's curly black hair was tamed in a tight bun, while her round face had become a little rounder since Clarissa had last seen her.

They rocked to and fro for a few moments before separating. "Oh, how I've missed you, Rissa. I can't believe it's been eleven years since I saw you in Boston. I wish your children were here so I could meet them too," Florence said. Her smile dimmed as she noted the tightness around Clarissa's mouth and the effort she made to smile. "I see we have much to discuss."

"Where's Sophie?" Clarissa glanced over Florence's shoulder, expecting to see their fierce suffragist mentor and friend.

"She's at the culmination of the march. She said she didn't have the energy to walk such a great distance, and she wanted to have the distinction of watching our triumphant arrival." Florence stumbled into Clarissa when jostled by a few of the women marchers preparing to line up. "Richard and Gabriel decided to sit with her, not march at the back of the parade with the other men. They said they wanted to cheer as we arrived."

"I was sorry I could not see you yesterday," Clarissa murmured as she half listened to instructions to form rows four abreast and to prepare to march forward in a few minutes. Rather than the white cap most women wore, Clarissa donned a purple hat with a yellow ribbon set at a jaunty angle atop her chestnut-colored chignon.

"I wasn't feeling well." At Clarissa's inquisitive stare when Florence blushed, she whispered, "I'm expecting again."

"Oh, how wonderful! Maybe a girl to go along with your five boys?" Clarissa pulled Flo into a tight embrace. "I can't imagine Richard was pleased you insisted on marching."

"No, he wanted me to sit next to Savannah but relented when he realized our impending argument would be far worse for the baby than me walking a few miles."

"I know Sav's disappointed not to be marching, but she's simply too weak." Clarissa shook her head as she thought of her other sister-in-law and cousin, Savannah Russell McLeod. "I still can't believe she insisted on traveling all this way."

"Jeremy was at a loss as to how to encourage her to care for herself when I saw him yesterday," Florence said. "I haven't seen such a hopeless look come into his eyes since his return from the Philippines."

"Savannah's persistent disappointment is devastating to them."

Florence gripped Clarissa's arm, correctly interpreting the well of emotion behind Clarissa's words. "I have a feeling it's not just Savannah's."

They took their places in the middle of their group, listening to the nearest band's discordant notes as it tuned up. When given a signal to begin, the band played a rousing John Phillips Sousa march, earning cheers from the crowd. The parade participants moved forward and, after a few minutes, marched down the middle of Pennsylvania Avenue. Clarissa waved her small yellow pennant and smiled, her spirit light, as the thick crowds behind the feeble chain barricades cheered while they walked past. Clarissa gripped Florence's hand, and they shared a smile, both overwhelmed and unable to speak at that moment.

"Where's Zylphia?" Clarissa asked. "I thought she'd traveled down with you, Sophie and Richard."

"She did. She's one of the beauties at the Treasury Department pageant. We should see her shortly, although I can only imagine how cold she'll be in that flimsy outfit they instructed her to wear."

"Is that why we didn't see her last night?"

"Yes. She had to practice the dance routine for all of them to do. Miss Paul has it timed perfectly so that their performance will culminate when Miss Milholland and the front of the parade marches past the Treasury Department. It should be something to see!"

"You know I'm thrilled to march. However, a part of me wishes I could see the parade too."

"I know," Florence said with a long sigh. "Savannah and Sophie are lucky to observe."

"Well, this way, we'll be able to share our experiences, as they'll all be slightly different. Even Zee will have something distinct to tell us about the day." Clarissa paused for a moment as their forward progression stalled. Her attention wandered, missing her children who were in Montana, missing Gabriel ... even though he was with her in Washington, DC. She shook her head to banish the thought. "How was Zylphia chosen?"

"You know Sophie. She's acquainted with everyone, and, when she discovered this march was planned, she obtained hotel rooms, a plum role for Zylphia and then ordered us to attend."

"I think she'd phrase it as a strongly worded invitation," Clarissa said with a giggle. "Although I am thankful she was able to book hotel rooms for us on the eve of the inauguration."

"And at one of the nicest hotels in the city." Florence looped her arm through Clarissa's, frowning as they swayed in place.

After about an hour, when they should have marched at least a mile, they had barely moved six blocks. During their slow movement forward, the broad lines of women four abreast in front of them had funneled into a narrow line, further barring their progression. Clarissa shared a worried glance with Florence, before remembering the words of one of the organizers *to smile and to project confidence.*

Clarissa straightened her shoulders, smiled and attempted to walk with a bold purpose. She nodded to one of the policemen at the side of the parade route and edged her way forward. However, each stride became shorter—to the point she was marching in place. Clarissa noted that the policemen on the sides, who were to separate the marchers from the unruly crowds, were thinning. One even appeared to be jeering at the marchers.

"Where are your husbands?" a man yelled in the increasingly restive crowd.

"I doubt they could get husbands," another jeered.

A balled-up wad of paper hit Clarissa, and she jumped but continued to smile and wave her pennant. She noted Florence doing the same, when, in an instant, they were surrounded by men, pushing and prodding them. Clarissa used her small pennant as a club to shove men away from her. One man spit on Florence, who reared back as a chicoreed splat of tobacco marred her cheek and the front of her white dress and purple coat.

"Flo!" Clarissa shrieked, momentarily distracted from protecting herself as she reached for her sister-in-law. She thrust out an arm, looping her hand through Florence's arm to keep them together, only to be grabbed by a pair of strong hands. At his strong tug, she was separated from Florence. Another man grasped Clarissa's pennant, and she didn't have the strength to hold on to it.

Suddenly Clarissa was jostled, encircled by a crowd of leering men, with not even her pennant for protection. She attempted to still her breathing but continued to pant, watching with wild eyes as men poked and prodded her. She had nowhere to turn for safety, and she pushed away hands touching her skirts or flicking at her purple cape. When she brushed a man's hand from her hat, she was slapped, her cheek aflame with pain, the man muttering that a woman such as her should be thankful for any sort of male attention.

A hand pawed her backside, and she flinched, unwittingly leaning toward a man in front of her. He jeered at her evident distress, reaching forward to tug at the front of her cape and dress. Clarissa reared backward, and his grip on her clothing tightened. She heard a loud ripping noise and glanced down at her torn bodice. She fought to rein in her panic, to find a way to fight back, determined to free herself from the mob.

All around her she heard whistles, shrieks and demands that the women be allowed to pass. No one seemed able to bring any semblance of order. One word, *hatpins*, carried on the breeze, and Clarissa thrust her elbow at a sneering man getting too near. She reached up, yanking on two long hatpins, freeing her purple hat, uncaring when it fell to the ground.

"Stay away from me!" Clarissa shrieked. Her chestnut hair remained in a tight chignon, although loose tendrils floated around her face and neck from her exertions. She grasped a hatpin in each hand and held them out toward the men circling her. One man sneered at her, his brazenness enhanced by drink, and she poked him in his hand, drawing blood. He yelped in pain and drew back. After a few more exchanges where Clarissa poked deserving men with her hatpins, the men near Clarissa kept their distance, searching for easier prey.

She turned around, frantic to find Florence. She saw her sister-in-law a few feet from her, elbowing men away from her. "Hatpins, Flo!"

Florence nodded, reaching to pull the pins from her hat. After a few well-placed piercings, Flo and Clarissa again stood next to each other. "Where are the police?" Florence asked. "Why aren't they doing anything to protect us?"

***

Zylphia McLeod inched toward a ray of sunlight to warm herself as she awaited her signal to begin her part of the allegorical dance on the treasury's steps. She was a participant in a Greek-styled play, showing the marchers and onlookers that a new period in women's history had begun. She stood alongside fifty women, facing another fifty, all in flimsy white dresses and sandals. Zylphia's jet-black hair formed a coronet on which a crown of flowers lay. However, their thin garments, suitable for a warm summer day, proved no match for the early March winds. The women and girls formed an honor guard of sorts for the main characters in the play, soon to be performed when the forefront of the parade marchers arrived.

Zylphia sighed with relief when she heard the herald of the first trumpet. With the final blast, the main performers danced. They represented Liberty, Justice, Charity, Hope and Peace, and they danced in harmony as they moved toward the front of the treasury's steps. When their dance ended, they raised their arms in triumph, expecting to see Miss Milholland and the first marchers below them. However, the street remained deserted.

After a few minutes they lowered their arms and peered up the street toward the Capitol. "That doesn't look right," Zylphia murmured to the woman standing next to her, as they broke formation and moved toward the edge of the steps. An angry roar crested and receded, depending on the wind, and the avenue was filled with an enraged mob, not the well-organized parade marchers.

"Something has gone terribly wrong," whispered the woman next to Zylphia.

***

Clarissa glared at a man smirking at her. She raised a hatpin and met his sneer with a determined glare. Slowly, step by agonizing step, they moved forward. A cold wind howled, and the day's bright rays faded. Long shadows now fell in certain places as the sun passed tall buildings, adding to the day's chill.

"At this rate, we'll reach the end of the parade route tomorrow," Florence said as she half shrieked when someone slapped her arm. She jumped away, trembling as the man gloated in his ability to unnerve her.

Clarissa shivered at a freezing gust of wind, wishing she wore something more substantial than her cape and a torn dress.

Florence saw Clarissa shiver and frowned. "Use one of the pins for your cape. Pin it closed."

"But one of the men may get ahold of a pin if he were too close again," she said. "It's not that cold." Another frigid blast of wind put to lie her statement as her teeth clattered. Clarissa pulled the purple cloak around herself, but it was more decorative than useful, and she gave up after a few moments as their forward momentum stalled.

The women near Florence and Clarissa had carved out an oasis of safety, their backs to each other as they protected themselves from any further attacks. The women held at least one hatpin in their hands, their eyes alert as they searched the crowd for any man brave enough to approach them now.

Clarissa glanced around, finally feeling safe enough to notice more than her immediate surroundings. Women lay on the cement, beaten, battered and bruised, some bleeding. Unruly men stumbled over many of them, causing further injury, while other women were fortunate enough to be helped from the ongoing mayhem. All the marchers near Clarissa carried a memento of the day's violence, from a bruise to a torn dress to a bleeding gash on a forehead. A fierce light of indignation and determination shone from their eyes as they surveyed the chaos around them.

"How could this happen?" Florence whispered. She flinched as she saw a man strike a woman with such force she fell, too. Her young daughter wailed as the man taunted her, calling her a disgrace to motherhood as he sneered over her prostrate form before kicking her stomach. Florence moved to render aid, but Clarissa gripped her arm.

"No, Flo, don't. He'll only hurt you too," Clarissa said. "Think of your babe." They watched as the woman struggled to her knees, and a pair of women closer to her than Florence and Clarissa helped her to stand. They led her through the crowd with her daughter clinging to her purple cape.

Ahead they heard a police whistle and the repeated demands to allow the women to pass, but the calls remained unheeded. The band, which had played rousing marches at the start of the parade, had dispersed into the crowd, disappearing as a morning mist when exposed to bright sunlight. Instead of uplifting songs, the roar of angry men and the shrieks of indignant women sounded on the breeze.

Suddenly a car honked behind the parade of women on the avenue, and they were forced momentarily to the side. Florence, Clarissa and the women near them cheered as a car passed with Alice Paul and Lucy Burns seated within, the car's frequent honking opening the crowd before the car. Lucy Burns leaned out the passenger window, ordering men to move aside and to allow the women to peacefully pass. Alice opened the door, her long black robes flowing as she jumped out, motioning for bystanders to move away. Another car joined the first, and a woman stood on the running board with a megaphone, ordering the onlookers to clear a path for the marchers. As a small swathe opened for them, the women hastily marched forward, filling the gap.

As they made true progress in their forward momentum, Clarissa saw groups of uniformed boys pushing and prodding men aside. The boys wielded their previously decorative staffs in a manner to clear the avenue but not to evoke more violence. "Look," she said to Florence. "It seems the Boy Scouts know what is proper, while their elders do not."

Florence shook her head ruefully and hastened to keep pace.

After a few blocks Florence gripped Clarissa's arm and motioned toward an alley with her head. An army truck had backed in there, and a group of soldiers unloaded. The women looked ahead to see their way cleared, soldiers joining the ranks of the Boy Scouts and bringing a semblance of order to the chaotic scene. The arrival of the bedraggled, weary group of suffragists at the terminus of the parade was unheralded as the grandstands were deserted.

"Hurrah," a hardy soul shouted.

Clarissa and Florence joined in the cheer, the momentary exultation easing their exhaustion.

As the crowd dispersed into the bitterly cold March evening, Clarissa gripped Florence's arm. "We did it, Flo. We made it. We showed them that women are serious about obtaining the vote."

"I doubt this parade will go down in the annals of suffragism as something to be proud of," Florence said. "What an unmitigated disaster."

They glanced around the terminal area of the parade route but didn't see tall McLeod men awaiting them.

"Flo!"

They spun to face Richard, racing toward them. He carried two heavy jackets, which he flung around their shoulders. "Richard," Florence murmured, embracing him a moment.

He traced her cheek, frowning at the dried tobacco stains there, plus on her coat and dress, before nodding. "I see you had an adventure, but you survived it."

"Where is everyone else?" Clarissa asked, shivering even with the added warmth of the jacket from Richard. They began the short walk to the nearby Willard Hotel, Richard and Florence arm in arm.

"Savannah was exhausted, while Sophie said she was frozen. Zylphia had to change out of that ridiculous costume. Jeremy and Gabriel accompanied them to the hotel, and they are awaiting the two of you in Sophie's suite," Richard said.

"I see," Clarissa murmured.

Richard patted her arm, as though understanding her disappointment that Gabriel hadn't accompanied him.

They entered the elaborate lobby of the Willard Hotel, the golden marble Corinthian pillars and marble floors gleaming under the chandelier light as they walked past potted ferns. Clarissa peered at the ornate coffered ceilings in gold and sage green before entering the elevator to Sophie's suite. Clarissa knocked on the door, quivering now as the warmth permeated her frozen limbs.

"What happened to you?" Sophie asked with a gasp as she stared at the two marchers.

Clarissa looked down at her hands clutching her coat together and glanced at Florence's stained cheek. Both women had lost their hats, and their hair was in a complete state of disarray. "Do we look that bad?" Clarissa asked, attempting to joke.

"Worse," Sophie intoned in her deep, scratchy voice, her aquamarine eyes filled with concern. "I knew it had been a difficult march, but I never imagined my girls would be so viciously abused. Alice and I will have words over the lack of police protection that she provided."

"I'm sure she did all she could," Clarissa said, the warmth of the suite seeping into her frozen bones. She shivered again at the delight of thawing and moved toward the radiator. She shrugged from her coat, dropped the ineffectual cape on a stool and clasped her bodice closed with one hand.

The ample sitting room was filled with gold and white silk-covered chairs and couches with tables and potted ferns scattered throughout. Red and blue throw pillows added splashes of color while delicate stained-glass lamps lent an inviting glow to the room.

Clarissa came to an abrupt halt when she saw Gabriel pacing in front of the windows, near the radiator. He glanced toward the doorway, his eyebrows furrowing as he must have noted a bruise forming on her right cheek, her tousled hair, her torn dress and bodice. His jaw firmed as Clarissa stiffened under his perusal.

Clarissa absently noted Richard exiting from the bathroom with a washcloth to swipe at the tobacco stains on Florence's cheek and dress, caressing her head, swiping away tears and enfolding her in a gentle embrace. Clarissa focused on Gabriel again, aware that he too had noted his brother's actions. However, Gabriel remained rooted in place across the room from her, as though awaiting some sign from Clarissa.

"I'll freshen up," Clarissa whispered. She shared another long, tortured glance with Gabriel before spinning and fleeing the room.

CHAPTER TWO

"Wait just a minute, young man," Sophronia Chickering demanded as Gabriel walked toward the sitting room door to follow Clarissa. "I've waited long enough to know why you and my girl are acting like a pair of circling pugilists, each waiting to land the next blow."

Gabriel halted at the doorway, his back to the room. "It will all work out in time."

Sophronia cackled humorlessly. "I doubt it. Whatever's bothering the two of you is in deep, a venom that grows more potent as time passes." She nodded to Richard and Florence as they sidled from the room, closing the sitting room door behind them. "Sit." Sophie's barked order hid her deep concern.

"Does everyone jump to do your bidding?" Gabriel asked with a glower.

"If they have any sense." She watched as he swore silently and exhaled a deep breath before throwing himself down into a sturdy chair.

After a few moments of tense silence, Gabriel rasped, "Get on with it then."

"With what?"

Sophie's air of serenity was like a match to the fuel of Gabriel's ire. "With whatever misbegotten advice you believe I need."

"No need to glower, growl or bluster at me, young man. However, if this is how you've been treating Clarissa, it's no wonder she didn't desire your comforting after such a trying day."

"Do you always meddle?" Gabriel rose, walking a few steps to the window, where he leaned a hip against the sill and stared vacantly at the distant street scene.

"Always. Especially when it pertains to those I love. You're making her miserable, Gabriel," Sophie murmured.

"Do you think I don't know that?" Gabriel spun around, his face a mask of agonized regret and wanting. "Do you think I don't know what an utter failure I am? In all regards?"

Sophie's eyes shimmered as though she fought tears, and she nodded. "So it's like that then. She's yet to understand the truth?"

"She understands it well enough." Gabriel came to sit on a chair next to Sophie, his head in his hands.

"She sees her version of the truth. That doesn't mean it's the correct one. We often harm those we love the most because we misinterpret what we perceive to have occurred. Or failed to have occurred."

"She's right. I failed her. I failed …" Gabriel choked, unable to say more.

Sophronia reached her hand toward Gabriel, stroking his head as though in a benediction. She met his devastated eyes. "Nothing will ever take away Clarissa's and your loss, Gabriel. Nothing will ever make you both whole in that way again." Her hand gripped his with a fierce intensity. "The only chance you have to move forward is by making your peace with Clarissa."

"I don't know how." Gabriel swiped at a tear and sniffed to forestall further crying.

"You have one path to move forward and heal. You need to make your peace with your wife, or you will never recover. You need her forgiveness and love. You can't heal without her. Clarissa has two paths. Don't let her choose the path without you."

****

Clarissa glared at the door, at the insistent tapping, before moving to open it. Her hair was loose, hanging to her waist, and she'd yet to change into a new dress. "Who is it?"

"Rissa, open up. It's Sav."

She flipped the lock and opened the door for her cousin to enter. She spun away to the closet before Savannah had a chance to study her. Clarissa pulled off her torn dress and flung it to the floor. After choosing and donning a simple sky-blue dress that she could pull on over her head and button up without help, she returned to the small room she shared with Gabriel.

"Aren't you attending the postparade function at the DAR Continental Hall?" Savannah asked, frowning as she stared at Clarissa's simple dress. Then she glanced up, noting the bruise on her cheek and blanched. "What happened, Rissa?" She sat in a chair, her already pale features turning more pallid as Clarissa described the march, the vicious attacks, the disparaging comments.

"Thank God for hatpins," Clarissa muttered.

"I never thought I'd hear you say something like that." Sav giggled.

"Me neither." Clarissa sighed as she finally relaxed. She fought a slight trembling at the realization that she was safe, that no one would yell at her, grope her or abuse her in any way.

"Where's Gabriel?" Savannah asked, unable to hide the concern in her voice. Her strawberry-blond hair fell in a braid down her back, and she wore a simple eggshell-blue dress, enhancing the blue of her eyes. A shawl in a shade darker than her dress covered her shoulders.

"Still speaking with Sophie." Clarissa thrummed her fingers on the table between them.

"Why should he be there, rather than here with you?"

Clarissa stared at the table, unwilling to meet her cousin's gaze. "I was fine without him." She raised her chin in defiance and false bravado.

"Maybe you were, and you marched to the end like the brave, determined woman we know you to be. And yet I imagine Gabriel would have liked the opportunity to hold you, ensure for himself you were well."

"He had no need," Clarissa snapped. When Savannah flinched at the harsh tone, she sighed. "Forgive me, Sav. Please?"

"Why can't you and Gabriel work to comfort each other, rather than continually causing each other pain and suffering?" Savannah watched her, concern mixed with disappointment.

Clarissa flushed under her cousin's close scrutiny, looking away, unable to meet her penetrating gaze. "I know you believe you understand what I'm feeling. But you can't. No one can."

Savannah's mouth puckered, and she stiffened. "You're not the only one to have lost a child, Rissa."

"And, if I recall correctly, it took you longer than four months to recover."

Savannah jerked as though Clarissa had slapped her, and Clarissa instantly regretted her words. "Sav, I'm truly sorry."

"No, as you've said, how could I possibly understand? Thus, there's no point in me even offering you solace when you so desperately desire to cling to your misery." She rose, quivering with indignation. "For, unlike you, Rissa, I relished the support Jeremy, Sophie, Aunt Betsy, *anyone* gave me. After being alone for so long, after enduring the terrible isolation thrust upon me by Jonas, I yearned for their succor as it slowly brought me back to myself."

For a moment Clarissa saw Savannah's despair, which she hid from everyone, except Jeremy.

Savannah murmured, "I know you will never recover. I know the pain is with you always. But you decide if the future you want is one filled with rancor."

Clarissa blinked away tears and looked toward her clenched hands, gripped so tightly they were white. "He won't talk to me," she whispered haltingly. "He won't touch me."

"Not even after a day like today?" Savannah eased into her chair again, her gaze focused on her cousin.

"No. The only time he touches me is when we are in public and when he feels he needs to offer me his elbow or steer me through a crowd with a hand on my back. Otherwise, nothing."

"That's not like Gabriel. He always held your hand, stroked your cheek or hugged you. He always found a reason to touch you."

"It's as though when ... Rory died"—her voice broke on his name—"our marriage did too." She bit her lip to fight the tears, but they streamed down her cheeks relentlessly as she finally admitted the truth to her cousin who was more like a sister. She leaned into Savannah and sobbed, acknowledging her grief for the first time in months.

When her sobs turned to stuttering breaths, Savannah spoke. "Do you want a marriage with Gabriel?"

Clarissa stiffened at her question.

"It's a legitimate inquiry." Savannah pushed away so she could meet Clarissa's gaze. "You must choose. Will you fight for your marriage and ultimately forgive Gabriel? Or remain married and become more bitter and angry with each passing day, affecting your children? Or will you leave and restart your life?"

Clarissa shuddered out a breath and shook her head. "I can't imagine a life without Gabriel. But I can't continue on like this. Not for years and years."

"As you said to me, it's only been a few months. Don't do anything rash." Savannah squeezed her shoulder. "However, I want you to know that, whatever you do, I will support you."

Clarissa smiled mirthlessly. "I doubt Jeremy would."

"You'd be surprised. He's feeling more like the eldest brother as Gabriel has fallen apart." Savannah's sky-blue eyes shone with her worry. "I want you to know you can depend on me, no matter what you decide."

***

"Zylphia!"

"Jeremy," Zylphia called out as she spun to face him. She walked toward him with her long stride, her jade silk evening dress swinging around her ankles and clinging to her hips. A black velvet cape at her shoulders provided minimal warmth on the cool early March evening. She wore her raven hair pulled back in the fashionable Gibson-girl style, while her blue eyes flashed with confusion as her cousin ceased pacing the lobby of the hotel. Over six feet tall, Jeremy towered above her five-foot-eight frame. "Why are you here, rather than with Savannah?"

"Because we didn't know where you were, and, as my wife wasn't threatened in that damned march, we decided I could keep watch for our errant cousin." He clasped her shoulders, his bright green eyes flashing their irritation. "Where have you been?"

She grinned at him when she sensed he wanted to give her a good shake but refrained. "I was at the after-parade party at the DAR's Continental Hall. It was extraordinary. I met so many wonderful women, and I even glimpsed Carrie Chapman Catt!"

"I can't imagine there was much to celebrate," Jeremy said with a glower.

"On the contrary, many of the leaders present believed that the actions by the women today, and the barbaric reactions of the drunken men, will help propel our cause in gaining the public's sentiments. There was even a call for a congressional investigation as to why we weren't better protected." She beamed at Jeremy. "Isn't that wonderful news?"

"Who would ever celebrate your fellow suffragists being sorely abused and unprotected?" Jeremy groaned at Zylphia's unrelenting optimism as he led her to a pair of chairs in the opulent lobby, where they both sat. He stretched out his long legs and flicked his fingers over the navy fabric of his suit coat. "Why didn't you return here first and inform us of your plans?"

"I did return, but no one was here. Besides, I thought everyone would be at the party, so why bother leaving a note when we'd meet up anyway?" Her blue eyes shone with sincerity.

Jeremy squinted as he studied her, sensing her cunning. "You're as much a McLeod as I am, thus just as capable of mischief. You know your father wanted one of us with you always whenever you left the hotel."

"Why would he possibly think I'd need a chaperone? I'm old enough." Zylphia attempted one of Sophie's harrumphs but fell short in the execution, sounding more like she was clearing her throat. She saw Jeremy bite his lip as though he understood what she'd tried and failed.

"I would think after the chaos of today's march, you'd understand your father's concern for you and his desire to see you safe." Jeremy's gentle scold provoked a soft blush on Zylphia's cheeks.

"Washington, DC, isn't any more dangerous than Boston, and I've been roaming Boston alone for years." Her gaze was calculating when she watched Jeremy. "Did cousin Savannah always have a chaperone every time she visited you before you married?"

"No, although she should've had one with her maniacal husband on the loose." Jeremy's jaw tightened, a sign he was either agitated or fighting a smile. "Listen, Zee, you're not getting out of a scold. Not this time."

"Fine, scold me, and then let's find something to eat. I'm famished." She slumped against the back of her chair in an unladylike fashion, watching her cousin in feigned boredom.

Jeremy coughed, and began a five-minute lecture on propriety and following a parent's instructions. He ended with "Your father's wish to see you with a chaperone, to see you safe, is just one of the many ways he shows you how much he cherishes you."

Zylphia smiled and sat up straight. "That was a fine scold. You've become more proficient with them these past few days. I'm glad I've been good practice for you when you'll need them for Melly in the future."

Jeremy laughed out loud and rose, offering his arm to Zylphia. "Let's find you some dinner, and you can regale me with tales of that party."

"I know Father had hoped my coming here would, in some way, lessen my desire to become such an active participant in this movement. Instead it's fueled my desire to become an ever-greater part of it."

"I know Uncle will only want for you to be content. If I know Uncle at all, he'll be enormously proud of what you want to accomplish. Just as he was when he attended your graduation from Radcliffe."

"I wish now I'd studied something other than English literature. I desire to know more about government policy and how to enact change." She paused as she ordered dinner, and Jeremy asked for a cup of coffee.

"God help us if you were any more adept," Jeremy muttered. "None of us would be safe from your plots to change the world."

"I only have energy for the women's movement."

"For now. When you've accomplished this goal, you'll find something else." He smiled his thanks to the waiter and took a small sip of his coffee. "Unless, of course, you decide to do something truly conventional, like marry."

Zylphia glared at him for a moment before laughing. "You know that I've never envisioned myself married with children."

He watched her intently, and she struggled not to squirm under his scrutiny as he said, "I've heard how you are with Richard's boys, how you dote and relish your time with them. Besides, I can't imagine you wish to go through life alone."

Zylphia flushed and played with her silverware, before tracing a finger along the starched white tablecloth. "There's a joy in knowing I can leave for the quiet of my own house while they have to remain in the chaos of their home."

"Zee." He raised an eyebrow, refusing to be waylaid by her attempt at levity.

"I find it nearly impossible to imagine having what you and Savannah have. What any of your brothers have. I don't think it's meant to be for me."

"You're quite young to decide you are against marriage forever," Jeremy teased. "Besides, didn't Uncle mention you were to have some sort of foray into society?"

"Yes, I'm to learn what I can from Sophie and a few of my friends before I join them at a house party in Newport this summer." Her eyes sparkled with her delight. "I'm hoping to make contacts that will help the movement."

Jeremy laughed. "Or you could enjoy yourself. You never know who you'll meet." He laughed again at her frown, nodding as her meal was served.

"Can you see one of those society men interested in me? I have no graces. I speak before thinking, and I fear I'll never learn to dance well."

"If your worst fear is that you don't waltz, I think you'll do just fine." He took another sip of his coffee as he watched Zylphia devour part of her dinner. "And, for what it's worth—as I'm your cousin, and I know my opinion doesn't count—any of those men would be fortunate to have a woman such as you in their lives."

Zylphia flushed at his compliment before turning the conversation to Savannah's and his adopted daughter, Melinda—Clarissa's and Colin's much younger half-sister by their father and his second wife. The older siblings persisted in calling their stepmother Mrs. Smythe as a sign of disrespect. At their father's death in 1902, their stepmother had placed Melinda in an orphanage. However, Colin had rescued his youngest sister and brought her to live with him while he remained in Boston after his father's funeral. When he decided to return to Montana in the spring of 1903, Jeremy and Savannah had joined him on the journey. During the train travel west from Boston to Missoula, Savannah and Jeremy had begun to consider Melinda their daughter and had raised her as such for the past ten years.

"We had a letter today from Araminta, who's minding the children while we are away. She said they're all doing well, although Melly misses us and her siblings, and wants us to return."

"I imagine she's jealous she wasn't able to travel with you."

"We didn't want her to miss so much school," Jeremy said. "Although I realize now that might have been an error. She would have learned a tremendous amount traveling here."

"You have the resources to travel with ease, Jeremy," Zylphia said with a wry turn of her lips.

"Yes, but Savannah and I decided that Melinda's education is what is most important. We want her to have every opportunity available to her."

"Which is the reason you support women obtaining the vote."

"Partially. I support it because I believe in Savannah." His eyes became distant, almost haunted. "I want her, and women like her, to have more rights when it comes to their lives. I know the vote won't change everything overnight, but I hope it will lead to an eventual transformation as to how we view women."

"That's quite advanced, cousin," Zylphia teased.

Jeremy shook his head. His sober countenance caused Zylphia to blush at her attempt at levity. "You didn't see her. Battered and soul weary from the treatment inflicted upon her by her first husband." He raised defiant, mutinous eyes. "When women have the vote, their concerns will be heard. Their abuse will no longer be brushed aside."

Zylphia clasped his hand. "I'm sorry for teasing you, Jeremy. Forgive me."

He sighed, the tension dissipating as the air left him. "Forgive me for becoming too serious. As you can see, everyone has a different reason for wanting to join this movement."

Zylphia toyed with her silverware a minute before asking in a halting voice, "How did you coax Savannah into trusting you? I'd think she'd have remained an unmarried woman rather than place her faith in any man after what she suffered with her first husband."

"With time and patience, she learned that not all men were like him." He smiled with fondness as he thought about the months he and Savannah had shared that led to their unique courtship. "I had to be patient, and she learned that I needed her as much as she could need me."

Zylphia rested against the back of her chair, lost in thought.

"You're too young to settle for a cause as your bedmate, Zee. Be patient." Jeremy winked at her and then sobered as he murmured, "Be brave."

***

The door creaked open, causing Jeremy to cringe and dispelling any hope for a stealthy entrance. A small lit lamp cast long shadows on the walls and the bed. Savannah stirred under the cream-colored coverlet, and he grimaced. "Forgive me for waking you, my love," he whispered as he changed out of his clothes.

"I meant to remain awake, but I was so sleepy." She leaned up on one elbow, her rumpled strawberry-blond hair cascading over one shoulder in a long, disheveled braid. "Did you find her?"

"As you suspected, she attended the party alone."

"I know you worry, but she is almost twenty-six. Besides, she was with a group of women." Savannah yawned as she reached out an arm to Jeremy.

"Women who were attacked on the march today. The streets remain filled with rowdy drunken men intent on mischief."

"Which, of course, you noticed outside while you were pacing in the lobby," Savannah said with warm humor lacing her voice. "Come to bed, my darling. It's been a long day." She lay on her side, waiting to snuggle into Jeremy's embrace.

He climbed under the covers, eliciting a shiver from Savannah as he tugged her into his arms, cradling her blanket-warmed body against him. He stroked a hand up and down her bare arm.

"How are you, my love?" he asked as he kissed the back of her head.

A stuttering sigh was his only response.

"I know it bothered you not being with your family today when they took to the streets."

"You know as well as I do that I wasn't strong enough for that," she whispered.

Jeremy heard her breath catch.

"Besides," she continued, "with what happened, … I wouldn't have made it to the end of the parade route."

Jeremy frowned as he felt the slight trembling of her body as she fought tears. "Talk to me, please, Savannah."

"I am filled with such a nearly … unutterable … rage."

Jeremy's quiet acceptance of her words, the persistent soft stroke of his hand over her arm, encouraged her to continue.

"And a sadness that seems boundless."

Jeremy coaxed her onto her back, stroking away silent tears, gazing with intense sincerity into her eyes. "Why the rage?" He bit back the question he most wanted to ask.

"At fate." She swallowed back a whimper. "At what I can't have."

He closed his eyes for a moment, before asking, "With me?" He felt Savannah soften in his arms and opened his eyes to meet her gaze, filled with a mixture of revelation, self-recrimination and wonder.

"Never with you." She stroked his cheek. "Every moment with you is a gift, Jeremy. I never knew I could be so fortunate as to meet a man like you. And to have a man such as you love me. I hate the limitations imposed on us by our recent loss and my slow recovery."

"When you almost died this last time"—he broke off as his eyes filled with tears—"I just can't lose you, my Savannah. Nothing, not making love with you, not even a baby, is worth that." He met her eyes with a pleading desperation. "Please tell me that you understand."

"I know we have Melinda, but I still yearn for more," Savannah whispered, leaning up and burying her face in the crook of his neck. "A little boy with your eyes, my smile and a mixture of my impulsiveness and your good sense."

"Ah, my love." Jeremy cradled her face between his palms, knowing she dared never to dream for another daughter after losing her daughter Hope. "How could we want for more? We have a beautiful daughter in Melly. A wonderful home in Missoula, near Clarissa and Gabe. You have causes you promote, and I have my work. What more could we want?"

"Rationally I know what you say is true."

"But the heart's not rational," Jeremy murmured, a deep love and understanding in his voice. "No matter what you want, no matter how I wish to give you your heart's desire, I can't bear to risk your life with another pregnancy."

Savannah stifled a sob and nodded. "I know. I understand. And a part of me, the part that clawed back from the brink of death after the last miscarriage, is relieved."

After a few moments while Jeremy held Savannah in his arms, stroking a hand over her head, her back, her arms, he felt her relax. "And the other part?"

"Continues to mourn the dream."

"It's nothing we can't face together, darling." Jeremy released a contented sigh as Savannah snuggled into his arms.

CHAPTER THREE

Clarissa sat at the table in Sophie's suite, sipping a cup of tea. Bright light streamed in through the curtain-free windows, casting a warm glow on the gold and green flowered rug. She perused the morning's newspaper, shaking her head in disgust as she read an editorial criticizing the women for marching. She flipped the page, featuring a picture of Inez Milholland on her white horse, and read the account of the violent march. She glowered as the reporter cast blame on the women marchers for enticing the men into acting in such a manner, although the reporter admitted that the men forced their way past the erected barricade.

Even though she'd lived through it, she shivered when reading how over one hundred women needed medical care after the march. Dozens remained hospitalized or incapacitated in some way. The varying calls for the return to a traditional home and values equaled that of the outrage voiced at the treatment of the women on the march. Calls for a congressional investigation were strong, although one opined his belief that the women who marched should expect no deferential treatment if they desired to move into the political realm.

Clarissa focused on a small notice of President-Elect Wilson's arrival in Washington the previous day. Her glower transformed into a smile as she read of his disgruntled realization that no crowds greeted his arrival because they were watching the women's march. "I hope this will help him understand the importance of our cause," she murmured as she flipped to another page.

She grimaced as she read about the disastrous sinking of a British passenger ship, the *Calvados*, sunk during a storm in the Marmara Sea near Istanbul, where all two hundred passengers perished. "So terrible." She momentarily thought of losing her family in such a way, but her mind shied away from such a tragedy. Losing one child had been painful enough. She couldn't imagine any harm coming to her three living children.

"Are you ready, dear?" Sophie asked as she emerged from her room. She raised an eyebrow at Clarissa's downcast expression.

"Of course. I was reading about the disaster in Turkey." She folded the paper and held out the article for Sophie to scan.

"Poor wretches," Sophie said. "Although I can't imagine anyone desirous of visiting that part of the world." She *thunk*ed her cane. "Come. We are meeting the others in the lobby, and I refuse to lose our seats along the inauguration route due to any dillydallying."

Clarissa smiled and rose. Her woolen sage-green dress highlighted her trim figure, chestnut hair and the bruise blooming on her cheek.

"I'm thankful you did not use any of those horrid so-called beauty products on your face to conceal your injury." She paused in the doorway to look at Clarissa's face. "It's coloring as I'd hoped it would."

"Sophie, how can you be pleased at my mistreatment?"

"I'm not. However, seeing as you were abused, it seems only proper you stand front and center of our group as we greet our new president. He should see what the actions of so-called *gentlemen* have wrought." She spun, her cane *thunk*ing with her determination as she strode down the carpeted hallway toward the elevator.

"Sophie!" Clarissa sputtered. Others were present in the elevator, preventing Clarissa from speaking freely. As the elevator stopped at each floor and filled, pleasantries were exchanged by those who boarded. Clarissa hid a flinch each time a stranger gawked at her bruise, tilting up her chin with false bravado.

They joined their group in the opulent foyer. Bright sunlight streamed through the high windows, enhancing the spacious feel of the entranceway. A shaft of sunlight enhanced the earthy tones of the mosaic and marble floors, while the golden marble columns gleamed. Hotel patrons streamed from the elevators and foyer, many carrying small flags, as they headed toward the inauguration and its parade. Their voices were excited, although subdued in comparison to the previous day's participants.

Clarissa stood next to Gabriel, flinching as his hand came to rest on the small of her back. She spoke to her family. "Sophie wishes me to sit at the front of our group, thus confronting President Wilson with the violence that occurred yesterday." She felt Gabriel stiffen behind her.

"I'm not certain this is the correct action to take," Gabriel said. "Clarissa and the other women marchers have already suffered plenty."

Zylphia clapped her hands together with barely contained excitement. "I think it a marvelous idea. Why should we cover up what men have done? They should feel ashamed, not us."

"I fear I must agree with Zee," Jeremy said. "The women had every right to march and expect protection. Now some sort of consequences should be levied against those who perpetrated such violence."

"Yes, that's all well and good, but it's not you who must be made an example of," Clarissa protested. "I'm thankful we are just watching the parade, rather than sitting through his inauguration."

"If I could have obtained seats, we would have been at the ceremony. However, the best I could do was convince a friend of mine to give us a block of seats along the parade route. I refuse to stand for hours on end at my age," Sophie said, ignoring Clarissa's complaint.

"You can do it, Rissa," Zylphia said, looping her arm through Clarissa's and dragging her forward with the force of her enthusiasm. "We'll all be with you and beside you to support you."

Sophie's striking eyes sparkled with mischief as she followed Zylphia and Clarissa from the hotel. Gabriel offered his arm to Sophie, and his brothers walked arm in arm with their wives.

Throngs of people filled the streets, crowding both sides of Pennsylvania Avenue. A large contingent of police ensured the avenue remained clear. The grandstands used for the previous day's procession were now filled with national and international dignitaries, and they awaited the new president's triumphant journey from his inauguration at the Capitol to his new home at the White House via the inaugural parade. The decorative red, white and blue bunting strung from the balconies and windowsills had doubled from the day before. Peddlers hawked commemorative inaugural coins and postcards of Washington, DC.

As the McLeod clan walked, Sophie used her cane to clear a path within the crowd, having taken the lead from Zylphia and Clarissa. Sophronia maneuvered their large group to a smaller grandstand with perfect views of the inaugural route. She pushed Clarissa, Florence, Savannah and Zylphia to the front of their group and stationed the McLeod brothers behind their wives, while Sophie sat behind Zylphia.

The sunny day had warmed to over fifty degrees, and they sat, awaiting the arrival of the president. They heard distant applause and then the sounding of a cannon followed by trumpets. Clarissa shared a bemused smile with Zylphia and leaned forward to find Pennsylvania Avenue empty.

"He'll arrive soon," Sophie said.

A large contingent of soldiers on shiny black horses appeared. Half of their number preceded a carriage, while the other half flanked the rear of the carriage.

"That will be the president," Sophie said. She gave Clarissa a nudge, and Clarissa raised her head and leaned forward in her seat from her family members. However, by the time President Wilson reached them, his carriage was moving quickly. He waved at the large crowd, his rapid pace precluding him from focusing on any one group.

After he passed, Sophie *harrumph*ed her displeasure. "That man must be made to see what was wrought yesterday."

"I'm afraid that, even if he's forced to acknowledge it, he may not understand it," Florence murmured. "After what I saw yesterday, too many believe the women received what they deserved for daring to demand more."

Richard laid a soothing hand on his wife's shoulder, and she leaned into his touch.

The group remained to listen to the marching bands interspersed with floats representative of every state in the nation. Montana's float depicting the industry of the state appeared, carrying a group of men dressed as miners and another as loggers. Four strong Percheron horses pulled the float. As they passed, the Montana McLeods cheered loudly, earning a salute from the men on the float.

This caused the McLeods to cheer even more loudly, their enthusiasm infectious to those around them. "Oh, how wonderful that Montana is represented," Clarissa said.

"They said every state in the nation would be, although I had my doubts they truly meant it," Gabriel said.

As the parade ended, the McLeod clan joined the slow-moving group leaving the parade route and returned to their hotel. "I'm planning a quiet evening tonight," Sophie said. "Those who would like to join me are welcome."

***

Sophie *harrumph*ed as she read the evening newspaper. "I hope Alice has something to say to our new president to alter his way of thinking."

"As do I. There is no excuse for how the women were treated on the march," Richard said.

"That's not what I mean. Listen to what he said in his Inaugural Address. They reprinted it in the paper." She cleared her throat of a portion of its raspiness and read aloud:

Men's hearts wait upon us; men's lives hang in the balance; men's hopes call upon us to say what we will do. Who shall live up to the great trust? Who dares fail to try? I summon all honest men, all patriotic, all forward-looking men, to my side.

Richard shared a perplexed glance with Jeremy. "I'm uncertain as to why you are offended. Seems a sound argument to me."

"*Men. Men. Men!*" Sophie barked. "Don't believe for a moment he was considering women in his speech when discussing his concern for men. I doubt that man remembers on many days that he was birthed by a woman, is married to one, nor that he has a daughter."

"That's uncharitable, Sophia," Savannah scolded.

"But true." Sophie slapped down the paper, glaring at the words. "I fear that man will refuse to be reasonable when it comes to women desiring the vote. If his only concern is for men, it is evident he fails to see the other half of the population."

"It makes sense for him to address those who voted him into office," Jeremy said, with a wink to Richard.

Sophie glowered at him. "Exactly, dear boy. Which is why he, and politicians who think like him, must come to understand that the struggle for universal enfranchisement is not one they can defeat. Their fists, their bullying and their patronizing will not keep us from attaining our objective."

"I don't know what more you can do," Savannah said.

"Thankfully we have young women who are intent on reaching the objectives my generation has failed to secure. I am convinced that, with their diligence and determination, we will succeed." She *thunk*ed her cane for good measure, discouraging disagreement.

"I fear they will promote violence," Jeremy said. "Zylphia is already enthralled with the women she's met here, and I'm concerned she will become even more so should she meet Miss Paul or Miss Burns."

"While it's true that Alice and Lucy learned numerous methods from the Pankhursts in England, many which would be considered objectionable, I remain convinced Alice will refrain from outward violence." Sophie shared a chagrined smile with those in her sitting room. "However, I cannot guarantee Alice won't defy conventions."

CHAPTER FOUR

The following day, Zylphia stood outside the bustling headquarters of the Congressional Committee Office of the National American Woman Suffrage Association, or NAWSA, headed by Alice Paul. Zylphia watched women enter and exit the basement office before she followed a woman down a half flight of stairs and stepped inside a doorway, just as another woman pushed past her, carrying a stack of letters. The scene was one of coordinated chaos. Women in the front office wrote letters by hand or typed them. Telephones rang. Impromptu meetings occurred, with decisions reached after only a few sentences.

"What can we do for you, miss?" a woman asked. Her dishwater-blond hair was pulled back and partially covered in a kerchief, while she wore a thinning gray sweater over a navy dress.

"I came to see if there was anything I could do for the movement." Zylphia jumped as her arm was gripped, and she was pulled to a table.

"Sit. You can help stuff these envelopes." The woman nodded to a chair next to her and then to a pile of papers and envelopes.

"What are these for?" Zylphia asked as she shed her jacket.

"After the success of the parade, we want to obtain as much support as possible from our backers."

"Financial support."

The woman rolled her eyes at Zylphia. "What other kind is there? Of course financial. To win this struggle, we must have funds. The antis have a war chest at their disposal, seeing as the majority of businessmen and wealthy women are against the suffrage movement."

"Not all wealthy women are against it," Zylphia murmured as she began her task of folding letters and then filling the envelopes. "I'm from Massachusetts, and a group of us are in favor of the vote."

"Well, you need to work harder, as there remains too much opposition."

They worked in silence a few moments. In between the folding and filling of envelopes, Zylphia glanced around the room. The secondhand furniture, scraped and battered from years of use, was still functional. Oak filing cabinets vied for space, while desks were nearly stacked atop each other. Framed pictures of the suffragist leaders, past and present, hung on the walls. Zylphia studied the photographs of Elizabeth Cady Stanton and Susan B. Anthony for a moment. Every woman here had a purpose, and Zylphia noted that many walked down the hallway to a small office in the back.

"What more do you need?" Zylphia asked after a moment.

"Besides money and political influence?" The woman shared a sardonic smile with Zylphia. "Our newspaper is always in need of artwork."

"I'm an artist."

"Do you draw caricatures?" At Zylphia's shake of her head, the woman sighed. "I'm afraid that's what we need. Grand paintings are of no use."

"That's what I do. Paintings."

"If you are truly committed to the cause, you will forego everything that distracts you from the movement."

"What do you mean?" Zylphia asked as she frowned.

"Do you think Miss Paul wastes her time on frivolous activities when she knows all her energies are needed to win this battle?" She nodded her head down the hallway. "She intentionally keeps her living quarters at such a cold temperature that she has no desire to read at night. And she is an avid reader of mysteries. However, she knows that this cause is more important than any mystery novel."

"Her dedication is admirable," Zylphia whispered. Her heart raced as she considered giving up her painting.

"As should all of ours be," the woman said as she rose. "I'll leave you to it."

Zylphia nodded and continued her task. She smiled at those who entered and tackled the stack of papers in front of her. When she departed a few hours later, she had a small sense of accomplishment, although she battled a growing sense of unease.

***

R ichard slammed down his glass of ale with more force than necessary as he shot another furtive glance toward the bar's entrance. He shared a long look with Jeremy before nodding to the bartender for another round. Although midday, the dark mahogany of the long bar and the dim lighting from the scattered light fixtures lent the establishment a late-evening feel.

"He'll come," Jeremy said, nodding his thanks as another beer was set in front of him. "He's as excited as we are to have time for just the three of us again."

"You'd think after fifteen years he wouldn't be late. We haven't all been together since you went away to fight in the war in '98."

"He's not the same Gabriel you remember, Rich." Jeremy took a long swig from his glass of beer. "None of us are the same as when we were last together."

Richard rolled his eyes. "Of course we aren't. We're all married, have children. You've survived a war. And the two of you abandoned me to live in Montana."

"We did not abandon you," Gabriel said from behind them.

"Gabe!" Richard said, leaping from his stool to embrace his brother. Jeremy joined them, and they slapped each other on the back a few times before standing awkwardly for a moment.

After collecting their mugs of beer, the McLeods moved to a small round table. Gabriel smiled as he looked at his brothers. "It's about time the three of us have a chance to talk about something other than women earning the vote or Wilson's inauguration."

Richard raised his glass to Gabe as Jeremy laughed. "We couldn't leave our womenfolk alone two nights ago as planned, seeing what a disaster the parade was, and yesterday was too chaotic with the inauguration," Richard said.

Gabriel grunted his agreement.

"What did you do the night of the women's parade, Gabe?" Jeremy asked. "I thought I saw you leaving the hotel while I was waiting for Zylphia."

"I took a short walk. I needed to clear my head."

"Was this before or after you comforted Clarissa?" Richard asked. He took a sip of his beer and shared a quick glance with Jeremy.

"Don't start, Rich," Gabriel warned. His gaze roamed the room, refusing to meet their eyes.

"It's about time somebody did," Jeremy muttered.

Richard grabbed Gabriel's arm as it flexed, preventing him from rising. "Gabe, it's just the three of us. Talk to us."

"There's nothing to say. Clarissa and I can't see past our … loss." Gabriel shook his head as though dispelling memories.

"You've always been able to do anything you desired if you wanted it badly enough, Gabe," Richard said, with Jeremy nodding beside him.

"You think that isn't my most cherished goal? To reconcile with Rissa?" He shook his head in exasperation.

"You found a way to free us from Mrs. Masterson. You struggled to eke out a survival so that Jeremy could finish school and I could have my full apprenticeship. You ensured we had a treat a week, knowing that would be enough to motivate us and prevent us from losing all hope." Richard watched Gabe with confusion. "You fought for Clarissa, accepting every obstacle laid in your path to reunite with her. I don't understand why you'd give in so easily now."

"Maybe I'm tired of the struggle." Gabriel took a deep sip of his beer.

"Bull," Jeremy said. "I've seen you come alive with each challenge. Something happened."

Gabriel raised tormented eyes to his brothers. "I know now what it is to lose the esteem of the one person who matters most to me in the world. And I find it difficult to care much about anything else."

"Then fight to regain it," Richard snapped. "Don't just sit here and bemoan your fate. That's not like you."

Gabriel barely nodded and took another swig of his beer.

When Richard took a deep breath, Jeremy kicked him in the leg and said, "Tell us how your business is, Rich."

"Like I write you every week, it continues to grow, and I have men—good, talented men—clamoring to work with me."

"Of course they are. They know you'll treat them fair and pay a decent wage." Gabe nodded as he beheld his middle brother with pride.

"Are you looking to expand further?" Jeremy asked. He stretched out his long legs in front of him, sighing.

"I don't think so. I've three shops to run, and it keeps me busier than I thought it would. I don't have as much time at home with Flo as I'd like."

"I'm sure she understands," Gabriel said.

"She says she does. But I miss the time with the children, the simple things. Listening to them bicker as they wash up for supper. Helping them with their homework or readying them for bed." Richard's gaze became distant as he thought of his five boys.

"The little things that make a family into a family," Gabriel whispered. He thought of his three living children, his mind shying away from a time when he had four.

"Yeah. I'm hoping to have a man in charge of each forge by the end of summer, and then I can simply oversee," Richard said.

"Won't you be bored? Shuffling paperwork around a desk rather than working at the anvil?" Gabriel asked.

"I've been doing that for nearly twenty years. Besides, I own three forges. Anytime I want to build something, I have access to the best smithies in Boston."

"Col's never resented you getting his family's forge," Jeremy murmured. "I think he's pleased to be in Missoula."

"It all worked out as it was meant to," Gabriel said. "Colin had his time where he didn't have any responsibility, just like he wanted. And now that he's older, he has a forge in Missoula. Seems to have turned out well for him." Gabriel sighed, mimicking Jeremy, kicking out his long legs, but moving them to the side so they wouldn't hit Jeremy's. "Remember when we'd meet in Old Man Harris's shop, and we'd eat those treats he saved for us?" His gaze was distant as he imagined the scene from twenty years ago.

"Most of them were barely edible, but we didn't know better," Richard said.

"What with the food we were eating at Aunt's house," Jeremy said with a shake of his head.

"Or not eating. I swear, if she had had her way, we would have starved." Gabriel shook his head. "Life was simpler."

"But not any better," Richard said. "I'd never trade the years I've had with Flo. Or the years without her, when I thought she'd betrayed me with Aunt Masterson."

"Do you remember the time we knocked cousin Nicholas into the fountain?" Richard asked, his eyes lit with glee.

Gabriel grinned. "When he came out of the water, covered in the mud and muck, leaves dripping off his pristine uniform ..." Gabriel chortled.

"Even when Aunt threatened us with life in an orphanage, I couldn't regret what had happened to him."

Gabriel shuddered. "That was one of the worst days for me. The thought that we'd be separated, intentionally, by Aunt."

"Well, we never were," Richard said.

"Thanks to you, Gabe," Jeremy said.

"I did what any elder brother would do. I'd do it again." He beheld his grown, prosperous brothers sitting in front of him. "I think Mum and Da would be proud of us."

Richard and Jeremy sobered as they considered their long-deceased parents. "They would," Richard said as Jeremy agreed.

Gabriel raised his nearly empty glass in a toast. "To the McLeod brothers. May we always know the value of hard work, friendship and family." He smiled at his brothers as they clinked glasses.

***

While the McLeod men settled in for a chat over a pint, the McLeod women, along with Sophie, gathered in the formal dining area of the Willard Hotel where tea was served each afternoon. Light streamed through the stained-glass dome, casting a kaleidoscope of colors onto the tables and floor. Paintings of the District of Columbia's bucolic past lined the gray-blue walls, romanticizing the once-swampy landscape of the nation's capital.

"I'm thankful you reserved a table for us, Sophie," Savannah murmured as she settled between Sophie and Zylphia. Clarissa sat next to Zylphia with Florence on her other side. They wore their most formal afternoon dresses, with hats titled at jaunty angles.

"I suspected many would linger the day after Wilson's inauguration, and I did not want us to be denied," Sophie said, her eyes sparkling, either with delight or mischief. "What did you think of yesterday?"

"It was rather sedate after the day before," Zylphia said.

Sophie choked on her sip of tea. "I'd hope a rabble of drunken men wouldn't think to attack the president of the United States."

"But it's acceptable to treat the women of this country in such a manner?" Florence asked, taking a dainty bite of a small sandwich.

"Of course not, but true men still know the bounds of propriety." Sophie squared her shoulders and *harrumph*ed. Her eyes twinkled again. "Besides, the fact they could behave for the president and didn't for us only helps the cause."

"I don't understand," Savannah said. She settled against the back of her chair, appearing paler than she had a few days ago.

"It shows a deference to men that wasn't shown to women." Sophie sighed as she settled in her chair.

"He's also the president, Sophie," Florence argued.

"Yes, he is. But, as we marched on the same route the day before, the police should have been able to provide equal protection. I'm sure there will be an investigation into the police commissioner's failing."

"President Wilson didn't appear to notice any of the women in the crowd who'd been harmed the day before," Zylphia said. She smiled slyly. "I heard that Alice Paul and Lucy Burns want to meet with President Wilson within the next few days to discuss the need for the amendment." At the women's curious glances, Zylphia shrugged. "I went by the headquarters this morning and spent a few hours stuffing envelopes."

"That was good of you, Zee, and I'm certain they appreciated the help." Savannah's smile of encouragement earned a frown from Zylphia.

"It seemed like I did so little. I wish we weren't leaving tomorrow, and I'd be able to attend the meeting with them," Zylphia said. "Of course, that is, assuming they'd want me to go with them as I'm virtually unknown to them." She rapped her fingers on the tabletop in agitation. "I want to do more."

"Zee, you did plenty. You attended the after-parade event, and you were one of the treasury's beauties," Florence soothed.

Zylphia made a face. "I want to do something other than stand and look pretty. Or stuff envelopes. Or ask my father for a donation."

"It's important that the voters of this nation realize that the women seeking the vote are young, successful, attractive women. You aren't dried-up old women, bitter at your lot in life," Sophie intoned. "What you provided during the march was essential." Sophie paused for a moment, deep in thought. "Why else would Alice and Lucy insist on meeting with President Wilson now?"

"I heard a rumor that Lucy wanted to force him to see her and some of the other women before their bruises faded," Clarissa said, sharing a wry smile with Sophie. "It seems you aren't the only one wishing to confront the president with what happened two days ago."

Sophronia appeared lost in thought. "I's been a long struggle. The two leaders of NAWSA, Anna Howard Shaw and Carrie Chapman Catt, worked tirelessly for years beside Susan B. Anthony and Elizabeth Cady Stanton with little to show for their efforts." Sophie suddenly cackled with glee. "Oh, that Alice is something. She'll give Anna and Carrie fits before it's over."

"I'd think you'd be appalled at her antics," Savannah said.

"I've waited my entire life for someone to come in and ruffle their feathers. To take action. If you think I'm about to be upset by Alice's and Lucy's initiative, you'd better think again." She smiled at the women around her. "There's no reason we can't support different tactics in gaining universal suffrage. The only thing I will not condone is violence. I will not see my girls hurt or threatening others."

"Don't worry, Sophie. Alice is a Quaker," Zylphia said.

"Yes, and I remain confident she'll remember that rather than her training at the hands of the Pankhursts," Sophie said. "I know I spoke positively in front of your husbands last night, but I do worry that Alice and Lucy were influenced more than they should have been by those radical women in England."

"Do you think Miss Paul will have success when she meets with President Wilson?" Florence asked, fiddling with the filigreed silverware.

"I believe his daughter is for the vote, although I'm not sure that is enough to sway him," Savannah said.

"My friend Parthena Tyler is for the vote, and her father couldn't be more conservative," Zylphia said with a shrug. "He remains convinced a daughter is nothing more than an arm ornament for her husband."

"Time will tell," Sophie said, grimacing at Zylphia's description of Mr. Tyler's view of women. "If President Wilson continues to postpone supporting universal suffrage, then we know he is against women voting and that he is not a man to support in the next election."

"I wish Teddy Roosevelt had won." Zylphia sighed. "At least his progressive party supported women obtaining the vote."

"Well, what a man says and what a man does are two very different things," Sophie said. "Roosevelt had his time in office, and we're still without the vote."

The women nodded, smiling ironically at Sophie's sage words.

A gilded clock across the room discreetly chimed the hour, prompting Florence to say, "Come. Let's prepare for dinner. It's our last night together, and I look forward to all of us gathering again like we used to in Boston."

***

Zylphia poked her head into the formal private dining room, sighing with relief. "Thank goodness. I strolled into another dining room, filled with men smoking cigars and discussing business." She laughed as she shared a rueful smile with Florence. "One of the men rose, as though they'd been expecting me."

"Oh, Zee," Flo said, hugging her warmly. Their private room had pale-pink wallpaper, white crown molding, two sideboards and an oak table with just enough seats for their group. The crisp damask tablecloth with white and gold china, crystal and silver all sparkled under the chandelier's bright light.

Sophie approached them, studying Zylphia. "What has you disconcerted?"

"If it's more nonsense about not doing enough for the movement, Zylphia, you need to realize that the next phase is only beginning," Clarissa said as she joined their group.

"Something was said while I was at headquarters. A woman there told me that Miss Paul has given up reading mystery novels so as to completely dedicate herself to the cause. She suggested I do the same."

Sophie squinted as she studied Zylphia. "What could she possibly mean?"

"You are not to give up your painting," Florence commanded. "You are far too talented to waste it on someone else's vision of what defines commitment."

"Shouldn't I be willing to make some sort of sacrifice for the cause?" Zylphia wrung her hands as she battled her mounting agitation.

"Would it make you feel as though you've contributed more to the cause to know you've given up the one thing that brings you pleasure?" Clarissa asked, her friendly smile doubtful as she watched Zylphia. "Besides, do you honestly believe you could cease painting?"

"It's like a compulsion. I wake up dreaming about my next project," Zylphia whispered.

"Exactly," Sophronia said. "Reading mysteries is a pastime. There is a difference between reading another's masterpiece and creating one yourself. You must nurture what you feel compelled to create, even if it takes time away from a cause you support."

"Come. Let's sit," Sophie ordered as she moved toward the table. She sat at one end and pointed at Zylphia to sit at the other. "It seems only appropriate that the eldest and youngest should bookend this table."

"Yes, the matriarch and her protégé of the movement," Jeremy said with a wry smile.

"Exactly, my boy," Sophie said, her aquamarine eyes sparkling. She smiled as everyone settled—Clarissa, Savannah and Jeremy on one side of the table, while Gabriel, Florence and Richard sat across from them. They passed around the large platters of food. "I dismissed the servants. I hate having them hover over us," Sophie said.

"Thank you, Sophie," Florence said. "You know how disconcerting I find that."

"It's a joy to have us all together, and I'm sure you are dreading the separation tomorrow," Sophie said, watching the McLeod brothers.

"We are, although I'm thankful we were together again." Gabriel cleared his throat as he looked at Richard.

"At last," Richard murmured. He gripped Florence's hand. "Next time we are together, the children must be with us. They need to meet their cousins."

Gabriel nodded, his eyes clouding at the mention of his children.

Sophie raised a glass. "May the bonds of friendship and family continue stronger today, forever more."

Everyone clinked glasses and settled in to enjoy their last evening together.

CHAPTER FIVE

The smell of baking bread permeated the immense kitchen at the rear of Savannah's large yellow Victorian house, with its turret and wraparound front porch. Savannah and Jeremy had purchased the home soon after their arrival in Missoula. Although it was designed to have numerous live-in staff, Savannah and Jeremy preferred to hire help as needed and otherwise manage on their own. Their home sat on a corner lot a few blocks from Clarissa's house on the university side of the river. A large maple table, crafted by Jeremy, was centered in the kitchen with six matching chairs encircling it. The tabletop was covered in flour after the bread-making endeavor.

"Sav, why don't we travel to Butte?" Clarissa said as she helped Savannah clean up the kitchen. After their return from Washington, DC, in mid-March, Clarissa had felt aimless. She no longer frequented the library due to the recent hire of a rancorous new librarian. Thus, Clarissa spent time with her three children, cleaned her house and was a daily visitor at Savannah's home. "A symphony is traveling there from Chicago that I'd like to see next week."

Savannah paused in scrubbing the wooden tabletop to stare at Clarissa a moment. Her cheeks were flushed a rosy red, her health having returned to her after months of illness. "You just arrived home. Why would you want to be away from your children again?"

Clarissa flushed and looked around the spacious kitchen, with its gleaming pine cabinets lining three walls, while green tiles covered the deep countertops. A window over the kitchen sink let in anemic light on this gray day, while the back wall was lined with curtained windows and a door to the side porch and back-yard.

Clarissa answered her cousin. "It's not that I desire to be away from them. However, it's a concert I've longed to hear."

"I've never known you to be that interested in music," Savannah said with a frown, moving to the sink to wash out her cloth. "Melinda would be upset if I were to leave again so soon. As would Jeremy."

"Please, Sav. Just this once come with me to Butte. We'll shop at Hennessy's, see the show and come home."

Savannah frowned. "We weren't able to do the shopping I'd hoped to in DC." She sat without her usual grace, battling a smile, and then shrugged. "Fine, I agree, although I don't understand the urgency."

Clarissa beamed at her and gripped her hand. "We'll have a wonderful time. I promise."

***

"**M**r. Pickens, I wish you wouldn't spend so much time at the library," Clarissa said as she set the bowl of beef stew on the table with a *clunk*. She had left the children with Araminta, playing in the park, to make a quick visit to see him.

"Did Minta make that?" he asked as he tottered over to the small polished oak table Gabriel had made him. He collapsed onto the chair with a sigh, catching his cane with a practiced move and hooking it on the chairback. He sniffed the food appreciatively before sighing with exasperation. "One thing ye'll find, Missy, is it ain't no fun gettin' old. I cain't smell like I used to, an', boy, does that take the joy out o' eatin'."

"You smell pies just fine," she said with a wry smile.

"Well, I ain't no fool, 'specially when it's one o' Minta's finest." He watched Clarissa with an amused glance. "She ever teach ye how to make one yet?"

"I can make a single-crust pie fine, but the double-crust pies are too hard," she said with a shrug of one shoulder. "Now you think you're sly, and you are, but you aren't distracting me from my original concern. Why are you spending so much time at the library? You've no need to now that you are at Gabriel's workshop a few times a week."

He raised his eyebrows with blatant amusement and flashed his near toothless smile before he took a bite of the stew. He shook his spoon at her, encouraging her to sit with him while he ate, rather than bustling around, tidying up as she usually did. "Why, I think my Missy's jealous o' the time I spend with Pester."

Clarissa choked out a laugh, not wanting to encourage him with his misspoken name for Hester Loken. "I would never be jealous of her."

"Course ye would. Ye see me with her, talkin' with her just like I used to talk with ye when ye ran the depository. Might make some wonder if I was fickle."

She sighed, glaring at his correct assessment. "Fine. I hate that you spend time there with her, and I can barely enter the place to ask for a book without her believing I'm undermining her authority."

"She's a bit prickly. Wants things done just so." He speared Clarissa with another amused glance. "Reminds me of a young woman come from Boston with ideas on how to reorganize a depository."

"I was nothing like her," Clarissa sputtered, her face reddening and hands clenching. "I always welcomed whatever help I could obtain."

"Well, just as ye were, Missy, I suspect Pester's runnin' from some sort of *scandalotorious* event in her past."

"There's no need for her to be rude to my children," she hissed. "I don't care if she's hiding a scandalous or notorious past. She has no right to slap Billy's hand for reaching for a book or for swatting at Myrtle for laughing. They're children and should be allowed to act as children."

"She comes from the belief children should be seen and not heard." Mr. A.J. chuckled. "An' yer children can always be heard."

"I know they are full of energy ..."

"*Runnin' wild* is how Pester would call it."

"They know their manners. They are filled with exuberance." She glared at A.J. "I don't appreciate her inability to accept help when offered."

"Missy, ye've got to understand ye ain't the librarian no more. Ye chose yer family, as was right. Pester's gotta learn how she wants to run things." He speared Clarissa with an intense stare. "Make her own mistakes."

Clarissa's attempted *harrumph* caused A.J. to chortle his accordion laugh. "Now, Missy, if ye were to offer friendship, instead of wantin' to be a mentor, I think ye could get along with Pester." He took a bite of the stew. "A friend would help her *maneuvipulate* the sisters."

She cringed as she envisioned the sisters Vaughan and Bouchard. "That is the best part about no longer working in the library. Not having to deal with them. Not having to maneuver around their backward plans nor manipulate them."

"I think Pester could use a friend. The sisters are throwin' their weight around." He shared an amused glance with Clarissa.

"Which is considerable," she muttered, causing A.J. to laugh.

Mr. A.J. pushed away his bowl and gave a dramatic sniff. "Can I have my pie now?"

She giggled, her irritated mood lifting. She brought over a piece of cherry pie for him, and he sighed with appreciation. "Ah, perfection." His eyes, now somber, met her gaze. "Why'd ye come by today, Missy?"

"I'm traveling to Butte tomorrow with Savannah. I wanted to visit with you before we left. I've barely seen you since I returned from Washington, DC."

"Runnin' away again?" He smacked his lips, either with delight at the delicious pie or with disgust at her upcoming travels.

Clarissa shook her head and closed her eyes.

"No peace with that man o' yours?"

She stilled and shook her head again. "No, no peace. He ran away from me when I tried to talk with him recently."

"When ye ambushed him," Mr. A.J. said with a grunt.

She blushed and nodded.

"Missy, after all this time, ye gotta learn that men don't like bein' pushed."

She sighed but was unable to prevent a tear from leaking out. "I don't know what to do," she whispered. "I'm filled with such anger at him, and yet I miss him." She gave a mirthless bark of laughter. "Which is ironic because we live in the same house."

Mr. A.J. held out a gnarled hand to her, gripping her fingers as tightly as he could although unable to hide a grimace of pain at his action. "I never was blessed with children. I have no idea how ye feel,." He gave her hand a slight squeeze before letting go. "But I can't imagine holdin' yer pain to ye like a shield will make anythin' better."

"I know," she whispered. "I don't know what to do." She lowered her head as a few more tears trickled free. "I'm afraid, if I don't have my anger, if I can't blame Gabriel, that I'll have nothing."

Mr. A.J. traced away her tears on one cheek, the skin of his fingers almost as soft as a baby's. "Ye have to decide that replacin' the anger with forgiveness, understandin' an' love is worth the pain of finally mournin' what ye lost."

***

On their arrival in Butte, Clarissa searched the platform for Jedediah Maloney but failed to see him. It had been twelve years since she'd been in Butte, but she'd hoped to see his familiar face. They instructed their porter to bring their trunks to the Finlen Hotel and boarded a streetcar.

"We could hire a cab," Savannah said.

"I know, but this was how I first traveled in Butte when I fled Boston, hoping to reunite with Gabriel. I'm feeling nostalgic."

Savannah squeezed her hand as she recalled the letter Clarissa had written, describing her journey to Butte all those years ago, only to find Gabriel had moved. "I just wish you would tell me why we had to travel to Butte today of all days. The real reason."

Clarissa shook her head, unable to hide a smile. When she met Savannah's gaze, she saw her arrested, shocked expression. "What?" Clarissa asked.

"For an instant, you looked happy. Like the old Rissa. And it made me sad."

"Sad?"

"Because I know the happy Rissa is fleeting and the new Rissa will be back soon." Sav sniffled and turned away, staring out the window as the streetcar trudged up a steep hill. "I always forget how ugly it is here."

The streetcar passed rows of brick multistoried buildings, the late-season snow covered in a fine covering of gray coal dust. The gallow frames in the distance dotted the horizon, while ash and coal spewed into the sky from tall smokestacks. The only flashes of color were on the signs painted on the sides of buildings.

Clarissa giggled, feeling lighthearted for the first time in months. "It is. Shockingly so." They disembarked on the corner of Main and Broadway and walked the short distance to the Finlen Hotel. "When I was here last time, Colin and I stayed in the same place, but it was a smaller hotel, called the McDermott. They tore it down and built the Finlen in its place." Clarissa pointed to another imposing brick building kitty-corner across the street from the Finlen. "Gabriel helped build that hotel."

"We should venture inside so we can let him know we've seen his work."

"Sav—"

"I'm teasing, Rissa. I know nothing so simple will bring harmony between you and Gabe." She turned toward the entrance to the Finlen. "Come. Let's get settled, and then you can share whatever this surprise is with me."

***

The plush red velvet seats sank a little as they sat, and Clarissa stared at the opulent ceiling design of gods and goddesses playing musical instruments, accompanied by white marble pillars and gold-gilded chandeliers. Clarissa had successfully maneuvered Savannah into the plush Empress Theater without her discovering why they were here. They sat in the front row of the first mezzanine level, slightly to the right side. When Clarissa refused to hand over her playbill, Savannah rolled her eyes.

"It's as grand in here as almost anything in Boston," Savannah whispered, unable to hide her awe.

"I know. Who would have thought? It shows that mining can be quite profitable." They shared a smile and then settled down to watch the performance as the red velvet curtain parted for one man to enter the front of the stage to address the crowd.

Savannah turned to Clarissa in confusion. Clarissa had told her they were coming to watch a traveling symphony, but no sounds of instruments tuning could be heard. "Rissa?"

"You'll see," Clarissa whispered, unable to hide either her delight or her bright smile.

The short, rotund man, his waistcoat bulging with his girth, waved at the crowd to hush them for his address. "Thank you, loyal patrons, for once again joining me on a night I'm certain will be unforgettable. For a night that will rival any that has come before and any to follow. For tonight, we have the incomparable talent of the pianist Mr. Lucas Russell, the man who's thrilled royalty and eastern society with his brilliance."

Savannah gasped at Lucas's name, gripping Clarissa's hand until she grimaced in pain.

"He's here to share with us tonight his latest compositions, all the way from Boston, Massachusetts. Please join me in giving him a warm Butte, America, welcome." He thrust his arms in the air, and the curtain rose, revealing a darkened stage with only a well-lit piano centered thereon.

Savannah leaned forward in her seat, her eyes lit with anticipation at seeing her brother perform on stage. The crowd around them broke into polite applause while Savannah and Clarissa clapped as though Mozart were to appear in front of them, earning a few curious stares from their neighbors.

For the past two years, they'd read clippings of articles sent by Uncle Martin, Savannah's and Lucas's father, about Lucas's successful tour through much of America and part of Europe. Savannah and Clarissa had established a routine where Savannah wouldn't open a letter from her parents without Clarissa present so that they could read about Lucas's latest success together. As they had sighed over the stories of Lucas mingling with the elite members of society after each successful performance, they had dreamed of seeing him perform.

On their return from Washington, DC, Clarissa had seen an advertisement for a one-time performance by Lucas in Butte, before he headed farther west to San Francisco via Seattle. With Jeremy's aid, she'd been able to obtain two tickets.

Lucas walked onto the stage, appearing taller in his tuxedo than his five foot eight, with his light-brown hair longer than fashionable, tucked behind his ears and free of any pomade. He bowed to the applause, flicked out the tails of his jacket and sat at the piano bench, his fingers stretched theatrically over the keys. After a momentary pause, he played.

Clarissa closed her eyes as a lilting lullaby floated around the audience. She heard wisps of the song he'd teased them with when Savannah had brought Jeremy to meet Uncle Martin over ten years ago. Lucas's composition evoked emotions from tenderness to anger to wistfulness to an aching regret. When he finished, nearly half an hour later, tears coursed down her cheeks.

He leaned away from the keyboard, lowered his hands and then turned toward the still-silent audience. After a moment, a deafening roar burst forth, the calls of "Bravo!" and "Encore!" competing with the whistles of approval. Lucas stood, smiled, bowed and exited the stage.

Savannah and Clarissa shared an incredulous look, sharing the joy at witnessing Lucas perform. They were on the verge of rising to leave when he emerged again. After a curt bow, he played another original piece, this one much faster paced, and Clarissa sighed as she sensed the rage and longing hidden in his music. He again stood to bow at the end of his song and sat again to play a much shorter piece by Mozart. After three such encores, the master of ceremonies emerged once more to thank the audience for coming, encouraging them to continue to patronize his fine establishment.

"We must find Lucas," Savannah said. "I doubt he knows we're here." They were jostled by the crowd and slowly made their way down the stairs to the main lobby area. White marble balustrades and pillars gleamed in the bright light of numerous chandeliers while gold-gilded mirrors along the walls reflected their brilliance throughout the room. Clarissa gripped Savannah's arm as they approached a porter.

"Sir, we need to see Mr. Russell. He is my brother," Savannah said.

The usher smirked as he looked from Savannah in a turquoise-blue silk dress with its fine lace overlay to Clarissa in a burgundy velvet dress that flared at her curvy waist. "And you're his cousin," he said with a roll of his eyes. "Do you think I haven't heard the likes of that before? Move along." He glanced pointedly at the exit behind them.

Savannah dug in her heels as though preparing for battle, but Clarissa pulled her away and out the front doors. "Come, Sav. If this opera house is anything like Boston's, there's a back entrance down an alley."

"You're suggesting we traipse around an alley?" Savannah asked as they skirted around a remnant of the mingling crowd, down Park Street and then came to an abrupt halt at the mouth of a darkened alleyway.

"If we want to see Lucas, yes," Clarissa said as she firmed her shoulders and dragged Savannah alongside her.

"You were always getting me in trouble," Savannah muttered, although humor laced her voice.

"And you always enjoyed it." Clarissa stifled a shriek as her foot sank into something soft.

They saw a lit entrance a few doors ahead and approached it, taking deep fortifying breaths before knocking.

A man with broad shoulders and well over six feet tall opened the door to peer down at them. He raised an eyebrow but didn't speak.

"Is this the back entrance to the Empress?" Clarissa asked.

When he stared at them with a mixture of amusement and malevolence, she barreled on. "This is Mrs. Savannah McLeod, but before she married she was Savannah Russell. Lucas's sister. I brought her here as a surprise. Is Lucas still here?"

"And you would be?"

"Clarissa. His cousin."

He broke into a smile at her introduction. "He wondered if you'd come to his performance. He's moping in the back because he thinks you weren't here."

He held open the door, and the two women entered the rear of the theater. Clarissa coughed at the stale air but did not pause.

The man led them down one poorly lit hallway to the left. They passed numerous closed doors before reaching one which the tall man pounded on a few times before thrusting it open.

"Damn it, Gil. Can't you leave me in peace for a few moments before I have to go to that infernal party?" Lucas groused.

"It's a soiree, and, no, I can't. Not when your relations come calling."

Lucas spun toward the door, sitting atop a stool in front of a small table where he appeared to have been writing. He dropped the pen, his mouth agape as he beheld them. "Sav? Rissa?" He whooped loudly as he jumped up and grabbed first Savannah, twirling her in a circle, and then repeated the same with Clarissa. She giggled as he finally set her on her feet again.

He stepped back, his hand still on Clarissa's arm, and reached out to link his other hand with Savannah's. "You came! Please tell me that you saw the performance."

"Of course we did. We'd just arrived home from Washington, DC, when I read you were to be here in Butte. You should have written and told us that you'd be so near," Clarissa chided as she ran a hand down his arm. The door clicked behind them, and they were granted privacy with Lucas.

"It was a last-minute addition to the tour. The decision was made only a few weeks ago. I'd forgotten about your trip to DC, or I would have insisted on performing here later this summer." His gaze moved from Savannah to Clarissa and back. "I can't believe you're both here."

"I can't believe I finally heard your gorgeous compositions performed in public," Savannah said, her eyes gleaming with pride. "I wanted to proclaim to everyone sitting near me that you were my brother."

"You liked them?" Lucas asked, unable to hide his childlike eagerness.

"I loved them," Savannah said.

"They were wondrous, Lucas. And to think you composed them too," Clarissa said.

Savannah and Clarissa sat on a small settee, and Lucas settled on a chair he had turned to face them. "I don't have long until I must go to the after-performance party. It's seen as acceptable to arrive late, but I'm pushing the limits of propriety already."

"We couldn't obtain tickets for that," Clarissa said. "It is a fund-raiser of some sort and quite expensive."

"Of course you're coming, as my guests," Lucas said with a smile. "The organizer will be delighted I'm willing to stay for longer than one drink, and he'll know it was due to the presence of you both."

"Why would he worry you'd leave early?" Savannah asked.

"I'm becoming known as a *difficult artist*." Lucas looked chagrined. "It's hard, night after night, to enter a room filled with people I don't know. To have them fawning over me. I always hope I'll see someone I know, but I never do. The only way I continue to attend these events is by bargaining with myself that I only have to stay for one drink."

"Well then," Clarissa said with a broad smile, "let's go prove your reputation wrong and shock them all." She rose, reaching her hand down for his as he stood.

***

They strode into the lobby of the Finlen Hotel, its crystal chandeliers sparkling, marble floor gleaming, and approached the entrance to the ballroom. They heard a gentle roar behind the closed mahogany doors, and Clarissa slowed her confident strides.

"It's all right, Rissa," Lucas soothed, pulling her forward. "I can guarantee the Butte society won't be like what you suffered in Boston." He stood between Savannah and Clarissa, each of them with an arm looped through one of his. He winked as he smiled, a carefree lightness in his spirit which Clarissa sensed he hadn't felt in too long. "They'll be shocked and then ravenously curious to discover how the reclusive pianist could have two beautiful women with him when he just arrived today."

Savannah rolled her eyes at him but couldn't help giggling. "Let's hope there's a reporter, so we can send a photo to our parents."

Lucas nodded to the man standing watch at the door a moment before it was flung open. A loud voice intoned, "Lucas Russell," and the threesome sauntered into the ballroom. A hush fell over the room as Clarissa saw members of Butte's elite strain for a view of them, and then the chatter slowly began its crescendo.

"Sauntering in late ..." one voice hissed.

"With two women," another whispered fiercely as the trio walked past.

"Well done, lad," murmured a man with a deep baritone.

Clarissa blushed but nodded, trying not to laugh. "Lucas, you must tell them the truth," she whispered in his ear.

"Why? People love the thought of a scandal much more than the boring truth. Besides, you keep whispering in my ear, and no one will believe you're my cousin," Lucas murmured.

She swatted his arm and then laughed. She shared an amused glance with Savannah, realizing she hadn't felt this free in spirit in months. Not since ... Her mind shied away from the thought, and she focused on the ballroom. On Lucas.

He smiled vaguely at those in the room and maneuvered his sister and his cousin so that they'd receive a glass of champagne. "Drink it," he muttered before they could protest. "Butte's far from a dry town, and you need to fit in. The ilk of Carrie Nation isn't all that welcome here."

Clarissa took a dainty sip and saw Savannah frown as she did the same. After a few minutes Lucas was separated from them by fans and patrons of the arts. Savannah and Clarissa stood there, a large swath of space around them as though surrounded by an impenetrable moat. "I never thought spending time with Lucas would paint me as a fallen woman," Clarissa murmured.

Savannah snorted. "Ironic, considering we're both married with children." Her eyes clouded after she said that. "And that we are truly related."

Clarissa glared at a man, swaying subtly as he approached them.

He appeared confused by their frigid welcome but walked away.

"I wonder how Lucas survives these events every day."

"He would find almost anything worthwhile as long as he could perform." Savannah stiffened as she watched the crowd surrounding Lucas. "Rissa, is that …" Her voice broke off as she frowned.

"What?" Clarissa followed her cousin's gaze and froze, her fingers going numb as her glass of champagne tumbled to the ground, splintering on the marble floor. She barely noticed the commotion around her as waitstaff rushed to clear the shards of glass while she stared into eyes she thought she'd never see again.

"It can't be," Clarissa mouthed, a tear coursing down her cheek.

A broad-shouldered man, with brown hair shot with gray, excused himself from his associates near Lucas and approached her. His brown eyes, lit with an incandescent joy, made them appear like molten chocolate.

"Patrick?" Clarissa croaked.

He beamed as she said his name, and he reached out a hand to clasp her shoulder.

She stroked a hand down his arm, her gaze taking in the subtle changes wrought by his thirteen-year absence. "Where have you been?" she asked, batting him on an arm in frustration.

He laughed, and another tear slipped out as she remembered their youth. "Here and there and everywhere in between." His deep voice was raspier, quieter. "I never thought to see you here in Montana, Rissa."

"Did you think I'd remain in Boston, living the life deemed appropriate by our stepmother?" She cleared her throat to forestall any more tears. "When you left, with only a note, I thought Da's heart would break."

Patrick's mouth tightened at her words, before he forced a smile. "Well, I needed to begin again."

She saw a flicker of something in his eyes but was prevented from questioning him further when Savannah interrupted them.

"Patrick, I can't believe it's really you," Savannah murmured, gripping his hand.

"Hi, Sav," he said, shaking his head. "I can't believe so much of my family is in Montana."

"Sav and I married two men from Boston with a penchant for adventure. We've lived here for years. Colin's with us too." Clarissa's breath hitched at the thought of them all being together again.

"I thought he'd stay with Da," Patrick said. He frowned as he watched Savannah. "I never would have thought Jonas Montgomery was adventurous."

Savannah blanched at Jonas's name.

"Have you had no news of Boston? During all those years away?" Clarissa asked.

"I moved around a lot. I ceased learning the latest news from a city I knew I'd never return to."

"Da died, Patrick. He had a heart seizure at the forge. Over ten years ago now." She paused, blinking away tears. "And Jonas died too. Savannah's here with her second husband." She saw Savannah half-smirk at Clarissa's whitewashed rendition of Savannah's tale.

"And you live in Butte?" Patrick asked as he smiled at an acquaintance. When the man approached, Patrick introduced Savannah and Clarissa, instantly reducing the intrigue surrounding them. "This is a good friend of mine, Mr. Samuel Sanders. He works at the Company with me and has helped me learn my way about."

"It's nice to meet you," the women said in near unison.

"I hadn't realized Patrick had family," Samuel said. "Did you travel all this way for a mere concert?"

Savannah bristled at his tone. "The concert was reason enough as my brother is Mr. Russell."

"How proud you must be."

Clarissa gripped Savannah's arm—to prevent her from doing Mr. Sanders any bodily harm at his dry, condescending tone—and pasted on a smile. "You sound as though you are from the East."

"I'm originally from Massachusetts."

"How fascinating," she said as she passed Savannah another glass of champagne and took one for herself. "We are from Boston, as are our husbands."

"I know quite a few people from there." He nodded his head at her as though commanding her to speak.

Clarissa shared an amused yet affronted glance with Savannah. "My husband is Gabriel McLeod, and my cousin is married to Jeremy McLeod. We reside in Missoula."

His smile dimmed for a moment before he shook his head. "No, I'm afraid I've never met them. They must not have been successful businessmen."

Clarissa turned to Patrick for support and to escape his friend, but he was occupied speaking with a pair of well-dressed men. "I believe we have different ideas of what constitutes success."

"Yes, I can imagine we do, seeing as you're content living in the backwaters of Missoula, rather than in the only place in the state where anything of import occurs."

Clarissa replied before Savannah said something untoward. "Again we must disagree."

Mr. Sanders sipped his champagne and smiled magnanimously at a group of people across the room. "I'd say your one good fortune would be to have a famous cousin, able to dredge you from obscurity."

Clarissa leaned forward, now ready to verbally battle with him, but was pulled away by Savannah who forcibly introduced Clarissa to Patrick's business associates and Lucas's benefactors. Clarissa watched as Samuel Sanders moved away, mingling with others not of their immediate group, finally taking a full breath when he was some distance from them.

CHAPTER SIX

"When's my Missy coming home?" Mr. Pickens asked, perched on his stool, leaning forward on his cane, seated in his now-customary spot near the workshop door where he greeted all those who entered, seeking to purchase furniture or cobbling. A.J. spent at least three mornings a week at the workshop, imparting advice, telling tall tales or encouraging the locals to purchase more than they'd intended.

"Either today or tomorrow," Gabriel said, the scraping of sandpaper sliding against wood sounding in the room.

Jeremy sat on a stool near Ronan.

"I'd think ye'd know when yer wife was expected home. Seems *unchivalierious* not to meet her."

Gabriel paused, frowning as he thought through Mr. Pickens's words. "Unchivalrous? Cavalier?"

"Exactly."

"You know, as you age, you're getting worse with your words," Ronan said, where he hammered at a shoe sole off to the side of the shop.

"Just 'cause I'm old, laddie, doesn't mean I can't continue to learn."

Ronan winked at Gabriel, who shook his head, a whisper of a smile flashing before he sobered and resumed his sanding.

Mr. Pickens slammed down his cane as he peered through the open door to the downpour outside. The mud streets were nearly impassible after a few days of steady rain, and few carts or horses passed by. "Reminds me of the time before the flood. *Whoo whee!*" he exclaimed with glee. "That was a sight to see. All that water an' muck pourin' into downtown. Never thought I'd see the day a bridge would wash away." He attempted to whistle, but it came out as a blowing sound. He waved his arm in front of him to demonstrate the destruction of the bridge. "Like a pile o' toothpicks. Broke up an' floated away."

Jeremy squinted as he watched Mr. Pickens and opened his mouth to speak but yelped instead as A.J. whacked him on his shin with his cane. A.J. nodded to Gabriel, who shook his head as though to silence Jeremy.

"Better a little rain than the infernal heat two years later in '10. Hard to believe all the forest that burned in a few days." Mr. Pickens slapped his palm on his thigh. "They even let the men outta jail to fight in that fire. The valley filled with smoke so thick ye couldn't see." He blew out a breath, shaking his head in wonder. "I'd hate to see another summer like that."

Gabriel slammed down his sanding paper. "Old Man ..." He paused as he took a deep breath and spun to face A.J. "We, all of us here, lived through the flood and the Big Blowup. Why talk about it again?"

"'Cause I think ye've failed to learn what ye could, Sonny, from those disasters." He pointed his cane at Gabriel, smacking his lips together, discontented that his cane couldn't reach far enough to poke Gabriel in his chest.

"What could I possibly have learned from two natural disasters?" Gabriel's voice rang with a resigned disinterest.

"Life continues, and only a fool, or an old man, remains in the past." He glared at Gabriel. "Set yer past to rights, Sonny, and move forward with yer life."

Gabriel shook his head, muttering about interfering old geezers. Jeremy nodded, watching Mr. Pickens with respect. Ronan threw down a pair of shoes, glaring at Gabriel as he ignored Mr. Pickens's advice.

"Be thankful ye got an ol' geezer who cares about a young whippersnapper like ye," Mr. A.J. said. "Yer hurtin' my Missy." He slammed down his cane with such force he bounced on his stool. "No one has a right to hurt my Missy." When

Gabriel turned his head to meet Mr. A.J.'s glowering gaze, he added, "Ye make it right, or ye skedaddle, 'cause all yer doin' is causin' more pain. Day by day."

***

Low clouds blanketed the mountains while a fine mist fell when Clarissa reached Missoula. She spoke with the porter about sending her trunk to the house and boarded a streetcar. Savannah had been convinced by Lucas to travel with him as far as Seattle before returning home. Lucas had hoped for her company to San Francisco and beyond, but she refused to leave Jeremy and Melly alone for that long.

As Clarissa walked up the front steps to her two-story house, it was nearly time for dinner. She entered the front door, hanging her coat on a peg in the front hall. She glared at the empty space where Gabriel was to make a hallstand but then moved on. She sniffed in appreciation as her stomach grumbled. Araminta had cooked dinner. Clarissa moved through the living room, filled with comfortable furniture, on to the dining room and paused outside the kitchen door, listening to laughter and voices a moment before she entered.

"I tell you, it's true," Colin said, his arms crossed over his chest, his steel-blue shirt opened at the collar and highlighting the blue of his eyes. He sat at the kitchen table while the woman in the room worked.

"No, your eyes are sparkling like they always do when you're in the midst of a great fib," Araminta said, shaking her head with disgust. Her thick sable colored hair was tied back in a braid, and her light brown eyes shone with exasperated humor. She walked with a barely discernable limp while moving around the kitchen.

"Cross my heart and all that." Colin had his innocent-but-guilty-as-sin look on his face. "Just ask Mr. A.J."

"As if I'd believe anything that old goat said," Araminta muttered.

Colin chuffed out a breath, and Clarissa knew he was trying hard to swallow a laugh.

"What's he convincing you of this time?" Clarissa asked, entering the kitchen.

"Rissa!" Colin said, rising and grabbing her in a tight hug and twirling her once before setting her down. "Why didn't you tell me that you were coming today? I'd have met you at the station. When'd you get back?"

"Just now, and it was easier to catch a streetcar in this rain than worry about having a wagon stuck in the mud." She smiled away a frown as Colin sobered. "Araminta, what are you making for dinner?"

"A simple pot roast. I thought you were expected back and wanted to have something for you and the children."

"Where are they?" she asked, looking around, expecting to hear their excited voices.

"They wanted to spend the day with Gabriel."

Clarissa instinctively tensed at the thought.

Colin reached forward and stroked a hand down her arm to calm her. "Instead they decided to go with Jeremy." He pushed a strand of her hair behind her ear. "I'm hopeful he finally wore them out."

"Have they been running you ragged?" Clarissa asked with an impish smile.

"First it was the time you spent in DC. Then it was Butte. I hope you're here for good now, Rissa," he said, no teasing in his voice.

"I am, Col. My children need me, and I need to be home." She gripped his hand. "The most wondrous thing happened in Butte."

"Besides hearing Lucas perform?" Colin asked.

She brushed a hand over his shoulder. "I'm sorry you couldn't attend. We only had two tickets."

"I know. I've promised myself that I'll hear him next time." Colin pulled out one of the chairs at the kitchen table and sat.

"Col, I found Patrick." She blinked away tears, watching as Colin jerked backward in his chair.

He raised a hand to his head and massaged his temples as though trying to understand what she'd said.

"Col?"

"How is that possible? I've thought, for so long, that he'd died too."

"I know, but he didn't. He's moved around a lot. Changed professions and is now working in Butte."

"Why'd he leave? Why'd he never say good-bye to us?" Colin asked, an old anger simmering in the depths of his light-blue eyes. "Why did he never write? He knew where to find us, at least in the beginning."

Clarissa sat across from him and covered his gripped hands, easing them open to clasp them. "I don't know. He wouldn't say, and then we were surrounded by his friends and Lucas and Sav. We didn't have time to talk."

"When's he coming to visit?"

"I don't know," she whispered again. "I ... I know he was excited to see me. But there's something holding him back from wanting to be with us again."

"He's been away for over a decade. He missed his own father's funeral. He missed ..." Colin broke off as he saw tears coursing down Clarissa's cheeks. "Dammit, forgive me, Rissa." He leaned forward, reaching across the table to first rub her cheek and then leaning farther to rub her shoulder.

"I want my family together again. I'm tired of strife."

Colin sighed, glancing around the kitchen, noting Araminta had slipped out at some point, unnoticed. "Then you'll have to forgive him."

She knew instinctively Colin wasn't referring to Patrick.

Clarissa shuddered out a sob, her shoulders bending forward as though to ward off a blow. "How can I forgive a man who won't ask for it?"

"You can't, not until you mean it," he whispered. He gripped her arm, his touch both soothing and irritating. "I know you, Rissa. You have a forgiving, loving nature. But you've held on to this hurt for far longer than is healthy. Neither of you can move forward until you confront what happened last October."

"I want ... I want ..." Her voice broke. She raised her hands, scrubbing at her face as she battled tears.

"Rory's never coming back, Rissa, no matter how much you want him to return to you."

Clarissa flinched as Colin said the name that was rarely spoken. She met Colin's implacable blue eyes and gave a nearly imperceptible nod.

"Your strength has always been a blessing. It helped you survive the torment of living with Mrs. Smythe and the abuse at Cameron's hands. But now that strength is turning you into someone who's untouchable. As though you no longer need anyone."

"That's ridiculous," she sputtered.

"No need to be indignant, Rissa. Just make sure that one of the things that Gabriel always loved most about you, your resilience, doesn't form an impenetrable wall around you. You have this ability to carry on when most would have cowered in a corner, and it's part of the reason you're so dreadfully lonely now."

"I don't know how *not* to be strong, Col." Her voice trembled at that admission.

"I know, Rissa. But letting Gabriel understand you need his support, his love, isn't a sign of weakness." He gripped her hand. "Forgiveness can be the greatest show of strength you ever do."

"I'm so filled with anger. I don't know if I'll be able to survive without my rage." She flushed at that admission.

"Think about your life in a year. In five years. Is this the woman you want to be? Is this how you want your children to remember you?"

She blanched. "Of course not. I'd want them to remember me like I remember Mama. Always laughing. Always encouraging my escapades."

"Not held so tight that they're afraid to do anything without looking to you for approval."

She flinched, acknowledged his just criticism. "Stay for dinner?" She rose, filling a glass of water.

"Please, Rissa. Don't keep ignoring your family's advice. We love you and want to see you and Gabe happy again."

She closed her eyes as she stared out her kitchen window. "I don't know as I'll ever be fully happy again, Col." She met his worried gaze. "But I'll try. For the children's sake."

He rose and brushed away an errant tear on her cheek. "For *your* sake, Rissa."

She set down her glass and wrapped her arms around him, welcoming his embrace, but unwilling to allow any further tears to fall.

***

Two weeks later in early May, Jeremy sat on a chair in the room he shared with Savannah and traced the stamps on Savannah's trunk at his feet, picking at a faded stamp from her honeymoon trip to France with Jonas.

"What has you so pensive?" Savannah asked as she swept into the room, her arms filled with folded linen.

"We never took a proper honeymoon." He flinched as he ripped a corner of the stamp.

"I've had no need of one. Why would you think, ten years later, that I've been pining for a honeymoon?" She set the linen on a chest and faced him.

"We spent one night at the Florence Hotel, and then we returned to my uncle's house to live with Melly, Colin and Amelia's family. We never had time alone," Jeremy said, his green eyes lit with a fierce intensity, and she moved to stand between his legs.

"We just spent weeks traveling to and from Washington, DC. Today I've just returned from traveling with Lucas. Why would you think I'd desire any more time on a train?"

He frowned. "I'd hoped you'd relish an adventure with me, where we could be together."

"Do you know what I dream of?" She leaned into him, as one of his arms wrapped around her middle. She rubbed his black hair, sighing with contentment, as he turned his face and nuzzled her belly. "I visited a doctor when I was in Seattle."

Jeremy tensed, pushing Savannah back and easing her down to sit on the trunk in front of him. "Why? Are you ill?"

"No." She blushed rosily. "I recalled our conversation in Washington, and I knew our time of … of—"

"Forced lack of intimacy," Jeremy said with tenderness.

"—was coming to an end. I want us to have a full marriage, but I wanted to speak with another doctor about the possibility of carrying a child."

Jeremy stiffened. "Savannah, you could speak to one hundred experts, and none of them could convince me that risking another pregnancy would be worth imperiling your health."

Savannah sighed. "I know. The new doctor didn't give me any further hope. He advised me to look to other means to grow my family."

"As we have already done with Melinda." Jeremy stroked her cheek, forcing her to meet his eyes. He tilted his head with inquisitiveness as she bit her lip and appeared uncomfortable.

"I inquired if there was a method or some manner to prevent pregnancy. Becoming pregnant hasn't been a problem …"

"Unlike what that specialist in Boston said," Jeremy said with rancor.

"Yes." She reached up and cupped her fingers around his face, meeting his gaze even though hers was filled with embarrassment. "I don't want us to be relegated to kisses on the forehead and pats on the arm. I want to continue as husband and wife to each other. That is my dream."

"I can't risk you, Savannah."

"I know. It's why I asked the doctor about a method. To ... to prevent pregnancy. He was concerned about breaking the Comstock Act, but, in the end, he was more concerned about my health. It's why I had to remain in Seattle a few extra days." She took a deep breath. "I had something made that will help prevent pregnancy."

"Only help?" Jeremy asked, turning his face to kiss her palm.

"Nothing is foolproof."

"Well, I thank this man for his aid and for defying the law, especially if it means preventing another near-death experience for you." He sobered. "If you asked it of me, I would continue to refrain from ... touching you."

Savannah's smile bloomed with wonder. "I know you would. But I'd suffer as much as you, and there's risk in life, Jeremy. I want to have a full life with you."

He leaned forward, nuzzling her neck. "I've missed you, darling." He sighed as he heard Melinda's excited shriek. "As has Melinda." He rose, stretching his hand down for her. "Let's join our daughter. We're preparing dinner for you."

Savannah smiled and followed him downstairs to the large kitchen.

"Mother!" Melinda called, dropping the paring knife as she ran to embrace Savannah. "You've been away forever."

"I know, my dearest one. I met my brother in Butte." Her eyes filled with wonder as she remembered seeing Lucas.

"When will I meet him?" Melinda asked, moving back to the sink where she was peeling potatoes.

"Soon I hope. He thinks he'll come to Missoula to play this fall." Savannah shared a contented smile with Jeremy and sat at the table as they prepared supper together. "Where is Araminta?"

"She's with Clarissa and the children," Jeremy said.

"Did Gabriel go with them?" Melinda asked.

"No, he was busy with projects." Jeremy smoothed a hand over his daughter's head. "Don't worry, Melly. Gabe's just fine."

"He's been so sad lately," Melinda said. "I miss hearing his laugh or him teasing Rissa."

Savannah shared a sad smile with Jeremy.

"All will be well soon," Jeremy soothed.

"You keep saying that, but it's been months. Even Colin is starting to become serious," Melinda said.

Jeremy laughed. "What more indication do you need than Colin losing his ability to laugh?" He chuckled again, tousling Melinda's hair as he helped her set the table. "I think Colin's having romantic troubles and is a sour old man due to that."

"Jeremy!" Savannah scolded.

"I've heard that he has become *entrancangled* with three women and doesn't know what to do," Melinda said, beaming after using such a large word.

"Have you been spending time again with Mr. A.J.? For only he could come up with such a word," Savannah said with a giggle as Melly nodded in confirmation.

"Although it does seem a good sort of word. *Entranced* and *entangled* all mashed together," Jeremy mused, sharing a wink with Savannah. "And most likely sums up Colin's predicament."

"I think Colin's smarter than that," Savannah said loyally.

"From what I heard, Mrs. Vaughan's daughter is pinning all her hopes on him." Melinda nodded, as though she spoke with the wisdom of an oracle.

"Where do you hear such tales?" Savannah asked.

"School of course. Mrs. Vaughan's niece, Victoria, is in my class." Melinda raised curious eyes as her parents groaned. "Now that Colin's running the forge, many women are interested in him."

Savannah's shoulders shook with laughter. "If Col doesn't know better to escape their nets …"

"Poor Minta," Jeremy murmured, then sobered, sharing a glance with Savannah. "At least he's not boring us."

"What I don't understand is why Colin needs to marry Victoria's aunt to make right the wrongs our family did to her family." Melinda scrunched up her forehead as though contemplating a puzzle.

"Where did you hear such nonsense?" Savannah demanded, stroking a hand over Melinda's curls to lessen the sting of her harsh tone.

"From Vicky. It's what they think."

Jeremy sighed and shared a long glance with Savannah. "Our families have a mixed-up history, Melly." He continued after Savannah subtly nodded to him. "Clarissa's ex-fiancée, Cameron, followed her here when she left Boston to reunite with Gabe. Clarissa had married Gabe before Cameron arrived, so she didn't have to worry about anything—"

"Why would she worry?" Melinda asked, her face contorted in a confused expression.

Jeremy pursed his lips for a moment as he searched for the words. "Not everyone appreciates your sister's independent spirit. And Cameron wanted the dowry her grandparents, her mother's parents, would have given her."

Melinda frowned. "He doesn't seem like a nice person."

Savannah laughed, easing the tension in the kitchen. "He wasn't. He was horrid and self-centered. He thought Clarissa should feel fortunate that a man such as him, from a supposedly wealthy family, would deign to marry her."

"He sounds *pomptuse*."

Jeremy snorted out a laugh. "*Pompous* and *obtuse*. A very apt description. And I appreciate you spending time with Mr. Pickens, but you shouldn't learn his poor English."

Melinda shook her head in disagreement but didn't argue further.

"At any rate, Clarissa's former fiancée remained here in Missoula, courting Mrs. Vaughan's daughter, on the verge of marrying her, before he framed our good friend Sebastian for theft. Clarissa discovered that Cameron had framed Sebastian and also murdered a man, so Cameron was sent to jail."

Melinda still frowned as she listened to her adopted father. "But why do the Vaughans dislike us? And why would they think Colin needs to marry their daughter?"

"They blamed Clarissa for ruining the daughter's chances of marrying an eligible man, even though I would think they'd be thanking Rissa for saving one of their own from a murdering thief," Savannah said. "Now that more than ten years have passed, and the daughter's that much older, their memories are fading and, Mrs. Vaughan in particular, is becoming bitter at her daughter's unmarried state."

"Some will always look to blame others," Jeremy said.

"I hope my brother's smart enough to avoid her." Melinda tipped her head to the side, mimicking her father. "Although I like her. She doesn't seem anything like her mother."

"Whether she is or isn't, Mrs. Vaughan would be a miserable woman to have as a mother-in-law," Jeremy said, earning a gentle pat from Savannah.

"Mother-in-laws are meant to be difficult," Savannah said.

"I wouldn't know as mine is thousands of miles away," he teased. "I presume Araminta is named as one of the three supposedly vying for Col's affections. Who's the third woman?"

"Oh, that new librarian, Miss Hester Loken."

Savannah gasped and coughed on a sip of water she had just swallowed. "He would never be interested in her. Not after the way she's treated Rissa."

Jeremy shook his head with amusement. "At least he'll keep us entertained." He rose and grabbed something off the kitchen counter. "Speaking of being entertained, here's a recent letter from Zylphia."

May 15, 1913
Dear Jeremy, Savannah and Melinda,
I trust you had an uneventful return journey to Montana, Jeremy and Savannah. I heard from Mother that you had the opportunity to hear your brother perform, Savannah. How marvelous! My friend Parthena will be green with envy, as she also plays the piano.

On my journey home, I had the opportunity to speak with a few women from New York who had attended the parade, and it was enjoyable. They are hopeful that there will be a referendum for the universal enfranchisement in New York in the next few years. I pray Massachusetts will also have a similar referendum, and we will move one step closer to full enfranchisement for all.

With Sophronia's tutelage, I'm now preparing for my journey to Newport, Rhode Island. Whereas my father merely wishes me to have an enjoyable time while I'm there, my goal is to meet influential women who will join our cause. However, I've yet to master numerous social rules, and I'm quite nervous about putting a foot out of place. As the time approaches for me to leave for Newport, the worse my dancing becomes! Three dancing instructors have quit, one claiming irreparable damage to his "most precious assets." While my father calmed him, the instructor muttered that mine was not an auspicious beginning as I foray into society. I have a few more months to master the popular dances, and my fourth dance Instructor starts tomorrow. Wish me luck!

As summer approaches, I hope you have a wonderful break from school, Melly. I look forward to hearing all about your adventures. I promise to write you about mine after my time in Newport. I miss you, dear cousins, and look forward to a time when we are again reunited.

Sincerely,
Zylphia

Savannah wiped at her eyes as she calmed her laughter. "If that doesn't sound like Zee—stomping on a poor man's feet as she attempts to learn to dance."

"Not all were born to that life, love," Jeremy said. At Melinda's curious expression, Jeremy explained. "Zylphia spent the first years of her life separated from her father, my uncle Aidan, and didn't learn the formal rules of the upper class from an early age."

"I'd wonder why she'd bother now," Savannah said. "I'm rather happy to be free of most of them." She sighed. "I fear Zee'll be disappointed by the monotony of it all."

"Why wouldn't Zee have already entered society if she's known her father for years?" Melinda asked.

"Well, she has, to an extent, but she's never done the whirl of balls and soirees like she'll do now," Savannah said. "It's very different from dinner parties. Besides, Delia remains so busy with the orphanage, they don't even have afternoon tea."

Jeremy and Melinda shared a confused stare before grinning at each other. "Why should that be important? Besides missing out on some delicious tea and cakes." He winked at Melinda, who giggled.

"It's where the women gather to share the important gossip. If you aren't hosting teas and attending those teas, you don't know what is truly occurring in that world." Savannah sighed, her face momentarily crinkled in thought. "So what are you two cooking us for dinner?"

"Fried chicken and boiled vegetables." Jeremy rose from the table. He finished chopping the potatoes and vegetables, placing them in the large cast-iron pot filled with water. He went to the icebox, removing the chicken he planned to panfry.

"Thank you, darling, for making dinner," Savannah murmured.

"Anything for you, love," Jeremy whispered as he stepped near to kiss her forehead before returning to finish dinner preparations.

Melinda chattered about school, her friends, the joy of the upcoming summer vacation and any thought that entered her mind as they prepared their meal and then sat to eat.

***

After dinner and quiet time spent in the family parlor, where they all read their favorite novels, Savannah ensured Melinda went to bed by nine. "Tomorrow will be another fun-filled day, my darling girl," Savannah said as she coaxed her daughter through her bedtime routine. After speaking with her about her dreams and saying their prayers, Savannah eased from her room, leaving Melinda's door ajar.

Savannah met Jeremy in the hallway, as he peeked in to see Melinda already asleep. "Settled for the night," she whispered to him.

He watched her with an ardent tenderness as he raised her hand and kissed her palm before leaning forward and kissing her mouth.

She sighed into him for a moment, before abruptly pushing him away. She reached down, grabbed his hand and led him along the hall toward their bedroom. "Show me how much you've missed me," she whispered as she quietly shut the door behind them.

CHAPTER SEVEN

"Sullivan," Samuel Sanders called out. "Let's call it a day." He nodded toward the door as he pulled on his gray coat. He ran a manicured hand over his immaculate smoky-blue tie, his pale-blue eyes lit with impatience as Patrick rose and grabbed his jacket off the hook by his desk.

"Why the rush?" Patrick asked as he followed Samuel out and down the stairs of the Hennessy Building.

Their office was on the sixth floor, and they clattered down a hallway lit by windows. They exited by a side entrance onto Granite Avenue, through an ornately carved brick door, and Patrick took a deep breath.

"I still can't believe you didn't tell me that your cousin was Lucas Russell," Samuel groused as they walked the short distance to the Amalgamated Copper Company's club in the Thornton Hotel.

They nodded to the doorman, smiled at the man guarding the reception and walked into the private club. The parquet floor gleamed, while the soothing mahogany-paneled walls gave the room the feel of an Old World study. A finely carved black-walnut bar along one wall was attended by two men, one behind the bar, the other running drinks to members scattered throughout the room seated in leather chairs. A haze of cigarette and cigar smoke hung in the air.

Patrick rolled his shoulders, sidling up to the bar. He nodded to the barman, who pulled two pints. "I wasn't sure he'd recognize me. It's been a long time since I've seen him." Patrick's gaze became distant for a moment. "Or anyone from Boston."

"I know how that is. I've not seen my family since the Panic."

Patrick watched as his friend paused upon mentioning the Panic of 1907. He recalled the run on the banks, the fear that Wall Street—and the entire financial system—would collapse. He shook his head at the irony of realizing the Panic had begun due to a failed attempt to corner the market of a Butte copper company, United Copper Company, owned by F. Augustus Heinze. "You landed on your feet," Patrick murmured around a sip of beer, licking at the foam along his upper lip.

"Well, we Ma ... Sanders always do. My mother would hardly recognize me if she saw me now." He shook his head. "I was a weak, pampered ass when I left Boston."

Patrick twitched his head to the side as he took in his friend's fine clothes, styled dull-brown hair and manicured hands. "They couldn't call you weak." Although lanky, his friend exuded a sense of lethal strength, akin to a rapier.

"Oh, I toughened up. Hard to believe I'm saying this, but the Panic was the best thing to happen to me. Made me much stronger. I realize now that a little adversity is good for the soul."

Patrick grunted as he followed Samuel to a pair of chairs. "You say that now because you've found success again. If you were still begging for notice, eking out a survival, you'd feel much differently."

Samuel lowered his voice to barely above a whisper. "I've warned you, none of that which could be misconstrued as Socialist nonsense."

Patrick raised an eyebrow. "In all your time with the Company, have you ever actually spoken to a miner? Listened to any of their concerns?"

"Why should I?" Samuel lit a cigarette and blew a puff of smoke above their heads, then spit out a piece of tar.

"I think you'd find it illuminating. They don't like this new rustling card system you've come up with at the Company. And it can only bring trouble if enough of them become agitated."

Started the previous year, the rustling card system required each man desiring to work in a mine to keep a card listing all the mines he had worked in. In theory, when he approached a new mine boss, the boss could easily determine that he was a good worker by what was written on the card by previous foremen. The miners didn't like it because they thought it unfairly favored the Irish and the members of the miners' union. Without being a paid member of the union, a miner couldn't obtain a card.

Samuel leaned forward, wagging his cigarette at Patrick. "Listen, I took you under my wing because I thought I saw a bit of me in you. Ambition. An understanding that sometimes ruthless measures must be taken for success. An unwillingness to accept defeat." He raised his eyebrows in a challenging manner. "Tell me if I'm wrong."

"Of course I want to succeed. I'm merely saying that your methods may end up hurting the Company, and that would end up hurting you."

"Ah, well." Samuel leaned back, relaxing against his chair and crossing his legs. The aged leather creaked with his movement. "I appreciate your loyalty. However, all it will do is cause the miners to fight among themselves. And discord among the miners is a good thing for the Company." He took another puff from his cigarette and spoke as he exhaled. "The worst thing is a unified group, speaking as one. When they're fractious, they're powerless." Samuel sighed and took another draw of his pint, nearly draining the entire glass in one gulp. He nodded to the nearby attendant for another pint. "How do you like your work?"

"It's mindless. It's fine." Patrick brushed at his slacks. "I'm thankful for the good work."

Samuel grunted. "As you should be. You never know what could come of it."

"Tallying numbers doesn't take a genius," Patrick grumbled.

"No, but honesty, integrity and loyalty are harder to find than you'd think."

Patrick nodded.

"I have the ear of those up above. Don't mess things up, and you could find yourself doing much more than tallying rows of figures."

Patrick nodded again, taking a deep sip from his glass of beer.

"Don't become enamored with any of the miners' twaddle you hear. The Company has all the power in this town and in this state. Don't worry about those who will always remain powerless."

***

Patrick slipped from the room he rented in an upscale boarding house in Uptown Butte on Quartz Street and wandered toward Main Street. He entered the Mile High Saloon on Granite Street, pushing his way to the bar. When he had the barman's attention, he ordered a pint, slapped down his coin and then moved toward the back wall. He leaned against it, ostensibly lost in his own thoughts, while he listened to his neighbors' conversations.

He hid his grin or grimace by taking sips of his pint, but an alert miner noticed him and propped a shoulder on the wall, facing him.

He was at least six-and-a-half-feet tall, with pale blond hair and striking blue eyes. "You find our talk humorous?" He spoke with a slight accent, although Patrick couldn't immediately place it.

"Not at all. Although I find your conversations illuminating."

"You aren't a miner," the man said in an accusatory manner.

"No. I'm the one who works on the payroll so you get paid," Patrick said with a droll smile.

"You work for the Company?" the man hissed.

Patrick glanced around, thankful the man's voice hadn't carried too far as Patrick didn't look forward to miners, angry with stagnant wages, inflation and ever-increasing mine profits, venting their anger on him. "Yeah." He took a sip of his beer.

"Did you implement that card system?"

"Hell, no," Patrick said with an emphatic shake of his head. "I didn't arrive until a few months ago, and I believe that started in December of '12. You believe I have more clout than I do. I have none with the Company. I'm a hired laborer, in many ways like a miner."

"No, you're not. You don't have to go down there and risk your life every day. You don't have to worry if your mine will be open or if the Company has decided to close it for some reason, leaving you no way to pay rent or buy food."

"Very true. I meant no offense." He held out his free hand. "I'm Patrick Sullivan."

"I'm Elias Laine, from Finntown."

"Ah, Finnish," he said. "I couldn't determine your accent."

"I've been in America for many years, and I've tried to become American." He shrugged. "Sometimes I succeed. Sometimes I fail." He waved his hand in a cutting manner.

"Have you always been a miner?"

"No, I was a farmer back home, but there's never enough land for a big family. So I left."

"So Butte's your home."

"For now. I come and go. When there's work, I work. When not, I move on."

Patrick nodded as he glanced around the crowded bar, everyone standing shoulder to shoulder, gripping at least one pint. He didn't relish pushing his way forward for another drink, so he relaxed against the wall, continuing his conversation with the talkative Elias. "Would seem a hard way to raise a family."

"If you had one. Life as a transient, indigent miner makes it hard to rear a family." He shook his head with chagrin. "Besides, women are smarter these days. They don't want a man going down the mine. Not when there's such a great risk of maiming and death." He stared at Patrick with a touch of envy. "They'd be looking for the likes of you."

Patrick laughed and shook his head. "No, I'm not the marrying kind."

"No family then."

Patrick's gaze became shadowed before he forced a smile. "Not really."

Elias was called away by his friends. Patrick stood among the crowd for a few more minutes before venturing forth to enjoy an evening in Butte.

***

Patrick reached out a hand, grabbing the woman by her arm an instant before she would have plummeted into the lake at the Columbia Gardens. "I wouldn't advise swimming, ma'am."

She stuttered out a laugh, her alarm-filled gaze shifting to one of recognition. "Mr. Sullivan?" At his curious stare, she nodded as she repeated, "It is Mr. Sullivan, isn't it?"

"Yes, it is," he said, his confusion evident in his gaze. "I'm sorry, but I don't know you."

"There's no reason you would. I'm Mr. Sanders's secretary, Miss O'Leary."

Patrick's memory cleared as he looked at her. Her red-gold hair was tied back in a loose bun, and she wore a light-blue linen walking-dress that enhanced rather than hid her curves.

Her cognac-colored eyes met his with appreciation for saving her from falling in the lake.

"Of course. Forgive me."

She shrugged. "It's nothing. When you are with Mr. Sanders, I'm certain you have more pressing things to note than his secretary."

Patrick flushed with chagrin, refusing to agree with her. "Do you come to the gardens often?"

"On every possible free day." She looked toward the mountains looming in the distance, for once not obscured by a thick haze of coal smoke. Saplings lined a few walkways, and green grass covered the area surrounding the lake. Nearby, a group played a game of baseball, and the players could be heard arguing about the rules. "It's the only place here that reminds me of home."

"You're from Ireland?" At her nod, he smiled. "So was my father." He leaned down and picked up the wicker basket at her feet, its lid firmly latched even after she had dropped it. He frowned as he hefted it. "Might I escort you to your destination? This seems too heavy for you to carry."

"Oh, I wouldn't want to impose." A soft blush highlighted her rosy complexion. When he waited patiently for her to take his elbow, she grinned at him and looped her arm through his. "I'm meeting my sister and a cousin at the far end of the lake."

"Why there?"

"We like to imagine, on days like today, with the mountains shining in the sun and the lake before us, that we are home again. 'Tis silly, I know."

"No, believe me. I understand. After the desire to forget home wears off, all you want to do is remember it."

She nodded her understanding. "Why don't you join us today, Mr. Sullivan? We always bring far too much, as you can tell by the weight of that hamper. It would be a nice change for us to have someone new to speak with." When he stuttered out an excuse, she interrupted him. "It will be no imposition, and I insist, especially as you almost pushed me into the lake. This is what I request as my boon for nearly drowning me."

Patrick laughed and agreed. "Then I don't know how I could refuse."

She led him toward a small hill near the far end of the lake and waved at two women sitting on a large blanket. They looked as though they were sisters, thin blond tendrils of hair artfully curling toward their napes as fine hats protected their fair skin from the sun. They waved as Miss O'Leary approached. She, in turn, had to tug at a reluctant Patrick, his steps slowing as he neared them.

"Come. We aren't scary," she teased, her lips upturned into a smile.

He realized she was always on the verge of smiling, reminding him of his brother Colin. He allowed himself to be led to the small hill and set the hamper on a corner of the blanket, anchoring it against any gusts of wind.

"Maeve, Shannon," Fiona said as she pointed at Patrick, "this is Mr. Sullivan. He prevented me from falling into the lake."

"We saw. He was most gallant," Maeve said with a flirtatious smile. She wore a light-green linen dress that highlighted her complexion and eyes.

Miss O'Leary added, "My younger sister, Maeve," pointing at the flirty one.

Her curves were subtler than those of Miss O'Leary.

"You're very welcome to join us," Maeve said.

Patrick sat and soon the hamper he'd carried and another the other women had brought were opened, revealing a feast of cold chicken, potato salad, green bean salad, crusty bread and bottles of cider. "Forgive me for not offering anything to this feast."

"Nonsense. It's nice to have someone join us for a change," Shannon said.

She was thinner than her two cousins and her nose slightly less rounded. Her brogue was more discernible, and she smiled less freely than her cousins. "Your contribution can be to entertain us with tales as we eat."

He froze, his gaze flitting from woman to woman. He then looked down at the blanket and frowned. "I'm afraid little I have to tell would entertain."

Fiona glared at her cousin. "Mr. Sullivan and I work together." She handed full plates around. "He's quite friendly with Mr. Sanders."

Maeve and Shannon stiffened at the mention of her boss, and Patrick's frown deepened further.

"Fiona, I know you don't like me speaking plainly about your boss," Maeve said, "but he reminds me of a wild panther we saw in one of those passing circuses." Maeve shared a mutinous glare with her sister.

Patrick laughed. "He's not as bad as all that. He's simply a man who's had to work hard for what he now has, like many of us." At their persistent looks of disbelief, he shrugged. "Although I'm sure you have reasons behind your opinions." He paused, hoping one of them would speak again, but they focused on their cold repast instead.

"Now, Mr. Sullivan, I refuse to believe a man such as you has no tales to tell of his journey to this fine town," Shannon said.

"I'm not a storyteller. That's my brother, Colin's, talent." Patrick set down his empty plate and reclined on his hands, his legs stretched in front of him and crossed at his ankles.

"Let us be the judge," Fiona said with a smile. She handed him another bottle of cider and curled her feet under her to one side as she watched him expectantly.

Patrick paused, his gaze distant. "I left Boston, where I'm from, not long after the turn of the century." His mind was consumed by his last days and hours at home. He shrugged as he regaled them about his travels from city to city, the differences in each place. "Somehow I managed to be in St. Louis for the World Fair in 1904. Wandering the expositions on my day off, I never saw everything. It was a spectacular site."

After a few moments' pause, Maeve giggled. "You're right, Mr. Sullivan. You're a terrible storyteller." As he flushed, Maeve giggled again.

"Tell me about Ireland," Patrick said. "My da was from there, but he rarely spoke of it."

Fiona gazed toward the glinting water on the lake. "It's always green. There's rarely a time when it doesn't rain for more than a few days. So 'tis often gray as well. But when the sun shines ..." She gave a faint nod. "The mountains rise as though from a mist, and the lakes shimmer."

"It sounds beautiful," Patrick murmured.

"It is. It was. But 'tis a poor country unable to support its people. Thus, we leave." Her smile held little of its earlier brilliance. "And cling to what we can remember and recreate it in our new homes."

They sat in silence for a few minutes. "Do any of you like music?" Patrick asked. "I heard the Minneapolis Symphony comes to town next week and thought to attend." The women shared glances, and he watched them with confusion at their silent communication.

"Are you asking any of us in particular?" Shannon asked.

He rolled his eyes. "No, I'd like to invite the three of you to thank you for sharing your picnic with me today."

Maeve laughed at his frustration. "We'd be delighted. I'm sure you'll be able to relate the particulars to Fee as she works with you."

Patrick sighed his relief as Fiona laughed her agreement, reaching farther into the hamper to extract an apple tart for dessert.

They joked and laughed as the afternoon wore on, finally rising to catch a trolley near suppertime.

CHAPTER EIGHT

Samuel Sanders paused at his secretary's desk, noting the gentle curve to her neck, the thin gold necklace nearly hidden under her dress collar. He admired her generous curves for a few moments before he tapped his fingers on the pile of papers beside her typewriter, meeting her startled cognac-colored eyes with amusement in his.

Her fingers stilled on the keys as she awaited his instruction. When he remained silent, watching her as though he were a bird of prey, she tensed. "Sir?" she asked.

"I find I have need of your expertise, Miss O'Leary," he said, an indulgent smirk flirting with his lips.

"I have nothing else to offer you, sir, beside my secretarial skills." She lowered her gaze to appear demure.

"I'm certain that is not true. I never realized I would come to you should I want to discuss the finer points of a musical composition." He motioned for her to precede him into his office.

She grabbed a pad of paper and a pencil and entered his office, sitting on the edge of one of the hard wooden chairs in front of his desk, her shoulders held so far back her shoulder blades nearly touched. She spared little time glancing around the room she'd seen numerous times but instead focused on the man shutting the door with a gentle *click*.

His manicured hands belied a hidden core of steel. His perfectly styled dish-water-brown hair, parted to one side, and his immaculately tailored gray suit with maroon waistcoat gave him the appearance of a pampered businessman. However, his light-brown eyes shone with the unapologetic acceptance of what he'd done to achieve such a position.

"I see you've become friendly with Mr. Sullivan," Samuel said as he moved with the stealth of a cat to stand behind her. He fingered the thin strand of her necklace, tugging on it. He smiled as he elicited a gasp of dismay.

"I'm sorry if it is against company policy," she whispered, her head bowed, her hand over the front of her neck.

"I'd hate to have to train a new secretary because you became enamored of him and decided to leave to marry him." He tugged further on the chain, smiling as it snapped.

She moaned as she grasped at the chain.

However, it slipped through her fingers as he lifted it over her head and clasped it in his palm. He sat in front of her on his desk. "What were you trying to hide so desperately from me?"

"Nothing." She tilted her face, throwing her chin up in defiance.

He smirked as he uncurled his fingers to look at her necklace and the charm that had dangled at the end of it. "I'm surprised, Miss O'Leary. Or should I say *Mrs.* O'Leary?" He held up the wedding ring that had nestled between her breasts moments before.

"It was my mother's."

In an instant, he leaned over, trapping her in her chair, his arms on either side of her, caging her in place. Although a thin man, menacing strength emanated from him. "Don't lie to me. Never to me."

She shook at the threat carried in his voice. "Let me go."

He moved closer, his whiskey-flavored breath washing over her cheeks. "Never. You owe me, missus." He traced a finger down her cheek, eliciting a shudder. "Do you react so to Mr. Sullivan's touch?" She moved as though to push past him, and he pressed on both of her shoulders with the palms of his hands, holding her in place, hard against the back of the chair, her head pinned by his thumb's hold on her chin. He smiled with satisfaction at the terror reflected in her eyes.

"I'll resign."

"Do you think anyplace else in this town will hire you? I'll make sure you are not worthy of anywhere but the Dumas," he said, referring to one of the brothels in the nearby red light district. He kept one hand on her neck and ran the other over the front of her bodice. "Personally."

She jerked as futile tears escaped. "Let me go!" She opened her mouth as if to scream, but he covered it with his palm and shook his head with disappointment.

"I expected better from you, Miss O'Leary. But then I don't know why. You are, after all, a woman." When she stilled underneath his hold, he leaned closer and whispered in her ear, his warm breath provoking more trembling. "A weak, soft, malleable woman." His hand coursed down her chest to her hip, then back up again to rest on her breast, holding her in place.

"Here is what you will agree to, my dear. And, if you don't, or if you think to cross me in any way, you will regret the day you left your lovely Ireland."

***

Fiona sat in the chair, caged by Samuel Sanders, and nodded as tears coursed down her cheeks. She shivered as he whispered in her ear threats to her sister. Her cousin. She recoiled at the pleasure her torment provoked in him as he promised pain and humiliation should she defy him. She shuddered as he licked and then bit the side of her neck. In that moment, she would agree to anything to escape him.

***

A few weeks later in early June, Patrick walked into a marginally less crowded Mile High Bar. He scanned the room for Elias but failed to see him. After obtaining a drink for this evening—a tumbler full of whiskey—Patrick moved again to what he considered his customary place along the rear brick wall. He sipped his whiskey, wincing at the burn and relishing the slow slide to oblivion. Tomorrow was a free day, and, other than a trip to the Columbia Gardens to see a patch of green and breathe fresh air, he had no plans.

"Do you believe this wall won't hold itself up if you don't help it?" Elias asked.

Patrick focused on him and smiled his welcome. He raised his glass by way of saluting his companion's dry humor. He'd met Elias a half dozen times in the past few weeks, their friendship slowly solidifying.

Plain electrical fixtures adorned a nondescript ceiling but provided bright light to the entire bar. The mirror behind the plainly carved long mahogany bar reflected the group of men awaiting their chance to purchase a drink. Casks of whiskey and ale filled the area behind the bar and below the mirror, and bartenders kept a close watch on patrons as they filled orders.

"Why are you always alone?" Elias asked.

"I don't know many people in this town. I have no idea how long I'll stay." Patrick shrugged his shoulders.

"Doesn't mean you can't make friends," Elias argued. "Besides, most who come here believe they'll only stay a short while before leaving. And then they settle here."

"I've begun to realize that." Patrick took another sip of his drink. "I don't know as I'm the settling type. I've moved around too much to ever feel like I belong anywhere."

"You have the luxury of being able to put down roots, knowing you have a steady job. Something us miners could only hope for." Elias gave Patrick a pointed stare. "Find a good woman to settle down with."

"Like I said, I'm not sure I'm the settling type." Patrick thought about Fiona and then shared a grin with Elias. "But I'll know when it's time to."

Elias laughed and slapped him on his back. "If it's that good-looking lady from the gardens I've seen you with a few times, you'd be a fool to not become better acquainted with her."

They stood in companionable silence a while, sipping their drinks.

Patrick broke the silence, saying, "I thought your union was strong. That Butte was a mining town where the miners set down roots and raised families."

"Not anymore. The union was strong when it was run for the Irish. When Marcus Daly was in town."

"He's been dead for years," Patrick said, taking a sip of whiskey and crossing one leg in front of the other as he leaned against the wall. "Didn't he die in 1900?"

"Ya, and those of us not from Ireland …" Elias shook his head with disgust. "They refused to strike last year when a group of Finns was fired. Refused to stand up for their own union members."

"What were they accused of?"

"Being Socialists."

Patrick smiled wryly. "You can see why the mining companies would be hesitant to have Socialists, eager to wreak havoc wherever they go, working in a mine. They could endanger the lives of many men." He thought of the daily mine accidents leading to maimings and death. He shook his head as he envisioned a group belowground, intent on causing harm. "I can't blame the Company for wanting to keep its people safe."

"Did the union stand up for five hundred of their members when they were fired?" Elias's eyes blazed. "No. Because they weren't Irish. Many were fired by their foremen, Irishmen, who didn't want Finns working with them."

Patrick frowned and was about to speak but held his tongue as Elias barreled on.

"Has the union demanded that the Company stop using the rustling card system? Of course not. We're all convinced they helped create the damn thing to keep us in our place and to force us to pay our dues to a union that doesn't represent us." He glared at Patrick. "They want to do all they can to help the Irish and keep the rest of us from any position of power."

"I'm sure it's more complicated than that," Patrick murmured.

"Just as I'm sure you don't want to see it as being that simple—what with a last name like Sullivan." Elias glared at him.

"Listen, I have no say over anything that happens in the Company." He frowned, staring into the amber liquid in his glass. "I only accepted the job here as I had hoped it would provide me with a fresh start."

"Well, if you have any friends who are in higher places, I'd think they'd be worried. The miners are restless, and they aren't happy."

Patrick shook his head. "I'd think that would make the miners more uneasy than the mine owners. If you aren't organized, you have no bargaining ability with the Company."

Elias snorted. "That's what the union keeps saying. That we must be a unified group. But they want us unified in their way. The old way. We aren't willing to accept that."

"I fear your union may be correct." Patrick speared Elias with an intense stare. "You splinter that union, and you may well lose all your influence with the Company."

Elias smiled ruefully and raised his glass to Patrick. "I never thought I'd have a drink with a man who works for them yet encourages me to remain in my union."

Patrick laughed. "I've never been conventional."

***

A warm breeze blew, bringing a respite to the day's even warmer temperature. Men sat on boardinghouse stoops or stood outside the bars to enjoy the evening. Patrick nodded to a few he knew and entered a small café for dinner. He waved off the hostess, moving toward a small booth along one wall. Large windows, opened to the night's breeze, let in the evening light and fresh air. "Hello, Miss O'Leary," Patrick said with a grin. He frowned as she jolted at his voice.

She met his gaze, any hint of discomfort replaced with delight at seeing him. "Mr. Sullivan. I was about to order supper. Would you like to join me?"

He nodded his agreement and sat with her. "I'm not certain this is altogether proper," he said, appearing uncertain.

She laughed. "There's no concern for my reputation. We're doing nothing untoward. Times are changing, Mr. Sullivan." Her cognac-colored eyes shone with amusement. "Why aren't you eating at your place of lodging? I thought it came with full room and board."

"After months of eating the same food on the same night of the week, I needed a break. Today would have been mutton with creamed peas and mashed turnips." He shook his head ruefully. "Have I ever told you how much I hate turnips?"

She laughed, their easy friendship solidifying. "I'll have to remember."

"I had hoped to see you last week. There was a silent film I thought you and your sister would enjoy." The joy in his eyes dimmed as she merely smiled at him. "Well, hopefully next time you'll be free."

She smiled at the waitress as they ordered—fried chicken for her and steak for him. "How are things at the office?" she asked.

"I'd think you'd know more about that than I do," Patrick said with a chuckle. "I merely tally numbers. Your boss is the one in charge."

"He wouldn't share anything of import with his secretary," she murmured.

Patrick paused from replying, studying her a moment.

She fiddled with the salt shaker, and her mouth had lost its customary uptilt at the corners. A slight frown marred the pale skin between her eyebrows, and her gaze had become unfocused.

He reached forward, stilling her hands' repetitive sliding of the shaker. "Miss O'Leary, are you well?" He frowned as he looked into her eyes. Devastation and despair met his concerned gaze for an instant before she blinked, and then all hint of such emotion disappeared.

"I'm perfectly well. There's no need for any worry," she said with a bright smile.

Patrick frowned, shaking his head in disbelief. "I know we are just becoming friends. But I want you to know you could come to me about anything, and I'd help you," he whispered. His frown turned to a near scowl as she refused to meet his eyes, instead focusing on the tabletop and nodding a few times in a dismissive manner.

"Of course."

"Miss O'Leary," he said, sliding from the booth. "I fear I'm interrupting what you'd hoped to be a solitary supper. I'll speak with the hostess about obtaining another seat." He rose, grabbing his jacket at the last moment before it slipped to the floor.

She reached out, grasping his hand so that he couldn't move past her. "Please don't leave. I'm horrible company tonight, but I don't want to be alone. Stay and tell me about your family in Missoula, your travels before arriving to Butte. Anything to distract me. Please?"

He reached forward, a finger stroking down one of her cheeks in a featherlight caress before nodding his agreement. He squeezed her hand once, then stepped toward the booth and slid back in. "What interests you the most?" he asked.

"Anything," she said, unable to hide a relieved smile.

Patrick laughed and regaled her of his journeys around the United States, noting the return of her good spirits moment by moment. He answered her inquisitive questions, and they laughed together at the ridiculous antics he'd participated in, and, for an instant, he knew joy.

***

"Sullivan," Samuel said as he stood across from Patrick's desk in the open workspace on the sixth floor of the Hennessy Building. Light streamed in from a nearby window, limning Patrick's desk covered with scattered papers, pencils and a slide rule.

Patrick raised his head, his gaze slowly focusing on Samuel. "Yes?" He cleared his throat and shook his head as though clearing it of rows of numbers.

"Please come to my office."

Patrick frowned at Samuel's brisk tone as he marched away. Patrick sighed, marking where he was in a long line of figures before dropping his pencil onto his desk. He rolled down his shirt sleeves and pulled his suit jacket from his chairback, slipping it on as he strode down the hall. He nodded to Fiona before entering the boss's office.

Samuel's office was shadowed this time of day and filled with heavy oak furniture. A neat stack of papers sat at the corner of his desk, while a pen lay beside it. A framed photograph of Boston sat on the opposite corner. A large framed photo of Columbia Gardens hung on the wall behind his desk, while smaller photos of Uptown Butte hung on the opposite wall. Two polished chairs sat in front of the desk. Samuel waved at Patrick to shut the door and to sit down. He did as he was bid, remaining silent.

"I'm certain you know why I've asked you here." He steepled his fingers in front of him as he propped his elbows on the arms of his wooden chair. At Patrick's perplexed frown, he glowered. "Your association with ruffians must come to an end."

"Ruffians?"

"Don't act innocent. Of course you know to whom I refer. Those dispensable, interchangeable miners."

"Have you been spying on me?"

"Don't be so dramatic. It has merely been noted that you have had quite a few conversations with miners recently. Specifically with the same miner."

"I don't see how that is any of your concern."

"Do you know he's a suspected Wobbly? That, bare minimum, he's a Socialist?" At Patrick's blank stare, Samuel slapped his desk. "I expected better of you." Samuel leaned forward, his brown eyes gleaming with indignation. "When you work for the Company, in your position, under me, with the amount of money passing through your desk to ensure proper tallying of funds, it is essential you be seen as aboveboard. Anything you do that is untoward reflects on me."

"And talking with a miner discredits me?"

"Of course. You cannot sympathize with them. They're a commodity, just like copper."

"They're people, Samuel. With hopes and dreams, like you or me." Patrick fought the urge to rise and kick at Samuel's desk. Instead he gripped his legs to the point of bruising.

"No, Patrick. They're the machine that allows us to extract the copper and make a good living. I'd hate to think you'd forget who writes your check each week." Samuel pointed a finger at Patrick. "And also remember, what discredits you, discredits me. I refuse to ever be forced to excuse your behavior again to the upper brass."

Patrick glared at him. "Of course. I apologize for placing you in such a position." He took a deep breath as his words had emerged as though choked by rage. "I'll remember to whom I owe my loyalty. I'm grateful for the work. For the new start."

"I took a chance on you. You owe me. Don't further your association with the likes of them."

Patrick bowed his head, hiding his momentary ire. He calmed his breathing, hoping the heat leaving his face meant his ruddy cheeks were slowly returning to their normal pale color.

"I believe you've been working too hard. Take a few days and visit your family in Missoula. When you return, I'm sure you'll see the correct action to take." Samuel flicked his hand toward the door as a dismissal.

Patrick rose, nodded and refrained from storming through the door as he would have preferred. Instead he quietly exited Samuel's office, burying any evidence of rage or shame behind a mask of indifference.

CHAPTER NINE

Patrick stood outside the door to the home on Front Street in Missoula, his hand raised but frozen in place, refraining from rapping on the battered wood. From Rissa's recent letters, he knew Colin visited his friend Ronan most evenings before heading home. Patrick had arrived after the smithy had closed and decided to pass by Ronan's house on the way to Colin's across the river. With his hand still hovering in front of the door, he glanced up and down the boardwalk, lowering his hand when uncertainty filled him. A bark of laughter floated through the door, and he canted forward, closing his eyes as long-ago memories flooded him. Colin teasing him. Colin telling a tall tale about someone from the smithy. Colin laughing with Da.

Patrick placed his hand on the door as he made out the rumble of low voices. As though against his will, his hand slammed against the door a few times, demanding entrance into his brother's life. He heard a groan and cajoling as boot steps sounded someone's approach. Patrick knew from Clarissa's letters that the other man, called Ronan O'Bara, was crippled and wouldn't have made such noise.

He stood tall, squaring his shoulders, as the door was flung open. His breath caught as Colin stood in front of him, then glanced over his shoulder as he called something to the man in the room. When Colin turned to face him, he studied him with a puzzled expression. "May I help you?"

"I hope so, Col." Patrick stood there, entreating Colin with his gaze for some sign of recognition.

Colin shook his head, his lips upturning as Ronan made a wisecrack before Colin stilled. He froze as he studied Patrick from head to toe. "Patrick?" he whispered. "Patrick Sullivan?"

At Patrick's nod, Colin launched himself into his arms, grasping him in a bear hug and slapping his back a few times. He then let go and belted him in the shoulder, sending Patrick off-kilter.

"Months! It's been two months since Rissa saw you in Butte. Did you think to write us? To let us know you were coming? It was as though you disappeared again. How could you?" Colin glared at him before letting out another whoop and grabbing him in another hug, his anger and joy forging a battle for supremacy. Colin dragged Patrick inside, kicking the door shut with his heel.

"Ro, this is my wandering brother, Patrick. Pat, this is my good friend, Ronan. His only defect is that he's a horrible cribbage player."

Ronan laughed. "If I remember correctly, you've had to buy the drinks the last three times we went to the saloon." Ronan rolled away from the table and the cribbage board to shake Patrick's hand. "It's nice to finally meet Colin's and Clarissa's brother."

"It's nice to finally be here." Patrick looked around the small room, the walls covered with tacked-up images from magazines of faraway places. A cot along one wall, two chairs, a small table and a miniscule wood stove made up the sparse furnishings. Patrick sat in the chair Ronan waved at, nodding his agreement to a glass of whiskey.

"What happened, Pat? What took you so long to come to us?" Colin watched him with hurt blue eyes.

"It's not as easy as you believe to get time off of work." He sighed, taking a sip of whiskey. "And I tried to write. But I didn't know what to say after all these years."

"You could start with why you ran off." Colin grunted as Ronan smacked him on his arm with a rolled-up newspaper.

Patrick closed his eyes as though world-weary and shook his head.

"Give him time, Col," Ronan hissed. "So, Pat, what do you do in Butte?"

Patrick's eyes remained closed as he answered. "I work for Amalgamated. I work as one of their accountants, ensuring the ledgers are balanced properly and payroll is correct." He opened his eyes upon noting the utter stillness in the room.

Ronan gripped his glass to the point it looked like it would shatter in his hand, and Colin frowned.

"You work for them?" Ronan asked in a voice barely above a whisper. "For *them?*"

"Yes. They were willing to take a chance on me. Give me a decent job, with hopes for a promotion."

"With no thought of those you'd be hurting with your glorified job sitting in the Hennessy Building in Uptown," Ronan said. "Crunching numbers and expanding their wealth as the men who break open the earth die for it underneath you."

"Please, not tonight," Patrick said, setting his whiskey on the table before propping his face in his hands. "I just need a break from it all."

"There's never a break from them. They are everywhere." Ronan waved his arm around expansively, his rapid breathing a sign of his agitation. "They run the newspapers. They rule the judges and politicians. They run this state. The sooner you understand that, the better."

"I fear he's correct," Colin said. "Very little is done to rein them in. As long as they provide jobs and produce a large amount of copper to spur along our rapid progress as a nation, no one will change the way things are."

"But what about the miners?" Patrick whispered. He looked up to see a flash of disbelief in Ronan's eyes.

"What about them?" Colin asked.

"I wonder, as I look over the tallies, as I see the number injured or who've died, what happens to them?" He looked at Ronan. "Are they all cared for?"

Ronan shook his head. "Few have as good a friends as I do. The union tries to see them cared for, but it's losing its power, and not as many are willing to pay their dues." Ronan shifted in his wheelchair. "Some bosses will find jobs aboveground for those who've been injured, but, if you're truly crippled, there's not much work you can do."

Patrick nodded.

"You look ready to fall over, Pat. Do you want to stay with me?" Colin asked.
"Would you mind?"

Colin smiled, gripping Patrick's shoulder and giving it a squeeze. "Not at all, as long as you don't care that it's just two bachelors sharing a place. Minta comes by every few days to make sure it's not a complete disaster, but, for the most part, it's mine." Colin looked toward Ronan. "Ro, sorry about interrupting cribbage. You'll have to wait another day for your trouncing."

"You mean, I have to wait another day for my free trip to the saloon," Ronan said with a laugh. He shook Patrick's hand and rolled over to the door to see them out.

When they stood in front of Ronan's, Colin turned right toward Higgins. "It's a short walk to my place. I live on the other side of the bridge, near Clarissa and Gabe, and Sav and Jeremy. They have new homes with most of the modern conveniences."

They walked down Higgins in a pleasant silence, Colin nodding here and there to those he knew. He picked up his pace, gripping Patrick's arm to hasten him along, when Colin saw a rotund woman in a lime-colored dress make her way toward him.

"What's your rush, Col?" Patrick asked, looking at the woman.

"She's one of Missoula's busybody mothers who hopes I'll marry her daughter," Colin said as he breathed a sigh of relief when they were halfway over the bridge. He slowed his pace, noting Patrick glancing toward the mountains, the river, the soft light of the evening sky before dusk.

"It's beautiful here," Patrick breathed. "I think I'd put up with a busybody mother-in-law if it meant I could stay."

Colin laughed. "You say that now, but you've never met her."

They continued their walk across the bridge, turning right onto Third Street. They approached Colin's house, a small Craftsman with a large front porch. Two rocking chairs sat to the right of the front door.

After unlocking the door, Colin ushered Patrick in, flipped on a light and beamed as he looked around his small living room. "Welcome."

Patrick paused near the threshold, his gaze wandering from the dormant brick fireplace to the cream-colored walls, worn leather furniture and finely carved side tables. An archway led into what appeared to be a dining room. Colin moved past Patrick, grabbed his coat and hung it on a peg behind the door with his, and motioned for Patrick to set his suitcase by the front door.

Colin propelled his brother into the living room, pushing him until he settled on the edge of a sofa. Colin moved to a small sidebar and fixed them a drink. "Seeing as it's just the two of us," he said with a playful smile. He handed Patrick a drink and sat down. "You sure you're too tired to see Rissa tonight?" At Patrick's nod, Colin sighed. "She'll be angry to have missed out on any of her time with you."

"I know, but I can't tonight. She's too …" He shared a knowing glance with his brother about their inquisitive sister, and their fragile bond of brotherhood strengthened with their mutual understanding of their sister. "You have a wonderful home, Col." Patrick looked around at the tidy living room that led into a small dining room.

White curtains covered the windows, and the walls were painted a soothing cream color. Painted built-in bookcases lined either side of the stone fireplace, and a painting of Union Park in the South End hung over the fireplace.

Patrick leaned forward, his hungry gaze taking in every romantic nuance of the painting of his former home in Boston.

"Thanks. I do. I worked hard for it." Colin glanced around his home with pride. He nodded to the painting. "Zee painted that—Aidan's daughter, Gabriel's and Jeremy's cousin. She's a tremendous artist, and she gave that to me and a similar one to Rissa a few years ago." He paused a moment, his gaze roving over the painting, reliving memories from his life in Boston.

"Why didn't you remain in Boston?"

"After Da died?" At Patrick's nod, Colin sighed and pinched the bridge of his nose. "Mrs. Smythe had plans to sell the smithy. It was her right as Da's widow. Thankfully Gabriel's uncle Aidan learned of her plan and bought it. Richard runs it now, along with two other shops."

Patrick squinted as he studied his younger brother. "I can't believe you're so unemotional about the loss of your birthright, the place you sweated over for years."

"Well, it seems we all lost the right to our birthright when we left. I forfeited any claim to it when I traveled with Clarissa so she could reunite with Gabe."

"I don't believe you truly felt that way." Patrick studied his brother, who had become a stranger to him after all these years.

"Believe what you will, Pat. I refuse to mourn what will not be. I have a good life here, with family and friends around me. I run a smithy of my own now. And my long-lost brother is sitting in front of me. I refuse to look backward and bemoan what could have been."

Patrick nodded, his gaze distant. "I can't believe I'm sitting here with you."

"How long can you stay?"

"I have to leave the day after tomorrow."

"That's not nearly long enough." Colin glowered at him, causing Patrick to laugh.

"It's very generous. I shouldn't have even been given that long, but they're hoping I'll … learn my place." Patrick shook his head. "I'm exhausted. Can you show me to my room?"

Colin bit back the multitude of questions he had and rose, motioning for Patrick to follow him. "Your room is through here," he said, crossing into the dining room and into a small hallway. He opened a door to a bedroom with a comfortable double bed covered by a duvet and wished his brother good-night.

***

A tapping on the window to her kitchen door jarred Clarissa from her thoughts. She turned and smiled as Colin stood outside. He had on his work clothes and dusty shoes, and she knew he wouldn't want to come inside. He motioned for her to join him outside, and she opened the door and walked into the small fenced-in backyard with two apple trees. Pink and yellow columbine dozed in one of the side beds beside the fence.

Colin paced under the trees, his movements erratic.

"What is it, Col?" Clarissa asked.

He spun and grabbed her in his arms and twirled her around. She shrieked and then laughed before he set her down. He watched her with an arrested expression for a moment. "That's the first time I've heard you laugh, really laugh, in months." He grinned. "I'll have to do that more often."

She batted away his hand as he made to pick her up again. "What's your surprise?"

"Patrick's here."

She glanced around but didn't see him. "That's not funny, Col."

"Not *here* here. He's at my house. He was passed out when I left, and I have to be at work soon. You remember how soundly he slept. We used to always joke his room could be on fire and he'd never notice." They shared a smile at the memory. "Will you drop by and see him?"

She grabbed both of his arms. "You're serious. He's here? He's finally come for a visit?"

"Yes!" Colin's exuberance faded. "Although I think he's troubled, Rissa. Something's not right with him." He pinned her with a deep stare. "Give him time. I don't want you scaring him away with all your questions before we've even had a chance to know him again."

"I promise I'll try," she said, biting her lip but unable to hide her elation at Patrick's presence in Missoula.

"Do you think …"

"What?"

"Do you think we'll finally have him back again?"

She reached forward and gripped his arm. "I hope so. He better have had a darned good reason for abandoning us all those years ago."

"Don't let your hurt keep you from welcoming him now." He watched Clarissa intently. "I mean it, Rissa. Please."

She nodded her agreement before spinning to face Gabriel, calling out to her.

"Are you all right, Rissa? I thought I heard a shriek," Gabriel asked as he poked his head out the back door.

She frowned as she looked at him. He appeared more gaunt as the days passed, with such deep shadows under his eyes they seemed tattooed in place. "Patrick's in town." She smiled then, her hope that he'd join them and share in their joy dimming as he nodded and backed away inside without a further word.

"Rissa, he did come to see if you were all right."

"I doubt he would have done anything if I weren't," she snapped and then grimaced at her words. She clamped her jaws together tightly, to prevent crying or venting further caustic comments.

"You don't mean that." Colin gripped her hands, now clasped so tightly into fists that they were white.

"I don't know what I believe. Sometimes I wonder if his solicitude is all a show for those present." She blinked away tears. "Because it's never gifted to me when we're alone." She took a deep breath and smiled. "I refuse to allow this to ruin your wonderful news."

"I'm off to work. Let's plan on dinner at my house tonight. Patrick has to leave tomorrow, and I want us all to be together again before he does."

"Col, you know your place is too small for all of us," she protested as he moved toward the gate.

"It may be small, but we'll have a wonderful time together!" he said, blowing her a kiss and departing.

***

After ensuring that Araminta could watch the children, Clarissa walked the few short blocks to Colin's house. Small trees were planted in front of every home, and a sidewalk ensured the pedestrians a safe path. Soon the trees would grow, providing shade and a sense of permanence to this new neighborhood.

She climbed the few steps to Colin's porch and knocked on his front door. When there was no answer, she let herself in. "Patrick!"

She heard a rustling in the kitchen and moved through the living and dining rooms to get there. She paused as she saw Patrick crawling into a cabinet and heard him muttering to himself. "What are you looking for?" she asked.

He jumped and looked over his shoulder. "The lid to that pan." He pointed to the one on the stove.

"It doesn't have one." She laughed as he rose and turned to face her. She approached him, her steps cautious, although she couldn't prevent him from seeing her wide smile or the joy in her eyes at seeing him again. She reached up and brushed the hair off his forehead before running her hand down his arm. "I'm so glad you've come to us."

He watched her intently a moment before pulling her close into a hard hug. They swayed side to side, and she felt him shudder.

"Dammit," Patrick muttered when he smelled the burning oatmeal, turning to the pot on the stove and pulling it off the heat. He sighed with frustration as he stared at his scorched, mushy oatmeal.

Clarissa laughed again and grabbed his hand. "Let's go for a walk. We'll pass a baker's, and you can buy a treat."

They locked up Colin's house and headed toward a favorite neighborhood bakery and café, The Last Drop. Patrick pulled open the door and followed her inside. After introducing him to the serving girl, Patrick opted for a hot breakfast, and Clarissa had coffee while he ate, choosing a seat next to the windows.

"What would you like to do today?" she asked, watching her neighbors and friends bustle by while she became reacquainted with her brother.

"I want to go someplace where I can forget that man is industrious. Where I can sit and listen to nature and smell something fresh."

She tried not to visibly grimace at his simple request. "I know just the place, and the streetcar will be passing soon." They hurried to Higgins, hopped on the electric streetcar that eventually took them down Broadway and rode it until the end of the line.

She looped her arm around his as they walked through a residential area toward a small creek. They bypassed the bear cage and entered the verdant area of Greenough Park. Soon the sounds of the modern world faded away as they walked beside the creek. Birds chirped and soared overhead, swooping to catch insects and to ride the breeze. Dappled light through the tree branches gave the creek an otherworldly feeling.

Clarissa approached a few boulders shaped like seats and settled on one. Patrick sat next to her, and she sensed him relax, moment by moment.

His breathing deepened, and he sighed with contentment. "Butte has the Columbia Gardens. I go there as often as I can. But it doesn't compare to this." He opened his eyes and met hers.

Rather than the peace she had hoped to see imbuing them, she saw torment and anguish. "What happened to you, Patrick? Why did you leave us?" She bit her lip to forestall any more questions.

Patrick laughed halfheartedly. "You just broke your promise to Col, didn't you?" At her guilty nod, he laughed more fully before looking as though he were choking back a sob. "You don't know what it means to find you again. To be welcomed by you."

She grasped his hand. "Why would you ever think we wouldn't welcome you?"

"Let's just say that I know what I've done, and … I shouldn't expect anything but your animosity."

"Now you're talking in riddles." She studied him a moment and knew he would say nothing further to her. "I understand if you won't talk with me. But talk to Col. Please. You shouldn't live with this guilt. There's no reason for it."

"Is there ever a moment when you didn't hate Mrs. Smythe?"

She sat back, considering for a few moments the sudden change in conversation and his desire to talk about their despised stepmother. "No. I always resented her. I hated how she treated me. How she changed our family. Worse, how she gave Melly away."

"Melly?"

"Her daughter, Melinda." Clarissa picked up a handful of multicolored pebbles and tossed them one by one into the creek. "She gave her to an orphanage rather than raise her. Thought the inconvenience and expense was more than she should have to bear."

Patrick nodded. "She and Da had no other children?"

"No, I doubted she …" Clarissa blushed and shook her head. "No." She took a deep breath, allowing the gurgle of the creek to soothe her. "I try not to think much about her and all she did. I haven't seen her in over ten years."

Patrick watched inquisitively. "What did she do to you?"

She shrugged her shoulders and then closed her eyes to ban the barrage of memories. "She left me alone with Cameron, who took advantage of the situation in an attempt to force me to marry him." She gasped as Patrick's large, strong hand gripped her knee.

"I'll kill him if …"

"He did, Patrick." She cleared her throat. "It's why I had to flee Boston. Why Colin came with me. I had to escape."

They shared a tortured glance for a few moments—anger, regret, anguish, all flashing across his face as he saw her stoic resignation to what had befallen her. "I'm sorry I failed you. That I wasn't there to protect you from her."

Clarissa's eyes filled, but she refused to allow the tears to fall.

"Does Gabriel know?"

She paled at the mention of Gabriel. "Yes, from the beginning he knew what happened to me. And still wanted me. Well, until now." She blinked away more tears. "We're having a few problems in our marriage."

Patrick scooted over on his boulder so that she could lean against him. "I'm sorry, Rissa. I'm sorry I wasn't there for you all this time."

She swatted him on his shoulder and then hit him again. "You should be," she whispered. She wanted to rail at him; instead she felt an overwhelming sense of loss. "I hated you." She felt him stiffen, although he continued to hold her. "I hated you for leaving. For not sending word as to your whereabouts. For abandoning me." She shuddered. "It seemed everyone always left, and I had to remain and continue on, as though everything was fine."

She buried her face in his shoulder and cried, the tears finally pouring from her. "I missed you so much." She leaned away and swiped at her tears. "From the day you left until the day I saw you in Butte, I never said your name. At first because Da was so angry that he forbade it, and I was so devastated and hurt that I agreed."

"And then?" He cleared his throat, perhaps thickened with the strong emotions he was dealing with now.

"And then it was habit. I had an irrational fear, if I said your name, if I spoke of you, it would mean you were truly gone, like all the others I spoke of and mourned." She pulled out a handkerchief and blew her nose. "But I never forgot you. I never stopped praying I'd see you again."

"Will you be able to forgive me for leaving?"

She leaned into his side, snuggling into his embrace. "All I've ever wanted was for you, Col and me to be reunited. Now we are, with Melly too. So, yes, I'll be able to forgive you." She hit him on the arm once more. "Just don't disappear again."

"I promise," he said.

They sat there, enjoying the peaceful location until her backside had grown numb. She sensed that the near solitude, listening to the creek's susurrus melody, breathing in the clear scent of the forest, soothed Patrick as he calmed minute by minute. Reluctantly she stirred, rousing him from a reverie as they returned to prepare for the evening's meal and Patrick's reentry into his extended family.

CHAPTER TEN

Patrick sat on Colin's porch later that afternoon, watching as a woman with a limp approached carrying two baskets filled to the brim. He leapt up and grasped the handle of one of them before opening the door for her. "You're Minta, I assume?"

Her eyes flashed a mixture of amusement and embarrassment. "Araminta, yes. I work for both Savannah and Clarissa." She smiled. "And Colin and Aidan at times."

"I imagine they keep you busy." He entered the kitchen, setting the basket filled with fresh vegetables on the countertop.

"I'd rather be busy than feel a burden." She nodded her thanks and then turned to the doorway, indicating she preferred to work alone.

He smiled and returned to the front porch. He continued the calming movement of rocking in one of the chairs by the door.

A short while later Clarissa arrived with her children. After a few stilted moments where Geraldine and Myrtle watched Patrick with wide eyes, he charmed Billy with a magic trick. The boy jumped up and down with enthusiasm, begging Patrick to teach him how to pull coins from his ears. While Patrick sat with his nephew on his lap, he glanced up to see Savannah walking up the porch stairs. He stood, set Billy on the rocker and moved toward Savannah.

"Hi, Sav." He crammed his hands in his pants pocket to still their nervous tapping on his legs.

"Patrick!" Savannah exclaimed, throwing herself into his arms for a hug. She pulled back and gave him a small tap on his shoulder. "It's about time you came for a visit. Rissa'd about given up hope of ever seeing you again."

"Give him space to breathe, Sav," said a tall man with ebony hair and piercing green eyes behind her. He held a girl's hand.

"You must be a McLeod," Patrick said, holding out a hand.

"Yes, I'm Jeremy. And this is our daughter, Melinda." He gripped Patrick's hand while his free hand ran over Melinda's head.

"Melinda?" Patrick asked in confusion. "I thought she was in an orphanage?"

"Oh, she was. For a few weeks back in 1903. We refused to allow her to be raised there. We adopted her, formally, five years ago."

"I see," Patrick said, his gaze raking over Melinda, from her yellow curls, blue eyes, pale skin to her lanky frame and polished black shoes. He cleared his throat. "I'm your brother. Patrick."

She moved forward and wrapped her arms around his middle, startling him. He patted her on her shoulders a few times before she backed away. "I'm so excited to have another brother! Can you tell good stories like Colin? Do you like to—"

"Melly, don't overwhelm your brother the first moment you meet him," Savannah said, her eyes alit with droll humor. "Come along. I'm sure there's plenty to do in the kitchen, and we want to help Minta and Rissa."

"Don't tell me Rissa's in the kitchen?" Patrick burst out.

All of them, including Billy on the rocker, laughed.

"Yes, she is," Savannah said. "You'd be surprised, Patrick. After twelve years of marriage, she's become a proficient cook. Well, except for pies." Savannah winked at Billy.

Colin arrived with a wagon, Ronan and an elderly man beside him. "Patrick and Jer, get over here and help," Colin bellowed as he jumped down.

Colin extracted Ronan's wheelchair from the back, put it on the porch, and Patrick and Jeremy carried Ronan the short distance and up the few stairs. Then they turned toward the wagon. "That's Mr. A.J. Pickens. He's one of Clarissa's oldest friends here. He's a bit ornery, but you'll come to love him like we do."

They helped him down, and Patrick gasped as Mr. A.J.'s cane found his shin.

"That's for leavin' my Missy to think ye were dead an' buried all these years. Ye darn fool." He shook his head in consternation and *thunk*ed his way up the walk, heaving himself up the stairs.

"See? He likes you already," Colin said with a laugh. "I'll be back in a minute."

Patrick entered Colin's house to find the children playing, the adults laughing and telling stories. He stood in the entranceway of the living room, marveling at such simple, essential human interactions.

"Just because you've been gone for years doesn't mean you don't belong in there, arguing like the rest of them." A man's deep voice rumbled behind him.

Patrick jolted and met a distantly familiar, amused gaze. "Gabriel McLeod."

"It's good to see you again, Patrick."

Gabriel pushed Patrick inside, and soon he found himself in the midst of all the conversations. He found, when he was with Ronan and Mr. A.J., Patrick's input wasn't much required, and he could simply enjoy their banter and ridiculous sense of humor. He watched as the women set the table, moving from the kitchen to the dining room, all while keeping an eye on the children. He watched Jeremy tease Savannah and noticed Gabriel settle into the living room, away from Clarissa.

"I know yer her big brother," Mr. A.J. said in his attempt at a whisper after he watched Patrick's gaze dart around the room. "But don't *interferee*." He evidently enjoyed drawing out the *EE* sound of the word.

"*Interfere?*"

"He probably means both *interfere* and *referee*," Ronan muttered. "He has a way of making up words that are ridiculous but wholly appropriate."

"Ah, there she is," Mr. A.J. said in his wispy way. "Pester, 'bout time ye showed up."

Ronan leaned in and whispered to Patrick. "Hester Loken is the new librarian here. She's been in Missoula over six months, but we still consider her new. She and Rissa had some mighty battles, but they've made their peace. For some reason Mr. A.J. likes her and has insisted she be adopted into our little group."

"And just in time," Savannah said as she moved toward Hester and gave her a hug. "Let's wash up and settle for dinner."

Hester brushed at her red hair, her fair skin sprinkled with freckles. Pale blue eyes watched the chaotic scene with trepidation, the fine lines around her eyes and mouth indicative of either frequent frowning or smiling. After a moment's hesitation, she followed Savannah into the kitchen, her navy skirt and starched cream-colored shirt oddly formal in the informal family gathering.

Soon Savannah herded the children to the kitchen to wash their hands, and they sat, adults and children, crammed around Colin's dining room table. Colin speared Clarissa with a glare before she could mutter an "I told you so" about the tight quarters. Savannah and Melinda giggled. Patrick stole surreptitious glances at Melinda, which made her squirm in her seat next to Savannah.

"How are things in Butte, Patrick?" Gabriel asked. He laid his arm along the back of Clarissa's chair, and she straightened to avoid any contact with him.

Patrick watched the interaction with confusion before answering, "Difficult. The Company, Amalgamated Copper, does not want anything to do with Socialists or the IWW. The Company believes this new card system they've created will help weed out miners they perceive as troublemakers." He shook his head as he considered the Industrial Workers of the World, their link to Socialist and anarchist beliefs, and their goal of altering capitalism to favor the worker with wage democracy.

"But you're not convinced," Jeremy said with an amused glance toward Gabriel and Ronan.

"I think it's not nearly as simple as they make it out to be."

"It never is, young man," Mr. Pickens wheezed. "'Specially when those like the IWW are involved."

"Do you remember when they came to Missoula?" Savannah asked with a shake of her head.

Patrick furrowed his brow inquisitively.

Savannah opened her mouth, as though she were to speak, and then settled into her chair and nodded to Mr. A.J.

"When those Wobblies steamed into town, they filled the wind with more hot air 'n woulda been needed to fire one o' Colin's bellows for a day. Never seen the likes of our good mayor so puffed up! An' all they was doin' was standin' on a street corner, proclaimin' their right to be there."

Mr. A.J. thumped his hand on the table, rattling the silverware and china, as there wasn't enough room to thump the floor with his cane. "Readin' such things as the Constitution!" He shook his head and then laughed with glee. "Made those stuffed shirts seem right ridiculous when the basic laws o' the land were spouted back to 'em."

"What happened to them?" Hester asked.

"They were arrested one by one. Placed in a jail cell, under a livery, with horse dung as their companion." Mr. A.J. shook his head. "But did that stop 'em? No. They filled those boxcars an' poured into town like a herd o' buffalo. Filled the jail too, until a proper criminal had nowhere to sleep."

Patrick laughed and shook his head. "Those men must have been good orators." He gasped as Clarissa kicked him in the shin. "What?"

"That's just like my Missy. Always defendin' her womenfolk. The best orator was a woman. A Miss Flynn. Her voice carried better'n any man's and was more convincin' too. By the time she finished speakin', she made ye ashamed for ever bein' proud of havin' personal success. Ah, a fine-lookin' lady. Reminded me of my Missy." He paused a moment as he squinted and looked down the table. "And of my Pester."

"Now, Mr. A.J.," Clarissa said, holding up her hands in protest. "I've never been a Wobbly, and I don't plan to join that party."

Hester nodded her agreement.

"Not sayin' ye were, Missy. Jus' sayin' there was somethin' 'bout her fire that reminded me of ye." He looked at Clarissa with pride.

"I think that's enough storytelling, Mr. Pickens," Hester said, a flush rising up her neck. "The IWW will never be considered appropriate suppertime conversation."

"Now don't become all squeamish, Pester," Mr. A.J. said.

Miss Loken blushed when hearing his nickname for her.

"They'll wreak havoc, even if only for the short term, if they can," Gabriel said.

"It's not that I don't agree with some of what they say. It's their methods," Jeremy said.

"I worry what it will all mean for the miners. The threat of IWW activity is making the bosses in Butte uneasy." Patrick played with his unused silverware.

"As they should," Clarissa said with a wry smile. "Heaven forbid the bosses lose a penny. Or have to share any more with the workers who bring forth the riches for them."

"See, there's my Missy." Mr. A.J. beamed his toothless grin at her.

"Enough serious talk," Savannah said, once the room fell silent for a few moments. "Let's clear the table and have coffee and dessert."

"I'm looking forward to Araminta's pies!" Colin said with a laugh. He winked at Minta, and she rolled her eyes at him.

The women rose, preparing for their after-dinner gossip session in the kitchen, ushering the men and children from the dining room.

***

Patrick sat in the living room while Savannah, Araminta, Clarissa and Melinda cleaned up the dining room table. The women had shooed away Hester, saying they wouldn't allow her to help as she was a guest. Hester sat in a chair with her hands clenched, hastily hidden in her skirts, as she listened to the women laugh and talk in the kitchen. Gabriel and Jeremy were outside on the front porch while Colin chatted with Ronan and Mr. Pickens at the dining room table.

"They don't intentionally exclude you," Patrick said, settling more comfortably on the sofa.

Hester sat upright and forced a calm expression to her face. "Whether it's intentional or not, it's evident I'm little more than a guest."

"I'd think it would be a privilege to be a guest here." Patrick watched a flush climb her neck. "Unless you have such a plentitude of friends that their consideration for you and their desire to see you feel honored holds little meaning."

"Of course I'm honored ... privileged to be here. These are generous, welcoming people, and I hope to call them friends."

"Is it me then, Miss Loken, that you find unsettling? For I can leave you in peace if you prefer."

"No, of course not." She slumped in her chair, her misery evident.

"What has you upset? Truly?"

She met his intense gaze and shook her head. "Nothing more than mere foolishness. It will pass."

"Loken is Scandinavian, is it not?"

"Norwegian." She smiled as Araminta brought her a cup of tea.

He studied her for a moment. "I have a friend in Butte who's Finnish. But he's tall and blonde, not a petite redhead." He watched as her blush intensified. "I beg your pardon. I'm unaccustomed to polite company. Where did you come from when you decided to move to Missoula?"

"I applied to numerous positions and Missoula's was the best offer," she said, setting her teacup down as it rattled in her hands. At his nod for her to continue, she cleared her throat. "I traveled here from Minneapolis."

"So you—"

"Patrick, quit acting like an inquisitor," Clarissa chastised as she and the other women approached. "Minta told me in the kitchen how you wouldn't stop pestering Hester with your questions." She smiled as Hester gave her a grateful glance.

Clarissa sat next to him on the sofa and dragged their sister Melinda to sit between her and Patrick. He stiffened as Melinda bumped into him and saw Savannah frown at his reaction. He tried to smile and relax again. Luckily, Melinda curled into Clarissa and ignored him. Jeremy and Gabriel joined them, with Jeremy standing behind a seated Savannah, gently stroking a hand over her shoulders. Gabriel stood to one side of the room, leaning against the window frame.

"We're fortunate to have Miss Loken here to run the library," Clarissa said.

"Mmm," Colin murmured, rising from the table. "We're thankful you've both finally made peace."

"It wasn't that bad," Clarissa argued, glaring at Colin over her shoulder and earning a wink from him.

"Bad enough. I'm glad to no longer feel guilty for signing out a book from the library and then hiding it from you when you visited," Savannah said. She laughed at Clarissa's gasp.

"I'm sorry my transition here wasn't a smooth one," Hester said, her hands gripping her skirts again.

"Ha, there ain't been no word invented for how awful yer arrival went," Mr. A.J. said with a cackle. "But that's all right, Pester. We like ye just fine now."

"Not that that's saying much," Ronan said with a laugh. "We're just a bunch of misfits who banded together to form our own sort of family. It's too bad Seb and Amelia aren't here too. Then we'd all be together."

"And Sebastian could play the fiddle for us," Clarissa said with a sigh of longing.

Colin nodded his agreement.

"Who are they?" Hester asked.

"Our friends who live in Darby. He runs a lumber mill there," Gabriel said.

"Amelia came here from Butte with us," Ronan said with the smile of one momentarily lost in memories. "Seb's her second husband. Her first husband, Liam, was our friend in Butte."

Patrick looked around the living and dining rooms filled with adults, knowing his nieces and nephew were most likely asleep on his bed, and a deep sense of gratitude filled him. He shook his head to make sure he wasn't dreaming. "For someone who's been alone as long as I have"—he cleared his throat of its raspiness—"I'll take your version of family any day."

Colin clasped him on the shoulder. "It's good to finally have you home, brother."

Patrick nodded, too overwhelmed to say much. "I won't stay away so long again."

"You better not, or we'll come and hunt you down," Clarissa said, causing everyone to laugh.

Patrick squeezed her outstretched hand, joining in with their laughter and fully feeling a part of their group at last.

CHAPTER ELEVEN

Gabriel climbed the stairs to the space over his workshop, his boot heels sounding on the wooden steps as he reached the space where he and Clarissa had lived when first married. The gentle tapping as Ronan cobbled a shoe and the sound of sanding as Jeremy worked on a rocking chair faded away as he entered their old home. As he stood at the edge of the kitchen, looking down the length of the room, memories flooded him. Of Clarissa poking her head into the oven with a hopeful smile as she looked to see if one of her latest dishes was edible. Of Clarissa sitting in her rocking chair, knitting late at night as they talked or he read to her. Of Clarissa writing at the desk they shared. Always of Clarissa.

He closed his eyes to stop the barrage of memories and emotions. He opened his eyes to see the space, no longer filled with the detritus of a life lived but with boxes and larger pieces of furniture to be sold. All their own furniture was now in their house on the other side of the river.

He moved toward the far end of the room, into what used to be their bedroom, and eased himself onto the windowsill. He could hear faint noises from the street below—the passing wagons, bickering voices and the rare sounds of an automobile.

"Gabriel," Aidan said in his low, authoritative voice. "I'm surprised to find you here, rather than at home or working."

"I wanted privacy."

"I suspected as much, seeing how you acted a few nights ago after our arrival dinner. Delia was quite offended by your cold welcome." Aidan and Gabriel exchanged glares. "However, when I learned you were up here, I decided to invade your solitude." He shared another long, stern look with Gabriel. "It's about time someone did."

Aidan moved into the loft, maneuvering around boxes until he stood near Gabriel. He scooted over so that Aidan could also perch on the windowsill, but he settled on a trunk facing Gabriel instead. "I wish I could say you looked well, Gabriel. But I can't. You look like hell. If possible, you look worse than a few nights ago."

Gabriel flinched at his uncle's assessment, knowing he would not sugarcoat his impressions to make Gabe feel better. "I'm fine."

"You're far from fine, and you know it. From all accounts, you're increasingly distant, barely speaking with anyone. Richard told me that he couldn't believe how things had changed between you and Clarissa when he saw you in March. That was four months ago, and I'm saddened to see you haven't improved."

"Dammit," Gabriel said, rising to pace around the items he and Jeremy had made to sell.

Aidan rose to settle against the windowsill, leaning against it, his gaze tracking Gabriel's movements. "There's no shame in missing your son, Gabriel. There is shame in causing undue suffering for those who also loved him."

"Don't you dare," Gabriel hissed.

"Dare what? To presume to understand the agony of losing a child?" Aidan's eyes flashed with long-buried torment. "Do you think all this self-flagellation will bring him back?"

Gabriel spun toward the exit, but his uncle anticipated that move and leapt to intercede, standing in his way. "No, Gabriel. You aren't leaving until you make me understand why you are acting like this. Why you won't comfort Clarissa. Why you fail to show any joy at your children's accomplishments. Why you leave the house before anyone rises and you return home after they are all abed."

Gabriel turned mutinous eyes to his uncle, his blue eyes flashing with desolation and resentment. His cheeks were flushed, and his jaw clenched tight.

Aidan sighed. "Oh, my dear boy. What happened?"

Gabriel reared as though struck, but Aidan gripped his shoulders, preventing him from spinning away. Gabriel stuttered out a sigh, and his body shook.

"Let go, Gabriel. My darling nephew. Beloved of Ian. You can't continue on thus," Aidan murmured as a sob burst from Gabriel's lips. Aidan tightened his hold on Gabriel's shoulder, and Gabriel collapsed into his uncle's embrace, heaving sobs onto his shoulder.

After many minutes, when Gabriel had calmed, Aidan pushed him back onto the windowsill he had vacated. He pulled a small silver flask with an intricate Celtic filigree from his pocket and handed it to Gabriel. "Times like this deserve fortification," Aidan murmured as he handed it to Gabriel.

Gabriel took a sip, wincing as the liquor burned his throat. He stared in front of him, his gaze unfocused, absently aware his uncle had sat beside him this time rather than on the trunk.

"I never understood what Clarissa felt, all those years ago," Gabriel whispered. "When she thought she was unworthy of me. Uncertain of our love. I remember feeling a righteous anger that she would doubt me. Doubt us." He paused, taking another sip from the flask. "I've always known Rissa was strong. It's an essential part of who she is. I never doubted she'd survive whatever life threw at her."

"She's barely surviving, Gabriel. The woman I saw a few nights ago at dinner is turning into a brittle, bitter woman. If she were to leave you or to decide she was no longer concerned about her marriage, I believe she would improve. However, as long as she remains with you, daring to hope for a future with you, she will deteriorate until she is a shell of the woman you fell in love with."

"The problem, Uncle, is that, although her belief that she wasn't worthy of me was utter nonsense, the belief that I am, isn't."

"Gabriel, what happened with Rory?"

Gabriel shuddered at his son's name. "He'd be alive today if I weren't his father."

"No one could love his children more than you did, Gabriel," Aidan said. He leaned forward, perching the silver flask on his thigh, the fingers of one hand strumming the side of the flask. "More than you *do*." The quiet reproach in his voice forced Gabriel to meet his uncle's gaze.

"I never want them to doubt I love them." Gabriel took a deep breath, closing his eyes for a moment.

"Disappearing the way you have only leads to doubts and confusion. They will begin to wonder as to their own worth."

"Damn you for implying I don't love my children," Gabriel growled. "They are everything to me."

"They'd never know it by how you've acted in recent months." Aidan met his nephew's glower, his calm diffusing Gabriel's ire.

Gabriel sighed in resignation. "I know you are eager to impart your advice, Uncle. Please tell me what you recommend."

"Speak with Clarissa. Tell her why you believe you are no longer worthy of being a member of your own family. For that is what it appears to be at the root of it all." Aidan pinned him with a severe stare, and Gabriel nodded his agreement, resigned to his uncle's insight of the situation.

"You accepted and loved her through her worst fears. There's no reason she won't do the same for you."

Gabriel shook his head. He reached out and took one last sip from the flask, hissing as he swallowed, before standing.

"You say I don't understand, even though I lost a wife and a child. Yet you're right. I don't understand, not fully, because you won't tell me what's truly bothering you. That's your right, Gabriel. However, you need to speak with Clarissa. If she rejects you or cannot forgive you for what you think you did, it's no worse than what you're already living through."

***

Gabriel entered his two-story house, hanging his coat on a peg near the kitchen door. He rubbed his boots on a small rug by the door and tiptoed so his boot heels wouldn't sound on the wooden floors as he crept to the kitchen door, peering into the dining room. He paused, watching the scene between Clarissa and their children unfold. His breath caught at the simple daily ritual of saying grace and at how much joy he felt watching them interact. At the regret for the number of such events he'd missed in the past months. "My family," he whispered in wonder, rather than despair.

"Amen," Clarissa said with a nod of her head and a wink to their youngest. She took their children's plates, adding a small piece of chicken, a serving of potatoes, green beans and beets to each.

"Not beets, Mama," their youngest, Billy, protested.

"You'll grow to love them," Clarissa soothed. "Tell me about your day. Did you have fun playing in the creek with Araminta?" She held up her plate to fill as she watched her children with an eager, excited expression.

Gabriel moaned at her question, with Clarissa and the children jerking their heads in his direction. He pushed away from leaning against the door jam and half smiled. "Do you mind if I join you?" Gabriel asked.

Clarissa's plate clattered to the table, spattering the pristine white cloth with beet juice. "Of course not." She nodded to his empty seat at the head of the table, a place set for him. "Please hand me your plate."

He sat, watching her movements become increasingly agitated as she served him dinner. "I'm sorry I missed the blessing," Gabriel murmured.

"Why are you home, Papa?" Geraldine, their eldest daughter, asked.

"I wanted to spend time with my family." He took a bite of his food as he heard a grunt of disbelief from Clarissa's end of the table. "I've missed hearing about how your days are."

Geraldine looked from her father fiddling with his fork to her mother studiously playing with her food on her plate. She mimicked her mother and looked at her plate, refraining from speaking with her father.

"Myrtle, how are you enjoying the summer?" Gabriel asked his youngest daughter. "Have you had any adventures?"

She watched him with large blue eyes and picked at her food. His son, Billy, wolfed down his food as though he were at the county pie-eating contest, refusing to pause for conversation. After fifteen minutes of tense silence, the children were excused to go upstairs to play in their rooms or to read, and Clarissa rose to clear the dining room table.

"Let me help you, Rissa." Gabriel reached for the children's plates.

"I wish you wouldn't, Gabriel," Clarissa said, her back to him as she approached the kitchen. "I'd rather do this myself."

He set the dishes on the table with a clatter and sat again at the chair at the head of the table. He watched Clarissa make three more trips to and from the kitchen before she had cleared the table. He had hoped to watch her in the kitchen, but she closed the door firmly behind her.

Gabriel sighed, uncertainty and frustration roiling through him as he felt a need for action after months of passivity. He rose, with the goal of forcing Clarissa to speak with him in their bedroom when he heard a quiet sob. He approached the kitchen door, opening it a fraction to behold Clarissa leaning over the sink, her shoulders shaking as she cried. "Clarissa," Gabriel murmured as he approached her, gripping her shoulders to turn her to enfold her in his arms.

"No! How dare you?" she gasped, beating on his chest with her hands and pushing him away with all her force. He stepped aside, and she fell to her knees, keening her sorrow.

Gabriel knelt in front of her, reaching out a hand to stroke her head and shoulder before lowering it to his side. "Rissa, forgive me."

"I've tried, Gabriel." She sobbed, hiccupping and smearing her wet face with her palms to clear her tears. "I've tried to understand why you'd refuse to comfort me. To refuse me to comfort you." She raised deadened eyes to him, and he reached out a hand, gripping one of hers tightly. "But I never will understand. When I most needed you, you abandoned me." She pushed away his hand and rose, swaying as she gained her feet, reaching out to the counter to regain her equilibrium.

"Clarissa, let me explain," Gabriel said, still in a kneeling position.

"Now you want to explain? Our son died eight months ago, and now you decide you want to reappear? Now you remember you have other children who need a father?" Her cheeks flushed with her indignation.

Gabriel rose and leaned against the counter.

She stabbed a finger in his chest as she spoke in an indignant whisper. "Where were you when I needed comforting? Where were you when our children woke in the middle of the night, crying, missing their brother and not understanding that death is forever? Where were you when I had to clean out Rory's things?"

She clenched her jaw as she watched him with resentful agony. "Nowhere to be found. Nowhere useful."

"Rissa," Gabriel rasped.

She closed her eyes and took a deep breath. "I've learned not to depend on you. I don't know why you'd want that to change now." She turned toward the kitchen sink again but was halted when Gabriel grasped her, pushing her against the counter, gripping her face fiercely, almost to the point of pain.

"Dammit, I'm sorry. I'm so goddamn sorry, Rissa." He leaned forward, resting his forehead on hers for a moment, before breaking that contact. "I always knew you were strong, and I'm sorry I wasn't what you needed through this. I couldn't bear to see our children who look so much like Rory." His voice cracked as he said his son's name for the first time since his death. "I couldn't look myself in the mirror, much less meet your gaze."

"I don't have it in me to sympathize with you for all you suffered."

"Dammit, don't become bitter," he pleaded. "I can't bear that I've caused you such pain."

Clarissa tried to move, to free herself from Gabriel's firm clasp, but he refused to release her. "Why do you think I want to listen to your empty words now?" she asked. "Nothing you say will ever bring him back. Will ever restore the months I lost when I needed you—" Her voice wavered as her lips quivered.

"I tried, that day. I tried." Gabriel rested his forehead against hers once more as tears leaked out and dripped off his chin. "As I held our boy in my arms, and you screamed and wailed, I tried to tell you."

Clarissa arched her back, at first to escape his implacable hold, then so as to meet his gaze.

"Dammit, I came in that day and begged you to listen to me. I begged you," Gabriel said, his brilliant blue eyes tear-brightened.

"How would you expect me to react? Calmly? Rationally? My son left with you for an adventure on his birthday and never came home." She raised a clenched fist, slamming it against his chest as she hiccupped through her sobs.

"Our son," Gabriel hissed, backing away, but grabbing her hand and holding it to his chest over his heart. "Dammit, he was ours." He bent forward, meeting her gaze.

"I know," she whispered after a moment. "It helped me cope with your disappearance by believing he'd been more mine than yours. That I'd loved him more."

"Rissa," he choked out, his body stiffening as though she'd stabbed him.

"But he worshipped you, Gabe. He was never happier than when he was with you."

He closed his eyes. "When I came home that day, covered in Rory's blood, to the decorations and cake and everyone shouting 'Happy Birthday,' I wished it had been me." He opened his eyes and stared into Clarissa's. "And then, when you attacked me, screaming over and over 'Why did it have to be Rory?' refusing me to comfort you ..." Gabriel cleared his throat, although he was unable to take the raspiness from his voice. "If Rory's death broke my heart, your screams tore it from my chest."

"Gabriel ..."

"You threw yourself at me. Called me a disgrace of a father. Said he'd have been alive if he'd been with anyone but me."

"No. I couldn't have," Clarissa whispered, her cheeks paling. "You have to know I didn't really mean it."

"And you were right," he whispered, leaning forward to kiss her forehead. "Rissa, forgive me." She shuddered, and he felt a nearly imperceptible softening of her shoulders and body. She leaned back, staring into his eyes for a long moment. He saw her gaze slowly alter from an irate disappointment to a reluctant concern.

Her hand held rigidly at her side now loosened and rose to brush his ebony hair off his forehead. "What else have you done that needs forgiveness, Gabriel?"

He grasped her hand, kissing her palm. She shook at his first show of tenderness since the morning their son died. "I'm so sorry, Rissa."

"Tell me. We can't continue like this." A tear slowly tracked down her cheek.

He forced himself to meet her gaze and stiffened as he took a deep breath. "Our son is dead because of me. I killed Rory."

Clarissa stared at him with unseeing eyes for a moment before collapsing to the ground.

He moved with her, kneeling in front of her.

She raised tormented eyes to his, her mouth opening and closing like a fish gasping when exposed to air, but no words emerged. When Gabriel rocked backward as though he were to rise and leave her, she grabbed his forearm and shook her head. "No, explain what you mean," she demanded in a hoarse whisper. "Explain how you could believe this."

"He was my responsibility. And I failed him. I—"

"Everyone, everyone including the doctor, said there was nothing we could have done to save him. How do you think you could have?" Clarissa asked, tears pouring from her eyes again. "It was a horrible accident."

Gabriel shook as he whispered his confession. "I heard his cry. I thought it was a shriek of joy. Because of that I didn't run to him as I should have. As you would have. I took my time. And in those moments, he drowned." Gabriel paused, swiping away tears. "He'd fallen, hit his head on a sharp rock and then fell into the stream. The minute I found him, I tried to revive him. I swear. But it was too late." At Clarissa's horrified expression, he gripped her arms tighter than he intended.

She jolted, her gaze meeting his as tears formed a stream down her cheeks. "Oh, Gabriel."

"I shouldn't have let him run ahead of me in the woods. If we hadn't been playing chase, if I hadn't encouraged him to run faster, he never would have fallen. He never would have hit his head. He never would have drowned if I'd reacted as I should have."

Clarissa raised a quivering hand, placing it over Gabriel's mouth. She shook her head. "Our baby died, Gabriel. He died." Her shoulders heaved as she held back a sob. "He tripped and fell and died. There's no one to blame."

"Dammit, I'm his father. Was his father," he growled as he had to use past tense. "I should have protected him. I failed him."

"Gabriel ..." Clarissa stroked his cheek, focused on him and his torment. "Chase was his favorite game to play with you. How many times did we hear that little shriek of joy of his as he ran away from us to play hide-and-seek or chase? He always made that sound. Why should you have known instinctively that this one was different?"

Gabriel shuddered at her understanding, at her soft caress. "How you can bear to look at me, knowing the truth?"

"Our son loved you, and you loved him. That is the truth I will keep in my heart." She traced away his tears. "Rory always dreamed of being as tall, as fast, as strong as you." She smiled as his eyes flashed with immense pain and longing. "He loved having you catch him and swing him in the air, even if he was growing so big it made it nearly impossible. He loved his time away with just you, imagining he could outsmart you and outrun you. He would have hated you encouraging caution."

"I failed you and my pledge to you on our wedding day." He closed his eyes as tears cascaded onto her palm. "I promised to love, honor and protect you. I've failed on all accounts."

"That's not true." She kissed him on his lips, causing him to shudder.

"It is." He opened his eyes, full of self-loathing, to meet her gaze.

She ran a hand over his cheek, into his hair and gripped his nape. "Whether you believe me or not, I love you." She stifled a sob. "I'd begun to fear I'd never say that again to you."

"Will you ever forgive me?" He forced himself to meet her eyes.

"It will take time, Gabriel. You hurt me. Dreadfully. Losing Rory nearly destroyed me. Losing you ..." She closed her eyes and shook her head. "It nearly killed me." She let out a deep sigh.

"I always prided myself on being strong. On meeting whatever challenge life threw at me." Gabriel's voice broke.

"There can be a strength in tears. In needing to lean on others as our world falls apart."

"I couldn't understand why you'd still want me when I was unable to protect Rory. To protect you in Washington. How could you have faith I'd be there for our children after I'd failed you and Rory?"

Clarissa took a deep breath. "You don't need my forgiveness, Gabriel. You need to forgive yourself. Until you do, I don't see us moving forward."

"Rissa, please," Gabriel begged.

She caressed his cheek, a forlorn smile moving over her face. She leaned forward and kissed his forehead before rising.

He gripped her hand, refusing to allow her to move away from him, coming to a crouched position now. "I've always tried to be strong for you. To protect you. To shield you as best I could." His voice shattered. "Now I need your strength, Rissa. I need your courage. I need …"

"You need me." Clarissa's voice broke as fresh tears coursed down her cheeks, lowering to sit again next to him.

"Desperately." Gabriel's shoulders shook with sobs he could not stifle.

"Cry, my love. Cry," Clarissa urged. She tugged Gabriel into her arms until he eventually laid his head against her lap and sobbed.

"I see him everywhere, Rissa. It's as though he's always with me, and I turn to answer a question or wink at him or ruffle his hair, and, only at that last instant, I realize he's gone. That I'll never see him again." He sniffled, rubbing his face into the cloth of her dress.

"Do you think it's not the same for me? For the children?" Her blue eyes haunted by the loss of their son met his. "At first we never discussed him, never spoke his name, because it only made me cry."

"What changed?"

"When we returned from Washington, I heard the children talking. Geraldine was telling Billy and Myrtle that, now we were home again, they must only speak of Rory when we were absent."

"Damn." Gabriel's voice was filled with regret and self-recrimination.

"I realized, in a way that neither Savannah nor Sophie had been able to show me, how my actions were harming those I loved most."

Gabriel raised curious eyes to his wife. "But the pain didn't go away?"

"Of course not. I learned how to bury it."

He nodded. "And it would have been a burden more easily carried had we shared it."

"Yes." Her whispered agreement acted as a pinion to Gabriel.

"How can we recover from such a loss?" Gabriel asked. He scooted around until he was leaning against the counter and Clarissa was sitting between his legs, half facing him.

"I don't know. Talking with each other, sharing our grief, remembering Rory will help, I think," Clarissa murmured as she burrowed into Gabriel's embrace.

"I've missed you so much, and the entire time you were right here." Her voice cracked as she fought fresh tears.

Gabriel's arms wrapped more firmly around her. "Thank you for loving me, darling." Gabriel kissed the top of her head.

"I think we should speak with Aidan and Savannah. They've both survived the loss of a child."

"I agree. I want us to have a full life again, my darling. And to do that, we need to somehow control our grief." He sighed again, this time with a hint of peace as Clarissa snuggled into his arms, his large palm caressing her head, shoulders and back. "Ah, my love," Gabriel murmured, kissing her beside her ear.

CHAPTER TWELVE

abriel and Clarissa were in Aidan and Delia's living room, the children at the park with Araminta. Jeremy and Savannah had settled on a settee across from Delia and Aidan, who sat on matching tufted wingback chairs while Colin stood, leaning against the wall to the dining room. Open windows allowed the gentle breeze to enter and cool the room, while a pitcher of untouched lemonade waited to be poured on a table in front of Delia.

Savannah studied Gabriel and Clarissa intently. They sat with the fingers of one hand interlaced. Gabriel reached over with his free hand to caress Clarissa's arm and their joined hands. Savannah smiled as she noted Jeremy relaxing after witnessing Gabriel's actions. It was the first public sign of true tenderness between the couple in eight months.

"Why did you want us to gather?" Colin asked. He frowned as he watched Clarissa and Gabriel.

Gabriel took a deep breath. "I wanted to thank everyone for your support and understanding after Rory died. I—Clarissa and I've finally spoken about what happened that day. I think it's helped."

"What did occur, Gabriel?" Aidan asked. "I understood your devastation at the loss of your beautiful boy but never your sense of self-hatred."

Gabriel closed his eyes, as though envisioning again what happened. "Rory and I went to the creek to spend time together alone while the house was prepared for his party." He opened his eyes to address his family. "You know how he loved to play hide-and-seek and run ahead of me to see if I could catch him. I wanted him to feel like a big boy as he turned seven and let him run farther ahead of me than I should have. He made that little shrieking sound. The one he always made."

Jeremy grunted his acknowledgment, and Colin shifted, his gaze distant, obviously thinking of his beloved deceased nephew.

"I thought it was because he was excited from our game." Gabriel shuddered.

Clarissa gripped his arm and then caressed it. "It's all right, darling. You did nothing wrong," she murmured.

Gabriel met his uncle's unwavering gaze. "It wasn't a chirp of joy. He'd fallen, near the creek. He hit his head, and, because I took too long to get to him, he drowned."

"Goddammit." Colin turned away and marched through the dining room and out the side door.

"Ignore him, Gabe," Jeremy commanded.

"You blame yourself." Aidan spoke with certainty, bringing Gabriel's attention back to those still in the room. "You think your inaction caused your son's death."

Gabriel nodded. "Yes, well, partly. I believed that until I spoke to Clarissa."

"You will always miss Rory," Savannah said. "You will always mark the time by how long it's been since you've held him or how old he would have been now." Savannah blinked her eyes to clear tears that had formed, as though she were thinking of her long-deceased daughter, Adelaide Hope.

"What I need ..." Gabriel paused, clearing his throat. "What I need is your support. You've lost children, and I—we—need your help as we come to terms with our loss."

Clarissa took a deep breath before speaking. "I've lived with a shroud of grief around me, and I realize I can't live this way. It's not the life I desire—not for my children, not for Gabriel, not for myself." She rubbed at her cheek as her tears fell. "I know I will always mourn Rory. There will be moments when I think the pain is insurmountable. But I must believe I can find joy in the future."

"Never lose your ability to hope, Rissa," Delia said. She rose from her chair and came to kneel by Clarissa's side. She stroked a gentle hand over Clarissa's head and then down her arm. "Never fear that we will not understand that grief comes in waves. That, no matter how long Rory's been ... dead, you'll still have days where the pain is almost as fresh as when you first heard the news. We'll be here for you."

Clarissa sniffled, glancing around the room to see Aidan, Savannah and Jeremy nodding.

Delia rose and moved to Gabriel's side. "As for you, Gabriel, I can only imagine what you suffered, discovering your son as you did, envisioning some way you could have saved him." She brushed the hair off his forehead, and he met her gaze with tears brimming in his eyes. "I wish you'd shared this burden sooner so that we could have prevented months of torment."

"Thank you, Delia," Gabriel said. "Thank you all." He nodded to everyone in the room before emitting a tired sigh. "When we return home tonight, I'll discover if the children will be as understanding."

"All they want is your love, Gabriel. Show them you love them, and they will forgive you," Aidan said with a gentle smile.

"Thank you, Uncle." Gabriel squeezed Clarissa's hand and then rose alone, striding through the dining room and exiting the kitchen door. He paused for a moment to enjoy the faint breeze as he searched for Colin. Gabe rounded the side of the stable, nearly tripping over Colin.

"Col?" Gabriel sat next to him in the stable's shadow, the quiet nickering of the horses soothing.

Colin sat with his knees bent and his head down.

A soft snuffling noise sounded, and Gabriel belatedly realized Colin was crying.

"I'm sorry, Gabe," he whispered.

"Why?"

"For not staying and listening to what else you had to say." Colin swiped at his cheeks and punched at the stable wall with his other hand as he stood, nervous energy not allowing him to sit for long. "I'm so damned angry."

"As long as you know your anger is best directed at me and not Rissa."

Colin spun to face Gabriel, his blue eyes widened in shock. "Of course it's not. It's directed at fate, at God, at whatever caused us to lose Rory. But never at you. I know you would never have harmed him." He squinted as he saw Gabriel shake his head in disbelief. "I've watched you wishing yourself dead these past months. I've seen you turn away from the support of those who care about you. I despaired at ever having back the man I considered brother, who was lost in a vortex of despair and self-hatred. I've witnessed Clarissa's transformation into a bitter woman I barely recognize." He met Gabriel's wounded gaze. "You have no need of my anger. You've done a good enough job on your own."

"Then why are you so upset now?"

"At the senselessness of it all!" Colin kicked at the stable wall. "I shouldn't have favorites. It's not right."

Gabriel stood at Colin's whispered admission and canted forward to better hear him.

Colin swiped at his nose as he faced Gabriel. "Although I tried to hide it, Rory was my favorite. I always dreamt that, when I had a little boy, he'd be like Rory. Eager to spend time with me. Loving, considerate, filled with enough mischief as is healthy in a young boy but never with any spite. I hate that he's gone." Colin turned away as his shoulders shook, his arms braced against the stable walls.

"Col, I'm sorry."

"If it's for Rory's death, save your breath. But, if it's for not being there for Clarissa—for any of us when we needed to mourn, to remember and to rejoice in what a miracle Rory was—then, yes, you should be begging our forgiveness."

Gabriel paled, holding a hand to his chest as though in physical pain.

"I may never know what it is to love a child of my own, and I pray every day that I never lose a child after seeing how you and Clarissa have suffered. But I hope, with every breath, that I never hurt those around me as you have in your agony at his loss."

"So you are angry at me," Gabriel said with a grim satisfaction.

Colin glared at him, firming his jaw. "For how you've acted, yes. For how you've thought you were the only one entitled to grieve. For forgetting you have three other children desperate for any sign of caring from you."

Gabriel nodded, taking a step back, his gaze haunted and distant. "I couldn't bear to be near them. To love them any more than I do. For what if something happened to them too?"

"Whether you loved them more or not, anything could happen to them, Gabe. And then you'd have to live with the fact that you'd ignored them for the better part of a year." Colin's stance became less belligerent, and he reached out to grip one of Gabriel's arms. "And I don't believe you could love them any less than you do."

"Of course not! They mean everything to me." He closed his eyes in defeat. "I couldn't live through losing any of them."

"You're stronger than you think, Gabe." Colin squeezed his brother-in-law's arm before letting go. "Just as I advised Clarissa not to swaddle them in a protective cocoon, stifling their childhood, I'd recommend you enrich their years with your presence. For that is all they desire."

Gabriel gripped Colin in a tight embrace, slapping his back a few times before releasing him. They turned to rejoin the others in the house, Gabriel fighting his panic at the upcoming reunion with his children.

***

"Gabriel, what are you doing?" Clarissa asked as she came to an abrupt halt upon entering their son's room, the room previously shared by Rory and Billy. Bright light entered the dormer window, casting sunlight on Billy's bed.

Gabriel sat on Rory's empty bed, against the far wall, his elbows on his knees, his eyes fixed with a distant gaze. They had just returned from his uncle's house, and he awaited the arrival of the children from the park. "Forgive me, Rissa," Gabriel said as he moved to rise.

"No, sit," she said as she pushed on his shoulder and settled next to him. "What are you doing in here? You've barely entered this room since Rory's death. Billy has to beg you to tell him a story before you'll creep inside."

"I'm sorry. I thought the room would still be filled with him." He glanced around. "But it isn't."

"I cleaned away his things months ago."

"Did you keep anything?" Gabriel couldn't hide the hopeful pleading in his voice.

"Yes." She rose, moving to a small trunk in a corner of the room. She lifted the lid, creaking from disuse. "I have his christening blanket, his favorite book. A few toys."

She moved aside as Gabriel knelt beside her. He lifted out the christening blanket and pulled it to his face, sniffing deeply. He lowered it, his shoulders stooping with disappointment.

"I had it laundered. I—I'm sorry, Gabriel," Clarissa whispered.

He shook his head, shoulders bowed as he looked at the few remaining items that had belonged to their son. "Forgive me." He raised wet eyes to meet her worried gaze. "For not being here with you when you had to clear away his things. For my reluctance to enter this room. For my disappointment that you laundered his christening blanket and I can't smell him." He choked. "I miss him so much, Rissa."

"I know, darling. So do I." She leaned toward Gabe, awkwardly moving so that she was nestled against him, tucking her neck under his chin.

"I know they say the pain will become bearable. I fear they lie." He pulled away, flushing at his admission. He glanced into the trunk, a wistful half smile flitting across his face as he reached in and pulled out a small train. "I remember whittling this for him. He always had it with him."

"It was his favorite."

Gabriel ducked his head as he cupped Clarissa's cheek with a shaking hand. "Thank you for saving this for me. Thank you for having faith, no matter how faint, that we would survive this. Together."

Clarissa leaned forward, her forehead resting against his for a brief moment. "I've missed us, Gabriel."

"So have I," he whispered. He kissed her gently on her forehead before leaning away as their son Billy raced into the room.

He came to a halt as he saw his parents on the floor in front of Rory's trunk, his light-blue eyes going round.

"Billy." Gabriel stood and walked toward him, picking him up. He frowned as Billy remained stiff in his arms. "What were you doing?" Gabriel turned toward the door, the approaching footsteps of his daughters thundering down the hall-way.

"We'll catch you, Billy!" Geraldine shrieked.

Billy's eyes widened in fear, and he squirmed to be released from Gabriel's hold.

"It's all right, son. Playing catch and hide-and-seek are fun games." He cleared his throat on the word *catch*. Holding Billy firmly with one arm, Gabriel raised his other hand to stroke Billy's head. "You've grown so much."

"I'm three!" Billy said, relaxing in his father's hold and resting his head on Gabriel's shoulder.

"Almost," Gabriel said, kissing the top of his head. He smiled at his daughters as they barreled into the bedroom. "I caught him first."

"Papa," Myrtle gasped.

"What are you doing in here?" Geraldine asked.

"Hoping to catch one of you," Gabriel said with a teasing smile as he set Billy down and lurched toward them with outstretched arms and a laugh.

Myrtle shrieked and jumped away, running down the hall. Geraldine stood rooted to the spot, her eyes luminescent with unshed tears before she beamed at her father and spun from his grasp a second before he reached her. Their delight-ed shrieks echoed down the hallway.

"I'll find you!" Gabriel called as he ran at half speed after his daughters. He stopped as he reached the hallway and turned to Billy. "Help me find them, Billy boy."

Billy grinned and ran toward him, nearly tripping in his excitement. Gabriel clasped his hand, and they raced down the hallway together. A few moments lat-er, shrieks and laughter could be heard as the girls were found.

Later that evening, Gabriel helped put the children to bed. He spoke in hushed tones to each of his children as he kissed them good-night and stroked the hair off their foreheads. Clarissa stood to one side, watching as a bedtime routine was reestablished.

Gabriel entered the bedroom he shared with Clarissa, shutting the door behind him. A large bed with a carved headboard stood against one wall, with a row of windows opposite the door. He moved toward their shared armoire, removing his shirt and pulling down his suspenders. Clarissa sat on the edge of the bed, already in a nightgown. She appeared deep in thought.

"I fear it'll be another unbearably hot evening," Gabriel said. He watched Clarissa nod absently. "Makes me wish we could sleep on the back lawn."

She nodded again.

"Naked." At her third nod, he chuffed out a laugh before moving toward her and kneeling by her side. "Darling, what's the matter?" He stroked her head. "For I know you'd never willingly sleep outside naked, no matter how hot you were."

Clarissa blushed as her distant gaze focused on him. "When did I say I'd do that?"

"Just now. But I think you were lost in thought." He watched her closely. "Have I done something to upset you?"

She gripped his hand, kissing his knuckles before holding it to her heart. "No." She cleared her throat. "No. I never thought to feel such contentment and joy again as I've felt today, watching you with our children."

"Neither did I." Gabriel lowered his head for a moment before meeting her gaze again. "I asked each of them to forgive me for not being the father they needed since Rory died. And they did."

"Of course they did." Clarissa freed his hand to stroke his face. "They love you. Just as I do."

Gabriel gripped Clarissa's head with both of his hands, moving forward to kiss her with a desperate passion. He attempted to show her only tenderness, but the desperation and longing of the past months burst forth. He grasped her tightly to him, his hands nearly rending her modest linen nightgown as he kissed her as though he would never be able to stop. Her moan of desire spurred him into action as he coaxed her nightgown from her shoulders, pushing it to her hips. She lifted, and he tugged, her gown dropping to the floor.

"Oh, God, how I've missed you." Gabriel peppered her face and neck with kisses while simultaneously divesting himself of his undershirt and pants. His and Clarissa's hands clashed a few times over buttons, but soon he was free of clothing too. Clarissa's hands roamed his chest, arms and back eagerly, as though remapping the planes of his body after their estrangement.

Clarissa scooted back on the bed, and he leaned over her, his mouth moving from her shoulders to her breasts to her belly. Clarissa arched into him, and her passionate acceptance of his desire fueled his own. He reached up, caressing her face, running a finger over her kiss-swollen lips. "I love you, Clarissa. In all my life, I've only ever loved you."

"I've waited months for you to return to me, my love," Clarissa said, a tear leaking out. "Don't make me wait any longer."

Gabriel groaned, losing himself in the joy of their reunion.

***

Clarissa snuggled in Gabriel's arms, unable to hold in a deep sigh of contentment. She kissed his collarbone, earning a grunt of pleasure from Gabriel.

"Thank you," he whispered. He coaxed her to her side, brushing her hair from her face to meet her gaze.

Clarissa blushed with womanly pride before smiling. "It should be mutual," she whispered huskily. "Hold me while I sleep, Gabriel. I've missed your arms around me," she murmured as she felt sleep approaching.

"Always, my love," he whispered, moving so her back settled against his front. "I've missed this. The simple contact of holding you in my arms." He nuzzled her nape.

She raised one of his hands, loosely fisted on her belly, to her lips and kissed it. "Sleep well, my darling."

"I no longer fear tomorrow," he whispered into her ear, his voice thickening as sleep beckoned.

Clarissa blinked away tears, pulling his arms more tightly around her. "Nor do I."

CHAPTER THIRTEEN

Zylphia McLeod laughed as Parthena Tyler and Rowena Clement whispered to her about the other guests attending the ball at Rosecliff, one of Newport's imposing summer mansions, frequently referred to as a "cottage." Zylphia sobered at the disapproving glower from another guest, Mr. Thurske, and then sighed in relief as the orchestra played, muffling their conversation and excess expressions of gaiety.

She leaned in to listen to her friends while looking around the room and taking in the splendor of a Newport mansion readied for a ball. Light from the two sparkling chandeliers reflected off mirrors adorning the long ballroom, and numerous doors on either side were flung open, inviting guests to escape from the stifling interior to patios outside.

Bouquets of white roses in crystal vases were set atop white pedestals throughout the room, their scent competing with myriad perfumes worn by the attendees. The crisp bright-white beauty of the room was highlighted against the brilliant blue color of the fresco on the ceiling and in sharp contrast to the entranceway decorated in a plush red velvet. The stairway leading to the private upper level formed the shape of a heart with the white marble stairs covered in the same thick red velvet.

Guests mingled in the entranceway, the ballroom and on the terraces, while staff moved among them with trays of champagne. A small group of musicians occupied one corner of the ballroom, unobtrusively supplying the music for the evening. Men exited a door at one end for the billiards room, rarely reemerging with a desire to dance.

"You know the others will wonder why our hosts invited us," Rowena whispered as she smiled vaguely at a matron across the room, attracting Zylphia's full attention.

"They invited us because they want to curry our fathers' esteem. And, to do that, they hoped to impress us with their sons," said Parthena, affectionately called P.T. by her friends. "Although I don't know how they'd imagine we'd attract anyone dressed all in white. Whose featherbrained idea was it to have a white ball?"

Rowena chuckled as she ran a hand down her pristine dress. "The hostess of this ball is something of an eccentric." She glanced at Zylphia with envy and nodded. "Some of us look striking in white."

Zylphia blushed, her raven hair pulled up into a chic layer of curls and her blue eyes sparkling with delight at her first Newport ball. "I think we all look lovely." She glanced at her friends, Rowena with her auburn hair and brandy-colored eyes and Parthena with her straw-blond hair and hazel eyes.

"Even if we don't look a fright, I can't see why dressing as though we were barely out of the schoolroom will entice interesting men," Parthena said.

"I'd think you'd want more than to just attract men," Zylphia whispered.

"Of course, but it doesn't mean I don't like to dance." Parthena tapped her feet to the music.

"Or flirt," Rowena teased.

"As long as it isn't with that horrid Mr. Wheeler," P.T. said with a dramatic shudder.

"I thought balls would be different here than in Boston," Zylphia murmured.

"Why should it be any different in Newport than attending a soiree or ball in Boston?" Rowena sipped at her punch, grimacing at its cloying sweetness. "Rich people gather, dance, drink excessively and then return again to repeat the whole series of events at another place the next night. If we have any luck, someone acts scandalously and adds a bit of gossip."

Zylphia snickered at Rowena's cynicism. "But New Yorkers are here too. Shouldn't it be more exciting?" Zylphia smiled wanly at a man with overly pomaded hair and turned her attention back to her friends.

"Well, all that I said might be done on a grander scale, but it really isn't much different," Rowena said. "Zee, at times like this I realize you weren't raised your whole life in money. This is how those of your father's class acts." Rowena glared at Zee. "Stop smiling at everyone who smiles at you. It only encourages them." Rowena frowned at the same man Zylphia had smiled at, and he approached another group of young women. "You must realize that those of the upper class act differently than those in an orphanage."

"Rich or poor, our needs are the same," Zylphia insisted. "As women, we need to be recognized as having rights. Full rights, equal to those of men."

"Zee, you know you'll never get her to agree with you," P.T. said. "For she's never been poor and never will be."

Rowena shuddered. "Thank God."

"You'll never be successful in having either of us believe that Socialist twaddle," P.T. said. "We couldn't be more different than those wretches at the orphanage."

"There are moments, like now, when I don't know how we are friends." Zylphia blew out a breath, her cheeks flushed with agitation.

"You like us because we aren't offended by your excessive liberal view for women. Besides, just because I never want to be poor doesn't mean I don't want rights of my own. I have my own thoughts and ideas, and I'd like to be able to express them," Rowena said.

"Being poor in spirit is worse than being poor," Zylphia said. "Believe me. I've—"

"Zee, we've all heard about your rich cousin who made a lucky escape from her husband. Although some would argue she wasn't a dutiful-enough wife." Parthena's eyes gleamed as though with enjoyment at goading Zylphia.

"I'd like to see you survive what my cousin Savannah suffered. But never fear, you'll be fine, as long as you marry who your father says and do what your husband wants," Zee hissed as Sophie towed a group of men toward them.

Parthena nudged her to silence her, and Zylphia glared at her.

"Zylphia, these men wish to be introduced to you and your friends," Sophronia Chickering said with her characteristic bluntness. She leaned heavily on her walking stick, although she appeared as sprightly at this evening's ball as she did over her first cup of coffee in the morning. Her eggplant-toned evening dress with black lace at the collar, bodice and wrists was a perfect counterpoint to her silver hair and aquamarine eyes. She had refused to wear white, proclaiming one of her great age should only don the color as a funeral shroud.

"Excuse us," said a young man, his blue-green eyes shining with merriment while his honey-gold hair fell just to his coat's collar. "We couldn't help but notice that you seemed the most interesting young women at this ball and wanted to meet you."

"This is Owen Hubbard of the Boston Hubbards. This is Theodore Goff"— Sophronia pointed at a tall, lanky man with sable hair and the appearance of a perpetual frown—"and these are Jeffrey Tindall and Morgan Wheeler." Sophronia *harrumph*ed after saying their names. "May I present Miss McLeod, Miss Clement and Miss Tyler? If you will excuse me, I'm certain you are intrepid enough to enjoy yourselves without my presence." She winked at Zylphia and moved to rejoin her friends.

Jeffrey's and Morgan's gazes traveled from the floor up the three women and then moved to other women in the room. After a nod, they departed, leaving their two friends, Owen Hubbard and Theodore Goff, with Zylphia and her friends. Parthena relaxed as Mr. Wheeler left their group.

"Pleased to meet you," Rowena said with a small curtsy to Owen and then to Theodore. She did not extend her hand.

Zylphia watched her carefully and then mimicked her actions.

Parthena merely nodded her head.

"What does it mean to be Mr. Hubbard of the Boston Hubbards?" Zylphia asked, tracing the stem of the empty crystal coupe glass in her hand.

"My father has found success with mining and the railways," Owen said.

"Have you?" Zylphia asked.

Rowena choked on her final sip of punch.

Theodore Goff watched Zylphia intently while handing Rowena a handkerchief. His inquisitive gray eyes were partially hidden behind wire-rimmed glasses.

"*Goff?*" Zylphia asked Theodore, before Owen could sputter an answer at her impertinent question. "Are you related to Mrs. Henrietta Goff?"

"She is my mother, yes," Theodore said with a curt nod, a hint of England in his voice.

"If I may be so bold as to inquire, Miss McLeod, how do you know Tedd's mother?" Owen asked with thinly veiled curiosity.

"She donates her time and resources to the orphanage my mother used to run," Zylphia said.

"That was very charitable of your mother," Owen said. "I'm surprised your father was keen to have his wife at such a place for longer than necessary to raise a few funds or hold a cake sale."

Parthena nudged Zylphia with her foot, a discrete attempt to dissuade her from speaking more on the topic. Zylphia blushed and nodded in a nearly imperceptible manner, flushing a bolder red when she noted Mr. Goff watching her.

"I've heard your mother's charity didn't cease even though she is no longer in charge of the orphanage," Theodore murmured in a deep voice.

"My mother and father will always concern themselves for those less fortunate among us." Zylphia bit her lip before schooling her features into one of bland inquisitiveness and politeness.

Tedd Goff's frown deepened as he noticed her action.

"As long as they don't invite them among us," Owen said with a smirk.

Zylphia blushed and glanced toward the dancers.

Rowena shared an amused glance with Parthena, whispering, "Then I hope he never calls at Zee's house." Parthena chuckled before focusing on the conversation again.

"Don't you live in the Montgomery mansion?" Theodore asked. He took a sip of champagne, a gold signet ring flashing with the movement.

"We call it the McLeod mansion now." Zylphia raised her chin as though daring him to comment.

"Fascinating history, from what I've learned," Owen said. "A murderess turned heiress runs away to hide in the wilds of Montana." His gaze sharpened as he focused on Zylphia. "Although of course you're related to her, aren't you?"

"Yes, well, my family is filled with people you might call eccentrics," Zylphia said with pride.

"Whose family isn't?" Parthena asked.

"Yes, we've all heard of your great-great-uncle who became a trapper and lived with the savages for a while." Owen turned from Parthena and reached out his hand to Zylphia. "Miss McLeod, will you join me in this dance?"

Zylphia smiled, stilling her foot that had tapped along with the lyrical music played by the musicians. "I'd be delighted to." She set her empty glass on a passing servant's tray and accepted his hand.

"Excellent." He gripped her gloved hand and led her onto the dance floor for a sedate waltz.

She glanced toward her friends to share a quick smile at her first dance at a Newport ball but sobered immediately when she saw Theodore Goff's glower. As Owen spoke his flowery praise of her dancing skills, she was unable to ignore the persistent stare from Theodore the entire time she remained in Owen's arms.

**

The following morning Theodore rambled along the walk clinging to Newport's cliffs. At points a well-maintained walkway, at others a rougher path with boulders in the way, the cliff walk highlighted nature's grandeur. Teddy huffed out a frustrated breath as he turned away from staring at the ocean to look up at one of the Vanderbilt mansions glistening in a rare beam of sunlight on this gray day before he continued on.

He approached a shrub and whacked at it with his stick to push it aside. A roiling unease filled him, while the hope that this walk would ease it diminished with each step. He swung his walking cane again in frustration. He took a few more steps, halting to find Miss McLeod perched on a low boulder. "Miss McLeod, are you harmed?"

She glared at him as tears leaked from her blue eyes. "No, I long to sit here in an undignified manner waiting for any sort of man to pass." She flushed at her frank words and blew out a breath. "Forgive me. I wasn't paying attention and twisted my ankle." She slapped away his hands when he attempted to lift her long sky-blue skirts to ascertain the damage.

"Please, let me help. I've studied quite a bit, and I would like to see how severely you are injured."

"Unless you have turned into a doctor overnight, no. I will not be caught in a scandalous position with you, raising my skirts." She blushed again at her blunt words and glanced around, belatedly realizing being alone with him on the path was true cause for scandal. "It's bad enough I'm sitting on the path with you hovering over me."

"There must be something I can do," he said, his hand reaching out to touch her ankle but dropping as she flinched away from him.

"Give me your hand and help me rise," she said, gritting her teeth and firming her jaw as she focused on moving. Although she stifled her moan of distress, she whimpered as she placed weight on her injured limb.

"*Oomph*," he gasped as he caught her against him when she collapsed into his arms after taking one step.

"Oh, that hurts," she whispered, another tear tracking down her cheeks. "Why did I have to pick now not to pay attention?"

He ran a palm down her back, feeling her tremble at his actions.

"I had the hope of dancing again tonight."

Teddy smiled at her frankness, easing her from his arms and pushing her to lean against the boulder. "Miss McLeod, I'm not certain how to assist you. We are a fair distance from the house, and I'm unable to carry you that far."

Zylphia flushed. "I'd never expect anyone to carry me. I know I'm not a dainty woman."

"No, you're not."

She glared at him at his ready agreement.

"I don't know why that would concern you. Rather than simpering in a socially acceptable emaciated manner in whatever god-awful room they've designated for tea or embroidery, you're out here. Hale and healthy."

"Except for the fact I can no longer walk," Zylphia muttered.

Teddy chuffed out a laugh. "Except for that, yes." He leaned on the boulder next to her, crossing his arms over his chest, and a peaceful silence ensued between them. The waves crashed against the rocks below, lending a soothing symphony, while songbirds trilled again in the adjacent bushes. A light breeze blew, ruffling his hair and tugging at her hat. The sky remained a dull silver, although no rainclouds threatened.

Zylphia sighed and pushed away from the boulder. Teddy stood, reaching out an arm to help her. She placed weight on her leg, grimacing, but then tried another step. "If I walk slowly, and if I can hold on to your arm, I think I can make it to the house."

"Are you sure?"

"I don't have much of a choice," she said with a determined tilt to her head.

They walked at the pace only slightly faster than a lazy turtle. Zylphia gripped his arm to the point he had to free her fingers and move them to a different point on his arm.

"You're in too much pain," Teddy murmured.

"No, I'll be fine. Tell me about your family. You don't sound like you're from Boston."

"Are you always this blunt?"

Zylphia blushed. "Yes, I'm afraid so. Sophie tried to teach me how to act, but I've always been plainspoken."

"And I highly doubt Mrs. Chickering is the one to turn to for sage advice on the proper ways a woman should behave."

Zylphia stiffened next to him. "She's an upstanding society matron who generously taught me the ways of polite society."

"Did she consider herself a success?"

Zylphia bristled at the hint of humor in his voice. "She deemed I had learned all I was capable of learning at this stage in my life, and then we focused on matters that concerned us."

"Why didn't your mother instill the basic knowledge of how to act in proper society when you were younger?"

"I wouldn't call it *proper* but *polite*." Zylphia breathed deeply, relaxing her grip on his arm as she exhaled. "She was occupied with the orphanage. Now, before you distract me further, tell me about your family."

"I'm from England, having arrived here when I was six."

"But you're an American now."

"No, I merely live here. I still consider myself a British citizen. As does England and the passport I have."

"You have a passport?" she asked, unable to hide the wistfulness from her voice. "I've always wanted to travel."

"I'm sure you will one day." The strengthening breeze ruffled his sable-colored hair, and she placed a hand on her hat to prevent it from blowing away.

"The farthest I've been is San Francisco."

"I imagine it was quite a journey." He helped her around a rough patch in the path, and they continued their slow progression to the house.

"I loved the train ride. I hated dusk because it meant all those hours where I wouldn't be able to catalog the different landscapes we were crossing."

"I've heard it's all quite similar. Flat plains for miles on end."

"That's what you would think, but then you notice how each area is unique. And mile after mile of wheat fields is hypnotizing in its beauty."

"What is San Francisco like?"

"Beautiful and boisterous. As though it has all this energy and vitality, and yet it's still determining what it will be. Boston is old and established, whereas, in San Francisco, there is a sense that anything could happen. I loved waking in the middle of the night and hearing the ships' horns sounding. Peering out my window at dawn and being surrounded by dense fog, as though enveloped in cotton candy. And then, when the fog finally lifted, to look out into the majestic bay toward Alcatraz Island and the village of Sausalito. Such beauty is unparalleled."

"When were you last there?"

"Oh, years ago. Our home was destroyed in the earthquake in 1906, and my father decided against rebuilding. He thought having two homes, one in Boston and the other in Montana, was sufficient."

"You sound as though you miss your San Francisco home." Teddy stilled her movement, encouraging her with a slight pressure to rest on a low rock for a moment.

"I miss the sense of possibilities. That I could be anyone or do anything. I feel stifled here." She flushed at that admission. "I've never been to Montana, and I don't know what kind of life my cousins live there."

"I can't imagine a well-bred, wealthy woman should ever feel stifled."

"As you said yourself, most woman of my class seek contentment over needlepoint or a cup of weak tea. That's not who I am." Zylphia frowned as she rubbed at her ankle.

"No. Although from what I know of your father, he would never stifle you." At Zylphia's curious stare, he smiled. "My family has business with him."

"What does your family do?"

"They are in the import-export business in England, and my father has an interest in the exchange here. When my parents moved to the United States, they planned to settle in New York City, rather than Boston. However, my mother preferred Boston and thus insisted they make it their home. They purchased a home in Cambridge, and they've been there since."

"You didn't mention what you do for work." Zylphia rose, putting more pressure on her leg. She nodded to Teddy, and he offered his other arm.

"I am working on a series of experiments to see if any of them are successful."

"For what?"

He smiled mysteriously but refused to elaborate. Their walk resumed again, this time at a faster rate.

"Do you know Mr. Hubbard from university?"

"No. We met by chance a few years ago when my mother insisted I attend a soiree." He glanced down at her inquisitive face. "I attended school in England."

"All of it?"

"Yes, from the age of eight on. I returned here only for long breaks from school."

"I loved university," Zylphia said on a long sigh. "I never minded the home-work. Well, except for math as I never much liked it." She sensed rather than heard him chuckle.

"I'm glad you were able to attend university, Miss McLeod. A mind such as yours should have the opportunity to never stop learning."

He paused at the edge of the expansive lawn leading up from the walk and the cliffs to the mansion. They were momentarily hidden in a hedge, separating the neighboring property from their hosts' land. The large gray-stoned multi-dormered mansion with its black mansard roof sat majestically in a rare ray of sunlight. "If you prefer, I shall leave you here to return on your own."

Zylphia's hand tightened on his arm for a moment before releasing it. "Thank you for your assistance, Mr. Goff."

He smiled with a hint of self-mocking humor. "I rarely have an opportunity to aid a damsel in distress. It was my pleasure."

Zylphia giggled before sobering.

He watched her with a fierce intensity as she transformed from the inquisitive, free-spirited woman who'd walked back with him to a demure woman of society.

She nodded to him before starting a slow, lumbering limp up the hill toward the house.

He settled into the hedge, listening as her friends called out for her, their ex-ultant hellos transforming into coos of worry. After fifteen minutes, when the voices had faded and the lulling waves and the chirping birds were his only com-panions, he strolled onto the lawn. Only as he neared the house did he realize his unremitting unease had dissipated.

***

A perfunctory knock sounded at the door a moment before it swung open. Sophronia strode in, only to halt as she beheld Zylphia resting on a chaise longue, a loose beige cotton wrap covering her.

"Why aren't you dressed for the evening?" Sophie shut the door and marched forward, her walking stick clicking on the exposed wooden aspects of the floor.

"I hurt my ankle. I couldn't possibly stand all evening and socialize. Never mind dance."

"Was the doctor called?" Sophie asked as she dragged over a chair to sit next to the chaise and face Zylphia.

"No. I believe it's simply a horrible sprain."

Sophie raised an eyebrow and pointed with her chin to the hem of Zylphia's wrap. "Show me."

Zylphia flicked up the long skirt of her wrap to reveal a reddened, swollen ankle.

"Good heavens. How did such a thing happen?"

"While on my ramble this morning along the cliff walk, I twisted my ankle. Thankfully I met Mr. Goff, who helped me return to the house."

"This is more than a slight sprain." Sophie reached forward and traced the swollen ankle, evoking a quiver of pain in Zylphia. "I'm thankful Mr. Goff was there to aid you. What did you think of him?"

"I'm uncertain. He excels at eliciting information while offering very little about himself."

"I've always thought him to be a shy man who hides in his laboratory, terrified of what might occur if he were to fully engage with the world."

"That's uncharitable, Sophie."

"*Hmph*. But true. He has a lot to offer but refuses to acknowledge it."

"Well, after my clumsiness, all I needed was his aid to return to the house. A walk that should have lasted fifteen minutes took nearly an hour."

"How chivalrous of him to ensure you arrived home safely." Sophie frowned again at Zylphia's leg. "Was it difficult to be in his presence for such a long duration?"

Zylphia collapsed against the chaise cushions, a long sigh escaping. "He almost had me admitting my orphanage origins and the fact I didn't meet father until I was sixteen."

Sophronia grimaced. "You have nothing to be ashamed of, but I'm afraid those here will be less than charitable if they realize the extent of your humble beginnings. For many, it's difficult enough your father is the first in his family to make his fortune."

"Hypocritical, if you ask me. All they care about is money, and Father has plenty of it."

Sophie smirked and then chuckled. "Which only proves the point, how you are unlike the rest. If all that concerned you was marrying the wealthiest man here, you'd have insisted Mr. Goff coerce his friend Morgan Wheeler to spend more time with you as a form of penance. Owen Hubbard might be wealthy, but Mr. Wheeler's family has begun to rival that of the Vanderbilts and Astors when it comes to wealth."

Zylphia rolled her eyes. "I don't understand why all these women are fixated on these men only for their money. Don't they want more from life?"

"Many do, but their mothers want them to marry well. For them, having financial security is important."

"Marrying a man with a steady job means having financial security."

Sophie's bark of laughter echoed through the room. "Ah, you are a breath of fresh air. Now if only you could befriend some of these young women and encourage them to our way of thinking with regard to the vote."

"I've tried, Sophie. Except for P.T. and Rowena, the rest think I'm a radical."

"Well, you are, darling. And Parthena and Rowena don't count because they were already your friends before you arrived." Sophie glanced toward the small clock on the dresser. "I must go down soon. Let me inquire if any ice could be spared. I think it might soothe the pain and ease the swelling."

"That would be lovely. I dread sleeping tonight." She raised an eyebrow and shook her head, cutting off Sophie's words. "And, no, I do not want a sleeping tonic or some nasty potion that will leave me in a confused state."

"As you wish, my dear. Let me also ensure that dinner is delivered to you. I imagine you are quite famished."

Zylphia smiled with a hint of guilt. "I had one of the maids steal a few scones for me at tea time."

Sophie shook her head in disgust, her distinctive eyes flashing with ire. "Our hostess should have ensured you were well taken care of when she learned you were ailing. I should have been informed too, as I am technically your chaperone. I can't believe Pamela has become so lax in her standards."

"I believe she is attentive to those she deems worthy." She patted Sophie's hand. "Don't bother yourself on my account. We always knew the upper echelons of society would never fully accept me due to my questionable origins. And my inability to learn how to follow all their rules. I'm simply thankful you were able to obtain an invitation for me so that my parents could travel to Montana for Gabriel and Clarissa."

"I still fail to understand why you refused to go with your parents."

"You remember what Gabe and Rissa were like in Washington, DC. I couldn't bear to be around that much tension again. Besides, I feared I'd never have another chance to experience the splendor of a Newport summer house party."

"And has it lived up to all your expectations?" Sophie stroked a hand over Zylphia's raven hair, fashioned in a loose braid over one shoulder.

"Yes! Everyone is exactly as I imagined they would be. Pompous, self-righteous and entertaining in their own way." She paused, breaking eye contact with Sophie as she raised an eyebrow at her brittle smile. "I had hoped they would be more accepting of me."

Sophronia frowned at her admission. "Those that matter accept you."

"You can't force your acquaintances to foist their sons at me in the hopes they would deign to dance with me. Or for them to willingly propel their daughters in my direction at tea time, hoping their polish will obscure my tarnish."

Sophie's eyes flashed with indignation. "There is nothing tarnished about you. You may have rough manners and say what you think—often before you think through what you truly believe or wish to say. However, there is no reason to believe that you wouldn't provide them with much-needed enlightenment from their limited viewpoints." Sophie studied her protégé. "As for finding a man to dance with and become entangled with, I've never believed you were eager to wed."

"I'm not. Not while I want to do so much. For myself and for the cause. A husband would prevent me from doing what I love."

"Not all men are tyrants, dearest. Look to your cousins and father. They allow their wives the freedom to do what they need, knowing that their wife's contentment will only lead to a more fulfilling marriage."

"Few men are as evolved," Zylphia grumbled.

Sophie cackled. "Very astute. However, I have every faith you'll find such a man." She patted Zylphia gently on the knee and heaved herself to her feet. "I must go down to dinner and give your excuses to Pamela. If you need anything, call for the maid."

"Thank you, Sophie."

When Zylphia settled on the chaise longue, a listlessness pervaded her. The open window next to her allowed wisps of conversations to enter. She closed her eyes, entertaining herself with what she imagined the guests discussed. The discordant notes of the small orchestra warming up soon eclipsed their conversations, and Zylphia listened as they played snippets of songs. She swayed in place, envisioning herself dancing with the handsome men present at the house party.

She shook herself from her reverie when a maid knocked at her door. After the maid entered, carrying a heavy tray overstuffed with more food than four people could eat, Zylphia settled at the vanity, converting it into her dining table for the evening.

After trying each dish, she settled on finishing the soup and chicken. A bowl of berry trifle awaited her for when she desired dessert. In her boredom, she stacked the dishes on the tray to tidy up and make it easier for the maid to carry away.

She picked up the bowl of trifle, setting it and a spoon aside to save for later. She frowned as she noted a folded sheet of thick cream-colored paper that had been hidden under the trifle bowl. She grasped it and hobbled back to her settee.

After arranging a small throw blanket on her legs, she opened the note.

My Dear Miss McLeod,

I am deeply saddened to learn the injury you sustained today will prevent you from joining the festivities this evening. I had hoped to have the pleasure of dancing with you, after watching you dance with such elegance last evening with Mr. Hubbard.

I wish you a quick recovery.

Tedd Goff

Zylphia raised the letter to her nose, catching a hint of sandalwood. She smiled, remembering that smell from her walk with Theodore Goff earlier in the day. She slipped the message inside her book to read again another day.

CHAPTER FOURTEEN

Zylphia walked with a barely discernible limp down the ornate stairs to meet Sophie, Parthena and Rowena in the main hall. The hall was three stories high, with a fresco covering the ceiling's large expanse. The doors facing the sea were open, and a light breeze cooled the expansive hall.

"About time," Sophie grumbled as she *thunk*ed her cane and walked toward the porte cochere. A white automobile with the cover pulled back awaited the women, and Sophronia sat comfortably in front while the three younger women crammed into the back of the car. They giggled when their wide brimmed hats bumped into each other as they settled in for the short ride down Bellevue Avenue. Their journey slowed to a near crawl as numerous cars merged onto the street in front of them.

Zylphia stared at the opulent houses they passed, enjoying their slow progression as it allowed her more time to stare. At their destination, their car drove through ornate black wrought-iron gates, along a driveway, pausing to drop them off in front of a large portico. Zylphia stepped out before the white marble building, its three white Corinthian pillars gleaming in the sunlight, and its large brass door opened invitingly. She followed Rowena, Parthena and Sophie into the mansion, stopping to marvel at the gold-brown marble covering the floor and walls in the entranceway, with a gilded room to the right and a room of pink marble to the left. A curved staircase wound its way up one side of the wall, and a fresco painting overhead was framed by golden florets.

She hastened to follow her group and emerged onto the back terrace, where crowds mingled, all discussing the need for universal suffrage. She started as someone approached her and affixed a Votes for Women pin on her coral-colored linen jacket covering her matching dress before moving on to the next person. She traced the pin, a satisfied smile escaping, as she ventured farther onto the terrace.

Zylphia moved to one side as she saw Sophie speak with members of her group, her cane waving haphazardly and smacking an unsuspecting bystander. Zylphia smiled at the woman's outrage and Sophie's unrepentant shrug as she argued for suffrage. Rowena and Parthena had disappeared into the crowd. Zylphia chose to lean against the back wall of the terrace, a place that maintained a good view of the speakers. She sighed as she glanced around the crowded terrace and back lawn.

***

"Why the sigh, Miss McLeod?"

She jumped in response to the voice beside her.

"Forgive me for startling you." Theodore Goff smiled as he leaned up against the marble wall.

"Mr. Goff, you surprised me." She took a deep breath. "How are you?"

"I should be asking you that question. How are you today after yesterday's incident?" His concerned gray eyes met her embarrassed blue eyes.

"I'm fine. Please, don't trouble yourself."

"I saw you walking with a limp." He frowned as he looked at her leg, covered in linen skirts in a vibrant coral. He frowned further as he watched Zylphia transform into a placid woman of leisure, any curiosity or vitality forcibly squelched.

She brushed at her skirts, probably to ensure her legs were covered, and folded her hands demurely in front of her. She held herself erect, no longer leaning against the marble wall. "There's no need for your concern. I'm perfectly fine today."

He studied her closely, battling to keep his face politely neutral, fighting the frown that wanted to transform into a glower. "Did you receive my note?"

Zylphia flushed. "I did, although I'm certain it wasn't proper."

Tedd bit back a smile. "I've never been known to follow conventions." He glanced over the crowd that had begun to hush as the speakers approached the podium. "Have you heard any of them before?" He watched as Zylphia shook her head no.

He watched her battle curiosity before she blurted out her question. "Why are you here? I wouldn't think your friends would approve."

Teddy chuckled. "I find that women often see sense before men do. I overheard you and your friends discussing suffragism the other evening and was curious. Besides, if you look closely, you'll see I'm not the only man here."

She looked away, her lips twitching as she noted a few well-dressed men scattered throughout the throngs of women. The speakers stepped up to the podium and Zylphia leaned forward, forgetting Teddy and all the others present, as the speakers touted the success of the parade in the spring at bringing much-needed attention to the ideals of the suffrage movement. She canted forward even more as Alva Vanderbilt Belmont, the owner of Marble House, began to speak. Zylphia stifled a giggle at a few of Alva's proclamations and clapped loudly when she finished speaking.

"Would your father approve?" Teddy asked as those gathered began to mingle. He knew the main goal was to encourage those present to donate to the cause, with various women moving through the crowd with donation baskets.

"Of course he approves of women obtaining the vote." Zylphia rose to her full height, grimacing as she placed weight on her injured ankle.

He reached forward, clasping her arm, his eyes filled with concern.

"Don't ask me again if I'm all right," she hissed. "I'm fine and recovering well. There's no reason for me not to be here."

She shrugged her arm, but, rather than release it, his grip firmed. She fought a desire to fidget as he studied her. "Why do you hide away who you really are?" he whispered.

She shook her head in denial. "What did you mean about my father?"

Teddy sighed in frustration at her reluctance to answer his question. "I wouldn't think any father would approve of the vow that Mrs. Belmont wishes you to take." He cast a spurious glance in Alva's direction.

"My father supports me in all I do." Zylphia tilted up her chin in defiance. She started as Parthena and Rowena approached her, unnoticed.

***

"Did you hear Mrs. Belmont, Zee?" Parthena asked with unbridled enthusiasm.

Before Zylphia could respond, Teddy had melted into the crowd, and then Rowena spoke. "I think we should take her vow. We three should promise not to marry until women have the right to vote. What do you think?" She turned from Parthena to Zylphia.

"I agree. No marriage for any of us until we have rights equal to that of men," Parthena declared.

"Although I like to believe that being granted the vote would also grant me equal rights, I'm far from delusional," Sophie said as she joined their group, her scratchy voice filled with wry humor.

"Zee?" Rowena asked.

Zylphia nodded. "Yes, it's our pact."

Sophie sighed. "You do realize that the woman advocating such a thing has already been divorced and remarried? It seems a strange thing to ask of women when it's not something she's willing to do herself."

"Alice Paul isn't married," Zylphia challenged.

Sophie *harrumph*ed before pinning her with a fierce gaze. "No, she isn't. But I had greater hopes for you, my dear, that you were able to forge your own road." She turned on her heel, her cane whacking innocent bystanders as she walked past in her agitated state.

"Don't listen to her, Zee," Parthena urged.

"She's always provided great counsel to my cousins." She watched Sophie's retreating form with a frown.

"Well, that's for them. For us, we have each other." Rowena linked arms with Parthena and Zylphia, leading them down the steps, across the lawn, to the edge of the cliff walk and away from the crowd near the elaborate Chinese tea house.

"What more do you think we can do?" Parthena asked.

"If you do more than attend a function like this, your father will disown you," Rowena warned her.

Zylphia ceased her own musings, turning with surprise at Rowena's words. "Certainly you speak in jest?"

"He barely tolerates my interest in music. He'd hardly condone such a terrible lapse in judgment," Parthena said, mimicking her father's tone.

Zylphia reached forward, clasping her friend's hand. "I'm sorry."

"Not all are as fortunate as you to have a father proud of his daughter and willing to support her in all she does." Rowena was unable to hide her envy or her bitterness. "At best, we are tolerated. At worst, we are seen as an expense until we are married off."

"I don't understand," Zylphia whispered.

"If your father had six daughters like mine, maybe you would." Parthena sniffed, breathing deeply of the salty air.

Zylphia turned away to face the sea, imagining a family with siblings. Instead of a glowering, domineering father, her father would be joyous and full of pride. She closed her eyes for a moment, giving thanks for Aidan McLeod.

CHAPTER FIFTEEN

Zylphia wandered the reading room at the Boston Public Library as she awaited the arrival of her requested book. She knew pacing the area appeared unladylike, and she should sit, with hands stacked on top of each other and ankles crossed as she passed the time. However, a restless energy filled her, and she was unable to do anything but stride back and forth.

She spun around to walk in the opposite direction, nearly running into another patron. "I beg your pardon," she whispered, failing to look at the man as she moved to step around him.

"Please do not bother yourself," said a man, his voice deep and distantly familiar.

She raised curious eyes and bit back a smile. "Mr. Goff! What are you doing here?" She flushed as he raised an eyebrow at her question while standing in the library.

He held up a book. "I just checked out this book and wanted to read a few pages before heading home." His gray eyes watched her with a keen intensity. "And you?"

"Oh, waiting for my selection. I already know I'll want to check it out, but it's taking forever for them to find it." Zylphia swayed in place. "I'm afraid I'm not a very patient person."

"Zylphia McLeod!" a loud voice rang out, and Zylphia jumped.

"Oh, that's me!" She reached out and gripped his arm for a minute before hastening toward the desk. She spoke with the librarian, smiling and laughing for a moment as she extracted her library card. When she finished, she turned toward Teddy, pointing to the exit with her head.

He walked toward her, opening the door for her into the heavy, humid air of a hot late-August afternoon. He steered her to the shaded part of the street, any decrease of the oppressive heat an illusion.

"I hate weather like today. I dream of a breeze that will blow all this away," Zylphia said as they walked at a sedate pace.

"Ah, but if we didn't have days like today, we wouldn't appreciate those perfect days." Teddy moved in front of her, subtly shielding her from two men marching down the street, their voices lowered as they discussed business or politics.

"I disagree. There were never days like this when I lived in San Francisco, and I didn't enjoy the weather there any less."

"I will have to bow to your experience," he said, giving her a mock tilt of his head. "What makes days like today bearable?"

"Thinking of cool gray days, like the day we walked along the cliffs in Newport. I envision the breeze cooling me, the sound of the waves soothing me." She sighed as she shook her head to clear the reverie.

"I greatly enjoyed my time in Newport, much more than I expected," he murmured. "I was disappointed to hear you were to depart before the end of the house party."

"Mrs. Chickering needed to leave, and, as she was my chaperone, I had to depart with her." Zylphia smiled at him. "I thank you for your chivalry, as I know my absence was not mourned."

"Ah, that is where you are wrong, Miss McLeod. I never had my dance with you, and, for that alone, I might be enticed into Boston society."

Zylphia laughed as she skirted past a boy peddling ices, melting faster than he could sell them, his cart leaving a trail of water as he pushed it down the street. "Now I know you are teasing me." She gripped his arm more tightly for a moment. "Is it true you are a recluse?"

"No. I'm out on the streets of Boston, walking beside you right now." She squeezed his arm again, prompting him to sigh. "No, I'm not a recluse, just quite selective of the company I choose to spend my time with. At society gatherings, I do not have the choice of who I will interact with."

"And yet you might meet fascinating people who become your friends."

"I can see you are an optimist, Miss McLeod." He was silent a few moments. "The only event I'm glad I was convinced to attend was the house party in Newport." He glanced down at her, the warmth in his eyes making her blush. "How is your ankle, Miss McLeod? I was saddened you departed before I was able to ascertain you had made a full recovery."

"I am quite well. I have no pain as I walk." He nodded his agreement as she strode next to him with no evident discomfort. "I thank you for your concern." She slowed as they approached her home. Trees yet to reach full maturity provided minimal shade as they walked up her street, passing brick bow-fronted houses with small front gardens protected by wrought-iron fences.

"Did you attend more suffragist meetings?"

"Yes, I attended a tea with Sophie, and it was wonderful." Her gaze was unfocused as she thought about that afternoon in Newport.

"What made it wonderful? I would think sitting around and bemoaning what you don't have rather tedious."

She shook her head in frustration. "That's not how it was at all. We reviewed the recent march in Washington, DC, and the subsequent burst of public support for our cause. We discussed various fund-raising efforts and the continuous challenge to remain on the forefront of the nation's conscience when so many other worthy causes are vying for attention. It was wonderful to be included and to have my voice heard."

"How do you plan to proceed?" Teddy stepped to the side to allow Zylphia to walk in front of him for a moment as the sidewalk narrowed. When they were shoulder to shoulder again, Zylphia slipped her gloved hand through his elbow.

"I'm uncertain how, but I'm confident we will succeed. Especially when we have women such as Alice Paul, Anna Howard Shaw and others working together to ensure our success."

"I wish you success, although I fear it will take some time to change the minds of most Americans." He glanced at Zylphia for a moment. "The only advice I'd give, as an outsider who is theoretically in favor of your cause, would be to avoid the use of the violence employed in England."

Zylphia turned to watch him a moment as he appeared lost in thought.

"I have a cousin, with more money and time than sense, who became entranced with the suffragettes in England. At first we supported her and the cause. However, when they used violence—blowing up mailboxes and smashing windows—and afterward she was imprisoned and force-fed, our support waned."

"How is she now?" Zylphia asked.

"Eugenie is a bit weaker, and my aunt fears she'll never fully recover from her time in jail. I'm merely thankful she was not strong enough to be at that horserace that killed Emily Davison." He shook his head as he thought of the suffragette who'd dashed onto a racetrack, was struck by the king's horse and died from the injuries sustained a few months before in England during the Derby.

"Had your cousin known her?" Zylphia asked.

Teddy smiled wanly at her. "Vaguely. I think they met in jail. She was terribly upset and wrote me about her." He sighed. "Thus I can see the merit to your cause, Miss McLeod. I merely hope you spare those who care for you, and the American people, such harrowing antics."

Zylphia nodded and motioned to a house across the street, a large four-storied corner-lot mansion with a mansard roof. The bricks shone in the bright midday sunlight while the front garden wilted under the unrelenting heat. Teddy walked across the street with Zylphia to her front door.

"Will you attend the Wheeler soiree?" Teddy asked as Zylphia turned to enter her house. "They are old friends, and if I knew I could dance with you ..."

"I might." She smiled at him over her shoulder as he watched her slip inside her home and out of sight.

Teddy waited until the door closed behind her before he crossed the street and headed toward the Charles River, Cambridge and home.

***

Zylphia sat with Rowena and Parthena in Parthena's private sitting room painted a soothing rose color with cream-colored wainscoting covering the lower half of the walls. A small piano sat in one corner, and comfortable settees and ladies' chairs formed two conversational areas. A fireplace lay dormant, and a vase filled with purple asters sat on the mantel. Clear curtains blunted the bright sunlight, and the open windows captured what breeze the day offered.

Zee's mind was not on her friend P.T.'s chatter about the proper way to obtain a man's interest. Zylphia sighed, reenvisioning the previous night's ball and her dances with Mr. Goff. The ballroom had had a romantic turn-of-the-century feel to it, as it was mainly lit by candle-filled candelabras. Electrical lights enhanced rather than overwhelmed the delicate candlelight, enriching the deep burgundy of the wallpaper. Twirling on the parquet dance floor, one side of the room lined by mirrors to enhance the sense of grandeur, Zylphia had felt as though she were royalty.

She bit back a chuckle as she recalled Mr. Goff's quick-witted humor, displayed only when they were alone. In a group, he became the taciturn, glowering man she'd first met in Newport. Now she sat with her friends, enjoying their teasing for having twice danced with the reclusive Mr. Goff.

Rowena lay on a settee, her legs tucked alongside her. She waved a fan lazily in front of her face. As it was just the three of them, they were much more relaxed than usual. "I'd think you'd find Mr. Hubbard much more intriguing than the glowering Mr. Goff," Rowena said.

"All he does is stare at my bodice or comment on my dancing skills." Zee snorted. "And you know they are deplorable. It's as though he can't reconcile himself with the reality that women are intelligent and can have their own opinions, independent of that of a man's." She glared at the still curtains as though conjuring a cooling breeze. "Teddy simply prefers to spend his time with his friends or closer acquaintances."

"Teddy?" Rowena asked, attempting unsuccessfully to quell her giggle.

"He asked me to call him by his given name. I told him Theodore made him sound like a commodore in the British Navy, and he compromised."

"I imagine the conversation was much more interesting if you're blushing about it," Parthena teased.

"It was nice to dance. To have someone pay attention to me for a change, rather than be a near-permanent fixture to the wall of the room." Zylphia stroked a hand down her burgundy-colored skirt.

"You know most men avoid you because they're afraid you'll convert them to your way of thinking. They believe you're a radical woman intent on upending society as they know it," Parthena said, any levity dissipating.

"I know. But I'd rather they knew who I am now, rather than have them become shocked to realize I'm a suffragist."

"Or worse, believe your beliefs aren't strongly felt and attempt to change you or them," Rowena said. She took a sip of water from a glass next to the settee and fanned herself a bit more vigorously. "I've had suitors believe that the prospect of marrying them would be inducement enough to alter my beliefs."

Zylphia shuddered while Parthena chuckled, then focused on Zylphia again. "Zee, you are sly, but I'm not letting you evade discussing your apparent fascination with this Teddy."

Zylphia resettled her skirts and played with her fan, although she didn't fan herself in a sophisticated, practiced manner like Rowena. Parthena squinted as she watched Zee, who was either attempting to find a more comfortable position or squirming in discomfort at P.T.'s question.

"He's a nice man. I like him." Zylphia flushed and attempted to fling open her fan in an elegant manner as she'd seen Rowena do, instead smacking herself in the leg. She grunted in pain as her friends giggled.

"Is he a suitor?" Rowena asked, slowly opening and closing her fan, demonstrating to Zylphia how to do it without bodily harm.

"We're friends. He actually listens when I speak and seems to care about my answers. He has a cousin in England who's a suffragette, and he seems to support her and the cause. He made me laugh, rather than want to run away and hide, when I tripped over my feet dancing." Zylphia shrugged her shoulders.

"He sounds much more gallant than I would have expected from his reputation," Parthena said. "Although we all know reputations are determined by those deemed popular and not by those with the most sense."

"At any rate, you can't be friends with him, Zee." Rowena frowned at Zylphia's infantile attempts to use a fan. "Unmarried women of our class simply aren't friends with men."

Zylphia dropped her fan and collapsed against the cushions on the settee. "At times like this I almost wish I were poor again." At her friends' horrified gasps, she said, "At least then I knew what to do, how to act and who I could befriend."

A tense silence pervaded the room for a moment before she relaxed. "I'd never give up the opportunity of meeting my father. Of seeing my mother filled with such joy. Of having been able to travel a little. Of having the freedom to work on the causes that mean so much to me." She paused for a moment. "But I no longer know where I belong in the world."

Rowena smiled as she tapped Zylphia gently on the knee with her fan. "If I know anything about you, Zee, it's that you don't back down from a challenge. I'm sure you'll determine where you fit in this world of ours and will thrive."

CHAPTER SIXTEEN

Araminta picked up a framed photograph of Aidan with Delia and Zylphia, running a cloth over the frame and along the tabletop where it sat before setting it back down. She wore a kerchief over her thick sable hair, pulled back in a tight bun. An apron faded to dull gray with tattered edges covered her serviceable navy blue dress. She dusted the room, moving quietly through Aidan's study. She did not startle as Delia entered but continued her quiet, efficient progress here.

"Araminta, there you are," Delia said, slightly out of breath. "I've been looking all over for you." She motioned for Araminta to put down the dusting cloth and join her in one of the comfortable chairs across from Aidan's desk.

Araminta settled, crossing her ankles and holding her hands in her lap, her anxiety belied only by a slight twitch at the corner of her left eye.

Delia smiled, reaching forward to clasp her hands for a moment before releasing them. "Please don't fret. There's nothing the matter."

"Then why won't you allow me to continue my chores, so I might move on to Savannah's home?"

"That's just it, Minta. I think you are working too hard, keeping three or four houses running simultaneously while also caring for the children." Delia exhaled deeply. "I wanted to speak with you before talking with the others."

"Do you find my work lacking? I've done all I could over the past ten years to show I'm a hard worker."

"Araminta, I fear you've been too diligent, to the point Clarissa, Savannah and Colin have come to rely on you too much." Delia leaned forward. She looked around the immaculately cleaned room. "*I* rely on you too much. You keep this home in ready expectation of our arrival, even though we only visit twice a year at most. Don't you want more from life than cleaning others' homes and caring for others' children?"

"I have more than I ever thought I'd have. I haven't had to worry about whether I'd have food or shelter since you sent me on the train ride west with Savannah and Jeremy ten years ago."

Delia watched her closely. "I know you have questions."

"Who were my parents? Why didn't they want me?" She bowed her head. "I know I would have been a burden to them with an incurable limp, but I've managed well here."

"You've done remarkably well," Delia soothed. "Better than I could have hoped. I worry that you're allowing your history to limit you."

Araminta raised her eyes to meet Delia's, her eyes filled with frustration. "You never answered my questions."

Delia grimaced. She reached forward and grasped her hand, cradling it with both of hers. "Your parents were unable to care for you, Araminta. I never knew who they were. They left you, with a note pinned on your clothing, on the doorstep of the orphanage, asking for aid in raising you."

Araminta sniffled and was silent a few moments. "What's my last name?"

"I don't know."

"Few have noticed I never mention a last name, but I wish I had one." She sniffled again, reaching into her pocket for a handkerchief. She wiped at her nose and dabbed at her eyes before placing it back in her pocket.

"Not having a last name doesn't mean you aren't worthy of respect, Minta."

Araminta moved to rise before stilling. "Did I even have a name pinned to me when you took me in?"

Delia paled. "No. I chose the name Araminta because, ... well, I'd always liked the name." She sighed and flushed with regret. "I have no excuse for not giving you a last name. I, more than most, know the importance of a last name."

"Thank you, Mrs. McLeod, for taking me in. For ensuring I traveled with Savannah and Jeremy." She raised luminous eyes to Delia. "For they've treated me like family, something I never had."

Delia nodded, patting Araminta's hand a few times before Araminta rose to finish her work.

"If you don't mind, Mrs. McLeod, I'll go to Colin's to help prepare for his brother's arrival tonight."

Delia nodded again, frowning as she watched Araminta walk from the room.

***

Araminta let herself into Colin's house, stilling when she heard a screeching sound coming from the kitchen area. She glanced around the living room and grabbed a brass candlestick. She crept toward the kitchen, raising the candlestick as she leapt into the room, stumbling as her weak leg gave out.

Colin's head jerked around, his startled expression changing to one of amusement as he beheld Araminta. "Did you think to bang me over the head with that?"

"What are you doing home?" she asked, her breath coming out in a gasp.

"I couldn't remember if I'd asked you to help me today, so I had one of the guys run the forge for me and came home early." He beamed at Araminta. "Now you're here, I can chat with you while you work."

She gave him a disgruntled look and rolled her eyes. "You can continue to clean, or whatever you were doing, while I work on another part of the house."

She shrieked as Colin grabbed her for an impromptu waltz.

"Patrick's coming back, and we'll all be together again," he sang, somehow forming a tune as he spun them around his small kitchen, easily compensating for the hitch in her stride. He frowned when he saw her battling tears. "Minta? Forgive me. Did I hurt you?" She shook her head, pushing away from him, but he held firm. "Talk to me, Minta." He pulled her closer, holding her to his chest.

A sob broke free before she swallowed her sorrow and pushed the top of her head against his chest to leverage herself away from him.

He allowed her to step back but reached forward to swipe at her tears. "What's wrong? You're never sad."

She gave an incredulous laugh. "There isn't a day of my life I'm not sad." She covered her mouth to prevent any further words from bursting forth.

He gripped her hands and pulled her through the kitchen door and the dining room to his living room and pushed her onto his comfortable, dilapidated sofa. He sat next to her, a frown furrowing the area between his brows. "I like to think we're friends, Minta. I hate to think all this time you've been sad and I had no idea."

He played with a loose strand of hair. "What happened today, Minta?"

"I talked with Mrs. McLeod. She's worried I'm doing too much for all of you."

"She's had the same complaint for years. Even when we've urged you to do less, it hasn't changed how much you do." He watched her intently. "That's not what upset you. What really happened?"

"It's nothing. I'm just being foolish."

"You're the least foolish woman I know. After evading Mrs. Vaughan and her daughter, believe me, I know what foolish is." His wry comment earned a slight uplifting of her lips. He raised a hand and stroked his palm over her head but said nothing further. His silence soothed her, and she met his eyes.

"I don't know who I am."

"You're Araminta. Our great friend, honorary aunt to the McLeod children," Colin said without a moment's hesitation.

She blinked away tears. "When I arrived at the orphanage, I had no name. My parents didn't want me."

Colin sighed, his body moving forward as though to take her burden and make it his own. "What matters is that we want you." He watched her closely. "If you never cooked or cleaned or cared for the children again, we'd want you with us. You're a part of our family. Surely you know that."

She lowered her head. "I know my worth stems from what I can do for all of you."

"No, Minta. You're valued because of who you are." He clenched his jaw. "Please, I want you to leave. I don't want you to clean here today."

"Colin—"

"No, I will not have you believe the only reason I value having you here is because you cook and clean. I refuse to have you see me in such a light." He rose, an angry flush on his cheeks. "Take the afternoon off and find something enjoyable to do, Minta. For once, think about yourself."

He strode to the door, opening it for her to leave. He watched as she left with hunched shoulders, refusing to meet his gaze. He stood on his porch, tracking her slow progression down his street. When he could no longer see her and had become quite cold, he reentered his home, slamming shut the front door and then kicking it for good measure.

***

Clarissa grabbed Patrick close for a moment before releasing him to march away to find Colin. Patrick shared an amused glance with Gabriel and followed Clarissa, leaving Gabriel to mind his children. Clarissa entered the kitchen, then walked into a side hallway toward Colin's bedroom and tapped on his door.

"Col," she said, as she rapped again.

"What do you want, Rissa?" Colin snapped as he opened his door. He rolled his eyes to find Patrick with his sister on the other side.

Clarissa pushed him back a step, frowning to see Patrick behind her before motioning him to shut the door. When the door was shut, she gave Colin a jab to his shoulder. "What do you think you were doing?" At Colin's blank stare, she jabbed him again. "Upsetting Minta like you did."

"I did no such thing. I was considerate for the first time in years. I gave her a free afternoon."

"A free afternoon? Do you know how she spent it?" Clarissa held her hands on her hips. "Crying in my kitchen that you no longer thought she was good enough to work in your house because you found out she was brought to the orphanage with no idea as to her parentage." Clarissa hit him again in his shoulder. "How could you be so unfeeling?"

Colin grabbed her hand, a dumbstruck expression on his face. "That's not what happened at all. I realized that we'd been using her. Having her do too much, just like Delia has been complaining about for years."

"Don't you think that's for Araminta to decide?" Patrick asked.

"Exactly," Clarissa said. "Do you know that you made her feel as though you no longer want her to be a part of our gatherings? That you no longer think she's good enough to be here with us?"

"No, she couldn't think that. I told her how she was an honorary aunt to all the McLeod children." Colin rubbed a hand over his face. "She's Minta. She's one of us."

"She's one of us who's always believed she had to prove her worth. And the only way she knows how to do it is by working in our homes and caring for our children. It's how she feels she belongs. When you took that from her today, you stripped her of who she's come to believe she is."

Colin sat on the edge of his unkempt bed. "I mucked up everything. I just wanted her to feel like there was more she could do. More to who she was. She didn't always have to be at our beck and call."

"Talk to her, Col. I had to forcibly drag her here tonight, telling her that I was feeling ill and couldn't possibly care for the children on my own without her."

Colin rubbed his shoulder, a wry grimace at the thought of his strong sister suffering an illness. "Where is she?"

"By now I imagine she's in the kitchen." Clarissa stood in front of him, preventing him from leaving his room. "I understand why you did what you did. But Minta's different. She doesn't have an inherent sense of worth that comes from being raised in a family who loves you."

"I hate that she feels she has to prove she's worthy of our attention. Of our care."

"I know," Clarissa said as she stroked a hand down from his shoulder, his arm, to his hand. She stepped aside and watched as he slipped from the room.

**

Colin entered the kitchen to find Savannah teasing a smile from Araminta. Savannah met Colin's gaze and gave him a worried smile. He approached Araminta and rested one of his hands on her shoulder, stiffening as she froze under his touch.

"Minta, could I talk with you outside a minute?"

"Of course," she murmured, turning to grab her wrap from the backdoor peg and following him out.

"Why do you have your wrap at the back door?" he asked, huffing out a frustrated breath.

"I always use the back door when I can," she said, head lowered.

"Ari," he whispered, using a nickname he rarely used. "I never meant to cause you distress this afternoon." When she refused to meet his gaze, he placed a finger under her chin, exerting pressure so she'd raise her head. "I never meant to make you think I didn't value all you do for me," he said, dropping his hand. "I'd be lost without your friendship, without you dropping by to tidy my place and ensuring I toed the line, lest my home look worse than a stall needing mucking out."

He frowned as a tear formed on her lower eyelash. "Don't cry, Ari." He pulled her into his embrace. "You're precious to all of us. If you find your worth in working, then we'll let you work." He held her a moment more before easing her away. "I merely wanted you to know I valued you as a friend. You don't need to clean or cook to be welcomed here." He let out a huff of frustration as she remained silent. "Talk to me, Ari."

"Without you, your family, I'd be nothing," she whispered.

"That's not true." Colin grimaced as his words came out harsher than he meant. "You'd still be a resourceful woman, able to survive."

"I'd have nothing."

Colin pulled her close again, holding her as she shuddered. "Forgive me my senselessness."

"I will because now I understand it wasn't meant out of spite."

"Never." He chucked her under her chin. "I only brought hardship on myself. For I denied all of us one of your pies."

She laughed, covering her mouth with her hand. "You have to make do with the one Rissa baked."

Colin laughed, slinging an arm over her shoulder and steering her inside. "God help us."

They reentered the kitchen, Colin ushering her in and sharing a relieved look with Savannah and Clarissa. They nodded their understanding, Clarissa's shoulders relaxing as she beheld Araminta's smile. "Come. Let's visit with Patrick a few minutes before we eat." She looped her arm through Araminta's, leading her into the living room, away from the kitchen and work.

***

Patrick sat on Colin's front porch, enjoying the brisk fall evening. He set his head against the back of the tall rocker and allowed the sound of the breeze soughing through the trees, the distant sounds of children playing and the rocker creaking to ease his tension. He fought to maintain his calm as he heard the front door squeak open and the slam of the screen door. The sound of Colin tumbling into the chair next to him caused him to smile.

"If you were going for subtlety, you failed." Patrick grinned as he turned his head toward his brother.

"It's good to finally see you relaxed." He rocked, and the two of them spent the next minutes in silent camaraderie.

"Did you make amends to Araminta?"

Colin sighed. "I think so." He muttered out a curse. "I hope so."

"What is she to you, Col?"

"A friend. A good friend."

"It seems she's more than that." Patrick ceased rocking and watched his brother grow tense. "I know I have no right to interfere in your life. You've only seen me a few times since I've reentered your life. I'm sorry to press you."

"You're my brother, Patrick. I might not like your questions, and I don't have to answer them, but we'll always be family."

Patrick stiffened at his words before taking a deep breath, forcing himself to relax. "I never thought you would welcome me back. Not after I left with no explanation." He met Colin's open, curious gaze and shook his head.

"So you still won't talk about why you left?" At Patrick's subtle shake of his head, Colin resumed rocking, this time with agitation. He stopped suddenly, pointing a finger at Patrick and spearing him with an intense stare, his blue eyes lit with a fiery intensity. "No matter what you could tell me, it would never make me want you to leave again."

Patrick closed his eyes, as though having received a benediction, but remained quiet. Colin rocked again, settling into his chair and whistling.

"Is that 'Come, Josephine, in My Flying Machine'?"

Colin nodded and continued. He moved from song to song, finally ending in a ribald rendition of "Row, Row, Row."

Patrick laughed, relaxing into his chair again. "Only you could make an innocent song sound licentious."

"If you think that's innocent, you haven't really listened to the lyrics," Colin said as he huffed out a laugh while taking a break from whistling. "How are things in Butte?"

"Good and bad." At Colin's raised eyebrow, Patrick said, "I'm making friends." He paused as he thought about Fiona.

"By the look in your eyes, one of these friends is female."

Patrick smiled, meeting Colin's amused grin. "Yes. Fiona O'Leary. She works for the same company I do as a secretary."

"Would the boss like you carrying on with his secretary?"

"We aren't carrying on. We meet at the Columbia Gardens or go to a show every once in a while, and her cousin or sister is always with us." He chuffed out a laugh at Colin's raised eyebrows, suddenly feeling like a young man back in Boston, sharing stories with his brother. "She's my boss's secretary, and he's not as fond of me as he was." When Colin remained silent, Patrick spoke freely. He recalled how Colin could always tease him and cajole him into laughing fits, but also had the ability to know when silence was needed.

"I like her, Col. I haven't allowed myself to like anyone in years. Not since I left." He stared in space for a few moments. "You have no idea what it is to be alone. To think you'll always be alone."

Colin leaned forward at the words wrenched from Patrick's soul and stabbed him in the shoulder with his finger. "You chose to be alone. We were here, waiting for you. Always." He sighed, his chair creaking as he leaned back into it. "Tell me about your Fiona."

Patrick half smiled at Colin referring to her in such a way. "I wish she were mine, Col. And that scares the hell out of me to admit it." He clasped his hands together as he thought about her. "She's open and warm and honest. Curious about the world and loyal to her family." He closed his eyes for a moment. "Living in one of the ugliest places in America, I see beauty again," he whispered.

Colin laughed and slapped him on his shoulder. "Well, then, it seems you know what you need to do, brother." He laughed harder as Patrick paled at the prospect. "Is this why you are so tense?"

"Partly. It's also that I'm not sure how long I'll remain employed. If I'm not working, I can't offer marriage. It wouldn't be honorable." He pinched the bridge of his nose. "I don't understand my boss. He's from Boston too and suffered from the Panic of '07. But rather than feel diminished from his financial losses, he's emboldened by them. He's brazen with money, with workers' lives. He sees them as nothing more than a commodity, like copper." He shared a look of chagrin with Colin. "He arrives in a few days with the expectation of meeting my family."

"Why would a suit from Butte come here?"

"He claims he has to meet with a man in Bonner about the lumber. I'd think it beneath him and far from his role, but it's not my place to question what he does."

Colin sat, his rocking little more than a soft swaying motion as he thought. "Lucas arrives the day after tomorrow. I doubt the family will want to spend time with a stranger." Colin met Patrick's worried gaze. "He didn't give you an option, did he?"

Colin swore under his breath again as he saw the answer in Patrick's eyes. "Well, we'll simply have to enjoy our time with Lucas and then welcome this man for a supper with us." As Patrick heaved out a sigh of relief, Colin slapped him on his arm. "You know we'd do much more than that for you, Pat."

CHAPTER SEVENTEEN

The following day, Patrick and Clarissa set out for Greenough Park. As they walked toward his favorite area along the creek, the fallen leaves crunched under their feet. A few bright yellow and burnished orange leaves clung desperately to the tree limbs.

"I love fall," Patrick said. "It always seems strange not to see the full range of colors here that we saw in Boston."

"I miss the vibrant red," Clarissa said. "But, when I travel down the Bitter Root Valley to see our friends, Amelia and Sebastian, it's extraordinary to see the hillsides filled with tamaracks turning gold. I hadn't realized until I moved here that trees could lose their needles each year."

They arrived at the place he had loved during the summer and found perches on rocks. Clarissa shivered as she settled and attempted to study Patrick from the corner of her eye but knew she had failed when he stiffened.

"What is it?" he asked, absently rubbing at his face.

"You've nothing on your face," she said with a laugh. "You seem less worried today than last night."

"I've finally realized that you and Colin truly want me to be a part of your life. That you still consider me family. When I spoke with Colin last night, I realized a part of me had remained skeptical and afraid to trust in you." His deep brown eyes were filled with gratitude. "Thank you."

"Of course you're part of my family and I want you to be a part of my life." She blinked away tears as she reached forward to clasp his hand. "I never want you to doubt it."

He gripped hers intently and nodded. "With each visit to Missoula, I believe it more and more."

They sat for a few moments, enjoying the peace of the creek. "Thank you for bringing me to this peaceful place. I imagine it must calm you to come here."

She shuddered as she looked around at the bucolic scene. "You couldn't be further from the truth."

He watched her with concern.

"I hate this place," she whispered. "I come here because I promised myself, not too long ago, that I was stronger than any memories."

"Rissa, what happened to you? To you and Gabe?" When she remained silent, he said, "I know when I left, I forfeited my right to act as your big brother." He cupped his hands together, interlocking his fingers. "But, dammit, I am your big brother. You and Gabe seem much better than this summer, but there always seems to be a shroud of sadness around you."

"You've changed," she whispered, fighting tears.

"How?"

"You aren't the domineering know-it-all from before. You always acted as though, if you pushed hard enough, people or the world would bend to your wishes."

"I grew up." His eyes were haunted with memories of the years they were apart.

"I think it's more than that." She cupped his cheek, and he closed his eyes for a moment.

"I lived, for over a decade, believing I'd never have family. That I was unworthy of family. I convinced myself that hard work, surviving at any cost, was enough."

"What changed?"

"I saw you and Sav." His gaze grew distant, wondrous. "I heard Lucas's music. I remembered I was more than a cog in a very large machine."

After a few moments of silence, she asked, "Why are you no longer an archi- tect?" At his hurt stare, she flinched. "You loved it so much. Talking about the—"

He held a hand to Clarissa's lips, stopping her words. "For me, to be a good architect, to envision the buildings and spaces, I needed to ..." His gaze flitted to the trees bowing over the creek, the rocks glistening in the sunlight, the leaves blowing in the breeze before falling into the stream. "I needed to be able to see beauty. And I couldn't. Not anymore. The world was a gray void instead of the kaleidoscope of colors firing my imagination. Everything I drew was an imitation of another's brilliant idea. I was empty, and I had nothing to offer."

He sighed, lowering his hand and head. "I moved constantly. I thought, if I changed scenery, inspiration would return. I roamed from New York City to Buf- falo to Cleveland, then on to St. Louis, eking out a survival, but slowly realizing I would never be an architect. Never build"—he shrugged—"anything. I finally returned to New York City. I was always good with numbers. The two worlds were separate, so those I had sought a job from in architecture didn't remember the dismal failure of Pat Sullivan, the architect. They saw Pat Sullivan, the eager accountant."

"And here you are," she murmured.

He nodded and took a deep breath. "So why do you hate this place, Rissa?"

She stiffened and then rose. "Come," she said. They rejoined the trail and walked a few minutes. Her body trembled, but she shook off Patrick's arm on her shoulder and walked down a small path toward the creek. She stood riveted, star- ing at the creek, her mind forcing her to see reality, not her nightmare.

"Rissa, sit down." Patrick pushed her onto the creek bank, moisture dampen- ing her skirt. "You're as white as a ghost. What's the matter?"

"Do you see that boulder over there?" She pointed to a place a short distance down the creek, partly in shadow.

"The one at the water's edge? Yes."

"My son died there."

"Oh, God," Patrick breathed. He grabbed her arm and forcefully pulled her up the trail and away as she hyperventilated. "Why would you force yourself to come here?"

"I need to be stronger than my ghosts," she whispered, shaking as he held her.

"Rissa, you've always been strong. You nursed Mama through her illness. You survived the likes of Mrs. Smythe to create a life where you thrive. Why would you need to prove anything to yourself?"

"He died when he was with Gabriel," she whispered against Patrick's chest.

"Which is why there was such a distance between you two this summer." Patrick eased her away. "You have to forgive him. He loves his family. He loves his children. He would never have wished harm to befall any of them."

She nodded her agreement. "I know. I thought, … if I could come here, my anger at fate, at whatever caused me to lose Rory, would release its hold on me."

Patrick pulled her close again, stroking a hand over her head and back. "You're smart enough to know that nothing will, Rissa. Time will lessen the ache, but it will always be there."

"His birthday is approaching," she whispered, refusing to mention the date.

"What do you want to do that day?"

"A part of me wants to celebrate it and remember him. The other part wants to hide in bed all day."

"What will you do?" Patrick asked.

She sighed, her crying abated. "I don't know, but I won't spend it in bed."

"There's the Rissa I remember," Patrick said. He released her, and she looped her arm through his, beginning a slow walk down the creek toward the streetcar stop.

***

The following day Patrick slipped into the kitchen, causing Clarissa to jump, dropping the baking pan and splattering the floor with batter.

"You're on edge today, Rissa," Patrick said.

She stared at the floor, then at Patrick, and burst into tears.

"I'm sorry, Rissa," he said, rushing forward, pulling her into his arms.

"It's not your fault," she whispered as she sniffled and pushed away from him, looking at the floor. She reached for a cloth and bent to scrub it. "Stand still or you'll step in the mess and spread it throughout the house. We're lucky you didn't already step in it."

Clarissa scrubbed the floor, rising to rinse the cloth and then bending back over to swipe at the floor. She wiped and wiped at it, even though it was clean.

"Rissa, there's nothing left," Patrick whispered.

She rose, nodding her head jerkily. "I know." She turned toward the sink and gripped the edge of it. "I can't imagine starting over again."

"I'm sure Araminta would help you." He rested a warm hand on her stiff shoulder.

"No. Not today. This is something I must do." She swiped at her runny nose, washed her hands and turned toward the dry ingredients she had set aside. "Please, Patrick, I'm not good company now."

She heard him ease from the room. Inhaling deep breaths to ease her tension, she battled her tears. Her grip on the countertop was a painful counterpoint to her inner turmoil, grounding her. She stiffened as the kitchen door eased open again. "Please, Patrick."

Fingers trailed down her back, then up again, coming to rest on her shoulders. She smelled musk and the scent of pine, the tension in her shoulders easing. "Gabriel," she whispered, leaning backward. He bent forward, nuzzling the side of her neck as he dropped his hands from her shoulders to her waist, linking them around her front.

"You were up this morning before I awoke," he whispered, a note of reproach in his voice.

"I'm sorry," Clarissa said. "I ... I didn't know how to face this day. I didn't sleep much last night and decided if I was busy ..." Her voice cracked.

He exerted gentle pressure on her side, until she spun to face him. His beautiful blue eyes were haunted, filled with pain and concern. "What are you doing in the kitchen?" he asked.

She raised a hand to trace his eyebrow, then his cheek. She tipped up on her toes, kissing him softly on his mouth. "I wanted to celebrate today, rather than mourn." She bit her trembling lip. "But it seems I'm unable to do anything other than cry."

"It's been one year, Rissa," Gabriel said. "Of course you are mourning. We all are." He looked at the kitchen countertop with its dirty pans and furrowed his brow. "Were you thinking of making a cake?"

She flushed at the incredulity she heard in his voice. "No matter what, I want to remember him. To celebrate him." Her breath hitched as tears coursed down her cheeks. "I …"

"Oh, love," he stuttered out, his voice shattering as he pulled her tight. He held her as she cried, shuddering in equal measure in her arms. "You don't have to do this. You don't have to prove you are strong," he whispered into her neck.

"Today will always be one of the worst days of my life. But I don't want to forget him. I don't want our children to believe they can't speak of him." She leaned away far enough that he ran shaking hands over her cheeks, smearing her tears.

"Let Minta make the cake. Let others help you today," he said. When she protested, he held up a finger to her lips. "I should have told you before, but I've always envisioned us spending the day together as a family, talking about Rory. Our adventures. What we loved about him." He rested his forehead against hers. "I think it would do the children good to have us all together, remembering him."

Clarissa shuddered. "Like a wake, but a year late."

"Something like that." He clasped her head between his palms. "Something we weren't capable of doing when he died." He paused, staring for endless moments into her eyes. "Our family wants to have a gathering tonight at Jeremy and Sav's, and I couldn't dissuade them. I think it will be good for us. But today I want time for us and our children."

She bit her lip, staring into his eyes.

"Please, Rissa." His entreaty provoked two new tears to trickle from her eyes.

She nodded, leaning forward again into his embrace. "Yes."

***

Patrick wandered through Savannah and Jeremy's first floor. The large living room and dining room were lit and ready for company. Colin's cajoling voice could be heard from the rear kitchen as he teased Araminta, with Melinda's high-pitched voice joining in. Patrick smiled at her youthful joviality. A darkened room to one side of the entranceway with a large bow-fronted window intrigued him, but he didn't enter.

"That's our office," Jeremy said with a smile as he joined Patrick and pushed him into the living room where a fire roared. "Savannah likes to write letters in there." He offered Patrick a drink, and Jeremy settled in a comfortable chair.

"Is there anything I could do to help?"

"No, not right now." Jeremy smiled to Ronan and A.J, handing them drinks as well. He answered another knock on the door. "Miss Loken, I wasn't expecting you tonight." He turned to frown at A.J.

A.J. thumped his cane. "She's part of our group, ain't she?"

Patrick watched as she stood to one side of the door, refraining from taking off her coat.

"If tonight's not a good evening, I can come another time." She gripped her purse in front of her until her knuckles were white.

"No, it's just that we're trying to cheer up Gabriel, Clarissa and the kids," Patrick said.

"If that's possible," Ronan muttered.

Jeremy nodded his agreement. "It's the one year anniversary of their son's death."

"Oh, I shouldn't be here," Hester protested. "Mr. Pickens, you should never have extended an invitation."

"Didn't know how else ye'd feel a part of our group unless ye were with us for the good an' the bad," he said. "Asides, Mr. Sullivan's visitin' from Butte. Seemed a pity ye wouldn't see 'im while he's here."

Patrick turned startled eyes to Mr. Pickens, who watched him with an owlish innocence. "Of course, you are very welcome," Patrick said to Hester.

Hester was pushed inside as Gabriel and Clarissa arrived with their children. Jeremy pulled Gabriel close for a long embrace, releasing him with a few hard pats to his back before enfolding Clarissa in his arms and holding her tightly. He murmured something in her ear, and she sniffled her thanks.

The children wandered off to play with Melinda, and Gabriel sniffed the scents of cooking. "Did Minta make a cake?" he asked.

"No, Sav did," Jeremy said. "She wanted to do something special for you and to remember her nephew by."

Clarissa nodded her thanks, too overcome to speak.

Gabriel kept a hand on her shoulder, and she leaned backward into him. He eased her into the living room and onto a settee. After stroking a hand down her arm, he whispered, "No one expects you to be good company tonight, darling."

She nodded again to show her agreement. She half listened as the conversation continued around her, paying attention to what was said when she heard Colin and Mr. Pickens speaking about Mrs. Vaughan and Mrs. Bouchard.

"As long as ye can steer clear of those pesky sisters!" A.J. said with glee, earning a half smile from Clarissa.

"Why would the sisters pester you, Mr. Sullivan?" Hester asked. She'd settled on a chair near Mr. A.J.

Colin flushed. "Ah, well, Mrs. Vaughan has come to the conclusion I should marry her daughter."

Hester bit back a smile at his unease. "What does her daughter think?"

Mr. A.J. *thunk*ed down his cane. "Now, I don't know as anyone's ever asked that poor girl. Seems she's still bein' told what she will or won't do by her mother."

"Well, it is often easier to do their bidding than to fight them," Clarissa said. "That's one of the best aspects of no longer working at the library."

"Do ye remember, Missy, when we worked in the depository? We could always hear her comin' 'cause she'd make as much noise as a herd o' buffalo walkin' up the stairs." He chortled. "Not so easy now yer in a proper building," he said to Hester.

Hester smiled. "I wouldn't mind a warning before they appeared." She glanced at Colin. "As for you, sir, I'd think you'd continue to evade them."

Colin nodded his agreement.

After a few moments, Hester was pulled into the kitchen, and Clarissa sat alone on the settee while most of the men wandered to the study for a drink. Mr. A.J. heaved himself to his feet, moving to her. He collapsed next to her, sinking into the cushions.

"*Whoo wee*, Missy, I'm gonna need all those young'uns to help me outta here," he said with a grin. He sobered as he watched her. "Now, Missy, how are ye?" He reached out a gnarled hand to pat hers.

"I'm all right. Gabriel, the children and I spent the day together, remembering Rory," Clarissa whispered. "It's hard to believe it's been a year."

"Ye did what ye needed to do," Mr. A.J. said. "Yer children needed to see their parents rememberin' their brother. Speakin' 'bout him with love."

"Rejoicing in what he was and all he brought us," Clarissa whispered.

"Exactly, Missy." He patted her hand again. "Take yer time to be sad but don't dwell in it. Yer too full o' joy."

"I worry this is who I'll forever be," Clarissa whispered.

"Well, course this is who ye'll be. Ye'll always be different. Loss leads to *altercations*." He grunted as she stifled a giggle at his word. "But it don't mean you have to cling to yer sorrow. Fight for yer joy instead."

Clarissa stilled, meeting his worried gaze. "I like that. And I will, Mr. A.J. Every day I'll fight for my joy." She leaned over to embrace him, stifling a sob as his arms came up around her.

***

Soon dinner was served, and they moved to Savannah's large dining room. Clarissa bit back a sob, turning to flee the dining room but ran into Gabriel. He held her against his chest but was as a stone wall, immobile in his constancy even as she exerted increasing pressure against him.

"Rissa, it's all right," he murmured against her head, kissing it softly.

"They made all his favorite foods."

"I know. I asked them to." He eased away and met her gaze. "I thought this would be a way to honor him."

"I don't know if I can do this," she whispered.

He watched her with steadfast love, softly tracing her cheeks and the errant tears that trickled from her eyes.

She took a deep breath and squared her shoulders. "I can, if you are beside me."

"Always, my love." He brushed a wisp of hair behind her ear and then clasped her hand, entering the room together. They sat near their children, and Gabriel gave them kisses on their heads before he sat down.

The meal consisted of roast beef, peas swimming in butter, steaming rolls, a casserole of creamed potatoes, raw carrots—because Rory hated them cooked—and creamed corn.

Clarissa took small portions of food, having little appetite. She smiled her encouragement to Myrtle and Geraldine, eating more as an example. Billy posed no concern as he ate two portions' worth of food.

"Do you think Montana women will be successful next year in finally obtaining the vote?" Ronan asked. He earned a nod of approval from Gabriel, as it was a topic of conversation that would engage Clarissa's interest.

"We will if men have any sense and support us," Savannah retorted, earning a chuckle from Mr. A.J.

"Ye've my vote," he said with a grin. "I want my Missy to vote."

"I think convincing the men at this table isn't the concern. It's the rest of the Montana men," Clarissa said with a smile, thankful the topic wasn't Rory.

"I'm surprised you're so fervently for suffrage," Hester said. It was as though everyone in the room froze, even the children.

"What do ye mean, Pester?" A.J. asked. "'Course we are."

"I'm uncertain it is the best course for women. It seems a radicalization, similar to what the IWW espouses."

Clarissa sputtered, unable to speak through her indignation.

Savannah laughed. "You are full of surprises, Miss Loken. To compare our upcoming suffrage campaign to the progressive radicals."

"When you read what the suffragettes are doing in England, I don't believe it is too great a leap to be concerned about your methods," Hester said.

"Well, first of all, no suffragist in the United States has ever espoused their English counterpart's violent tactics." Clarissa held up a hand to forestall Hester from interrupting her. "I know, as well as you, that Alice Paul learned their tactics and likely met the Pankhursts. However, she is a Quaker. I highly doubt she'll become violent and turn her back on her nonviolent antecedents." Clarissa took in a deep breath to calm her rising anger. "Do you believe that women should forever be denied the right to determine their own futures? That women should forever be dependent on men, hoping that they will remain benevolent and espouse causes that are important to women?"

"I merely believe you have no idea how the simple act of voting will alter our society."

"Alter it!" Jeremy roared, slamming his hand onto the table. "If it means that a man can no longer treat his wife as my Savannah was treated, then I will support it. If it means that I will know my Melinda will be protected under laws that are meant to protect all, not just men, then I will support it. If it means that my granddaughters have a future where they can choose what they want, independent of the need to marry due to economic gain, I will support it," Jeremy said.

"We already do much more than we did in the past," Hester argued.

"Do you think, if men had to work in the same conditions that women do, that the Triangle Shirtwaist Factory tragedy in New York City two years ago would have happened?" Savannah argued. "That doors would have been barred and escape routes locked shut so that women were left to either jump or burn to their deaths?"

"The men in power aren't voting to change our reality," Clarissa said. "Look how Congress failed to act, even after hundreds of women were brutally attacked in our march. We need to have a voice. Right now we don't have one."

"And the voice you have is seen as radical and discredited due to that," Ronan said.

"Exactly," Clarissa said.

Hester leaned against her chair, and Clarissa saw her quiver. "Forgive us, Hester. We're forceful in our beliefs," Clarissa said, then frowned when she found Hester's eyes filled with sorrow and tears.

"You don't know what it is to have your family torn apart by strife." She rose, fleeing the room, and they heard the front door slam shut.

Colin jumped up and ran after her, calling her name as he opened the front door. He reentered the dining room with a shake of his head. "I wasn't fast enough to catch her. Seems she was determined to escape to her home."

Clarissa glanced around the dining room table, staring at her family. "Mr. Pickens? You invited her and know her best. What was that all about?"

"Don't know, Missy. She's alone in this world, no family that I know of." He shook his head, clamping his jaw as though chomping on his pipe.

"She might choose to spend less time with us," Colin said. He frowned as he glanced first at Patrick before watching Araminta. "Which would be unfair. I was reminded recently that I don't know what it is to be alone in this world. I'd like to think she would no longer have to feel such abject loneliness."

Patrick nodded his agreement. "You should visit her soon, Rissa, and ensure she understands that she is welcome among you."

Clarissa nodded. "I will. I promise."

Patrick smiled at Savannah. "When does Lucas arrive? I thought it was to-day."

"He was delayed. He should be here tomorrow," Savannah said, unable to hide her joy at the thought of her brother coming to Missoula for the first time.

"Here's to family reunions," Jeremy said. "It's been far too long since the cousins have all been together." The room filled with a resounding chorus of cheers as they clinked glasses.

CHAPTER EIGHTEEN

A warm wind blew on the late October afternoon as Gabriel and his family walked the short distance to Jeremy and Savannah's house. Gabriel held Billy's hand as Clarissa gripped their daughters' hands, playing games with the shadows and cracks in the sidewalk, jumping and hopping and shrieking their joy.

"I'm glad Lucas chose to visit us now," Gabriel said. "He's fortunate we're having a warm spell rather than early snow."

"With Patrick here too," Clarissa said, unable to hide her joy, "it will be the first time we're all together in almost fourteen years."

Gabriel grunted as he picked up Billy and transferred him to his other arm, tickling him as he moved him. He smiled at his son's giggles. "Why would a friend of his visit now from Butte?"

"Colin mentioned something about it being his boss, and he wasn't given a choice." Clarissa shared a long look with Gabriel. "We'll be gracious and welcoming as usual."

Gabriel smiled and winked his agreement.

After saying their hellos to Araminta and freeing their children to play with Melly in a small room set up solely for them, they moved into the living room. Clarissa and Gabriel turned toward the doorway at the loud footsteps.

"Lucas!" Clarissa shrieked, throwing herself in his arms.

He lifted her up and then swayed side to side with her.

"It's wonderful to have you in Missoula at last."

"I can't believe it's been six months since I saw you in Butte," he said. He set her down and stared deeply into her eyes. "You look better, Rissa."

She smiled and squeezed his arm. "I am."

Lucas nodded and reached forward to clasp Gabriel's hand and then clapped him on one shoulder with his free hand. "I'm sorry to have missed yesterday's gathering. A problem with the train delayed me in Spokane."

Clarissa waved away his apology, content he'd finally arrived.

"I would have thought you'd be busy this time of year," Gabriel said as he smiled his thanks to Araminta when she handed out glasses of apple cider. "Why did you travel here now?"

"Thankfully I'm always busy if I desire to be. However, I wanted to be here for you and Rissa. It was important to me to be here this fall." He ran a hand down Clarissa's arm. "Don't worry though. I'll be back. Sav mentioned a fund-raiser for the vote sometime next year, so I'm sure I'll return to help raise money."

"Thank you for wanting to be with us. My Uncle and Aunt were unable to prolong their stay with us and had to start their return journey to Boston last week," Gabriel said. "Fall can be a fickle time to visit. You should plan to come in the summer and take time off from touring. This would be a good place for you to compose. There wouldn't be as many distractions for you." He settled on the settee with Clarissa next to him, his arm over her shoulder.

Lucas smiled his agreement, turning expectantly to the door as footsteps were heard behind him.

"How are things in Boston?" Clarissa asked, smiling a hello to Savannah and Jeremy who entered the living room.

"My music is going well. I've given quite a few successful performances." Lucas took a sip of his coffee.

"That wasn't what I meant, and you know it," Clarissa said with a frown. "How are Aunt Matilda and Uncle Martin?"

Lucas grimaced. "Father is well. He's considering selling the shop as he has no children who are interested in running it. I think he dreams of a life where his time is not dictated by the shop nor the current fashions and cut of cloth."

Clarissa waited a moment, but he remained quiet. "And Aunt Matilda?"

"Remains as she ever was." Lucas attempted a smile, which emerged regretful and tinged with bitterness. "I'm a disappointment because I refuse to take the mantle of shopkeeping from my father. I waste my life, tinkering away with music, loitering with those of questionable antecedents."

"Oh, Lucas," Clarissa said, reaching forward to grasp his hand.

"It's of no consequence." He smiled fully. "I've discovered what joy there is in doing what I love."

Clarissa settled more comfortably on the settee with Gabriel as Araminta entered the room to join them. She sat for a moment before pacing to the front window. "It's not like Colin to be late," Araminta said.

"Minta, he's fine. He probably was busy with a last-minute item at the shop," Gabriel said.

She nodded and moved into the room to refill their glasses. Lucas watched her intently, and Clarissa shook her head at the question in his eyes.

In a moment, Colin burst through the front door, his laughter infectious as he motioned for the men with him to enter the living room. "Sorry we're late," Colin said. "It took me longer to finish a project than usual at the shop." He scooped up Billy, who'd run for the door at the entrance of his uncle, swinging him high over his head and earning a giggle as he tickled his belly. "What's for dinner?" He winked at Araminta's exasperated expression at his concern for dinner and his stomach.

He stopped short as Gabriel, who had risen at his entrance, and Jeremy stood side by side, their shoulders back and posture rigid. They wore impenetrable expressions, making it impossible to discern their feelings. "Jer? Gabe?" Colin asked in confusion as he studied the room, setting Billy down to run to play with his sisters and cousin. "I know I'm late, but that shouldn't make you this upset."

"Why are you here?" Gabriel asked in a glacial tone that evoked a shiver in Clarissa. He glared at the man past Colin's shoulder.

Clarissa forced herself to face Patrick's guest, and she squinted as though trying to place the memory of him. She rose and walked toward Gabriel, clasping his hand. "Gabe?" She hadn't seen him like this since Cameron.

"Dammit, why are you here?" Gabriel demanded again, anger now lacing his tone.

"I was invited," the brown-haired man with pale brown eyes said. His voice held a hint of upper-crust Boston.

"We met him in Butte, at Lucas's concert in April," Clarissa said to diffuse the tension. "It's nice to see you again, Mr. Sanders." She laid a hand on Gabriel's arm, but, rather than soothing him, he appeared more tightly strung by her words.

"You've met him? You and Savannah?" Gabriel asked.

Clarissa frowned as he looked at her with a hint of betrayal. Clarissa nodded.

Gabriel and Jeremy stiffened, as though readying for battle.

"Did you think it a game, toying with our wives who didn't know who you were?" Jeremy asked. He clenched and unclenched his hands, either preparing for a fight or attempting to relax himself.

Patrick looked from his boss to his brothers-in-law in confusion. "I know this isn't the ideal time for a visit from someone who isn't family, but I know I spoke with you about my boss visiting Missoula and his desire to meet my family. I'd hoped you'd welcome him as you do all guests."

"You think he's not family?" Gabriel asked, shaking his head in bitter wonder and disillusionment. "He's more family to me than you are."

Savannah edged away from the group and stood next to Lucas against the wall near the dining room door. Lucas clasped her hand, although it failed to soothe the subtle trembling coursing through her. "Who are you? Why are you upsetting our husbands?" she asked.

Their guest brushed a hand down his finely tailored brown suit. "Imagine my surprise when I realized Patrick Sullivan was related to the likes of you." His eyes glowed with a mixture of triumph and animosity as he looked at Gabriel. "Cousin."

Clarissa gasped as her racing memory finally placed him. "You. You from the coffee shop all those years ago."

"Yes, all those years ago. I can see I was correct in his fascination with you. I'm just surprised he was content to accept damaged goods." He grinned as his barb hit its mark, his eyes gleaming with satisfaction as she flinched.

Gabriel growled and leapt forward, only held back by Jeremy and Colin from landing a crushing blow.

Patrick stood watching the milieu with frowning confusion.

"You've filled out some," Jeremy hissed. "You were a scrawny bastard, barely able to stand without your mother's support the last time I saw you."

"Ah, the war veteran who nearly went mad. Terrible to see they didn't have the common decency to put you down like the rabid animal you are to save us from your presence."

Jeremy released Gabriel and clenched his fist. He moved toward Samuel, only stopping when he saw Savannah flinch from the corner of his eye. He stilled, holding himself rigid, his green eyes lit with a virulent hatred.

"How fitting the man who fought in the war butchering innocents has married a murderess. I wonder how you sleep at night," Samuel said. His smile broadened as he watched Savannah shake next to Lucas.

However, it didn't take long for Savannah to find her resolve as she firmed her shoulders and moved from the wall. "I've survived worse than mean-spirited words from a man who hides behind his own false sense of importance." Although she fought subtle trembling, she no longer cowered in the corner.

Mr. Sanders's appreciative gaze roamed over her before homing in on Gabriel. "I was informed these few days were to be days of remembrance. For the son you cared so little about, you let him die. Pity you couldn't have died with him."

Clarissa gasped. "You vile, hateful man. You have no right to speak to my husband in such a manner." She reached forward and slapped him hard across his face.

His head jerked to the side, but his hand reached up reflexively and clasped her wrist. He gripped it until he saw her eyes fill with trepidation. "That was very foolish," he said.

Clarissa stomped on his foot with the heel of her shoe, smiling with satisfaction at his grunt of pain as he released her. She massaged her wrist, backing away from him toward Gabriel.

"Enough!" Colin roared, grunting with exertion as he held onto Gabriel, still straining to leap at the man. He watched as Patrick held back Jeremy. "Who are you and why are you acting like this to men I consider brothers? To my sister and cousin?"

"I'm Henry Masterson. Their cousin," he said with a touch of triumph as he pointed at Jeremy and Gabriel. "Imagine the joy I'll have in writing mother that I've discovered the McLeod brothers living such inconsequential lives in this backwater town with their second-rate wives. She'll be delighted."

"How could you?" Clarissa asked, glaring at Patrick as she stroked a hand down Gabriel's back to soothe him, his muscles rippling as he fought against Colin's hold. "How could you bring him here?"

"I had no idea," Patrick said, staring with dawning horror at the man he'd known as Samuel Sanders.

"You remember her, Mrs. Masterson, from that horrible day when Gabriel was forced away from me." Clarissa stared at her brother with a deep disappointment.

"Of course I do," Patrick said, shock replacing confusion. "But he calls himself Samuel Sanders. He's my boss. He was my friend."

"You'd lie about your identity?" Jeremy growled, rolling his shoulders to free himself from Patrick's hold.

"When you survive a financial crash like I did in '07, it is frequently beneficial to reinvent oneself. Even in such a minor way. For who would take advice from Henry Masterson, the man who lost millions?" He smiled. "But Samuel Sanders, there's a man who can be trusted."

"You snake," Gabriel rasped.

"No, I'm like the phoenix, able to rise again," he murmured as he strolled toward Araminta, standing as though transfixed in the corner as she watched the scene unfold.

She hastened away from him, her limp more obvious due to her rush to evade him, moving to stand beside Colin.

"It seems all the men in this pathetic family have a penchant for those considered second-best, if that."

"This is my house, and you are not welcome in it. You will never be welcomed here," Jeremy said in a low voice.

"You are no longer welcome at my home, either," Colin said, aligning himself with Jeremy and Gabriel. "You will need to find some other lodging for your stay."

Henry turned a speculative glance at Patrick. "I would think you'd reconsider any such hasty actions, as I'd hate for it to have negative repercussions on your dear Patrick. His position is quite precarious, dependent upon my generosity."

Clarissa paled, although her hand remained on Gabriel's arm. "Patrick has family now. He's not alone, and we'll ensure he is taken care of," she snapped. "He doesn't depend on your charity."

Patrick's eyes flashed with a deep emotion. "Sam—Henry—why didn't you tell me who you were?"

"For all intents, I am Samuel Sanders, your superior at the Company." He flashed gloating, amused eyes at Clarissa. "I realized how dull-witted you must be to not recognize your husband's dead mother's name. Although, of course, why anyone would mourn her is beyond me. Stupid cow, marrying that worthless Irish peasant."

Gabriel roared, breaking free of the hold Colin had on him and leapt at Henry, slamming his fist into his jaw and then his belly. "Don't you ever speak of my mother, your *aunt*, in such a disrespectful way again." He watched as Henry stood with his hands on his knees, pulling in gasps of air. "Don't you dare touch my wife again, either."

The tension slowly faded from Gabriel as Clarissa rubbed a hand down his back. "Darling," she whispered. "He isn't worth it."

Gabriel glanced around, blanching to realize his children had seen him attack Henry. Savannah stood against the far wall, quivering after watching his exhibition of violence. "Forgive me," he said, pushing past Henry and rushing from the room.

Araminta sprang into action, herding the children into a back room and shutting the door behind her.

Patrick released Jeremy, and he rolled his shoulders a few times, easing the tension and loosening his muscles in case he needed to further the work begun by his brother. Jeremy approached and knelt so his face was even with Henry's as Henry remained bent over in pain after Gabriel's blows.

"You remember what this feels like, cousin? Always on the losing end of a McLeod fist." His smile a mixture of pride and a sneer, he goaded his cousin. "We should write Richard so he could come visit. He always enjoyed beating on you the most."

Henry reared up, fists flying, but Jeremy dodged his wild jabs and grabbed him by the lapels, slamming him against the nearby wall, the force of impact dislodging a decorative plate. It crashed to the floor, a counterpoint to the men's groans as they struggled against one another.

"You might still have the fancy clothes. You might still have a position of power. But you have no hold over us. Not anymore." They shared a long, malevolent glare as Jeremy held him against the wall so that Henry stood on his tiptoes. He gave him a final shake, Henry's head thwacking against the wooden wall before Jeremy released him.

Henry stroked a shaking hand over his previously pristine brown jacket. He straightened his tie and smoothed his pomaded hair. "You are making a grave mistake, treating me in such a manner."

Lucas stared at Patrick a moment, but Patrick remained mute, standing to one side of the room. "What do you think you could possibly do now? You might have had influence and power in Boston, but this isn't Boston." Lucas smiled at Savannah to reassure her. "My sister and her husband have successful, prosperous lives here."

"Built from her murdered husband's money. The man she skewered to death. How do you think the townsfolk would react if they knew the truth?" He watched them with malicious glee at the thought of sharing such a tale.

Savannah laughed. "Do you think the tale of my actions didn't precede my arrival? That I haven't had to prove I won't murder the townsfolk over the past decade? That's an old tale, Mr. Sanders."

He frowned as he looked at the group. "I'll find a way. And I'll make you sorry you ever treated me in such a vile manner."

Patrick stepped forward and raised a hand for silence. "Do you expect me to believe that, all those months ago, when you befriended me, you did so out of kindness?" His brown eyes hardened to the point they appeared as dark as coal. "From the moment you met me, you were plotting how to harm those I cared about. You never intended friendship." Patrick took a step forward, his breathing quickening. "You didn't come here tonight hoping to reestablish a connection with your cousins. You wanted to cause pain and discord."

Henry stood in front of them, disheveled and alone in his defiance. "I refuse to live in a world where a McLeod, or one of their family members, is more content than I am. Believe me. You will regret this." He glared at those in the room, before spinning on his heel and storming out the front door.

***

Gabriel roamed the upstairs of the workshop, pacing the familiar space as his mind raced. He paused, reaching back to massage his shoulders as he fought painful memories—Henry taunting him, calling him an orphan. Henry destroying the boxful of treasures he and his brothers cherished the night before they fled their aunt's house. Henry discovering Gabriel with Clarissa in a coffee shop in Boston years later. He sat on an overturned crate, sighing as he attempted to banish the turmoil and anger Henry had evoked.

"Thought I'd find you up here," Jeremy said.

"I thought you were spending the morning with Lucas."

"No way am I leaving you alone with your thoughts today, the day after seeing Henry again." He pulled out a large box and sat on it. His roving gaze took in Gabriel's disheveled clothes and day's growth of beard. "Did you even go home last night?"

"No."

Jeremy looked toward a small pallet near the far wall and frowned. "You're letting him win, Gabe."

Gabriel firmed his jaw, his eyes ice cold. "I hate that he's here in Montana. I hate that, after fourteen years, he's come to this place where I sought to escape him and his mother."

"It's a horrible irony he's in Butte. Yet he doesn't matter anymore. He never really did."

Gabriel took a deep breath, willing the tension to leave him. "Do you know what it was like when we were younger, to know, at any instant, one word from him could separate us? Could have forced us to an orphanage, where we would have had no say as to our future?" Gabriel asked. "That he's a large part of the reason I left Boston? Left Clarissa? Left her to that fiend, Cameron?"

He stood, turning to stare out the window, gripping the windowsill. "I hate him with everything I am." Gabriel's confession sounded as though ripped from him. "And I hate him even more for that." He took a deep breath, his exhalation stuttering. "Every time he had the opportunity to show compassion, he showed us contempt. Every chance for kindness, he demonstrated malice."

"He taught us what we never wanted to be, Gabe," Jeremy argued. "And he didn't separate us. You wouldn't have allowed it. Even if we had ended up in an orphanage, you would have found a way to keep us together."

Gabriel turned to Jeremy, his eyes lit with anger. "Why is he here? He has no reason to be here. Amalgamated is in Butte, not Missoula."

Jeremy sighed and shook his head. "I don't know. He's always enjoyed riling you, and you're allowing him to get what he wants." Jeremy watched him intently. "Henry left, Gabe. On the first train out this morning back to Butte. I ensured he was on it." Jeremy frowned at Gabriel's lack of reaction to his news.

Gabriel raised his head as he heard a few *thunk*s from downstairs. "Mr. A.J.'s here."

"Good. Maybe he'll be able to talk some sense into you." He slung an arm around Gabriel's shoulders and tugged him away from the window and down the stairs. "A.J., we have a problem and need your help."

"What's the problem, Sonny?" he asked, frowning as he beheld Gabriel. "Don't tell me yer fightin' with Missy again? I cain't believe I was sick yesterday an' missed the gatherin'."

"No, everything is fine with her," Gabriel said. He walked to the door and shut it, placing the room largely in darkness. He pulled over an unvarnished chair and sat next to Mr. Pickens. Jeremy did the same.

"Well, what's got ye so upset?" Mr. A.J. smacked his lips as he fought a frown.

"Our cousin was in town. He befriended Clarissa's brother, Patrick, in Butte, using a different name. Unbeknownst to her brother, he's our cousin who relished tormenting us when we were children," Gabriel said as he fisted and unfisted one of his hands repeatedly, as though to ease his tension.

Mr. A.J. frowned. "Sonny, ye ain't that boy no more. Yer brothers are grown men, able to care for themselves. There ain't no need for such bitterness." He reached out a hand to Gabriel, setting it atop his hand to still his movement.

"I know what you say is true. But seeing him again ..." He paused as he shook his head, his voice shattered. "It's like I'm twelve, fighting to keep my family together."

"What'd ye do to save yer family, Sonny?"

"Gave up school, apprenticed with Old Man Harris. Ensured we had a place to go each day where we felt wanted." Gabriel's eyes squinted shut.

"Knowin' ye as I do, seein' how ye treat my Missy with the care ye do, ye could never doubt ye did enough for yer brothers."

"I know. I never wanted to see any of my mother's family again. They have no right to come here, to tarnish the memories I have with my family here."

"Seems to me they're only tarnished if ye let 'em be," Mr. A.J. said with a *thunk* of his cane. "Only if ye allow him to affect ye so."

"I don't know if I'm capable of not hating him."

"I know Preacher won't agree with me, but it's all right to hate, Sonny. Some people do us enough harm, we can't ever like 'em. Just don't be consumed by it," he cautioned.

"You have a good life, Gabe," Jeremy urged. "Focus on all you have, not on the hurts from the past."

"I'm worried about what his presence could mean. What sort of mischief he will wreak," Gabriel said. "For wherever Henry goes, he brings with him calamities."

"At least with regard to us," Jeremy said with a wry smile.

"As I told my Missy, don't go lookin' for trouble. It'll find ye easy enough," Mr. A.J. said. "Enjoy what ye have, Sonny. A beautiful wife and children. Friends. A home."

Gabriel opened eyes filled with embarrassment to A.J. "I struck him yesterday."

"Good," A.J. proclaimed with a resounding *thunk*. "Sounds like he needed it."

Gabriel shook his head with remorse. "My children saw me act like a barbarian. I scared Savannah. I hated myself reacting like that. It's not who I am."

Mr. A.J. raised his cane, prompting Gabriel to lean away, lest he be hit in the chest with the tip of it. "Not goin' home at night for the comfort my Missy could give ye ain't like ye either, Sonny. Ye need to ignore this man. He ain't nothin' to ye now."

Gabriel ran a tired hand over his face. "I know."

Jeremy slapped him on his back. "Go home, Gabe. Sav's already forgiven you. She hates violence, mainly because it reminds her of what she lived through. But she understands it's necessary at times. She forgave me for fighting him after you left."

"Violence never solves anything," Gabriel said with a rueful shake of his head.

"Don't know about that, Sonny. I imagine ye felt mighty good givin' that whippersnapper a wallop or two." He chortled with glee. "Just wish I coulda seen it!"

Gabriel stood and slapped A.J. on his shoulder. "Thanks, Old Man."

"Anytime, Sonny," he wheezed, beaming his toothless smile.

***

Gabriel walked the short distance home, his mind racing. He entered through the kitchen door to find it empty. Dishes sat out to dry on the rack by the sink, the only sign of breakfast from that morning. He walked through the house, devoid of his children's voices and laughter. He crept up the stairs, poking his head into his children's rooms to find them empty. He sighed, walking into his room, coming to a halt to find Clarissa sitting at her vanity.

She raised startled eyes to his but didn't turn to him or stand. "How was your evening?" She fidgeted with the jewelry on top of her vanity.

"Rissa, I'm sorry. I was ..." He sighed and approached her. She finally turned to face him, and he sat on the edge of the bed, their legs tangling. "Ashamed."

She frowned. "Why?"

"The children saw me. I never wanted them to see me like that." He lowered his face into his palms, resting his elbows on his knees.

She reached forward to massage his head, running her fingers through his thick black mane of hair. Her hands moved to his nape, massaging his shoulders. "Darling, they weren't afraid of you. Billy thought you were dashing and brave. Geraldine wanted to know who the mean man was who said horrible things about your mother. Myrtle waited with me in the rocking chair until she fell asleep because she wanted to hug you before bed."

He raised shocked eyes to her. "You can't be serious."

She smiled, tracing her hands over his cheeks. "Of course I am. He's a horrible person, and he hurt you dreadfully. But, just as I had to put Cameron firmly in my past, so must you with Henry."

Gabriel groaned as he pulled Clarissa from the bench and hauled her onto his lap. "I'm humbled, over and over again, at your strength. Your resilience," he whispered into her ear. "Forgive me for not coming home."

"There's no need for forgiveness," she said as she nuzzled his ear, kissing down his neck, along his jaw and then raising up to kiss him on the lips. He groaned, clasping her head between his palms as the kiss deepened.

"Where are the children?" he asked, easing away to pepper her jaw, collarbone and chest with kisses.

"With Araminta. They won't be home for hours."

She shrieked as he rose, toppling her onto the bed. "Good." His eyes gleamed with passionate intent, and he kissed her once before he rose and strode to the door, closing and locking it. He paused, as he beheld her on their bed, hair mussed and lips swollen from his caresses and kisses. "I need you, darling."

She beamed at him, holding a hand out to him. He grasped her hand, tugging her up to quickly shuck her of her clothes before easing her back to the bed, a bright shaft of sunlight limning her body. His hands followed the beam of light, his whisper-soft touches eliciting sighs and broken pleas.

She pushed at his shoulders, earning a laugh as he tumbled to the side. She moved to stretch atop him, smoothing her hands over his arms and chest. He leaned up, nipping her on her mouth. She backed away, holding his searing gaze with hers. "He'll never take away what we have. As long as we continue to fight, day by day, for this, we'll always have more than he could ever imagine."

Gabriel groaned, rolling with her so she was underneath him and kissed her deeply. "I love you, Rissa. I always will."

She kissed him again, easing the torment in his heart, helping him to forget the world outside their room for a few short hours.

CHAPTER NINETEEN

Boston, October 1913

Zylphia wandered the formal sitting room, tracing a finger along the polished mahogany side tables before walking to a bookshelf, eyeing porcelain knickknacks, then moved to sit on a cushioned window seat. Sheer curtains covered the windows, allowing in a muted light from the front garden. The scent of late-season roses wafted inside, and she closed her eyes as she listened to the trilling of the songbirds.

"Five minutes. I will allow five more minutes," she murmured to herself.

"Five more minutes for what?" a man with a deep voice asked, startling her from her musings as she jerked her head toward the doorway.

"To await the arrival of your mother for tea." She frowned at Theodore Goff, dressed casually in faded gray pants, a wrinkled white linen shirt with a loosely knotted tie and a misbuttoned cranberry-colored waistcoat.

"You'll be waiting longer than five minutes." His sardonic smile eased her tension. "I spoke with the butler, and Mother's out until she must return to change for a dinner function. Are you sure you are here on the correct day?"

"She wrote me a note inviting me to tea on October 27 to discuss her exciting ideas about the orphanage. As my mother is out of town, I believe your mother wished to speak with me."

199

Teddy frowned. "I'm sorry, Zylphia. My mother is … impulsive at times. She must have received another invitation and forgot her desire to speak with you."

Zylphia rose, her forest-green tea-dress settling at her ankles. "I have no wish to interrupt your afternoon, Mr. Go—Teddy. If you will excuse me …"

"Stay for tea with me?" he asked, flushing at his impulsive request. "I know it's not entirely proper, but the house is filled with staff, and I'd hate for you to leave without having refreshments." He motioned for her to sit again while moving to the hallway to speak with someone about a tea tray.

Teddy sat on a chair near hers, hooking his foot under a nearby table so the soon-to-arrive tray would be near them.

"I've heard your stories of being raised in England, but you don't seem nearly proper enough," Zylphia murmured.

Teddy flinched. "My mother despairs of me having proper manners. I know how to act when necessary, and I hope I won't embarrass you with any unforgiveable faux pas."

Zylphia laughed. "I must admit that I'm always afraid I'll say or do something wrong, so not having to worry that I'll stir my tea in an inappropriate manner is a relief."

He watched her with a warm light in his eyes. "Is there an improper way to stir tea?"

"Yes, and I've done it."

Teddy laughed, relaxing into his chair as the tea was delivered. He motioned to the table in front of them and indicated with a nod of his head for the maid to leave.

"I find it impressive how well you communicate without speaking," Zylphia said as she poured them each a cup. He nodded as she held up the sugar, holding up his hand to indicate enough after two cubes had been added.

"I am known as the absentminded inventor who locks himself away in his laboratory. I wouldn't want to waste words if I don't have to."

Zylphia held her teacup halfway to her lips, studying him, as if to decipher if he were in earnest. "Even scientists must need to communicate."

He shrugged.

Zylphia took a sip of tea, holding her cup by the handle in a dainty manner rather than cupping it in her hand. "My theory, if I were a scientist, would be that you act as you do to increase your mystique."

He choked on a laugh, his eyes sparkling with merriment. "I fear you'll find few who would agree with that theory."

"But has anyone done their research?" She wriggled her eyebrows at him, smiling without guile and leaning forward.

He sobered as he watched her. "Is that how you see me? As a subject for research?" Any levity disappeared as he tensed, awaiting her response.

She stilled, belatedly realizing she'd offended him in some way. "Of course not. Forgive me." She looked down at her now-clenched hand on her lap. "I often speak rashly, unwittingly causing distress with my comments."

"Please do not concern yourself on my account, Zylphia." He half smiled. "You don't regret our agreement at the Wheeler ball that I am permitted to call you Zylphia in private?"

"Of course not. It means I can call you Teddy rather than Theodore."

"I still think it would remind you of your former president."

"I have no need to think of a president." She laughed.

He watched her with a small smile. "You might, as you continue your crusade on behalf of women and universal suffrage."

Zylphia watched him with an arrested expression.

"I'd like to think I could be of some help," said Teddy. At Zylphia's prolonged silence, he set his empty teacup on the table, the brief sense of camaraderie dissipating. "I don't imagine you'd be interested in seeing my laboratory?"

"I would. Very much so." Zylphia set down her cup and rose.

He stood, showing her the way to the hallway and stairs, which they took in silence. "The third floor is my domain," he said as they reached the landing. "My parents didn't have much use for it, and, when I returned from England, it was the perfect space for me. My private study is down there." He pointed to a closed door at the end of the hall on the right.

He thrust open a door, ushering her into a space filled with tables covered in metal pieces, wires, nuts and bolts, and an assortment of tools.

"How do you know where everything is?" Zylphia asked as she took in the disorganized space. "I imagined it to be"—she waved her arm around—"tidier." She wandered toward a desk near a window, a drawing pad with a pencil on top, its pages fluttering in the breeze.

"I imagine most people create best in an orderly environment. I thrive on chaos and clutter."

"Well, you've succeeded here." They shared a rueful smile. She walked from table to table, deciphering what made each table's experiment different from the previous. She raised a confused gaze to his.

He walked to where she stood. "If you look closely, this wire is twisted three times while the one over there, four. I'm testing if that has any bearing on my project."

"Have you noted any difference?"

"Not yet but I'm not done with my quality checks."

She nodded and moved again toward his drawings. "Don't you miss living in England?"

"No. Although I spent most of my youth there, I've spent enough time here to know this is where I want to be. Boston is my home now. I don't feel guilty for having no desire to live in England. That is, until my grandparents visit." He smiled with a distant look in his eyes.

"Why?"

He focused on her, his gray eyes penetrating and intense even through his wire-rimmed glasses, yet kindled with a gentle warmth as he met her curious stare. "Because they discuss the important familial antecedents, the inspiring feats performed by generations past, and it makes me wish, for an instant, I were that sort of person."

"Rather than the sort who tinkers away in solitude in a lab."

"It's not all I do." He smirked at her raised eyebrow. "I know they wish I'd return to England and perform some glorious deed to increase their sense of esteem among their peers."

"You mean, fighting in duels and wars." Zylphia crinkled her nose in disgust.

He laughed. "You think it's unimportant, but those actions by men were as significant at the time as what your fellow suffragettes are currently doing in

England. What you'd like to do here." He raised an eyebrow, challenging her to disagree with him.

"I'd hardly call dueling and the struggle for universal suffrage remotely equal," Zylphia scoffed.

"Maybe not to you but, to men, attacks on their honor or against those they love, are powerful motivators. Just as the desire to show women are deserving of the rights of full citizenship is a powerful motivator for many women now."

"You've never sounded more English."

"You've never sounded more scornful of the fact." His delight faded as their discussion continued. "Zylphia, I'm not saying I agree in any way with warring or dueling, but I can understand what prompts a man to act as he does. Just as I'm beginning to understand what motivates you."

Zylphia stilled in her movement around his laboratory. "No need to make me one of your experiments. I'm not that difficult to understand."

"On the contrary." He smiled, the tenderness in his gaze intended to soothe her. "You're more intricate than any experiment I could fathom."

"I don't want to be viewed as something to be studied in a laboratory." Her eyes flashed mutinously, her discomfort obvious.

"Just as I don't wish to be seen as a pet project, only worthy of a report back to your friends."

"Is that how you see me? That I only deign to show you interest because I see you as an oddity?"

He reached forward, clasping her shoulders, preventing her from spinning away and rushing through the open doorway. "No, of course not. Forgive me." She stilled under the gentle caress of his fingers down her cheek. "I'd hoped we were friends."

"I've been advised unmarried women of my class can't be friends with men."

He chuffed out a laugh. "Why would the two unconventional misfits of Boston society play by their rules?" His smile widened as she reluctantly grinned back. "Be my friend, Zylphia."

"My friends call me Zee," she whispered.

His body relaxed, and he released her. "Zee, I'm so glad we're friends."

"So am I."

***

"Are you certain Clarissa and Gabriel have reconciled?" Zylphia asked, curled in an oversize chair in the front parlor.

A gentle fire glowed in the fireplace, adding more warmth to the mint-green wallpaper. Thick cream-colored drapes covered the front windows. The ceiling was decorated with a mural of contented cherubs, and a thick oriental carpet covered the wooden floors.

"When I saw them in Washington, DC, in the spring, it seemed as though they'd never find peace again." Her gaze roved over her parents, silently celebrating their presence in Boston on their return from Montana. Aidan held a tumbler of whiskey in one hand, his other stroking Delia's fingers as they settled into a comfortable settee.

Aidan sighed, stretching his long legs toward the warmth of the coal fire. "Ask you mother, but I believe all is finally well in Montana."

Delia nodded her agreement.

"At last I felt it was time to come home. We'd left you alone long enough. We were saddened to miss the first anniversary of Rory's death, but we wanted to return home before any inclement weather impeded train travel."

"I was fine, Father. I had my adventure in Newport, and I've continued my other activities."

"I'm certain Sophie has kept you busy," Delia said with a smile.

A pounding on the door interrupted their conversation. Aidan glanced first to Delia and then Zylphia before rising with a sigh. "I'm afraid our butler is too busy flirting with the maid to be of much use right now."

"Aidan, don't be too hard on him," Delia pled. "He's still learning the role, and he's terrified of being sent back to the orphanage."

"I know. And I'd never turn him out," Aidan said with a frustrated sigh. "If he could have served under our previous butler for a while, I think that would have been more suitable." Aidan strode from the room, a faint light from a wall sconce casting shadows on the carpet as he approached the front door.

He wrenched open the door, a glower already on his face for the person interrupting his reunion with his daughter. "Yes," he snapped.

"Uncle," Richard said. "Thank God you're home." He stood, swaying in front of Aidan, pale and shaking as though he were in the throes of shock.

"Richard." Aidan pulled him into the warmth of the large foyer before clasping him momentarily into a strong embrace. "Are you all right? No, I can see you're not." He swung an arm around his shoulder and propelled him into the front parlor with Delia and Zee.

"Richard," Zylphia said as he entered. "How lovely to see you."

Delia studied his swaying form for a moment before sharing a silent look with Aidan. When Richard collapsed into a chair next to Zylphia, Delia asked, "Is it Florence? Or the children?"

"Yes. No," Richard said. "Forgive me." He paused, glancing at them all for a moment. "The children are fine. They are with our wonderful neighbor, who acts like their grandmother."

"Yes, Mrs. O'Connell," Delia murmured.

"Florence had the baby today," Richard whispered.

Rather than shouting exclamations of joy, Delia tensed, while Zylphia frowned, and Aidan stood at attention, as though waiting to learn what was needed from him.

"She's always so valiant when it's her time."

Zylphia reached over and grasped his hand, giving quiet solace. "It's all right, Richard."

"They wouldn't let me see her. Florence didn't really want me there, and, by the time I arrived from the smithy, she was already far along." He let out a stuttering exhalation. "Our little girl never took a breath. She was born ..."

"Oh, no," Zylphia whispered, tears coursing down her cheeks.

"They told me the cord was wrapped around her neck. There was nothing anyone could have done." He swiped at his eyes.

"How is Florence?" Delia asked.

"Devastated. She'd always wanted a little girl, and, after five sons, to know this was our chance ..." He took a deep breath. "They wouldn't let me spend the night. It's against hospital policy, even though I begged." His shoulders shook.

Aidan shared another look with Delia, who rose and coaxed Zylphia from the room. Aidan took Zylphia's seat. "Richard," Aidan said. As the door clicked closed behind them, Richard collapsed into his uncle's arms.

Aidan held him for the few moments Richard leaned on him. "Forgive me," Richard croaked.

"What should I forgive?" Aidan asked. "A father mourning the loss of his child? You must mourn, Richard."

"I must be strong for Florence." His eyes became distant. "You didn't hear her shrieking, her begging for the doctor to help her baby."

"What happened at the hospital?" Aidan placed a hand on Richard's shoulder, before moving it around to cup the back of his neck to encourage him to meet his gaze.

"I shouldn't have heard her screaming, but I'd become restless, and I snuck into the back area where I wasn't supposed to go. I thought I was fortunate the nurses were lax in guarding the front." He gave a bitter laugh. "Turns out they were restraining an inconsolable mother.

"When I realized it was Florence, nothing would have kept me from her. The doctor and nurses were appalled that I barged in, but all I could focus on was Florence. Keening. As though her heart were breaking." Richard bowed his head as tears trickled down his cheeks.

"I'm so sorry, Richard."

"So am I, Uncle." He sniffed as he attempted to control his tears. "I saw her, our daughter, for a moment. She was perfect but for the fact she wasn't breathing."

"How is Florence now?"

"They had to sedate her. I'll return tomorrow morning at the earliest moment they'll let me be with her." He took a deep breath before he met his uncle's gaze. "I know I've asked many favors from you over the years, and I'm sorry to burden you."

"You've always been one of my life's greatest joys. Never a burden," Aidan whispered.

"Will you come with me as I tell my boys there will be no baby?" He sniffed again and straightened his shoulders. "I must tell them myself, but, afterward, when they are calm, it would help me to have you there."

Aidan squeezed his shoulder and nodded. "Of course. I'm honored you'd ask me. Let me speak with Delia, and then we'll be off."

Aidan left the room, striding with purpose until he saw Zylphia sitting on the stairs and Delia pacing in the foyer. "I'm to travel with him to be there after he tells his boys. I'll most likely spend the night there."

As Delia and Aidan walked upstairs to pack a small overnight bag for him, Zylphia approached the parlor.

Richard sat stock-still, an expression of intense anguish and fatigue on his face.

"Cousin," Zylphia whispered as she approached. "What can I do?"

Richard jerked at her voice, attempted and failed to smile his welcome at her in the room, instead grimacing at her presence. "Visit Florence soon. She'll need the company. And the distraction. Talk about the struggle for the vote. Your friends. Anything to get her mind off what just happened."

"I promise," Zylphia whispered, leaning forward to enfold him in her embrace for a few moments. She held him until a gentle clearing of Aidan's throat heralded the men could leave. "Take care of yourself, Richard."

He squeezed her arm before following his uncle from the room and out of the house.

CHAPTER TWENTY

Z ylphia exited the streetcar in Dorchester, straightening her pale-yellow ribbed day-dress and navy blue coat. Her raven hair was held by a few pins in a loose chignon and covered by a matching hat. She tugged on her ivory gloves, tucked her handbag under an arm and began the short walk past rows of triple-decker houses to her cousins' house, enjoying the short walk in the sunshine on a late-November day. Children played on the sidewalks and streets, calling out a warning to clear the road when a carriage or car passed.

She knocked on the door of the first-floor unit of a three-story house, painted a blue-gray.

"Zee!" her cousin Thomas shrieked when he opened the door. He gave her a quick hug before dragging her inside.

"Thomas! What have I said about not opening the door to strangers?" Florence called down the rear kitchen hallway that led to the front entranceway with rooms on either side. White and green floral wallpaper lined the walls in the hallway.

"It's no stranger, Mama. It's Zee!" he said, emphasizing the vowel sound of her name with glee.

A clatter was heard from the kitchen before the click of her shoes sounded down the hallway. "Zylphia."

Florence approached with a broad smile, her expression lit with joy upon seeing Zylphia. However, deep circles under Flo's eyes hinted at her recent anguish. She swiped at flour on the apron covering her gray day-dress.

"What a wonderful surprise." She hugged Zylphia close for a moment before leading her to the kitchen. "I'm baking a cake. Why don't you keep me company?"

"What kind?" Zylphia asked as she handed her coat to little Thomas and followed Florence.

"Nothing fancy. A simple white one with plain icing. Richard hopes today is the day he takes charge of the Hartley forge. If it goes well, I want to have a cake to celebrate. If it doesn't, one to commiserate." She shared a rueful smile with Zylphia.

"Thus, not much decoration."

"Exactly." She moved to the stove, put the kettle on for tea and motioned for Zylphia to settle at one of the kitchen table chairs. "How did you get here? Did your father's driver bring you to us?"

"No, I took the streetcar."

"Zee, you shouldn't have. Take advantage of what your father can offer you now."

"I know, but it seemed excessive to have his driver travel to the garage to drive me here and then to wait during my visit. I'll be fine. Besides, I enjoy the adventure and the people-watching."

"I imagine there's always something to see," Florence said with a half smile. Her gaze darted out the doorway, listening as her sons played in the front room. She measured flour, vanilla and milk while Zylphia settled at the table. "Somehow I thought, when we moved, we'd spend all of our time in the living room." She laughed to herself as her gaze became distant for a moment. "I had insisted on a formal dining room."

"I remember the arguments you and Richard had," Zylphia murmured, motioning for Florence to continue with the cake as Zylphia rose to fill the teapot with tea and boiling water.

"And look at us. Just like before, everything of import occurs in the kitchen! The children study in here. We eat almost every meal here. That dining room would be wasted space if we hadn't turned it into a bedroom for the children." She gave a chagrined laugh, before choking back a sob at her last word.

Zylphia watched her closely but avoided speaking about the loss of her daughter that had brought Florence nearly to tears. "It seems to me, as a family, you know what's important. Being together."

Florence cleared her throat. "Well, Richard works more than I'd like, but he seems to relish each new challenge, and he's quite adept at managing the three blacksmith shops we own."

"How have you adjusted to living here rather than the North End?"

"We've been here long enough now that it doesn't feel quite so strange. I still miss living nearer to the central part of the city, but we're not far. And I think this is a better place to raise the children. One day, we hope our children will live upstairs rather than renting out the units." Florence laughed. "I never could have imagined any of this when I married Richard."

"What do you mean?"

Florence gave the cake batter one last mix with her spoon before approaching the baking tin. "I was content to live in the North End, married to a simple black-smith. I never would have imagined we'd eventually own three blacksmithing shops, perhaps four, and a triple-decker in Dorchester."

"It seems he takes after my father," Zylphia said with a wry smile.

"I've often wondered if it is a McLeod trait."

After a few moments of silence, Zylphia asked in a gentle voice, "How are you feeling, Flo?"

Florence stilled for a moment before finishing her work on the cake. She set the cake in the oven and sat across from Zylphia. Her forced joviality dissipated, leaving an expression of numb grief in its wake. "I'm all right. I remind myself, daily, how fortunate I am for every blessing I have in my life. I give thanks for what I have, rather than focus on what I don't." She looked at her hands, gripped together on the table, refusing to meet Zylphia's gaze.

"Flo?"

"It's foolish, I know. To yearn for a little girl I never truly knew. I think poor Richard is at his wit's end with me."

"I think he mourns too."

At Zylphia's soft words, Florence met her gaze.

"He's visited my father a few times last week, and he's always appeared shaken."

"I remind myself it's nothing like what Savannah or Clarissa have suffered. They had memories with their children." She bit her lip. "I can't imagine having memories to mourn."

"Whereas you had the hope of memories to be made. The dream of what was to come."

"Yes. And it's so hard. But Richard holds me when I need to cry. There's a solace in that which words can't explain." She paused as she sniffed, wrapping her hands around the mug Zylphia set in front of her. "Knowing that this is something I don't have to go through alone."

"I'm so sorry, Flo." Zylphia squeezed her hand.

Florence met her gaze as tears coursed down her cheeks. "I desperately wanted a daughter." She placed her hands over her face for a minute before scrubbing them. She took a deep breath as though to rein in her grief and pulled a handkerchief from her skirt pocket, wiping her face clear of any signs of sorrow. "Thank you for visiting, Zee. It helps to have company during the day." Florence watched her curiously. "Why did you call today?"

Zylphia flushed and took a sip of her scalding tea, gasping as it burned her tongue. "I wanted to see how you were doing." At Florence's increasingly inquisitive gaze, Zee admitted, "I felt like doing something different today."

"No, *something different* for you is finding a new way to agitate for the vote, not visiting a mourning relative. What's wrong?"

"Entering society isn't what I thought it would be." She slumped into her chair.

"You mean, the men aren't as dashing as you'd hoped?" Florence teased, her customary good humor returning as the subject turned from her and her stillborn daughter.

"They're quite dashing, I assure you. I'm simply not what they expected."

"I don't know why that should surprise you. You're not what most anyone would expect, Zee. Why should you want to be? You're a remarkable woman who has much to offer."

She pushed one of her black curls behind her ear. "I'd hoped to meet others who would be interested in joining the suffragist movement. However, when they see me approach, they ignore me or flee."

Florence laughed. "Then you'll have to find another way to approach them. Sometimes barreling in isn't what people need. The truth, or our vision of the truth, can blind us, Zee. When others sense such passion or purpose, they automatically shy away."

"I don't understand why." Zee blew out her breath with agitation.

"Imagine someone continually approaching you, extolling the virtues of a world where women never voted. How would you react?"

"I'd argue with them." After a moment's pause, she said, "And, if they continued to approach me, I'd do what I could to avoid them."

"Exactly. You need to be more subtle in your approach. I think it's wonderful you have such zeal for the vote. I wish I had more time to dedicate to it. However, it is still considered a radical belief. If you want to convince others to your way of thinking, you must find a gentler, less confrontational way to induce them to listen to you."

"You sound like Anna Howard Shaw," Zylphia grumbled.

Florence laughed again. "Yes, and I imagine you espouse the more aggressive tactics of Miss Paul. However, I think both methods are needed, and, when one way isn't working, you must look to a different tactic."

"Unfortunately they all know I'm a firebrand radical now." Zylphia raised her eyebrow at Florence's snort of amusement. "And I can see of no way to approach them so as to convince them to my way of thinking."

"Perhaps there are others you could speak with. Besides, if you temper your words for a while, you might find that they are willing to be near you. Once you've formed an acquaintance, then you could broach the subject again."

Zylphia groaned as she leaned back in her chair. "It seems pointless, but, if it will help in any way, I'll do it. Biting my tongue has never been easy."

"I wish I could be there to see it," Florence said, humor lighting her eyes. She tilted her head to one side, idly running her fingertip around the rim of her mug. "Are there any men who interest you, Zee?"

"Ugh, not you too," Zylphia said with a deep sigh. She propped her head on her hand and glared at Florence before shaking her head ruefully.

"I know you espouse the idea that you will never marry, but that's never seemed realistic to me."

"Why? Numerous suffragists have never married. Why shouldn't I be one of them?"

"I see how you watch your parents. How you watch Richard and me together. It's always seemed something you yearned for."

"I marvel at your friendships. At how you communicate even though you aren't talking." She smiled to herself for a moment. "In a way it seems magical."

"It is, when you find a person you connect with. I would hate to think you'd become wedded to a cause and lose out on the joys of a full life, spent toiling away with little thought for what you truly want or need."

"I shouldn't marry until women have the vote."

"What an utter bunch of rubbish." Florence tapped her spoon against the edge of her mug. "No woman should advocate for other women to act in such a way that she herself isn't willing to act."

At Zylphia's surprise, Florence nodded. "I had a visit from Sophie recently, and she informed me of your juvenile agreement with your friends after hearing Alva Belmont speak. You are mistaken if you think a pact with your friends will bring about the enfranchisement for women nor will it bring you happiness. Especially if you choose it over love."

"There's no one I'm interested in, Flo."

"You say that now, but this struggle is far from over, and you could lose many years if you follow through with your agreement." She pointed her spoon at Zylphia. "I would also caution you that, if you believe you'll receive the counsel you require from your friends, rather than from Sophie, you are sorely mistaken."

Zylphia stiffened in her chair. "Why is it that you all act as though she is an oracle?"

Florence smiled. "Perhaps she is, and we were simply fortunate enough to meet her. In any case, you'd be foolish not to seek her out when you need to, rather than rely on your younger friends."

***

A few weeks after visiting Florence in early December, Zylphia stood on the side of the dance floor, attempting not to sway to the lilting music as she watched her friends laugh and flirt with their partners. The gold-gilded ballroom sparkled under a multitude of lights from the chandeliers while the colorful dresses worn by the women added splashes of color. She held a half-filled punch glass in her hand. The long ballroom opened onto the dining room and backed into a glass conservatory.

"No Mr. Goff this evening?" a man with a low voice asked from behind her.

She jumped at the voice intruding her thoughts before smiling at the teasing glance from Mr. Hubbard. "Good evening, Mr. Hubbard," she said with a tilt of her head.

He raised an eyebrow, his honey-blond hair artfully disheveled. "Where's your faithful companion?"

"You make him sound like a ..." Zylphia stopped at her near-disparaging comment about Teddy.

"Well, he does follow you around like one. One has to hope he doesn't have fleas." His blue-green eyes flashed with humor.

"Oh, stop. Not one more mean word."

His eyes lit with appreciation. "You are as loyal as they say," he murmured. "I'm merely thankful he's not dancing attendance on you this evening. It seems he's by your side at every function these days." He took a sip of the punch and grimaced. When Zylphia frowned her confusion at him, he lowered his voice. "I don't have to compete for your notice tonight."

Zylphia rolled her eyes, her cheeks blushing at his attention. "I'm sure Miss Perkins will be most disappointed when you fail to dote on her."

He laughed. "She just became engaged to Mr. Young yesterday."

"Really?"

"Yes, although don't bandy it about. A large notice is to be in the papers tomorrow. I believe they're hoping for a big wedding in Newport this summer."

"How wonderful for her. I wish them very happy." Zylphia smiled in the woman's direction, earning a confused glower from the woman and her friends.

"They're terrified you'll approach them and turn them into radicals."

"Simply because I believe women deserve the vote, as much as any man, does not mean I'm a radical." Zylphia then remembered Florence's advice to temper her words and to try a different tact.

"Believing that your beliefs have as much merit as a man's is radical though, Miss McLeod."

She flushed, this time with irritation, at the gentle censure she heard in his tone. "It's not as though it's a disease. They believe that merely being in my presence gives them incurable notions. Heaven forbid they had a thought of their own one day." Rather than the usual chuckle she was used to from Teddy, she sensed Mr. Hubbard stiffen before feigning a smile.

"You are rather forceful in what you believe." He nodded at an acquaintance as the dance ended. "Men like to know there will be some sort of order in their home and that their word is to be followed. And plenty of women are still fond of the world as it is."

"I suppose what you say has merit," Zylphia said as she attempted to heed Florence's advice. "A soothing home environment is conducive to the raising of children." She shook her head to avoid laughing out loud at speaking that bit of nonsense she'd read in a lady's magazine a few weeks ago. She imagined her disparate family's boisterous homes and the happy, healthy children growing in them.

"Miss McLeod," Owen said in his most charming voice. "I'm pleased to note you are seeing sense and that there's no need to argue. It's refreshing to hear you realize we all desire the same thing."

"And what would that be?"

"A secure home. A secure future."

Zylphia looked toward the dance floor, her stance more rigid even though she feigned ease. She gasped as he gripped her hand, placed her cup of punch on a side table and towed her toward the floor for a waltz. "Mr. Hubbard, this is not a good idea. I can't dance the waltz with any grace." She stumbled as he came to a halt, his hand holding hers. She belatedly placed her other hand on his shoulder, while she tried not to fidget at his hand on her waist, all the while stilling her panic.

"I'm certain you're merely being modest. You don't have nearly the opportunity you should to dance." He swung her into motion, nearly toppling over as she misstepped and tangled her feet in his.

"I beg your pardon," Zylphia gasped as they righted themselves, inches away from careening into a potted plant. "I warned you that I've never mastered the waltz."

Rather than glower at her, a smile flirted with his lips, and he whispered, "One, two, three," as he twirled her around the periphery of the ballroom. Zylphia relaxed and was soon able to concentrate on something other than the placement of her feet.

"Why did you want to dance with me?" she asked. She stifled a squeak as he pulled her closer than was proper. She met his intense stare, his blue-green eyes devoid of their customary merriment, instead filled with a singular focus and warmth.

"I couldn't imagine one of the prettiest girls here not dancing." He smiled as they now twirled effortlessly. "I know you are trying to assuage my fears as to your views, and I can hope that you will come to truly recognize the merit to my beliefs. However, I fail to see why any difference in our beliefs should be an impediment to our ... friendship."

"Mr. Hubbard ..."

"You know I'm a stodgy man of business, but that doesn't mean I can't change." His eyes held a silent entreaty. "I realize the world is changing. I understand there is unjustness. I might not want the world to alter in as radical a fashion as you, but I recognize that the world we live in will not remain as it is. Even as we waltz around a grand room, I understand that."

Zylphia's eyes glowed with pleasure at his words. She gripped his shoulder more tightly, her last thought on her awkward feet.

"I hope, as my friend, you'll help me to see other ways of envisioning this world."

She blushed as he twirled them to a stop, and he ran a finger quickly over her cheek. She gave a small curtsy as he bowed to her and offered his arm, walking her to the side of the ballroom.

He nodded to a passing servant, and two coupe glasses were delivered. "Come on. It's not like you to be silent," he coaxed as he took a sip of his drink.

"I find I don't know what to say." She studied him a moment as she took a sip of the drink, her nose crinkling as she realized it was champagne. "I would like for you to understand the difficulties faced by those less fortunate." She held back from expounding on the merits of universal suffrage.

"But you fear that one, such as me, cannot alter my way of thinking." His wry smile evoked an embarrassed nod of agreement.

"I fear that it's not you who'll be coaxed into changing, Mr. Hubbard. I like myself, and my beliefs, as they are." She bit her lip, this time with no intent to hide a secret smile. She sighed at her rash tongue, at the truth she'd inadvertently spoken about her intractable beliefs. They set their glasses on a passing servant's tray and backed farther away from the dance floor. They now stood in a small alcove, buffeted on three sides by palm fronds.

"Give me a chance, Zylphia," he whispered, her eyes flaring with surprise as he used her first name. "I believe you've come to accept the only sort of man you could entice is Mr. Goff. We both know you could do better."

She stiffened at his criticism of Teddy. "Please do not speak poorly of him. He's a friend who does not warrant such ridicule."

"Forgive me," he said with apparent contrition. "I merely wanted you to know that there are others who admire you."

"Of course," she murmured.

He glanced around, and they were largely ignored by the others. He grasped her hand and pulled her out a side door to the small glass conservatory. Although heated, the early winter's cold seeped in through the sealed windows. The December chill caused her to shiver in her dress. He pulled off his jacket and slung it over her shoulders.

"What are you doing?" she asked, jerking away from him to return to the overheated, crowded ballroom.

"I don't know how else to have any time with you. You seem to either always be with your mother or your friends. How else could we be alone?" he asked, maintaining a gentle hand on her forearm.

At any moment she could have broken away from him, but she remained in the conservatory with him. For a fleeting second, she thought of her stolen interludes with Teddy, only returning to the present moment when Owen cupped her cheeks.

He frowned for a moment before a warmth lit his eyes when she focused on him again. One hand reached to cup the back of her head, and he leaned forward, kissing her forcefully.

She leaned into him, although she maintained her hands at her sides. When he dropped the hand from her cheek to her shoulder and moved lower, she stiffened and pushed him away. She held a hand to her lips, panting as she backed up with startled blue eyes.

"This is why I think we'll suit. You've a passion in you," he said with a satisfied smile. "A passion for life. For all things."

"I don't want a husband." She blushed at her rash words. "That didn't come out right."

His eyes flared with interest, and she backed up a step. "I want nothing illicit," she whispered.

"I want you to share your passion with me, Zylphia," he whispered. He stroked a finger over her cheek, tracing it down her neck to her collarbone.

She shivered before backing up another step. "What I have is a passion for things you'll never appreciate." She shrugged out of his jacket and handed it back to him. She shivered once before sidling into the ballroom, her momentary absence unnoticed.

CHAPTER TWENTY-ONE

"What I would like to know," Parthena said four days after the ball at the Greaves' house, "is why Mr. Hubbard danced with you."

The three young women sat in the large glass conservatory at the back of the former Montgomery mansion, now the McLeod mansion, where Zylphia lived with her parents. The room was as warm as a summer's day from the heat generated by the potbellied stove and the heating vents hidden in the floor. Throughout the room, ferns sprouted from pots and lent a tropical feel on a dreary mid-December day.

Rowena picked through a pile of cookies and scones, searching for the least-burnt option. She finally decided on one and raised it, shaking it at Zylphia. "What I want to know is what happened in their small conservatory to cause you to look so flustered?"

"Ro!" Zee hissed as her eyes flared. She rose and flipped the lock on the glass-paneled door. She settled on a mint-green-cushioned wicker chair, tucking one foot underneath her. At her friends' expectant gazes, she flung herself backward with a sigh of exasperation.

"If a Hubbard were to show you interest, that would be quite a coup," Parthena said, shaking her head no as Rowena held up the plate of burnt cookies and scones.

"He said he wants a friendship with me. Wanted to get to know me better."

"A Hubbard would never approve of your beliefs," Rowena said, taking a sip of tea to wash down the dry scone.

Zylphia flushed. "I had visited my cousin Florence recently, and we discussed my lack of success in encouraging those I'd met at the balls and in society to join the cause. Florence suggested that I temper my arguments and become friends with people first before persuading them to my way of thinking."

"Does this mean he believes you are no longer a suffragist?" Parthena asked with wide eyes.

"No, but I fear the impression I gave was that my beliefs weren't as strong as I had portrayed them to be. He said he wanted me to help him learn about a new way of envisioning the world," Zylphia said as she curled into a more comfortable position on her chair.

"A new way of envisioning …" Rowena sputtered. "Please tell me that you set him straight that the only vision he needs is one where his wife has as much to say as he does."

"I didn't," Zylphia whispered. "He seemed to like me better. And he kissed me."

Rowena shared a quick glance with Parthena. "And?"

At Zylphia's prolonged silence, Rowena said, "What's bothering you, Zee?"

"He acted as though he had every right to drag me to another room. Grab me and kiss me."

"Did you not enjoy it?" Parthena asked.

"It … he kisses fine, but I wanted some thought, some consideration for me." She closed her eyes as she envisioned the scene in the cold conservatory. She flushed as she recalled her embrace with Owen. "I enjoyed his kiss. And he didn't hold me against my will. But there was no tenderness, nothing that made me feel like I was special to him."

"If he shows you such little consideration now, it will only become worse if you encourage him." Rowena reached over and stroked a hand down Zylphia's arm.

"I know. It's as though he believes I'm a weak-willed woman because I'm no longer fervently espousing my beliefs. As though I could easily be manipulated." Zylphia shuddered. "I think he wasn't entirely certain of my change of heart because he spoke of his awareness that the world constantly transforms itself and that he too could change."

"Thus, making it seem as though he's interested in change for himself, when he truly wants you to change. As he hopes you have already." Rowena tapped the saucer with such force that Zylphia glanced at the china to see if it were chipped.

"For you to give up your beliefs," Parthena said with a near growl.

"The entire time that I didn't say what I truly believed, I felt sick to my stomach." Zylphia looked at her friends mournfully. "I felt like I'd betrayed myself."

Both Rowena and Parthena reached out to Zylphia. "You didn't permanently betray yourself," Rowena said with a glower. "You followed your cousin's erroneous advice. Now you know that's not the correct action."

"It made me feel ill, but, in a way, it worked. He'd never said more than a few sentences to me before tonight. He'd never danced with me again since Newport." Zylphia held a hand to her head. "I'm so confused."

"Do you want to proceed through life feeling a fraud? Living a lie to the point you forget what you truly believe?" Parthena asked.

"Of course not," Zylphia sputtered.

Rowena asked, "What I want to know is why are you confused? It seems like you know exactly what you should do in the future."

Zylphia blushed. After exhaling a deep breath, she raised her eyes to meet her friends' curious gazes. "I liked the attention. I enjoyed no longer being the woman scorned, exiled to the side of the dance floor, instead someone worthy of notice."

Parthena frowned. "Well, you now know the cost of such attention."

Zylphia nodded.

"Did you agree to see him again?" Rowena asked.

"I was flustered after I left him in the conservatory. When we were leaving, he spoke with my mother as we collected our wraps. We're to go to the New Year's Ball in a few weeks at your house," Zylphia said with a nod to Parthena.

"Ugh, that infernal ball. It's all my mother will talk about. She's already concocting some necessity for me to dance with that horrid Mr. Wheeler." Parthena shuddered at the thought.

"It should be entertaining to watch," Zylphia said, hiding a giggle.

"I hope your Mr. Goff doesn't attend. He's such a boor." Rowena settled into her chair, the burnt cookies and scones abandoned while she held her teacup.

"There is much you don't understand about him," Zylphia said.

"So you say, but we never see it. Whenever he's out, he's as a petulant child. Grumpy and incommunicative." Parthena gave Zylphia a sly smile. "Unless he's with you."

"Stop it. He's just a friend." She sobered. "That's all he can be."

Rowena watched her intently. "Why? Did something happen between the two of you that you didn't share with us?"

"You know I have no desire to marry." She absently traced a piece of wicker with her finger.

"What would that have to do with the reclusive Theodore Goff?" Parthena asked. "I can't imagine anyone wanting to marry him." She gave a theatrical shudder, provoking a snicker from Rowena.

"Stop speaking so poorly of him," Zylphia snapped. "He's a brilliant scientist, and I ..."

"Oh my," Rowena murmured. "You're interested in Teddy?" She gaped at Zylphia. "Socially awkward, hides in his lab, reclusive *Teddy*?"

"I don't know! One moment all I can think about is the movement and how I'll help garner the vote for women. The next, all I can think about is my time with Teddy." She massaged her temples as she leaned forward, her elbows on her knees. "If I thought I knew one thing, it was that I had no interest in marriage and a family of my own until women earned the right to vote. Until I earned the right to my own voice."

"You've always had the right to your own voice, Zee. And of your opinion," Parthena said.

"Not by the law. The minute I marry, I hate the fact that I become nothing more than an extension of my husband. I want to count too." Zylphia sighed. "I never expected entering society would prove to be so confusing."

Parthena and Rowena laughed. "You forget that you come from a very wealthy family. Of course you'd be of some interest to the men." Parthena tapped her fingers on her chair's arm as though she were playing a piano. "What you can't forget is that Owen Hubbard knows you are wealthy and will most likely want that wealth for himself."

Zylphia sighed. "I wonder if any of these men would still want me if they realized I come with no dowry?"

Parthena choked on the bite of cookie she had finally chosen as Rowena nearly dropped her cup and saucer before recovering and setting it on a nearby glass-topped table. "What?"

"I thought you both had stated that having dowries was antiquated and offensive," Zylphia said with a sparkle in her deep blue eyes. At their persistent silence, she laughed. "I have no dowry. When I marry, I go with nothing. That's what my father has told me."

"He must be joking," Parthena said.

"Why? He believes it is the only way to ensure that a man wants me and not my father's influence or his money."

Rowena sat back in her chair, a dazed expression on her face. "It's a wicked thing to do. Dangle you in front of society, with the expectation of wealth should one of them marry you, and then not offer anything." She shook her head.

"Some will say your father is ashamed of you and, thus, refuses to dower you," Parthena said.

"Those who know him will know that's complete nonsense."

"Careful not to tell anyone else this, Zee. You know how cruel people can be," Rowena said as Parthena nodded her agreement.

"I won't. Besides, I know if I should ever marry, my father will be extraordinarily generous. He simply doesn't want the promise of wealth to be the sole reason a man would wish to align himself with me."

Rowena studied Zylphia a moment before glancing around the elaborate conservatory. "It seems he's afraid of the past repeating itself."

Zylphia thought of her cousin Savannah and the stories she had heard about Savannah's first marriage to Jonas Montgomery as she glanced around a room that had once been theirs. Only after the wedding had Savannah realized he'd married her for the generous dowry promised by her grandparents. Another of Savannah's cousins, Clarissa, had barely evaded a similar fate. "Exactly." She smiled at her friends. "Besides, I don't know why we're worried about marriage when we've our pact."

Rowena shook her head. "You know as well as I do that the pact was foolish. We'll have to marry before women are granted the vote."

Parthena nodded her agreement to Rowena's words.

"I refuse to live as a pauper while my father moans about the expense of having me under his roof. His threats are becoming more frequent." Parthena shuddered.

Rowena smiled gently at Zylphia who appeared crestfallen. "You know it was juvenile, Zee. It had no basis to it other than a momentary exuberance for a preposterous idea."

Zylphia sighed. "If I'm honest, I can say I agree. I liked having a ready excuse to have at hand when my family discussed the many potential suitors I would meet at the balls."

"Well, unlike my family, yours wants to see you happy," Parthena said. "They'd never threaten you with penury."

"No, but I sometimes think they doubt my ability to know my own dreams," Zylphia said.

"I think they refuse to allow you to limit yourself," Rowena said with a smile. "When you think about it, that's a truly wonderful thing."

***

"What brings you by?" Teddy asked as he watched Zylphia wander his laboratory. He raised an eyebrow at her maid dozing in a chair by the door.

Zylphia took note of his focus. "My mother insisted I not come alone. She doesn't want me running as freely around the city as I like." She waved him to sit while she roamed about. "Ever since her return in November, she's been much more concerned about propriety. She doesn't understand it's January 1914. Times are changing."

"For your mother, I imagine times are changing too rapidly." He smiled with sardonic humor. "I know my mother still imagines she lives in 1890 and attempts to behave in the same manner. Did you enjoy the New Year's Eve party?"

"As you can imagine, it was filled to the brim with the most important members of Boston society. Miss Tyler's mother wouldn't have it any other way." She glared at him. "Although you weren't there."

"I've never been particularly fond of New Year's. Seems an arbitrary thing to celebrate." He shared an amused smile with Zylphia. "I'd rather we persisted in celebrating the solstices."

Zylphia couldn't help but snicker. "You're already enough of an oddity, no need to espouse any more odd notions." Her mouth firmed as she thought of the party. "You didn't miss much, although an enormous fountain was in the center of one of the large rooms off the ballroom, and Mr. Wheeler tripped and fell into it."

Teddy's smile broadened. "I'm sure there's more to the story than that."

Zylphia giggled and clapped her hands together. "You know how P.T.—Miss Tyler—and he can't bear to be in the same room? Well, her mother somehow forced him to waltz with her. She attempted to walk away from him on the dance floor, but he clung to her like a burr, and they argued while she steered him from the floor. I don't know what they were talking about, but I heard her call him 'a conceited, misinformed buffoon,' and then she pushed him, and he went flying. Rather than help him, everyone jumped out of the way, and he landed with a splash in the fountain, the goddess on top pouring water on his head."

Teddy laughed. "I wish I'd been there solely for that." He watched her as she appeared lost in memories. "Did you dance, Zee?"

"Yes, many times. Mr. Hubbard introduced me to a few of his friends, and I had a wonderful evening."

"Did you stub anyone's toes?" he teased.

"Teddy!" She flushed, before waving her hand as though it were of no consequence. "It makes me wonder why I bothered with all those dance lessons."

He laughed again at her silent admission of her inability to dance with ease. "I'm surprised Owen Hubbard would favor you with your views on suffragism." At her prolonged silence, he frowned. "Zee?"

"He may have formed the opinion that my views are not as fervent as they once were."

Teddy's frown deepened. "How could that have come about? Everyone knows of your beliefs."

Zylphia paused her pacing to face him. "But that's just the problem, Teddy. Everyone knows I'm outspoken for universal suffrage. If I tone down my rhetoric, maybe I'll be able to persuade others to my way of thinking."

"You actually liked the attention at the ball."

Zylphia flinched at the accusation and the hint of disappointment in his voice. "It was refreshing to not be the only woman who didn't dance for an entire evening for a change." She tilted up her chin as her eyes flashed. "I have as much desire to be liked as anyone else."

"For God's sake, Zee, of course I know that. Everyone does, but not at the expense of what you believe. Not at the expense of what drives you." He watched as she paced his laboratory again. "Is that what has you upset?"

She moved farther from the door.

"That you've begun to doubt your beliefs?"

"I have all this nervous energy thrumming through me, and I needed to escape home. My mother is having a special tea this afternoon to raise funds for the orphanage, and I couldn't handle listening to the simpering obsequiousness needed to lighten the patronesses' purses."

She roamed, stopping in front of his desk and flipping through his drawings. She stilled at a few and then continued flipping pages. She slammed the book shut and moved through the room again, her nervous energy preventing her from remaining in one place for long. This time she paused in front of one of his long workbenches.

He smiled, his gaze following her as she picked up and set down one object after another. He winced as she slammed down a piece of metal on one of the tables. "Careful, Zee. Some of those take a long time to piece together. I don't want my labors wasted due to one of your bad moods."

"What are you working on?"

"I don't like talking about my experiments until I'm more certain they'll turn into something useful. However, I'll make an exception for you." He smiled as she traced one of his projects with a finger. "I'm working on perfecting wireless transmission."

"Wireless transmission? Why would anyone want that?"

"I suspect many will, starting with the military." He watched as her movements became less frenetic. "What's wrong, Zee?"

She sank onto a stool, her teal silk skirt covering her legs, her vitality fading. "I loved that feeling of being accepted at the ball, Teddy," she whispered. "But I hated that they only wanted to be near me because they didn't know or accept the parts of me that made me who I am. They didn't know me, and they didn't care to. I felt a fraud. A popular fraud but a fraud all the same."

Teddy reached out a large callused hand and stroked it down her forearm before gently squeezing one of her hands tightly gripping her knees.

She relaxed at his touch. "I want to do something with my life. My mother has her life's work helping the unwanted children of this city. My cousins in Montana are busy preparing their campaign petitioning for the vote there. And here I am, wearing pretty dresses, acting vapid as I enjoy circling a dance floor, doing nothing. I thought things would change after the march in Washington, but that was nearly a year ago! However, nothing's happened, at least not for me."

"Don't be so hard on yourself."

The scraping sound of him pulling up another stool to sit near Zylphia momentarily woke the maid. Zylphia and Teddy sat in a narrow aisle, obscured from view by objects littering the tops of the elevated lab tables.

"I have a feeling the struggle for the vote will be an on-going endeavor. Besides, you have your work at the orphanage."

"That's my mother's work, not mine. I should be doing something for the women's cause, other than tricking the unsuspecting into joining it. I should be doing more than sitting here with you, complaining I've yet to make a difference in garnering the vote."

"Then why don't you travel to Montana? Be with your cousins and help them?" He smiled gently. "That way you'll work for a cause you believe in while not having to forswear those beliefs to a group of people who have little interest in altering their long-held prejudices."

She froze, arrested in place at his suggestion. "My father would never allow me to go alone."

"I know you're clever enough to find a way to persuade your father and mother into traveling there with you."

"Are you that desperate to see me gone?" She sobered when he failed to smile at her weak attempt at humor.

"I'll never be happy to be separated from you. You're one of my rare, true friends. But I will know joy to see you with a sense of fulfillment."

His eyes, usually a brilliant gray, appeared almost silver behind his glasses, as he reached forward to push back a tendril of her raven hair.

***

He watched her with the same blind intensity that overcame him when working on his inventions. When she didn't flinch or move away from his soft caress to her cheek, he leaned forward, kissing her.

His eyes fluttered closed as their lips touched, and his hand moved from her cheek to her nape to hold her still as he kissed her first with featherlight brushings of his lips and then firmer kisses. He leaned forward, his long legs tangling in her skirts, and pulled her closer, one arm wrapping around her and the other moving up to caress her face.

He deepened the kiss, moving his hand down her neck and fluttering it over her collarbone. She gasped, but his roving hand went no farther. He pulled away, filled with passion as he attempted to control his breathing. He dropped his hands, although he was unable to completely break contact as he stroked one of her forearms.

She leaned back, holding fingers to her lips, a bemused expression flitting over her face before masking it. "You kiss differently."

He stiffened, breaking all contact with her. "What do you mean? And who have you been kissing?" At her hiss, he whispered to not alert the maid to any distress, although it appeared all the distress was on his part. "Zee?"

"You're not the first man I kissed, and I doubt you'll be the last. I don't know why you're shocked."

He flushed, gripping his hands together as he hardened his gaze. "And how was it different?"

Zylphia merely smiled, patted him on his shoulder and rose.

He gripped her hands, tugging her back down to sit across from him. "Don't play a coquette, Zee. That's not who you are. That's not who we are."

"We aren't anything." She flushed after her rash words.

He leaned forward, gripping her hands. "Is that why you continually visit me? Why you seek me out at functions? Because you feel nothing for me?" He frowned as he saw panic enter her eyes before she lowered her head. "I know we agreed on friendship, but—"

She held up her hand, stopping his words with her fingers to his lips. "I barely know you, Teddy."

He had to lean forward to hear her breathed words. He then kissed her fingers before easing back and freeing himself from her touch. "Because you've never wanted to look below the surface. That fault lies with you."

She raised eyes nearly overflowing with tears.

He grimaced, reaching to stroke her cheek.

She leaned into his caress for a moment before her movements became erratic. "You're right. I need to stop visiting you and seeking you out. I must avoid your company at upcoming functions. There can be no reason for us to see each other."

She rose, but he prevented her from moving past him by standing and blocking the narrow aisle and her exit from his lab. "Dammit, Zee. I'm not some toy you can come and play with when the mood suits you."

"I've never thought of you in such a way. Please forgive me if I've ever given you that impression." She raised her head, her eyes flashing with defiance, anger and hurt. "This is why I was advised women and men can never be friends."

When he stiffened at her words, she pushed past him, and he watched her leave with her maid on her heels, the laboratory door slamming on her way out.

CHAPTER TWENTY-TWO

Zylphia burst into Parthena's private sitting room, having charged ahead of the butler in her enthusiasm to share the news. She halted upon hearing the lyrical, lilting music P.T. played on the piano. Zee tilted her head to one side, closing her eyes as she listened more closely to the song. When the music stopped, she clapped and whistled her approval, earning a roll of the eyes from Parthena. "Isn't that one of my cousin's songs?"

"It's a Lucas Russell song, yes," Parthena said, idly caressing the keyboards. "If he's ever back in Boston and you don't introduce me, I will do you bodily harm."

Zylphia laughed, then laughed even more when she realized Parthena was serious.

"What has you so excited that you barged in here? I know we weren't planning on meeting today."

Zylphia held up a periodical, swinging it around in such an agitated manner there was no hope of reading it. "Alice has broken with NAWSA!"

"Oh my," Parthena breathed, turning away from the piano keys and reaching forward to grab the *Woman's Journal*.

"What will this mean for the movement?" Zylphia frowned. "I fear we'll lose momentum again, as we did with the split in 1869."

"Or it could be that Alice knows what she is doing and isn't willing to compromise on her vision of how to proceed."

"I think Carrie Chapman Catt and Anna Howard Shaw couldn't handle the fact that Alice was as popular—"

"Or more."

"—than they were. And I hate that we'll be forced to choose sides when we all desire the same thing, the enfranchisement of women." Zylphia grabbed the magazine back to stare at the small article, hidden on page six.

"I hate to think what the press will make of this," Parthena said with a long sigh, moving to join Zylphia on the settee near the roaring fire.

"They've never been positive before, so I don't know why we should concern ourselves now." The two friends shared a long look before sharing a smile.

"If you had to choose a side to support, whose would it be?" Parthena asked.

"Alice Paul's," Zylphia said without a moment's worth of hesitation. "I believe she has a true plan on how to succeed."

"She is radical. And she believes in hunger strikes."

Zylphia shivered. "I can't imagine being force-fed, like I've read about the suffragettes suffering in England. I'm certain it won't come to that here."

"I imagine force-feeding is better than starvation," Parthena mused. "However, I agree with you. Anna's vision of winning the vote state by state would take us into the twenty-first century to accomplish."

"What will we tell our parents when we join the more radical aspect of the suffragist movement?"

"I doubt your parents will be all that surprised. I'm certain your father would help fund it for you," Parthena said with a touch of envy in her voice. "My father will attempt to gag me as he convinces Mr. Wheeler to marry me."

Zylphia snickered at the vision of her friend married to Mr. Wheeler. "You'd murder each other within a month. He still hasn't forgiven you for the fountain incident last month."

"That's just one of many unfortunate episodes we've suffered together," Parthena said. "And, yes, without a doubt, one of us wouldn't make the one-month anniversary." Parthena shuddered at the prospect. "We must keep my interest in Alice quiet lest I suffer a fate worse than death."

"I think we should speak with Sophie. She always seems to know what to do." Zylphia frowned. "Although I think she's still disappointed in me from last summer. I can only imagine what she'll think when she learns of my recent actions."

"Sophronia is three-quarters bluster. Once she realizes you've come to believe as she does, she'll forgive you."

"How do you know Sophie so well?" Zylphia played with a tassel on a pillow.

"My uncle married one of her daughters."

Zylphia gaped at her. "I never knew you were related. Why didn't she take you under her wing?"

"She knew my father would never countenance it. He can barely tolerate her presence in a ballroom filled with two hundred other guests. He'd never have allowed me to spend time with her alone. He has yet to realize she was in Newport with us last summer." She shared an amused smile with Zylphia. "Besides, she came to fear I'd always be glued to a piano stool."

"You are talented." Zylphia's gaze became distant. "With two groups vying for funding, I'm sure Alice will need all the support she can obtain. Perhaps you could have a recital that would raise funds."

"Zee, you speak utter nonsense. My father would never agree to me playing in public, never mind for money." She raised an eyebrow as she widened her eyes dramatically at the thought. "It simply would not be borne for a Tyler to be seen asking for money."

Zylphia waved away her comment. "We need to brainstorm, and I think Sophie's the one to help us."

***

Zylphia, Rowena and Parthena sat in Sophie's rear sitting room overlooking her neighbor's gardens, with her desk and its small vase of hothouse flowers sitting in front of the windows. A rocking chair and a lady's chair were angled to the side of the fireplace where a fire roared, while more heat pumped from the vents in the floor. Zylphia sat upright on the settee as the *thunk*ing of a cane heralded Sophie's arrival.

"It's about time you paid me a visit," Sophie barked as she entered the room. She waved to the maid on her heels to place the tray on the table before the settee and then motioned for her to leave. The door clicked shut behind the maid as Sophie settled in the armchair near the fireplace. "Forgive me for not entertaining you in my formal parlor. I'm having it redecorated, and it is turning into a monumental task."

"I've always liked this room," Parthena said.

"I should think so. It's where you always came to escape your parents, the few times you were forced to call on me." She nodded to Zylphia. "I see you continue to perpetuate the folly you're no longer interested in the movement."

"Sophie, it was Florence's idea," Zylphia said.

"It's about time you had ideas of your own. First it was that peabrained suggestion by Alva. Now Flo's notion to act as though you're no longer a suffragist. I nearly came to blows with Mr. Hubbard's mother when she proclaimed your change of heart and newfound acceptability." She glared at Zylphia. "I did not appreciate learning I was in the wrong."

"I'm sorry, Sophie."

"As you should be. Having popularity when based on a falsehood is a waste of energy, time and emotion." She patted Zee on her knee. "If they don't like you for who you truly are, then they aren't worth knowing, Zee." She turned her fierce aquamarine eyes to the other women present. "It's the same for you two."

"Sophie, we're here because we want to know how we could help Alice. We read a few days ago how she broke with NAWSA."

"Anyone with sense knew that break was coming. Anna and Carrie could not abide her popularity or her unwillingness to bow to their model of garnering the vote."

"They perceive that their notion is the superior notion, not realizing that there could be more than one way to lead toward full enfranchisement," Rowena said.

"Well said," Sophie agreed with a nod. She took a sip of tea and then tapped a fingernail against the neck of her cane. "As you can imagine, Alice will need money. She'll need women willing to work with her and follow her instructions."

"Would we need to move to Washington, DC?" Zylphia asked.

"Not yet. Today I received a letter from Alice, and she did not mention any need for more women in Washington."

"I didn't know you were that close to her," Parthena said.

"I like to think I'll remain open to all possibilities. I plan to attend the NAWSA events in Boston, but I also will remain abreast of Alice's plans in Washington."

"I doubt that would make you popular with Anna or Carrie," Parthena said with a smirk.

"I doubt it would, which is why I hope it won't be bandied about." Sophie looked at Zee. "I have an idea for you, Zee, to become more involved in the struggle. However, I'm uncertain yet as to what it will entail. I'll keep you informed. For now I suggest you limit your time with that Hubbard boy."

"What about Mr. Goff?" Rowena asked.

Sophie's eyes sparkled as Zylphia flushed. "You've yet to discover all there is to know about him. I think you'll be pleasantly surprised."

***

Zylphia sat in her office in the orphanage, one she also shared with her mother, Delia. Now that Delia's role was mainly to find benefactors among Aiden's contacts, Delia had vacated the small, yet comfortable, office and rooms that had been their home for years. This tiny space was like a converted closet, with no windows and a bare lightbulb dangling from the ceiling to illuminate the sparse space.

Zylphia visited the orphanage a few times a week at the request of the new matron to review the books and to boost the morale of some of the younger residents. Although she and her mother had moved eleven years ago into the mansion her father had bought, the orphanage had been her home for the first sixteen years of her life.

"I wondered if I'd find you here," Theodore said, leaning against the doorjamb.

Zylphia started, her gaze shifting to the doorway filled by him. She frowned before attempting a weak smile.

"May I come in?" His gray eyes showed his hesitation, and he fidgeted with his hat.

"Yes, although I don't know where you'll go." She smiled as she looked around the cramped office.

He entered, stooping under the lintel, cleared off a chair of its pile of papers and deposited them on the floor and then sat in front of her desk. "How do you get behind the desk?"

Zylphia flushed. "I crawl over it."

He chuckled. "I'd like to see that."

"Generally I keep the door shut so no one witnesses my unladylike behavior, but today the room felt too small."

He glanced around the narrow room painted a stark white, lit harshly by one lightbulb. The desk Zylphia sat behind was the width of the room.

"I have to remember to clear the desk first, or I'll knock everything to the floor." They shared a rueful smile.

"Why don't you have the desk sideways?" He seemed to studied the dimensions of the room as he asked his question.

"We tried that, but it was a little tight with the desk and the chair. When my mother is here, a lot of people are coming and going, and she didn't like always looking to the side. She prefers to see people head-on."

"Do you mean your mother crawls over the desk too?"

"Yes." Zylphia giggled. "She claims it keeps her young." She sobered again.

"I thought you said you hated math," Teddy said, looking at the ledger in front of Zee.

"I didn't like the advanced classes I took. Basic math is easy." Zee shrugged. "Why are you here?"

"I wanted to apologize for my behavior the last time, when I saw you a month ago." His gaze never left hers. "I'd hoped to see you before now, but I realize you are quite adept at avoiding those you don't wish to see." He watched her curiously as she flushed.

"Apologize? It was of no consequence." She cleared her throat and tapped her pen on the desk.

"Exactly. Because it was of no consequence to you, I should never have acted in such a way. My apologies."

"There's nothing to forgive."

"I think there is, on both our parts." When she remained mutinously quiet, her expression imploring him to remain silent, he closed his eyes before holding out his hand, as though pleading with her to understand. "Zylphia, I never meant to overstep the boundaries of propriety. Of those of friendship. To inaccurately read your sentiments toward me." His gaze trailed over her raven hair in a perfect bun, her cream-colored blouse perfectly starched. "You for ..."

"For becoming as bristly as a hedgehog," Zylphia whispered.

He nodded. "Why won't you let anyone close, Zee?"

She flinched at his question.

"Why do you keep everyone at arm's length? Even your parents?"

She swallowed. "I'm capable on my own."

He stifled a laugh. "You misinterpreted my words. Let me clarify. You're the most independent, capable woman I've ever met. How could you doubt your-self?"

She refused to be charmed by the pride shining in his voice. "I will not be left behind, as though an afterthought."

He sat back in his chair, stunned to silence for a moment. "Is that what you think I'd do? Proclaim I had feelings for you and then leave you?" He glared at her.

"Not openly, no, but you are your father's son, and I don't see him present in Boston. How do you know he doesn't lead a duplicitous life in New York City? I'm sure I should expect no better, should I consider someone from your class."

"Is that how you see me?" His face flushed, almost matching the burgundy of his waistcoat. He slammed his hand down on her desk. "Dammit, is that how you think I'd treat you?" At her persistent silence, he stood, only a few paces from the door.

His movement broke Zylphia's forced calm. She swore under her breath and launched herself onto her desk, knocking papers and pens to the floor as she slid across it, coming to stand beside him. She grabbed the door and slammed it shut. "No. You can't leave when our conversation isn't finished."

He held himself with rigid control and leaned forward, rasping in a harsh voice, "You think you know me, Zee, but you only know part of me. You don't know my ambitions. You don't know my dreams. You don't know the why be-hind the who. I thought you wanted to. Forgive me my presumption."

She leaned into him, refusing to be cowed by his ire. Their agitated breaths mingled, and she caught a whiff of sandalwood and coffee. "And I can't believe you presume to know me so well as to believe I'd want to know you more intimately. I know as much about you as I need to know."

He paled, a stricken expression flitting behind his eyes before masking his emotions. "What is it that you've learned?"

"You tinker away for hours over meaningless experiments. You can barely hold a decent conversation when there are more than two people in the room. You are disdainful of anyone seen having a good time at a dance or a soiree."

"That's how you take the measure of a man?" Teddy whispered. "I can see I was mistaken in you, Zee. Forgive me."

Zylphia flushed, shaking her head. When he moved to leave, she backed up against the door, preventing him from departing. "No, no," she said, clearing her throat. "Forgive me. You know I say rash things I don't mean."

"Unfortunately I think those might be the truest words you've ever said to me."

"Teddy." She reached forward and gripped his hand. "I never meant to hurt you. It's just …"

"What?" His gray eyes were filled with pain and confusion as they met hers.

"I feel like you want something from me that I cannot give you. And it makes me lash out."

"Only you can decide what you will or will not give, Zee," he murmured, reaching forward to trace a finger down one side of her cheek.

"Why do you have drawings of me in your experiment notebook in your lab?" She flinched after asking the question.

He flushed. "You don't visit as often as I'd like, and it was my way of remembering you. Of not missing you."

"What do you want from me?" Her voice trembled as she forced herself to meet his impassioned gaze.

"More than you could imagine," he murmured, leaning forward to kiss her forehead. He gripped her shoulders, carefully pushing her to the side so he could ease open the door. "Good-bye, Zee." He gave her shoulder a soft caress and slipped through the door.

***

Zylphia sat on the chair Teddy had sat on three days before. Her mother sat behind the desk, having crawled behind it an hour earlier. Zylphia slouched in her chair, glaring at her mother as she refused to comply with her mother's wishes.

"I don't understand your reticence, Zee." Delia tapped the tip of her pen on a piece of paper, the rate of tapping increasing with her agitation.

"Stop abusing the pen, Mother. You have to know by now that has no effect on me. Nor does staring me down."

"I don't understand why you won't let us use one of your paintings." Delia slammed the pen onto the desk. "Is it wrong for a mother to be proud of her daughter and her accomplishments? I believe your art is worthy of display, not be hidden away in your studio."

"They're nowhere near good enough, for one. Find a professional artist." Her mother watched steadily, her silence prompting Zylphia to babble as she straightened to sit with perfect posture. "I paint for me, Mother. Not for anyone else. I refuse to allow my paintings to be found lacking."

Delia nodded once as though she'd deciphered a riddle. "Hmm."

Zylphia held herself with rigid control, her clothes perfectly pressed and her black hair styled into a chignon with no hair out of place.

"Since you've been found lacking by society ..." Delia's gaze softened. "No matter what you do, someone will judge you."

Zylphia shook her head and remained mutinously silent.

"No matter how much you change yourself, it will never be enough for some. Do you think because you hide your exuberance for life, for art, for suffragism, that you will become accepted? That a little spit and polish on the outside really matters?" Delia watched her daughter with a hint of sorrow. "If it makes you happy, Zee, then by all means change. However, you don't seem content sitting across from me." She paused for a moment. "There is something else we must discuss. Shut the door."

Zylphia leaned forward, clasped the side of the door and swung it shut. "What is so important that you want privacy?"

"What were you doing in this office, with the door shut, with Mr. Goff?" The staccato tapping of the pen began again and became more pronounced. "Why would you have him here, in this office, in a place where your reputation, *our* reputation, must be above repute?"

"We had argued. He came to apologize." Zylphia leaned forward, rubbing her temples, sighing with relief when her mother stilled her pen. "I acted like a deranged harpy, insulting him."

Delia settled against the back of her chair, the aged wood creaking with the movement. "You pushed him away. Or attempted to at least."

Zylphia shrugged a shoulder in silent agreement.

"Do you like him? Does he interest you?"

"I'm not ready for a man like Teddy." She blushed as her mother raised an eyebrow at the use of his nickname and at Zylphia's inadvertent admission of the truth. "I want meaningless flirtations with men like Owen Hubbard. Men who'd never truly be interested in me."

"And why wouldn't Mr. Hubbard desire to become better acquainted with you?"

"You know as well as I do that no man of that social standing would want a wife with minimal social graces. Who spent her youth learning about the rough-and-tumble realities of life while living in an orphanage."

"I think you do yourself and any man who paid attention to you a disservice. You assume no man would be interested in you below the surface. Or beyond what he believes your father could help him attain."

Zylphia remained silent as her mother watched her.

Delia raised a challenging eyebrow to her daughter. "You claim it's because you don't want to be a wife, but I think you do so to prevent disappointment on your part."

Zylphia's mutinous blue eyes glared at her mother.

"Rather than dare to dream."

"It's better to accept reality as it is."

"No, Zylphia. That's not who you are. You're allowing your fears to limit your ability to see a future where you aren't alone. For if that were truly how you felt, if you were a realist as you proclaim you are, you'd never agitate for women to obtain full rights of citizenship. It's as though you are willing to accept less for yourself but not for women in general." When Zylphia flinched, Delia gentled her voice. "I find that tragic for you, my talented, brilliant daughter."

"It's easy for you to say, when things have resolved so well for you."

"No need to become spiteful. And I know you'd never resent the return of your father." She tapped a finger on the desk. "Do you think I regretted having met Aidan? For my relationship with him, even though I had years alone afterward?" A tender smile washed over her face. "During moments when I wasn't consumed with grief, or concerns over the orphanage or you, I remembered our interactions. I gave thanks that, although our time together was brief, I'd had that time with him.

"I won't lie to you, Zee, and say it was easy to trust him again. To trust in him. That he wouldn't suddenly disappear again. He's never given me, or you, a reason to doubt him since his return eleven years ago."

Zylphia raised a hand to her face, wiping away a tear. "I know. And yet I still think the only person I should count on is me."

"Then I believe you will be very lonely. And, I fear, you'll come to rue that belief."

CHAPTER TWENTY-THREE

Teddy pushed into a room that was never occupied and peered inside to see who had trespassed. Curtains covered the long windows lining one side of the rectangular room, dimming the bright afternoon sun. No furniture filled this room, and the wooden floors gleamed where the sunlight slipped past the curtains. He gripped his hands, unable to hold back a growl of frustration as he saw who was wandering the room. "What are you doing in here?" His sharp question rent the stillness of the room as he strode into the long, dimly lit gallery, his polished shoes clicking on the wooden floor.

Zylphia spun to stare at him, her gaze unfocused. "Teddy—Mr. Goff. Forgive me."

"You have no right to be in here." He reached for her arm as though to tow her from the room. "And you know by now to call me Teddy when it's just the two of us."

She dug in her heels and leaned away from him. "Your mother invited me to come study the paintings in your collection."

"Yes, but this is our private collection. Not for anyone but family to see. What she had in mind is next door."

Zylphia blanched. "I beg your pardon. I had begun to think your mother was mistaken in her belief she owned a Constable."

"No, we own one. It's next door." He tilted his head to an adjacent room behind the wall where one of the late British master's paintings was on private display. "Come." He grasped her arm and tugged her in that direction.

Zylphia shook her head, her eyes transfixed by a painting. "Who are these young men? They look like younger versions of you, but I've never met a brother. Are they your uncles?"

Teddy's gray eyes hardened as his body stiffened. He released her arm, his fingers tapping a nervous tattoo on his thigh, all the while refraining from looking at the portrait. "No, that's a picture of me with … with … He was my brother. My twin. Lawrence."

"Was?" She reached forward and brushed a hand down his arm, eliciting a subtle shudder.

"Yes." He closed his eyes for a moment before meeting her gaze.

"What happened, Teddy?"

"It's not something I discuss."

"Talk to me, Teddy." She ran a soothing hand down his arm again, provoking another shudder. "I know we've had our differences, but I still want to be your friend."

He glared at her as she spoke.

"I think you could use a friend, Teddy. I know I do."

He studied her gaze for a moment before looking away again. She made a small sound of distress, but, instead of moving away from her, he reached forward and gripped her hand as he spoke in a low voice. "Lawrence and I shared everything. Toys, ideas, homework. Dreams for the future." His voice dipped. "Measles." He cleared his throat. "I hadn't even realized I was ill until, all of a sudden, I was bedbound. Everything hurt, and I couldn't bear to open my eyes. I remember darkness, and Larry on the other side of the door, reading to me, and telling me jokes and stories. He entertained me as I slowly improved, ensured I wasn't alone, even though I was ill at boarding school.

"I was quarantined but not well enough." His voice rang with bitterness. "I woke up one morning feeling better only to realize my roommate was Larry. And he was more ill than I'd ever been. He had a brain fever and died within days."

"Oh, Teddy, I'm so sorry. At least you were with him, and he wasn't alone."

He shook his head violently. He saw the far distant scene, of him in his weakened state clawing at the doctor, fighting to remain next to Larry. Of him pounding on the door, kicking and screaming for entrance. He took a deep breath, his voice shattered. "He was. Alone, that is. When they realized how sick he was, they banned me from the room. They didn't want me to see him suffer."

Zylphia watched him with rounded eyes. "That's the worst thing they could have done, isn't it?" His nod of agreement at her whispered question caused her to fight a sob.

"My grandparents were summoned. I was excused from exams because of his death and my illness, and sent off for my mourning period."

Zylphia grabbed his hand, holding it in both of hers, as he looked at a space over her shoulder. When he didn't respond to her gentle touch, she pushed herself into his arms, wrapping her arms around his waist. "It's not your fault he died." Her voice was muffled against his chest.

"I know. It's the measles' fault. It's the luck of the draw. I *know* that. But it doesn't take away my missing him or wishing him back. Wishing he were here to enliven my days." He shuddered as he finally moved to hold Zylphia close. "It's been nearly twenty years since he died. I miss him, every day." He took a stuttering breath. "He'd be sorely disappointed in who I've become."

"Why? What were you like before he died?" She stroked a hand down his back.

"We were known as the Goff Gale. We were hellions and proud of it. My father encouraged us to daring feats, and we loved innocent pranks. There's nothing we wouldn't have done for a laugh." He sighed, lowering his face into her hair, relaxing as he breathed deeply. "We knew what the other was thinking without having to speak. He was brilliant at arts and languages, and I preferred science. Together we could accomplish anything."

"And alone?"

"It's as though I'm always searching for my best friend. And yet I know I'll never find him because I've already lost him."

"That's unutterably sad," Zylphia whispered as she sniffled. "I know my words are useless, but I'm so sorry, Teddy. I don't know what it's like to lose someone I love." She eased away but his hold tightened.

"Thank you for easing my torment, even if only in a small way," Teddy murmured.

"I can't stand that you hurt like this." She leaned back, swiping her palm at his damp cheeks.

"Why are you really here, Zee?" His gray eyes glowed with intense curiosity and emotion. "We've avoided each other for the better part of a month. I don't understand why you'd come to my house now."

She stiffened, dropping her hand to his arm, as her blue eyes became guarded. "For art of course."

"There's no reason for you to be here. If you wanted to see decent art, you would have visited the Museum of Fine Arts, not my mother's haphazard collection based on personal taste rather than any merit on the artists' part."

"I've been to that museum more times than I can count. I wanted to see something new."

"Why not ensure I was out before you called?"

"You're never out," Zylphia said irritably. "Besides, I assumed if I didn't disturb you in your laboratory, you wouldn't even know I was here."

"Did you want to see me?" he asked in a husky voice.

"Of course not!" Zylphia flushed and then paled as his hold on her arms loosened. This time she held on tight. "That's not what I meant. I wanted to see the paintings, not act like some ... some floozy who can't even make up her own mind."

Teddy's eyes flashed with humor as he pulled her close. "Do you even know what that means?" he asked, a hint of amusement and relief in his voice and eyes as she shook her head no. "Then I wouldn't banter it around in good company." He grinned at her. "Do you desire my company?"

"Teddy, I like you. You know I do—"

He swooped down, moving his hands from her arms to the nape of her neck to hold her in place as he kissed her. His lips pressed firmly on hers, deepening the kiss on her sigh of pleasure. He stroked a hand through her hair, freeing it from its pins, and massaged her scalp as he pulled her more tightly to him.

Zylphia clung to him, her hands fisted in his coat, her knuckles turning white as she kissed him back. She moaned as he broke the kiss and peppered her jawline and neck with kisses. She arched to give him better access, allowing one of his hands to move down her chest, cupping her breast. She gasped, her eyes flying open to meet his intense gaze. His eyes were like molten silver, and she shivered into his touch before arching farther away. "No, no." She pushed against him roughly, startling him, while she tripped and fell backward, landing on her bottom with a loud thud.

"Zee!" He dropped to his knees by her side but refrained from touching her as she held up a hand to ward him off.

"Stop. Just stop," she gasped, hating that her voice wavered and had emerged as a weak plea.

"I'd never hurt you, Zee," he said with a frown as he watched her struggle to stand without any help from him. "I'll always respect what you desire."

"Don't, Teddy." Zee turned around, brushing away tears.

"Why would … caring for me be so horrible?" he asked, suddenly irate. "How can you go from desiring my touch one moment, craving it even, to looking at me with such loathing the next?"

"I don't loathe you, Teddy. I loathe myself," she whispered. "I shouldn't want this. I need to focus on my goals. On what I want to accomplish in my life."

"And being loved doesn't enter into that equation?" He blanched after his words emerged and backed up a step. His expression hardened, and he became increasingly distant as he watched her collect hairpins off the floor. He glared at her as she styled her long raven hair into a neat chignon, pushing in pins to keep it in place and transforming into the remote woman of society again.

"I value your friendship, Teddy," Zylphia whispered, refusing to meet his gaze.

"Did you find my kisses any more satisfactory this time than the last? Are you hoping to have the opportunity to compare them with your other beau?"

"That's cruel," she breathed. "That's beneath you."

"Just as this is beneath you. Beneath us."

"I can't be what you want. What you believe you need." Zylphia blinked rapidly, but tears tracked down her cheeks.

He shook his head in frustration. "You of all people could be whatever you wanted to be. The agony is realizing you refuse to want to be what I want. What I need." He spun on his heels and marched toward the door, flinging it open. He turned to her, raking his gaze over her. "I'm sure you can find your way out as you were intrepid enough to discover this room." He spun, the diminishing sound of his footsteps a sign of his retreat to another part of the house.

Zylphia collapsed to the floor, a quiet sob escaping as she traced her lips with her fingers. She willed the gentle shaking to stop as she rose, departing with as little notice as possible.

***

Teddy alit from his automobile and paused when he recognized the auto behind him. He waited as it rolled to a halt, before opening the passenger door, nodding to Owen's chauffeur.

"Good to see you, Goff," Owen Hubbard said as he gripped Teddy's hand.

Teddy inclined his head in acknowledgment. Owen smiled a triumphant smile as he turned toward his automobile and held out a hand for Zylphia. He placed a proprietary hand to her back as he propelled her up the marble stairs into the Opera House. Teddy followed, hiding a glower, as Zylphia turned back to smile at him.

"I'm delighted you could join our group," she said to Teddy. "Miss Clement and Miss Tyler are also joining us."

"Delightful," Teddy murmured in a near growl.

"I hadn't realized opera was to your taste," Owen said as he helped Zylphia from her burgundy velvet cape. She slipped a gloved hand through his elbow, her burgundy skirts with black lace overlay swirling around her ankles, and began the slow walk down the long hallway and the stairs to their box.

"I delight in many things," Teddy said as he tugged on the black jacket sleeve of his tuxedo. He half smiled at Zylphia's attempt to hide her laugh behind a cough, meeting her amused gaze. His amusement faded as she walked up the white marble staircase with Owen, leaving Teddy to walk behind them alone.

Upon their arrival, Parthena and Rowena were already in the luxurious box. Scallop-shaped light fixtures infused a gentle light throughout the space, while the rich red velvet fabric, mahogany wood of the seats and the gold-filigreed wallpaper added to the sense of elegance. Mr. Wheeler and Mr. Tindall moved to welcome the newcomers and signaled a waiting attendant for glasses of champagne.

"Do you know much about this opera, Goff?" Morgan Wheeler asked as he glanced into the cavernous opera house.

"No, although it must be popular as it seems to have sold out," Teddy said, nodding to the rapidly filling seats below.

"It's *Madame Butterfly*. Of course it would sell out. It's a masterpiece," Parthena said with unveiled exasperation.

"Have you seen it before, Miss Tyler?" Morgan asked her.

"I have, in New York City at the Metropolitan."

"I imagine it was much grander there than here," Teddy said with an amused raise of his eyebrows.

She laughed. "You'd be surprised. The stage here is just as big as the one there, if not larger. And the acoustics here are glorious." She sighed with pleasure as the sounds of the orchestra tuning melded with the cacophony of myriad voices within the hall.

"I'd forgotten. You fancy yourself as something of a musician," Morgan said, his mouth turned up in what could be interpreted as either a teasing smile or an attempt to hide a sneer.

Parthena glared at him. "I greatly enjoy music, yes. I play the piano."

"Your mother should have a recital of sorts for you someday," Morgan said, earning a snicker from Owen, who, while standing next to Zylphia and caressing her arm at frequent intervals, failed to pay full attention to her conversation with Rowena.

"I'm sure it would delight all present to hear you perform," Teddy said, earning a nod of approval from Zylphia, whose group had become silent.

The lights dimmed for the second time, and they settled, with Rowena, Mr. Tindall, Owen and Zylphia sitting in the front of the box. Behind them, Parthena and Morgan sat in stilted silence, while Teddy settled next to a vacant seat.

As the lights dimmed, Teddy took a deep breath, watching the stage, while surreptitiously noting Zylphia's reaction to the opera. He fisted his hand as Owen patted her arm at a haunting aria, noting the sheen of tears Zylphia fought. When

they reached the first intermission, Teddy rose with the intent of escorting Zylphia for a refreshment, only to find Owen leading her out.

"You'll have to be more cunning if you want to head that one off," Parthena
murmured as she brushed by Teddy. She took Morgan's elbow with a sniff and
followed in her friend's wake. Teddy, the last to leave the box, watched as
Zylphia placed distance between her and Owen, even though she walked with her
arm through his. Teddy stopped near their group as he watched the other groups
mingling around him.

"Why the long face, Goff? It's not as though you were ever truly interested in
the McLeod girl. She's an oddity but a wealthy one at that," Morgan said as they
watched Owen tease a smile from her. "Besides, there's much that a man would
countenance to obtain access to Aidan McLeod's influence."

"I thought he'd care that she's a suffragist," Teddy murmured.

"Come. Women think they believe such nonsense until they can be persuaded
otherwise. I'm sure Owen, with his charm and standing in society, will prove to
be much more interesting than any social cause."

"Do any of you know her? Know her friends and what they believe in?" Teddy asked, his jovial tone underlaid with a hint of steel.

"Parthena believes she can defy her father, but she'll soon learn that's not the
case. Besides, marriage to a respectable man is a far less onerous future than
many I could think of for her." He watched Parthena speculatively.

"Do you mean you?" Teddy asked, choking on his drink. "She can't stand
you."

"A minor hiccough we'll overcome. She fails to remember the good aspects
of our youth together."

"You mean, she only remembers when you were a beast to her," Teddy said
with a wry grin.

"Exactly," Morgan said with a laugh as he slapped Teddy on the shoulder.
"Forget Miss McLeod. Owen has set his sights on her, and he'll stop at nothing
to have her." He eased to move away from Teddy.

"Why?" Teddy demanded, stepping in front of him and preventing him from
joining Mr. Tindall and Rowena.

"An alliance with Aidan McLeod would only benefit him. Or any of us. But especially the Hubbards."

"Why?" Teddy asked again, sifting through the recent gossip he'd heard about the Hubbards. He shook his head in frustration to realize he should have paid greater attention to his mother's prattling.

"Not all emerged as unscathed from the Panic of '07 as they'd like you to believe," Morgan murmured as he sidestepped Teddy to join Parthena, Rowena and Mr. Tindall with a chuckle and a joke.

Upon returning to the box, their group took their same seats. Teddy watched Zylphia, although he now knew that Parthena was aware of his interest in Zylphia. During one particularly haunting aria, where the heroine sang of her dream to reunite with her husband, he saw Zylphia take a stuttering breath and bite her lip. A moment later, tears coursed down her cheeks. Teddy stiffened when he saw Owen swipe away her tears with a handkerchief, and then Teddy clenched his teeth as she clasped Owen's arm for a moment.

When the lights came on for the second intermission, Teddy rose, following close on the heels of Zylphia and Owen. He stifled a growl as he saw Owen's hand linger longer than it should at the small of Zylphia's back before moving to brush her arm. Teddy approached them, hearing the tail end of their conversation.

"I'd think she'd understand he's never coming back to her," Owen said.

"It's unutterably sad that she'll be deceived by him," she said.

"Not all men act in such dishonorable ways. Although there are many men who leave on ships, who fail to return." Owen watched her with a speculative look in his eyes.

Zylphia stiffened and refused to comment.

"Give me a chance to prove to you that I am a different sort of man, Zylphia. Let me show you the fervency of my admiration."

"*Men were deceivers ever,*" Teddy muttered as he approached them.

Zylphia heard him and raised an eyebrow.

"I'd be fascinated to know what you plan to show her as your demonstration of such fervency."

Owen glared at him. "Goff, your pathetic attempts at humor are wearing thin."

"Miss McLeod," Teddy said as he turned to her. "Aren't you curious about what Mr. Hubbard means?"

"I'm warning you, Goff," Owen hissed.

"And I'm warning you that you'd better only ever treat her in an honorable fashion." His voice came out in a low growl, and his eyes were as flint behind his glasses. He gripped his hands at his sides as though preparing for battle.

In an instant the two men were toe-to-toe, with Zylphia watching on. "This is ridiculous," Zylphia hissed. "You're causing a scene." She pushed at Teddy's shoulder, barely budging him. "Teddy, stop this."

He flicked a glance toward her, a flash of confusion and pain in his eyes before focusing again on Owen. Rather than backing away, he took a step forward as Owen leaned into him.

"Stop it, both of you. There's no reason to act like boors." She put a hand out to each of their chests to separate them further and to prevent them from coming to blows.

"She's not yours to guard, Tedd," Owen said.

Teddy flushed, his breaths stuttering from him as Owen taunted Teddy under his breath about his bookish ways, his inferior looks, his dependence on glasses, his lack of social graces. When Owen saw Zylphia's attention was otherwise engaged, motioning to Mr. Wheeler, he said, "You're a fool to think a woman like Zylphia would want you."

***

Zylphia had glanced away, looking for some sort of aid. When she turned to watch the two men again, she gasped with horror to see Teddy landing a forceful blow to Owen's jaw. The resounding *smack* caught the attention of nearby operagoers.

"Teddy, no!" She gripped his arm, preventing a further escalation of their argument.

He stilled under her touch and backed up a step. "I'd never mean to harm you, Miss McLeod," he said, his breath coming out in agitated pants. "I beg your pardon."

"You should be asking it of Mr. Hubbard," she hissed, her blue eyes lit with anger.

Morgan slipped between the two men, forcing Zylphia to the periphery and toward her friends. His presence effectively ended the brewing brawl, although the resentment and anger lingered. "Why don't you go home?" he whispered to Teddy. "I'll ensure Miss McLeod arrives home without incident. We'll travel with Miss Tyler, so there will be no whisper of impropriety."

Teddy nodded, noting Zylphia was firmly ensconced with her friends, the two women forming a wall in front of her and curious gazes. Parthena glared at him and shook her head, as though with disappointment.

Teddy bowed slightly toward Zylphia and her friends before turning on his heels, his long tuxedo coat snapping behind him. He pushed through the inquisitive throng, not taking a full breath until he'd exited into the cool March night.

CHAPTER TWENTY-FOUR

"What's wrong with Zee?" Aidan asked over breakfast the following morning. He took a sip of strong coffee as he studied his wife, Delia. Her hair, more gray than black now, was pulled back in a loose bun, and she wore a comfortable day-dress in navy. Bright morning light poured in through the windows, hinting at the warmer months to come on this springlike day in early March.

"I think she's interested in that Theodore Goff, against her better judgment. She visited his home recently to look at art, and last night she was at the opera while he was also in attendance. She appears to have had some sort of interaction with him during both occasions."

Aidan stiffened. "Interaction?" He calmed only marginally when Delia gripped his hand.

"From everything I've seen of the man, he wouldn't hurt her. However, I believe he's capable of confronting her on her beliefs of what she desires for her future."

"I would have thought Zee intelligent enough to realize she can marry and have a fulfilling life." Aidan raised Delia's hand and kissed it.

Delia lowered her gaze and played with the silverware by her china plate. "I fear not having a father for the first part of her life has affected her."

Aidan sobered. "I've done all I can to atone for not being here for her. For you."

Delia blinked away tears at his husky, remorseful tone. "My love, I'm not chastising you. I want you to be aware that the effects of being raised in the orphanage with the fear of being alone are still present. She wants to be self-sufficient because she fears that, at any moment, all of this could be taken from her."

"She has a family now. She will always have someone to care for her and care about her should anything ever happen to us." Aidan frowned. "How can she not understand this after the past decade together?"

"Not everything is rational, least of all our emotions or fears." Delia took a sip of tea. "Imagine, dearest. Right when she had accustomed herself to living this new life, with a home in Boston and San Francisco, the earthquake struck. To say it rattled her is not an overstatement."

Aidan's gaze became distant before focusing on Delia. "Those were the longest days for me. Longer than when I had lost my first wife and our baby. Longer than when I was first separated from you. When I couldn't find you and Zee for days afterward, I thought I'd go mad."

Delia nodded, lost in the memory of raging fires and overwhelming smoke, and the fear that she'd lost Aidan again. The destruction of their home had barely registered as she and Zylphia raced from the house, evading the roaring blaze while battling fear as aftershocks struck. When they were offered seats on a train out of the city, she'd eagerly accepted them, if only to ease Zylphia's torment.

"I'm sorry it took us so long to be reunited. However, this is just another reason why Zee is determined not to need anyone."

Aidan nodded, his shoulders stooping. "I feel as though I have failed her in some way. Rationally I know I haven't. Not since I've returned. And yet I've never been able to ease her of this irrational fear." His piercing blue eyes focused on Delia. "This Goff lad. What do you make of him?"

"I don't know him well. He's often in the company of Owen Hubbard." She raised an eyebrow at Aidan's *hmph*. "And he's very dedicated to experiments. His mother wishes he would take a more active role in running the business, but he appears to have no interest in it."

"Mr. Goff, his father, is a sage investor, although he spends the majority of his time in New York."

"Mrs. Goff preferred Boston. She did not like the hustle of such a large city. I suspect theirs is a marriage where they do not mind spending time apart."

Aidan grunted. "I do not want the same for Zee. She deserves more than a distant man, lost to his experiments." He pushed away his plate and drummed his fingers on the dining room table. "What can we do to help her?"

"Nothing. She must decide what she desires. I fear at the moment she wants her life to continue as it always has. And she wants to become more involved in the women's suffrage movement."

Aidan sighed. "Then I have to admit that, in many ways, I'm hopeful this Goff lad can continue to rile her. I want my girl to live a full life, not one hampered by fears fostered from growing up in an orphanage." He met his wife's gaze and raised both palms up. "I promise not to interfere in any way, but I can't say I'm not rooting for the lad."

***

Zylphia stood in the room she considered her studio. Savannah had written how it used to be her private sitting room and had hoped Zee would find a better use for it. The dreary wallpaper had been removed, replaced by bright cream-colored paint. All the drapes covering the front and side windows had been repurposed for the servants' quarters, leaving the windows bare and allowing bright sunlight to shine in. Two tufted red velvet chairs and a matching chaise longue were scattered throughout the room, along with a few tables and lamps. Haphazardly stacked paintings lining the wall were the only other flashes of color inside the room.

Zylphia stood, studying her canvas, squinting at it. "It's missing something," she murmured to herself. She tapped her paintbrush against the palette and squinted with frustration.

"It looks beautiful to me," a man with a deep voice said behind her.

She squealed, nearly upending the palette she held of its mixture of browns, grays and blacks onto the canvas. She spun, facing the amused gaze of Theodore Goff. "Teddy, what are you doing here?"

"I thought I'd call for tea and apologize for my behavior at the opera last night." His alert gaze took in the paint splattered on her apron, cheek and hair.

"Tea? What made you think we had tea here?" Zylphia asked as she placed the palette on a side table and scrubbed her hands in a basin. The clear water was soon discolored, and her hands were only marginally cleaner. "My mother only deigns to act that conventional when she has matrons over for meetings about the orphanage. My friends know when they call it will be a culinary adventure, at best." She grabbed a nearby rag and rubbed her hands dry and relaxed at Teddy's soft chuckle.

He roamed the room, bending over to study her paintings. He pulled canvases forward to see the ones behind them. "This is why my mother invited you to see our collection. She knew you were an artist. A very talented artist."

"My mother shared that information with her during one of their discussions at the orphanage. They thought to auction off a piece of art as part of a fund-raiser, and my mother mentioned my paintings."

"I can see why she did. Why aren't these displayed somewhere? They're magnificent." He stopped in front of one with a cherry tree in bloom, its colors muted and melded as though seen through gauze or a wet windowpane.

"I just dabble at painting."

Teddy raised his eyebrows before shaking his head. "This isn't dabbling, Zee. Most professional artists can only dream of accomplishing what you have. It's like you studied the Impressionists and then formed your own interpretation." His smile softened at her embarrassed blush. His gaze turned to her current project. "This is quite different."

"I've read a lot about the current trend in Paris, and I've seen a few of the lesser paintings. It fascinates me how art is changing, and I wanted to attempt my own version."

Teddy tilted his head and clasped his hands behind his back as he studied the painting of a couple, formed from cubes and geometrical shapes. The hues were more subdued than the vibrant work stacked along the walls of the room.

"It's called Cubism. Picasso is painting like this." Zylphia was unable to hide the excitement from her voice. "Or at least I think he is."

"And do you desire to be like Picasso?"

"I'll never know what it is to have his talent, but I enjoy creating art in his style."

"Why?" He moved to one of the tufted chairs and leaned against the chair-back.

She waved at him, silently giving him permission to sit even though she re-mained standing. "What do you mean?"

"Why should you stifle your art by copying other great artists? Why shouldn't you use what you know, use your talent, to create something new? Art à la Zylphia?"

She laughed for a moment before sobering when she realized he was serious. "I'm not an artist. I just tinker away here when I have time."

He motioned to all the paintings on the floor. "This isn't an idle hobby, Zee. This is your passion. Embrace it. Share it."

"No. My passion is to see women obtain the vote." She spoke resolutely, as though challenging him to contradict her.

"You can have more than one passion in your life. In fact, it will make your life much more interesting."

"You only have your inventing." She frowned as she detected a note of petu-lance in her voice.

"That's only what you know of me, Zee. There's much left to discover." He glanced over her shoulder, seeing a girl hovering in the shadows.

Zylphia turned. "Yes, Bridget?"

"Should I bring tea?" the maid asked.

Zylphia laughed. "Yes. Why not? Today is a different sort of day."

After Bridget departed, Teddy said, "She seems a bit young for a maid. And a bit uncertain of her role."

"She's from the orphanage. You'll find every servant here is an orphan who used to live there. Our butler, Jimmy, was one of my best friends growing up."

Teddy frowned as Zylphia flushed and busied herself with washing her paint-brushes. "That explains why he was lax in his duties."

Zylphia raised an eyebrow.

"He should have had me wait in a side parlor or, at the bare minimum, should have escorted me here to introduce me."

"Well, it's a learning process."

"Why would you be friends with an orphan? I would think your mother would shelter you from such a reality."

Zylphia tugged the other chair nearer to his and collapsed into it. "Do you ever wonder why I'm always looking to Miss Tyler and Miss Clement for the proper way to act? That I never say the correct thing at the correct time? That I'm always a little off?"

"You're an eccentric. Everyone knows that."

"No, I'm not. Well, maybe I am. Mainly it's because, until I was sixteen, I lived in the orphanage. In a small room, behind the matron's office, with my mother."

"I've seen you with Aidan McLeod. There could be no mistaking you're his daughter."

"I know. I am." She paused as Bridget returned with a laden tea tray. She thanked her with a smile, whispering to her to close the door on her way out. She faced Teddy, watching him beseechingly. "Please, what I'm about to tell you, I don't want it bandied about. Parthena and Rowena know, but I'd rather not have society gossiping any more about me than they already do."

Teddy nodded, accepting the cup of tea she handed him.

She hesitated and gripped her hands together.

He reached forward with his free hand, resting it atop hers. "There's nothing you could tell me that would stop me from wanting us to remain friends."

She sighed with apparent relief. "My father and mother were in love, many years ago. He was a sailor and would be gone for months at a time. Once, he returned home to find his brother and nephews dead. Then, during his grief, my mother demanded he give up seafaring. They had a magnificent argument, said hateful things, and he departed. He thought he'd never return to Boston.

"He did return, many years later, to discover that his nephews hadn't perished in that fire. A few years after that discovery, while helping one of his nephews, he met my mother again." She took a deep breath. "And realized he had a daughter."

Teddy smiled. "And then he married your mother, ensured you left the orphanage, and provided you with a home and his name."

"And his love," Zylphia whispered. She blinked away tears. "I'd dreamt for so long of a father, and then to have one, one as grand as Aidan McLeod, was as though a miracle."

"Do you believe because you spent the first years of your life in an orphanage, although you weren't an orphan, that I would think any less of you?" He frowned as Zylphia remained quiet. "That I would consider you less worthy of my friendship or esteem because you didn't have the benefit of your father's name or protection for the first years of your life?"

Zylphia nodded.

"None of that matters to me."

"I don't understand why it doesn't. You spent the majority of your life in England. You, more than anyone, should be prejudiced against me."

"Because I'm English? Because my family is wealthy and I come from a long line of aristocrats on my mother's side?" When Zylphia nodded again at his statements, he grimaced. "So you believe I shouldn't associate with someone like you because your past wasn't perfect?"

"Exactly."

"Do you know why I defied my grandparents and returned to America? To Boston? Even though I had no prospects here? My father and mother were content with my absence. In fact, they hardly register my presence now even though I reside in their home."

"That's horrible."

He shook his head as in frustration. "That's not my point. Do you know why I came back?"

Zylphia frowned. "No."

They were now holding hands. Teddy set aside his teacup and traced a pattern over the back of her hand with his free hand. "I returned because I believed the myth, the promise that, in America, I could be anyone. That I wouldn't be judged by my antecedents. That here I could determine who I wanted to be." He watched his hand caressing hers.

"Have you found the lie to the myth yet?"

"Nearly upon my return." He half smiled, one of regret and self-mockery. "I thought I'd remake myself into the son my parents wanted. Instead I ..." He broke off, shaking his head.

"Sometimes you need to go to an unknown place to find yourself."

"Is that what happens to you when you paint?"

She stiffened at his perceptiveness. "Yes. I'm transported to somewhere I've only imagined, and I feel as though a different person."

"That's how I feel when I'm working on my inventions."

They shared a smile, as though reaching a deeper understanding.

"If you love inventing so much, why don't you work with an inventor like Edison? I'm sure he'd be eager to have someone with your talent and education work with him."

"If there's one thing to know about me, it's that I'm independent. I couldn't imagine taking orders from anyone else. Even one so great as Edison himself."

"How is your invention progressing?" Zylphia asked, absently running her thumb over the back of his hand.

He flushed, either from her question or her caress. "Slower than I would like. It's as though I discover something that will solve one of my problems, but then it only raises three more contradictions and concerns."

"Why are you focused on wireless transmission?"

He released her hand. "I've always enjoyed technology, and I believe wireless will become one of the marvels of communication of our time."

Zylphia laughed. "I doubt it. Wireless? As though every home would have one? Newspapers are sufficient and always will be."

"For someone who is progressive with her art and beliefs for women, you are remarkably slow to embrace change when it comes to technology." He traced her cheek before leaning away. He glanced out the drape-free windows, noting the long shadows. "I'm sorry to have taken up so much of your time, losing the decent light for today."

"I enjoyed your visit," Zylphia said, rising.

He stood, moving toward the painting of the cherry tree. He looked at it as though in a trance.

"Why don't you take it as you like it so much?"

He spun to face her, his forehead furrowed. "I couldn't. It's too much."

"No, it's not. Just the dabblings of a young woman." She reached down, gripping it on the sides, careful not to touch the actual painting. "Here. It would please me to know you have it."

"Thank you. I shall treasure it. I hope this means you've forgiven me my behavior last night." He set down the painting, leaning it against the wall again.

"I can't believe you assaulted Mr. Hubbard. He meant no offense."

Teddy shook his head. His silver eyes flashed with irritation and disappointment. "There we'll have to disagree. I beg your pardon for lacking in all social graces." Teddy ran a hand through his hair.

"It's nothing you haven't been accused of before," she teased, only sobering when she noted his distress. "It was a simple misunderstanding."

"I would never mean to offend you in any way, Zee."

She became mesmerized by the intense sincerity in his eyes. "I know. Nor I you."

"I didn't like it when you defended him," he whispered.

She frowned as she met his injured gaze. "I wasn't. I was angry at the scene you caused. Not because I wished to have more time with him." She smiled as his eyes lit with understanding.

As though of its own volition, his hand raised to cup her cheek, his thumb stroking her soft skin. Her cheeks flushed while she leaned toward him. He watched her closely, a relieved smile escaping a moment before he lowered his head to kiss her.

Almost instantly the kiss deepened, her sigh melding with his groan as he pulled her tighter and she gripped his jacket. She moved her hands underneath his jacket and mewled in frustration when she couldn't place her hands under his well-tailored waistcoat. Settling for stroking her hands over his silk-covered back, she raised herself on her toes to better meet his kisses.

He pulled away with a gasp. "Zee," he panted. "We can't keep doing this." His fingers traced her lips, her chin, her neck, before dipping his hand to her loosened collar, eliciting a shiver as his fingers touched her bare collarbone.

"I only feel like this with you," she whispered, her head falling back as his lips followed the path of his fingers.

Inadvertently her words extinguished his ardor, and he released her. "I beg your pardon, Zee." His laugh lacked all traces of humor. "It seems all I do is ask your forgiveness lately."

She backed up a step after he released her, shaking her head as though to clear it of the vestiges of passion. "What did I say now?" Her luminous blue eyes followed his erratic movement as he moved toward the cherry tree painting.

"I'm sorry to disappoint you, but I have no desire to be used only to further your personal experiments as you compare me to your other suitors."

She gripped his arm, moving to stand in front of the door as he strode to leave. "That's not what I meant at all, Teddy." She raised a free hand to her forehead as she attempted to remember what she had said to lose his touch. "I thought you'd like to know no other man affects me as you do."

His eyes flashed, and she backed up until she was leaning against the door as he towered over her. "It will never please me to know that you have allowed other men to touch you."

"I have the right to want to experience life. As much as any man."

"So now you espouse free love? Do you believe that will bring you happiness?"

"More than the bonds of marriage to an overbearing tyrant would," Zylphia snapped, rising on her toes.

He leaned away, paling. "I—I must be going."

"Teddy, forgive me." Zylphia grabbed his arm as he maneuvered around her, creaking the door open.

"You speak your truth when you are rash, Zee. I must force myself to heed those words, rather than ignore them as I long to." He raised his palm, held it near her cheek but failed to caress her. She leaned her head forward to feel his touch again, but he lowered his hand and backed farther away. "Good day to you, Zee."

The door closed behind her on a soft click. She leaned against it, stifling a sigh. After a moment, she pushed herself from the door to collapse onto the chaise longue, gripping a throw pillow to her chest. Tears leaked out as she surveyed the controlled chaos of her studio. The comfort she sensed every time she entered her studio was elusive now, replaced with inquietude at the memory of Teddy and her unremitting fascination with him.

CHAPTER TWENTY-FIVE

"Fiona! Miss O'Leary!" Patrick called out as he raced after her retreating form down Galena Street. The wind howled on a cold March evening, and the streetlights' anemic glow did little to battle the early darkness. He slipped on a piece of ice, swearing under his breath as he slid into a well-dressed businessman, and Fiona strayed farther from view. He saw her turn into a stairwell leading up to apartments over a bakery and hastened after her.

The outside door failed to latch due to the freezing weather, and he pushed open the door. He heard a door close above him to the rear, and he rushed up the worn steps. He approached the rear of the hallway and knocked on the door, forcing himself to stand with an air of calm, even though he wanted to shift from foot to foot.

The door opened to a harried Fiona. Her irritation persisted when she saw Patrick on her doorstep. "Mr. Sullivan, I wasn't expecting you. And I'm afraid I don't have long before I must leave again."

"I'm sorry to bother you on such a cold evening, but I haven't had the opportunity to speak with you recently." He stared into her cognac-colored eyes, devoid of their usual brilliancy.

She waved him inside. Her sister sat on a wooden rocking chair darning socks while her cousin knitted on a stool in front of the stove. They looked at him with a mixture of curiosity and disappointment before rising and moving into a room toward the back of the apartment. Fiona slung his winter jacket over a dining room chair before following him into the living room.

"I didn't mean for them to leave," Patrick said.

She shrugged her shoulders and motioned for him to enter the sparsely furnished living room with threadbare carpets and dilapidated furniture. The wallpaper had faded to yellow, and the ceiling showed signs of previous water damage. He shivered as the stove failed to fully heat the room, rubbing his hands together to warm them.

"I'm certain you've followed me home for some reason," Fiona said as she perched on the edge of the settee, hands clasped together tightly.

Patrick moved toward a small upholstered chair, jumping up as the springs gave out from his weight. He decided to remain standing as he spoke with her. "Fiona." Patrick shook his head. "I beg your pardon. I have no right to address you in such a familiar manner. Miss O'Leary, I can't help but notice you've avoided me lately."

She smiled indulgently, although she failed to meet his gaze. "You're mistaken. I have a busy life here and have had much to occupy my time. I'm sorry if you've felt I've neglected you lately or if I've inadvertently hurt your feelings."

Patrick frowned, his muscles bunching underneath his suit coat. He studied her as she sat on the settee. She was more tightly wound than one of the whirl top toys he'd given his nephew for Christmas. "I'm sorry if I'm intruding this evening. I must admit I have missed your company. I'd hoped you missed mine." He clamped his jaw tight when she shook her head subtly and stared at the floor.

He turned and glanced around her sparse apartment. "I thought you'd be able to afford better living accommodations as a secretary to Mr. Sanders." He watched as she grew even more rigid. "I've heard things, Miss O'Leary." He met her startled, desperate gaze. "Things that make me worried for you."

At his whispered sentence, she jumped up from the settee and paced toward the potbellied coal stove. "I thank you for your concern, but I assure you that I am fine."

"Just as I can assure you, the man you are dealing with is not what he seems," Patrick murmured. He watched as her shoulders shivered, although he couldn't decipher if it were from emotion or the cold. "Samuel Sanders has no regard for anyone but himself."

"If you think I don't know that, then you don't know me at all," she said.

"What game are you playing, Fiona, to become involved with such a man?" Patrick asked. He reached for her, spinning her around to face him, no longer able to hide his fury. He gripped her shoulders. "Why him? Why wouldn't you at least give me a chance?"

"Why should I go for the lackey when I can have the man with all the power?" Her eyes glimmered with anger and poorly hidden desolation. "Why wouldn't I want a strong, successful man? It's what every woman wants. Why should I be any different?"

Patrick shook his head in confusion as he watched her. "Because you are different. This doesn't make sense. The woman standing in front of me isn't the same woman I met last summer."

"Do you think I dream of living like this, in a barren room, barely able to afford heat for the rest of my life?"

He glared at her, his hold on her shoulders tightening. "Do you think I want to remain in a job where I am demeaned on a nearly daily basis, merely because it amused my boss?"

"Why'd you stay?"

"For you. Because I was worried about you, working in close proximity to such a man." He traced a finger down her cheek. "I would have helped you, in any way I could have, Fee. All you had to do was ask."

She jerked in his hold as though he'd slapped her and blinked rapidly as she fought tears. "Let me go."

He immediately dropped his hands and backed away from her, frowning again as he saw surprise flit across her face. "Why would you expect me to ignore your wishes?"

She brushed a hand across her damp cheek. "Most men don't care much for women's desires."

He leaned forward until they were eye to eye, sharing the same breath. "I'm not most men." He watched her with an impotent fury. "No matter what he promised you, he'll betray you. He's not a man worth trusting."

Fiona nodded once, and he opened his mouth to speak but then shook his head at the futility of it. He spun, grabbed his coat and flung open the door, departing without a backward glance.

***

Patrick pushed his way into the crowded bar, already bustling in the early evening. The wood of the long bar was nicked and dulled after years of heavy use, innumerable glasses having crossed over it. He ordered his drink, remaining at the bar. He took his tumbler of whiskey, draining it in one long swallow, and nodded at the barman for another.

He jolted as a hand clapped him on the shoulder. "What's got you in such a sour mood?" Elias asked with a chuckle. "I bet you're still having woman problems." At Patrick's glare, he laughed. "Ya, that's what it is."

Patrick rolled his eyes and nodded. "Why would a woman change overnight?"

"Ah, so your missus has no interest in you now," Elias said with a half smile. He sobered when he saw the frustration on his friend's face.

"Something like that." Patrick frowned as his recent scene with her played through his mind again.

"Let her go. If she's found someone new, let her be. Plenty of women in Butte are interested in an aboveground man." Elias watched Patrick with a mixture of pity and amusement. "But of course you won't take my advice. It looks like you are hell-bent on drinking yourself to oblivion."

Patrick raised his nearly empty tumbler of whiskey in a salute before catching the barkeep's eye again to refill it.

Elias rolled his eyes before smiling. "I just hope she's worth the agony of the headache tomorrow."

"How can a woman want to be with a man like that?" Patrick asked as he slammed his hand onto the wooden bar. "A heartless, manipulative, evil bastard."

"You've just described most successful men in this town." Elias chuckled as Patrick glared at him. "Why else would a woman want a man like that unless he were rich? I'm not surprised she'd catch herself such a man. It would only be for her benefit."

"Nothing he does will ever be to her benefit. Besides, she's living in near poverty, when she should know riches if she were profiting from her arrangement," Patrick said as he hissed after taking a large swig of whiskey. He swayed subtly as he set down his glass with a *thunk*, and Elias eyed his misstep. "I'm no lightweight."

"Ya, I'm sure that's true." He nodded for a man to vacate his seat at a nearby table and pushed Patrick into it. He took the one across from him and watched his anger simmering below the surface of well-honed indifference.

"I stayed at that miserable job, month after month, accepting a demotion, refusing to rise to his abuse, for her. And how does she repay me? She ignores me. Ignores my offer to help her, as though I were a nuisance."

In his anger, he failed to see Elias indicate to the barman to send them further glasses of whiskey.

"And this is how she thanks me? By saying she'd never want anything to do with someone as lowly as I am?" Patrick asked. He clamped his jaw, his anger seeping from him. "I hate that I ever came to care," he whispered.

Elias thumped him on the shoulder and pushed another tumbler of whiskey toward him. "Soon you won't remember her name." He winked at Patrick as he raised a glass and saluted. "To all the fickle women who will rue the day they forswore us."

***

Fiona knocked on the elaborately carved door, entering silently as the butler opened it for her. She took off her coat, handing it to him before taking a deep breath. She stood as tall as her five-foot-three frame would allow and walked with measured calm toward the rear parlor. She knocked on the door twice, waited to be called to enter and donned a mask of impassivity as she did.

"I'm disappointed in you this evening," the man said, his soft voice in opposition to his words, an inadvertent shiver coursing down her spine. "You're late."

"I was detained." Fiona moved toward the settee but didn't sit. She knew by now to do nothing without permission.

"Yes, by another man. How pathetic he is to still want you, even though I let others know you're mine." Samuel Sanders smirked at the idea.

Fiona ducked her head, masking the shame and anger in her eyes. He chucked her under her chin, forcing up her eyes. "We have a bargain, lest you forget the repercussions for breaking it."

She nodded, her eyes deadened as she looked at him. She stilled awaiting his next move. She jumped as his hand rose, startling her as he traced it down the side of her head in a mockery of a caress. Rather than his fingertips brushing gently over her skin, his manicured nails dug into her skin, creating reddened grooves in their wake. She fought an instinctive flinch, remaining impassive.

His brown eyes flashed with anger at her control, and he pushed her onto the settee behind her. "Enough with the preliminaries," he said, rucking up her dress and ripping at her underclothes. She quelled her instinctive urge to fight him and forced herself to remain motionless as his hands bruised her. She was unable to stifle a gasp of pain as he forced himself inside her. She fought the tears that burned at the back of her eyes, praying that once would be enough this week.

CHAPTER TWENTY-SIX

Patrick weaved through the crowd, which grew more boisterous by the minute. The well-liquored populace of Butte was on its way toward celebrating another unforgettable Saint Patrick's Day with the parade about to begin. He paused as the throng of people impeded his movement and opted to remain here to watch the parade. His height gave him a perfect view of the marchers and floats.

He smiled as a band approached, playing marching tunes by Sousa. Although already over a decade old, they remained the favorites for marching bands. Then groups of miners from the different mines approached. They waved to the crowd, to their wives and sweethearts, if they were lucky enough to have one, and the crowd cheered.

Floats passed him by, highlighting the numerous ethnic groups in Butte. Many of those riding on the floats threw out trinkets to the crowd, earning a roar of approval. Patrick whooped when he saw his friend Elias. The large Amalgamated float went by, carrying miners from numerous mines.

He stiffened when a hand gripped his shoulder.

"Sullivan, it appears you haven't freed yourself of your unfortunate tendency to support the losers."

Patrick shrugged the hand off his shoulder, turning to face Samuel. "I don't base a person's worth on the size of their bank account. Or the amount of influence they wield."

"Which goes to show why I'll always be the boss and you the day laborer." He looked past Patrick to the passing parade. "I'd hoped to teach you something of value while under my tutelage, but I can see now you were a hopeless cause."

"You saw me as a way to harm your cousins, Henry," Patrick said, spitting out his original given name. "You never meant to offer me true friendship."

He smirked. "You still could have learned something of value from me." He sighed. "As it is, I've had to use my expertise on a more willing pupil."

Patrick became rigid. "If you mean Miss O'Leary …"

Samuel smiled with satisfaction. "If I do, it is surely none of your concern." He leaned toward Patrick as though he were sharing a secret. "She is delightful. It's a pity you never got to know her as I have. She's quite … sensual."

"You bastard." Patrick grabbed him by the lapels. He released him when those around them gasped and murmured their disapproval.

Samuel straightened his jacket and patted Patrick on the shoulder, as though in consolation. "Best of luck to you, Pat. I'm sure you'll be someone worthwhile before you die." He gave him a jaunty wave and sauntered off.

Patrick watched him leave with an impotent fury, the innocent joy of the parade lost to him. He pushed through the crowd, heading toward his local bar, hopeful for a visit with Elias.

***

Patrick looked up from his desk, his gaze belatedly focusing on Fiona as she brought him a stack of papers. "Miss O'Leary," he said with a small nod before focusing again on his ledger.

"Would you be so kind as to look through these today, Mr. Sullivan?" Fiona asked. "I've been advised there is an urgent nature to them."

"Of course," he murmured, pointing to a free corner on his desk. He heaved out a breath as she walked away. He refrained from glaring at her retreating back as he didn't want to provoke any further gossip among his colleagues. He flipped through the paperwork, sighing to see the number of pages to be tallied. He paused when he came to a slip of paper hidden amid the pages. He glanced around furtively, but no one paid him any attention now that he was no longer Mr. Sanders's protégé. After extracting the note, he picked up his pencil as though he were merely dealing with another accounting issue. *P. Please meet me tonight after work. F.*

He glared at the paper as he flipped it over to see if he'd missed where he was meant to go. He slipped the note into his pocket and refocused on his work. As the workday neared its end, he heard Fiona speaking with a colleague. She laughed about having to go home to see her sister.

Fifteen minutes after Fiona had departed, Patrick stood and donned his winter coat, hat, scarf and gloves. He passed Fiona's desk, Samuel's empty office and exited the building to walk to Fiona's apartment.

The scarred outside door was again ajar, and he soundlessly walked up the wooden stairs to her rear apartment. He stood in front of her door a few moments, glaring at it and berating himself for heeding her call the minute he received it. After heaving out a sigh, he rapped with more vehemence than necessary and fought a frown as he listened to her approach.

He catalogued the subtle changes in her. Her previously lush figure appeared on the verge of emaciation with her curves now prompted by a well-tied corset. Her eyes lacked all vibrancy, and she moved with a hesitancy that bespoke a familiarity with discord. The only aspect of her that shone was her hair—thicker and more lustrous than ever—even though she'd tamed it in a tight bun.

He moved past her, brushing against her arm and earning a slight tremble. He again stood as he waited for her to speak. However, she became increasingly agitated and remained silent. "Fiona, whatever it is you have to say, it can't be worse than anything I've already imagined," he said.

She closed her eyes for a moment, then met his gaze. "I asked you here to beg you for your forgiveness."

"You've done nothing to harm me."

She flinched at his cold tone. "Perhaps not but I feel I have." She took a deep, stuttering breath that made her more uptight rather than calm her. "Will you let me explain?"

He nodded, moving to settle onto a wooden chair, his outward display of a relaxed gentleman masking his growing unease.

"Samuel Sanders discovered my secret," she whispered. "And I agreed to a devil's bargain to protect myself. Or so I thought."

"What could you possibly have to hide?" Patrick canted forward, his interest piqued against his will.

"I agreed to tell him everything I learned about you. Your family. Anything he asked, I agreed to relate." She shook her head, her eyes pleading with him for understanding. "I didn't realize he knew your cousins. I should have known how evil he was then, but I only thought of myself."

"It's because of you how he knew about Rory." Patrick clamped his jaw as he fought his anger. "Gabriel's never trusted me, not fully, since that day. And it was all because of you."

She battled tears and nodded. "When I realized what he'd done, how much harm he'd caused you, I told him that I could no longer agree to the bargain. Things were all right for a little while, and then ... Then it all changed."

"Was this right around Christmas?" he asked. "When you no longer wanted to spend as much time with me? When you refused my gift and asked me to never call on you again?"

"Yes." She blinked away tears. "But it—"

"Because I was no longer of any use to you."

"No! Because I was ashamed. I couldn't bear for you to ..."

He watched her as she pleated and unpleated a piece of lace on the edge of her shirtsleeve, nearly ripping it off. "He would never have let you go once he could blackmail you." He glowered as he saw her shiver. "What did he demand of you?"

"All that matters is that I'm terribly sorry for how I treated you, Pa—Mr. Sullivan."

He knelt by the settee and reached forward, stilling her nervous hands, his grip firm yet gentle. "No, Fiona, what did he do to you?"

She fought a sob, her face contorting as the tears poured out against her volition. "It's not of your concern."

"Yes, it is," he whispered, moving to sit beside her on the settee. He put an arm around her shoulder and urged her into his side. "It's all right," he soothed.

"It will never be all right." She sobbed, unable to stop. "I've ruined everything."

"Can you tell me what happened?" he whispered, kissing the top of her head. He inhaled a hint of lavender and brushed a hand down her arm.

She spoke in a halting whisper, and he stilled to better hear her. "No one would ever interrupt him when his door is closed. Only fire or death of a superior were reasons to knock on his door when it was closed." She laughed without mirth. "He didn't even bother to lock the door the first time."

Patrick stiffened next to her. He ran a hand down her back and made circles on her shoulder, belatedly realizing he was soothing himself as much as her with his soft caresses. "What did he do?"

"He said, if I refused to be the informant I'd agreed to be, he'd have to find another use for me."

"He assaulted you." Patrick stilled his hands a moment in his anger before continuing their pattern over her back, shoulder and arm.

"Yes. When I said I'd report him, he advised me no one would believe me and that, if I wanted to still work as a secretary rather than at the Dumas, I needed to report to his house every Tuesday evening at 8:00 p.m."

"I was last here on a Tuesday," Patrick murmured.

"Yes." She shivered. "I knew I had to go there. I couldn't handle any kindness from you."

He pushed her back and stared into her eyes. "Why? Why allow him to abuse you? You know I'd have helped you in an instant."

He saw her deflate in front of him, and his brow furrowed in confusion as he thought through his words. "I'd help you now if you'd let me." When she moved back into his arms, he held her away from him. "I'd remove you completely from his sphere of influence. Marry me, Fee."

She paled and shook her head. "No, Patrick. No."

"You haven't thought it through. It's the best way to protect you from him." He raised one of her hands to his lips and gifted her with a half smile, filled with hopeful longing. "I was already dreaming of a proposal when I was in Missoula last fall."

Tears poured from her eyes. "No, I can't marry you." When he stiffened and moved to rise from her, she clung to him. "There's nothing more I would like than to marry you. To join that large family you talk about." She swallowed a sob. "I'd love to have a big family around me again."

"Then why won't you?" he demanded.

"Because I'm already married." She met his shocked gaze as she lifted a chain from around her neck, extracting it and the ring at the end of it.

He touched the ring still warm from hanging between her breasts, staring dumbly.

"I have been for six years."

"Where is he?"

"I don't know. I last saw him in Chicago."

Patrick shook his head. "It doesn't make sense. If you left him, then why become entangled with Samuel Sanders? Why lead me on last summer and fall?" He clasped her elbow, preventing her from rising. "Fiona, speak with me."

"That was my first mistake," she whispered. "Using my name."

He swiped at her tears, pulling her into his arms as she cried in earnest.

"When I think of all the times you were worried about my reputation ..." She stuttered out a laugh lacking in all humor. "I had no reputation left to defend."

"I refuse to believe that." He clasped her to him, urging her to find solace in his arms. "From the moment we first met, I knew you were a woman worthy of respect."

"Mr. Sanders discovered I was married, hired an investigator and found my husband. A man who's been searching for me." She shivered. "Mr. Sanders threatened to contact him and inform him where I am if I renege on my bargain with him."

"What's your real name?"

"Fiona Flaherty." She shuddered as she said the name. "I haven't said that name in over three years."

He cooed as he felt her tremble. "No one will harm you." He kissed her head resting on his shoulder. "I don't understand why you don't divorce such a man."

"Divorce means he knows where I am. If he knows where I am, he'll kill me." She pushed away and met his confused gaze. "I know you don't understand. I don't, and I married him. Any sweetness faded once I was proclaimed his wife, and he became possessive and cruel. And then ..."

Patrick waited, nodding his encouragement for her to continue.

"And then I heard him speaking with a friend of his. They were both mostly drunk. But Peter was at his most lucid right before he became insensate. He wanted to do away with his pesky wife in a manner where no one would question her death." She stuttered out a laugh. "Me! They were talking about me. Do you know what that is like, to realize the man you've married is plotting your demise?

"They talked about accidental falls downstairs, an innocent trip in front of a streetcar and then considered poisoning my food." She gave an indignant snort. "I knew we were in debt. I worked two jobs, lying to both employers about my marital status so I could work. Whereas he drank away the proceeds."

Her jaw firmed as she thought about her husband. "He'd taken out a life policy for me when we married. At the time I thought it showed his concern for my well-being. When I heard him with his friend, I understood the entire time he'd been awaiting his opportunity to collect what he saw as his due." She heaved out a sigh, resting once more against Patrick's chest.

He played with strands of her hair that had loosened from her bun but kept his own counsel.

"I disappeared three days later, moving around, never setting down roots."

"Why come to Butte?" Patrick asked.

"I thought I could be lost in the multitude here. And there's work. I could be with my cousin and sister." She winced. "I was so stupid. All he had to do was look for any member of my family to find me."

Patrick shushed her. "You're not stupid for not wanting to be alone forever. Our bravery can only take us so far before we need others we can lean on." He sighed into her hair as he thought. "I don't understand why you didn't say you were a widow."

"Men have expectations of a widow that they don't have for a single, unmarried woman." Her voice was filled with rancor. "I only made that mistake once."

His hold on her tightened at her shudder. "Why wait to tell me everything now? I would have helped you at any point."

She flinched at the hurt she heard in his voice. "I thought, after I pushed you away in December, you would no longer care about me. That you'd have the sense to let a woman like me go."

"Why not tell Samuel everything about my family? It would hurt you much less than the abuse of the past few months."

"No matter what you think about me, Patrick, I couldn't continue to harm you or your family. When he spoke with such joy about the distress he had caused your brothers-in-law, it sickened me. I realized I was the source of their pain."

"Believe me, if he'd never forced you into such a bargain, he would have still created as much pain as he did that night in Missoula. He thrives on discord and when those around him are discontent."

He pulled her against him, settling her until she leaned against his chest. "We'll figure it all out, Fee. I promise."

CHAPTER TWENTY-SEVEN

Clarissa sat at the kitchen table in her Missoula home, a cup of tea cooling while she read the mail. She smiled at Zylphia's latest adventures at the opera, wincing as Zee described the fight between two of her suitors. Clarissa picked up Patrick's letter next, her smile fading the more she read.

She rose, ignoring her tea, and moved to the front hall to don her winter jacket, hat, gloves and boots. Billy had gone to work with Gabriel this morning to spend time with him, and the girls were at school. Clarissa shivered as she hurried across the Higgins Street Bridge, the howling wind from Hellgate Canyon provoking a shudder.

She turned down Main Street and burst into Gabriel's workshop, teeth rattling as she thawed in the warm space.

Two workbenches lined the wall to the left of the door where Gabriel and Jeremy worked. Ronan had a small workspace to the right of the door for his cobbling business. Pieces of unfinished wood stood scattered throughout the room, waiting minor alterations, to be sanded or varnished.

Gabriel looked up from helping Billy hammer a small nail into a child-size rocking chair. "Darling," he said with joy as he saw her. "You're frozen through." He pulled her to him, and his warmth seeped into her frozen limbs.

"I should have waited for you to come home tonight," she said, her teeth chattering. "Where's Mr. Pickens?"

"Seems he had the sense to stay home in this cold," Ronan said with a laugh.

Clarissa murmured her agreement as she snuggled into Gabriel's embrace. She smiled at Jeremy as he took over helping Billy for a moment.

"What had you so worried that you braved the cold?" Gabriel said into her ear.

"Patrick." She gripped Gabe's arm at his instinctual stiffening. "He sounded deeply troubled in his letter I received today. Here." She pushed away from him and extracted the letter from her pocket, thrusting it at him.

He raised an eyebrow before opening the letter and reading it. He frowned as he read farther, pointing Clarissa to two specific lines in the letter.

I know Gabriel has been wary of me since my visit in October, but I find I need his counsel. Is there any chance he could visit me in Butte?

"Does he really mean this?"

"Yes, he does. He needs you in Butte, Gabriel. Will you go?"

Gabriel met her hopeful gaze and sighed. "Of course I will. No matter what occurred in October, he's still my brother-in-law." He reread part of the letter again. "I think Col should come, too. Whatever Patrick has to tell me, I think Pat needs family."

"Thank you," she whispered, shivering again as he enfolded her into his arms.

***

Gabriel stood with a distant gaze as he looked at the crowds of well-dressed residents walking the streets of Butte. He searched their faces and then closed his eyes. "Dammit," he muttered.

"Are you all right, Gabe?" Colin asked. He stared at the impressive brick buildings lining Main Street, slightly out of breath due to Gabriel's wish to walk partway.

"I keep thinking I'll see them. Hear them call out to me, 'Ah, Gabriel, I've a story to tell ye today about wee Matthew!'" Gabriel whispered, mimicking his long-lost friend Liam Egan. He turned to meet Colin's even stare. "I've never been back here. Never wanted to return."

Colin nodded. "I feel the same way about Boston, but I'm glad you did return because you came to help my brother."

"He better have a damn good reason for making me call forth these ghosts." Gabriel continued the short walk to the Leggat Hotel.

After checking in, they went to their room. Gabriel glanced around it and sighed. "Clarissa said we should stay at the Finlen, but I didn't want to spend the money."

"It's not like you came to Butte for the hotel room," Colin said as he slapped Gabriel on his back. "All we need are two beds."

"Well, that's about all we've got," Gabriel said with a chuckle as he put his bag on the floor next to the lone chair. He moved toward the window and glanced down at the busy street. Colin refrained from speaking, understanding Gabriel was lost to his memories. At the loud rapping on the door, Gabriel stiffened before taking a deep breath to relax.

He turned to watch Colin embrace Patrick and pull him into the room. Patrick was as composed as ever, and Gabriel frowned. "I expected to see you in some sort of distress," he grumbled as he shook hands with him.

Colin stiffened at Gabe's tone, earning a scowl from him.

"You asked me to come, Patrick, and I'm here. What couldn't you write in a letter?"

"I know you're upset with me, Gabriel. I used to think it was unfounded, which only made me angry. I've since learned I was wrong." He paced to the window, his gaze unseeing. "A friend betrayed my confidence. Told Samuel— Henry—about your family. About Rory. Things that she had learned from me."

Colin squinted as he watched his brother. "Not that woman you were interested in?"

"The very one." He turned to face them, leaning against the windowsill. "What I need to know, Gabriel, is how you managed to live in a town with the man who harmed Clarissa and not kill him."

Gabriel went rigid at the mention of Cameron. "What does he have to do with this?" His eyes narrowed. "What's Henry done to your friend?"

Patrick's hands clenched, and his jaw tightened. "He's abused her, weekly, since mid-December." He shared a bleak look with his brother.

Gabriel flushed with anger. "Why?"

"She refused to report any further about my family. She hadn't realized there was any relation between me and Henry and hadn't known she was causing me harm."

Gabriel gripped the back of his nape, massaging it as it tensed. "So instead of feeding that snake more information, she allowed herself to be abused?"

"It makes no sense," Colin whispered with a shake of his head. "Unless she's not the sort of woman you thought she was."

In an instant Colin's back was against a wall with Patrick leaning against him. "Don't you speak against her. You have no idea what she's suffered."

Rather than responding in rage, Colin smiled sadly. "I fear that Gabe's cousin has been successful in making you miserable too, as well as your woman."

Patrick released Colin with a small pat to his shoulder in apology and backed away. He rubbed at his hair, collapsing onto the only chair in the room. "I hate that she's been hurt in such a way. And yet I'm filled with such anger."

Gabriel sighed his understanding, perching on the edge of one of the beds and leaning his elbows on his knees. "That's why you wanted me here. Because you knew I'd gone through something similar with Clarissa."

Patrick nodded, his eyes bleak.

"You're angry at Henry but also at yourself." Gabriel paused, cocking his head to one side. "And at her." At Patrick's reluctant nod, Gabriel sighed. "There is no correct answer. No one way to see yourself through this, Pat."

At Gabriel's pause, Colin spoke up. "Do you still want her after all this?"

Patrick clenched his jaw, but the men's silence coaxed him to speak. "I think I want her more. I wanted her before because she was open and bright, and I saw beauty again when I was with her. I began to draw again." He met Colin's gaze, noting the flash of pain and regret in Colin's eyes.

"And now?" Colin asked.

"Now, now I realize she's strong, as strong as Rissa. There's nothing she won't do to protect those she cares about. Maybe all women have that inner strength, but it's not something women are encouraged to show us." He scrubbed at his face. "But I don't know if I can get past my anger."

"Why are you so mad?" Gabriel asked.

"She wouldn't have had to do any of that if she'd come to me first. Spoken to me. I hate that she didn't trust me."

"You have no idea what fear does. It takes away all rational thought, and all you can consider is the worst that could happen," Gabriel murmured.

Patrick stared bleakly at Gabriel. "Would you have been able to"—he closed his eyes a moment—"been able to accept a child not your own?"

"Goddamn him to hell!" Gabriel roared as he stood and paced to the window. He took a deep breath to calm his roiling emotions. "I despise my cousin. I always will for how he treated me and my brothers when we were children. But I never thought I could hate him with such virulence as I do now for what you describe he's done to this woman."

"She's pregnant?" Colin whispered. "By him?"

Patrick nodded, dropping his head into his hands. "She won't marry me." He chuffed out a humorless laugh. "She can't marry me because she's already married."

"What kind of woman is she?" Gabriel asked, meeting Patrick's irate gaze with one of cold calmness. "I mean no offense. However, as you stated, she's led you on, involved herself with my cousin to the point she's carrying his child, and she's already married to another man?"

"God, Pat, you never did do things by half, did you?" Colin said with a sigh, sitting on the other bed and collapsing backward for a minute as he stared at the ceiling. He shook his head side to side as he contemplated his brother's predicament.

"If I were rational, I would walk away and have nothing more to do with her. But I can't." Patrick pinched the bridge of his nose. "Her first husband, a drunkard, took out a life insurance policy on her and then plotted various ways to kill her in an innocent-looking manner to collect the policy. She fled before he could succeed, and she lives in fear that he'll find her."

"Thus the blackmail," Gabriel growled. "She has to know she can divorce him and all such hold over her is void."

"She was terrified of him finding her. However, I think her association with your cousin has taught her there are worse men in this world. Henry's made her husband seem an amateur when it comes to cruelty."

"What a mess," Gabriel muttered. "I thought Clarissa and I had a complicated beginning, but it's nothing compared to this."

"Why do you still want to be with her, Pat?" Colin asked. "It doesn't make sense to me why you don't look for someone else."

While Patrick sat in silence, Gabriel sighed and said, "To answer one of your questions, the reason why Cameron didn't die at my hand was that I refused to allow him to separate me from Rissa. He'd already done enough damage to our relationship. I vowed not to allow him further influence over it."

"Did you ever forgive him?" Patrick asked.

"Hell, no. Every time she flinches when someone mentions her past, every time I see that distant lost look in her eyes and I know she's been reminded of that sitting room, I want to rip his head off his shoulders." He closed his eyes and clenched his fists a moment before exhaling a deep breath and forcing himself to relax. "But I know she doesn't need my rage or to feel that there's any further need for rancor. She doesn't need to have one moment's worth of doubt about my decision to wed her."

"How do you handle it?" Colin asked, propping himself on his elbows on the bed, studying Gabriel with a mixture of curiosity and fascination.

"By putting her needs first always. Long walks in the woods helped, until Rory's death." His gaze became distant. "Focusing on the future, rather than the past."

"You make it sound simple," Patrick said.

"It's the hardest thing I've ever done or will continue to do. I've come to realize life will never be as I imagined it. But that doesn't mean it's not filled with moments of joy."

Patrick nodded and shared a long look of understanding with Gabriel. "I worry I won't be that person for Fiona."

"If you think you'll mention it in an argument, even once, then don't continue with her. Don't provoke such pain in her or yourself."

**

"What does Gabriel write?" Savannah asked Clarissa as they scurried around her living room in preparation for the meeting to organize the canvassing for the vote in Missoula. "I thought they'd be home by now."

"It seems that Patrick's predicament is much more complicated than we were led to believe. Thus, he and Colin will remain in Butte, for a few more days at least, to try to help him." She shared a long glance with Savannah. "I wish Col had written, but I have a feeling Gabe told him not to. Colin has a way of writing more than he should and informing me of what is truly going on. Gabriel just tells me all is well and that he'll explain when he sees me."

"I'm thankful that Jeremy wasn't asked to travel to Butte."

"I think Gabriel wanted to ask him to join them but knew you'd want him here to complain to after our suffragist meeting today," Clarissa teased. She rose, surveying the room. A small desk stood under the front window, the early afternoon sun limning the maple wood. Rows of chairs faced the desk, awaiting the arrival of the women.

"What if no one comes?" Savannah asked.

"They'll come, if for no other reason than to eat a delicious tea," Clarissa said. "Few can pass up the opportunity to eat Minta's treats." She smiled at Araminta, who entered from the kitchen door to place a plate of cookies on a rear table.

Soon women arrived, and they placed their coats in the office on the opposite side of the front hallway to the living room. By the time the meeting began, all the seats were filled, and Clarissa had dragged in a few more chairs from the library for those who'd arrived late.

Clarissa and Savannah stood toward the front of the room as they discussed their strategy for canvassing for the vote. "Unfortunately Miss Rankin is unable to be here today. Important committee work in Butte prevented her from being here. However, she sent us a letter, detailing what she envisions." Savannah held up a letter from Jeannette Rankin, the state's leader for the cause. Although from Missoula, she hadn't spent much time in the area of late due to her statewide duties.

"We believe it is imperative that we visit each home and discuss with everyone the importance of voting rights for women and for our society as a whole," Clarissa said. Before she could speak further, she was interrupted.

Mrs. Vaughan, attired in a brilliant shade of tangerine, snickered her disapproval. "You weaken the movement by breaking it up and doing it piecemeal. You should have a large rally in each city and town."

"I agree that having rallies and gatherings are a good idea," Savannah said, subtly elbowing Clarissa in the side to remain silent as she inhaled to contradict Mrs. Vaughan. "However, a significant number of families, of women, children and men will always be unable or unwilling to attend such gatherings. We need to visit them in their homes, on their farms and ranches. Everyone needs to understand why we believe in universal suffrage and why we believe that their vote matters. Why the women who live in that household should have a vote and a political voice."

Mrs. Bouchard huffed as she and her sister shook their heads in disagreement. "You waste your time visiting those not in a city. Their numbers aren't important. You should focus where the majority of the people are."

"I don't understand how you can say that, Mrs. Bouchard," Clarissa argued. "Montana has a significant rural population, even with its large cities of Butte and Helena. We need more than to appeal to those living in a city. We want this to be successful statewide, so that all residents will look at what transpired and be proud of what occurred, not resentful of what those in the city forced them to accept."

"I think you intentionally choose this path because you're hopeful this referendum won't pass. You're working as saboteurs," Mrs. Vaughan snapped, vibrating with indignation, her suit puckering as though she were an overripe fruit.

"Rissa," Savannah whispered in warning as Clarissa flushed, clamped her jaw and leaned forward for verbal battle with a woman who'd been her nemesis for years.

"You have it backward, Mrs. Vaughan," Clarissa said. "I've always been for suffrage, since I read my first *Woman's Journal* in 1900. I believe so greatly in this cause I have my young daughters here today." She pointed to Geraldine and Myrtle, sitting on the left side of the room toward the front. "You are the recent convert, seeing as you railed against my modern eastern convictions upon my arrival and every day since. Your presence here today could be construed as suspect, especially since your own daughter is notably absent."

Savannah stepped in front of Clarissa as her rage built. Savannah smiled magnanimously while waving Miss Rankin's letter, now in her hand. "These are the goals set forth by Miss Rankin, and, although they might appear ambitious, I believe they are attainable. However, we want all to feel welcome, doing whatever they can for the movement. If that means speaking to your friends and family, that is wonderful. The more you can do, the better." She stared pointedly at a disgruntled Mrs. Vaughan, who kept her silence.

"One aspect of this crusade troubling our leaders is the issue of raising funds. To place newspaper advertisements, to run our own newspaper, to print pamphlets—it all costs money," Savannah said.

"Why raise women's hopes when it's doomed to fail?" Mrs. Bouchard muttered.

"I refuse to believe we are doomed to fail," Clarissa replied. "I refuse to believe the good men of Montana will not listen with a fair conscience to our arguments and then vote accordingly. *You* have little faith," Clarissa said pointedly to Mrs. Bouchard and her sister. "We have always known that this would be a long crusade, but it doesn't mean it is any less worthwhile." She looked around the room and saw the majority of the women nodding.

"With regard to fund-raising, my brother, the estimable pianist Lucas Russell, has agreed to perform a series of concerts throughout the state and donate all proceeds to our cause. He will be here in the month of June, and his performance in Missoula will be at the Opera House."

The women in the room gasped and clasped their hands together at the news.

A worried-looking young woman raised her hand. "As it will be a fund-raiser, I'm sure the tickets will cost quite a bit of money."

"I will ask him if he will be able to perform a small at-home performance for our members—as long as the fund-raising concert sells a suitable number of tickets," Savannah said.

The women of the room whispered among themselves in excited voices. Savannah and Clarissa shared amused glances.

Clarissa added, "For now, what I would suggest is that you discuss with us and among yourselves what you envision doing for the movement, and enjoy the tea awaiting you. For any of you who would like to read Miss Rankin's letter, it will be here on the desk for you to see," Clarissa said.

The silence lasted only a few seconds before the room was filled with excited female voices. Clarissa and Savannah were separated, speaking with various women about ideas for promoting suffrage. They discussed forming committees on the proper way to canvass, on practicing a prepared speech for the first few times they approached constituents and the joy of planning for victory.

Clarissa shared a glare with Mrs. Vaughan who left after partaking of a plateful of Araminta's delicious food.

"Don't let her bother you, missus," a young woman whispered. "She's a lot of bluster but not much bite there. I think that's what makes her even angrier."

Clarissa laughed and nodded. "I'm sure that's part of it. Tell me. What do you plan on doing for the cause?" She focused on the young woman and nodded her encouragement as she forgot about the Mrs. Vaughans of the world and focused on the woman before her and the future.

***

Gabriel stood in front of the ornate mansion with its covered portico entrance, the black walnut door gleaming from a recent polishing. He studied the carvings thereon, shaking his head at the mythical scenes from ancient Greece and Rome. He rapped on the door, meeting the butler's dour expression with an equally grim one, refusing to be denied entrance. He entered a front hall devoid of warmth or charm, its impersonal, expensive art intending to raise the occupant's sense of social status scattered throughout.

Gabriel followed the butler into a small side room, darkly paneled with mahogany wood. A small bar stood at the far end of the room, near a desk. Heavy burgundy curtains half covered the windows, allowing in only a fraction of the day's bright daylight. A thick oriental carpet covered the floor, silencing the sound of Gabriel's pacing.

"Ah, so the prodigal cousin couldn't keep away," Henry murmured as he strolled into the room. His finely tailored navy suit had precise creases down his pant legs, and his starched collar appeared so stiff as to force his neck upward.

His silent, stealthy movement reminded Gabriel of a cat before striking out at prey.

"Have you come to congratulate me on my impending fatherhood?" Henry asked, his eyes sparkling with devious delight.

"I would never find joy in the fact that any Masterson had the ability to procreate. I would have thought you unable to—due to your natural inclinations."

Gabriel examined his cousin from head to foot. "Although I imagine you were only able to … provoke your interest in a woman … if you were causing her physical harm. I imagine raping Fiona would excite you unnaturally."

Henry sneered at Gabriel. "You're just upset that I took away your brother-in-law's toy. She's a worthless woman. He'll soon find another."

Gabriel clenched his fists as his cousin moved toward the small bar at one side of the room. "Why not simply destroy me or Jeremy?"

"It wouldn't have been nearly as much fun." Henry saluted him with his glass of whiskey. "I'll congratulate myself to a job well done, even if you won't."

"You feed off her fear." Gabriel released his clenched fists, not wanting to give Henry any more reason to gloat.

"She's pathetic. Anyone who allows someone to control her in such a manner is not worth your concern."

"Will you acknowledge your child? Provide funds?" Gabriel frowned as Henry moved behind the desk in the room.

"Why should I? She was willing enough to allow for my … pleasure, meager though it was, as long as I kept my part of the bargain. I can only assume by your visit today that the bargain is null and void."

"You truly are a bastard. You'd leave her destitute, pregnant and at the mercy of a man who plots her murder." At Henry's gleeful smile, Gabriel snapped. He reached across the desk, heaving Henry across it by his lapels. Gabriel slammed his cousin onto the rug and then spun him so Henry was facedown, with Gabe's knee in Henry's lower back.

"You think you're so high and mighty, with your exemplary values. But when it comes down to it, you're a barbarian, no better than the men blasting copper day after day." Henry wheezed out a breath as Gabriel exerted more pressure on his back. "No matter what you do, no matter who you speak with, no law will force me to support that whore. No law will coerce me into giving her or her child my name."

"You'd ruin a child's life?"

"Yes." Henry shifted enough so he could move his head and meet Gabriel's irate gaze. "Because I can. Men like me always end up on top. I can do what I like, and I always will."

"I've wondered, since the day my parents died, what I did to deserve such heartless relations." Gabriel grasped his cousin's head, smashing it into the carpet with a resounding thud before rising. "You may think you've succeeded, Henry, but this is far from over."

Henry sat, his eyes lit with challenge. "I'm hopeful that's true."

***

G abriel stormed toward the Leggat Hotel, nearly plowing down those in front of him in his agitation. When a hand gripped his arm, he spun, ready to fight.

"Whoa, Gabe," Colin said, letting go to hold up his hands. "Come on." He pointed with his head to a nearby bar, and Gabriel followed him inside.

The bar was a dive. Dark, smoke stained, with blackened patches hinting of distant fires on the walls and ceilings, it matched Gabriel's mood. The dim lights enhanced the sense of stepping into a cave.

Gabriel and Colin headed to a table toward the rear where Patrick sat, sipping on a beer.

"I'd try something stronger if I were you," Gabriel muttered as he flopped on-to one of the chairs to Patrick's left. Colin sat to Patrick's right, having picked up two more pints at the bar.

Patrick rubbed at his forehead. "No luck?"

"How could I ever have hoped to have a gentlemen's discussion with the likes of him? No one can give morals to an immoral man. Besides, we've hated each other since we were children. It was a stupid idea." Gabriel rapped his fingers on the tabletop in his agitation.

"He said something that upset you," Colin said, licking away the foam from his lip.

"When doesn't he say things that upset me?" Gabriel sighed. "He intentional-ly abused her, merely because he could. He has no plans to aid her in any way or the child. It brings him joy to have harmed her and to have ruined the child's life."

"What kind of person does that?" Colin asked.

"A very sick man," Gabriel said. "I always thought he was … more interested in men. But I realize now he only cares about causing pain. As long as he could harm your Fiona, he found her attractive."

"What will you do, Pat?" Colin asked, sharing a worried glance with Gabriel as Patrick remained quiet through their discussion.

"I used to see no color in this world. I saw no beauty and was unable to work as an architect. You need to appreciate beauty, to see the soft curves, the importance of light, to envision space." He pinched the bridge of his nose. "When I met Fiona, I again dreamed in color, imagining a time when my life did not consist of row after row of numbers."

"And now?" Gabriel asked.

"Now I only see red. Every shade of it." He shared a long look with Gabriel.

"No matter how you feel, you can't kill him," Gabriel said as Colin nodded. Gabe sat back in his chair and stared at the stained ceiling. "I keep asking myself what Uncle Aidan would do. He'd hire the best lawyer money could buy and free your Fiona from her first husband. And then he'd find someone to protect her."

"Sav has the money for an attorney, and I'm sure she'd be happy to give it to you," Colin said.

When Patrick protested, Gabriel said, "She'd be the first to want to help a woman escape an abusive man. Besides, you need to realize you have family around you again, and we refuse to allow you to suffer when we can help you.

After a long moment, Patrick nodded. "I need to write her a letter."

"We have to return to Missoula tomorrow, so we can deliver it for you," Gabriel said. He speared Patrick with an intense stare. "This is the easy part—hiring the lawyer and freeing Fiona from her murderous husband. It's deciding what you want to do afterward that'll be the true challenge."

CHAPTER TWENTY-EIGHT

Zylphia rushed into the crowded parlor of a mansion on Commonwealth Avenue, rows of chairs filled with women avidly listening to the speaker at the front of the room. Zylphia frowned as she saw all the seats around Parthena and Rowena were occupied, noting their apologetic smiles as Zylphia came to an abrupt halt. She looked around for another seat, smiling as Sophie waved her over.

"About time you arrived," Sophie grumbled. "I've had to be most injudicious with my cane in order to save you this seat."

Zylphia smothered a laugh as she imagined the women who'd had the temerity to approach Sophie and who'd left with a bruised shin. Zylphia sat with a satisfied sigh, her purse held on her lap. "I was painting and forgot the hour."

"You've all but missed the meeting," Sophie murmured. However, she smiled graciously as the women in front of the group nodded toward her and said they thought Mrs. Chickering's idea had the most merit.

After which the group of women relaxed in their seats and talked among themselves. Tea and snacks were made available in a side room, and the crowd slowly dispersed.

"What was that all about?" Zylphia asked.

"A measure will be on next year's ballot, asking the men of Massachusetts to grant suffrage to women."

"Finally," Zylphia breathed.

"There is concern the result will be as dismal as 1895, and we refuse to be thwarted this time."

"Excellent. I'm sure you have a wonderful plan." She smiled at Parthena and Rowena who joined them, pulling now-empty chairs from a nearby row to sit with them.

"Will you do it?" Parthena asked Zee.

"What do I have to do with anything?" Zylphia asked, confused.

"You are essential, dear girl, to my proposition," Sophie said. "We must learn the tactics of successful states seeking the vote. I'm certain, with women such as your cousins petitioning for the vote, that there will be success in Montana this November."

"You want me to travel to Montana?" Zylphia asked.

"Yes. You're the only one here with family there. It makes the most sense." She watched Zylphia with wry humor in her eyes. "Besides, I believe a change of scenery could be what you need."

"You don't want me here?" Zylphia whispered.

"Come now. None of that nonsense," Sophie said, her voice tinged with impatience. "I thought you'd rather travel there than the other states where the question is on the ballot."

Zylphia ticked them off in her mind: Nevada, Nebraska, Ohio, Missouri, and North and South Dakota. She nodded at Sophie.

"You've often spoken of your desire to do more for the movement, and this is your chance."

"Of course I'd prefer to be with my family in Montana," Zylphia said, "and if I can help earn us the vote, too ..." Her voice trailed away.

"It won't be as difficult for you, Zee. You'll be able to travel around with women who are already accepted among the suffragists and the townsfolk there," Rowena said.

Sophronia watched Zylphia with a knowing glint in her eye. "Excellent. All you must do is convince your father. And be in Montana by the first part of June, I should think."

"That's barely two months away."

"As you have nothing keeping you here, it should pose no difficulties for you," Sophie said, leaning forward to heave upright.

"I don't know if I can leave so suddenly," Zylphia sputtered.

"It will only benefit the men of this town to realize you are a woman of purpose and that you and your beliefs should not be trifled with."

Zylphia nodded absently at Sophie's edict.

"Besides, I've been informed that Mr. Hubbard has become a bit brazen, and I should think you'd relish a reprieve from his company."

Zylphia met Sophie's knowing gaze and acquiesced with a long sigh. Zylphia, Parthena and Rowena walked together with Sophie and paused as a group of women approached them. "Aren't you excited, Miss McLeod?" one of them gushed.

"I heard you might even have the opportunity to meet Dr. Shaw herself," another enthused.

Zylphia stiffened as Sophie gave her shin a nudge with her cane. "Of course, I'm quite pleased about my upcoming travels and any opportunity I might have to meet those in leadership of our movement."

The women bustled past them, leaving Zylphia with her friends. "Well spoken, Zee," Parthena said.

"None of them would know you'd rather meet Alice than Anna," Sophie said, with a small cackle of laughter. "Seeing as this group is aligned with NAWSA, best not to ruffle their feathers." Sophie turned to Parthena and Rowena. "You two should prepare yourself for some sort of work this summer. However, I realize your families aren't as progressive as Zee's, and I wouldn't want to hasten any unfortunate events." She *harrumph*ed as she turned to walk down the front stairs to her waiting automobile.

***

"I don't understand why you insist on bothering me here," Zylphia snapped. She flopped onto one of the tufted red velvet chairs in her studio and glared at her mother.

Delia sighed as she wandered toward the front windows, glancing at the discordant colors and shapes in Zylphia's most recent paintings. "These are different." She traced a line down one side of a cube meant to be an eye and frowned. "Why?"

"It's art, Mother. It's not always meant to be beautiful."

"Why waste your talent on something so … mediocre?" She watched as Zylphia flinched at her criticism. "They're not nearly as good as your other work. Something I'm sure you realize, as you are honest with yourself about your art."

Zylphia covered her face a moment before lowering her hands. "I simply haven't discovered what will make them … make them …"

"You can't even determine what you want them to be. They'll never be beautiful. They'll never cause someone to stop what they're doing and lose all sense of themselves staring at your painting. Not like your other work." Delia turned from the newest paintings and studied Zylphia, her frown deepening. "Zylphia, you must see it yourself too. How your inherent vitality has dimmed. Your eyes that used to sparkle with merriment or mischief are dulled and filled with disillusionment. What's bothering you, dearest?"

Zylphia shook her head as she battled tears. "Sophie wants me to go to Montana. Learn from Sav and Rissa how to successfully wage a battle for the vote."

"Why should that upset you?" Delia moved toward the matching chair near Zylphia and reached out a hand to stroke her arm.

"I feel as though she's banishing me. It's irrational, I know."

"You feel safe and secure here, in this home, when you've had little security in your life," Delia murmured.

Zee nodded, exhaling a loud sigh. "It's childish, but I have this irrational fear that, if I leave you and Father behind now, something will happen, and everything will be different when I come home."

"Or that your father or I won't be here," Delia whispered.

Zylphia lost her battle with tears as they trickled out, forming silver tracks down her cheeks. "It's stupid."

Delia moved closer, kneeling on the floor by her daughter and pulling her into her arms. "It's not, my dearest, beloved daughter." She ran a hand over Zylphia's disheveled hair. "Is it because you don't want to leave someone else here, too?"

Zylphia closed her eyes for a moment. "It doesn't matter. I'm not what any man here would want. Should want. In the end I'd only be a disappointment."

"What utter nonsense," Delia hissed. "I knew I should never have agreed to your desire to enter society. There was little to gain and much to lose, as I feared."

"I know what I am, Mother."

"And what is that?" Delia demanded, anger lighting her eyes at Zylphia's resigned tone. "A brave woman, willing to fight for others' rights and her own? A brilliant artist?" Delia's jaw firmed with her ire. "I hope you know better than to limit your sense of self due to your youth spent at the orphanage."

"It has repercussions, Mother. I'm not like the other women I meet."

"No, you aren't, thank God." Delia smiled as she swiped a hand down the side of her daughter's cheek and rested it on her shoulder. "Zylphia, I can't promise you nothing will happen to your father or to me—or any other person. That this house will always be here. Life is precarious. Which is why it is precious. Yet I can promise that you'll never be without those who love and cherish you."

Zylphia leaned forward, hugging her mother. "I know." She leaned away. "I want to be of some use for the movement, but I hate the thought of leaving right now."

"There's never a good time for leave-taking, Zee." She squeezed Zylphia's hand before she gave a small groan as she rose. "I'm getting too old to kneel on floors."

Zylphia chuckled and gripped her mother's hand for a moment. "Thank you, Mother."

Delia gently squeezed hers and left, closing the door softly behind her as Zylphia remained lost in thought.

***

Aidan sat in his comfortable chair in the family parlor, reading the newspaper, a low fire burning in the grate. Delia grumbled over paperwork from the orphanage at her desk, and Zylphia lay curled on a settee, a book held in her hands for show, staring into space. Every few lines of the paper he read, Aidan would glance toward his daughter, frowning more fiercely as he noted her mood.

"Your mother tells me that you're to travel to Montana to aid in canvassing for the vote," he said, setting aside the paper and the disturbing news about the Saint Martin in the Fields church bombing the day before in London—with British suffragettes the main suspects. He pointed at the paper even though she was unable to see the article. "I hope you'll continue to focus on nonviolent ways to achieve your goals."

Zylphia rolled her eyes at her father. "How many times must I tell you that I don't condone violence?" Then she smiled at her father. "Would you mind if I traveled to Montana soon?"

"Of course I'll mind. I hate it when you are away from home. However, I think it will be good for you and important for you to feel a more active participant in the movement you espouse." He shared a look with Delia. "Will Mr. Hubbard miss you?"

"I doubt it. He's not truly interested in me but you. I wish men could court each other and leave us poor women alone," Zylphia grumbled, provoking a startled gasp from Delia and a snicker from Aidan.

"I wouldn't say that outside this room," Aidan said as he controlled his mirth. "Although I understand your sentiment. I imagine women tire of feeling like pawns in men's games."

Zylphia grunted her agreement. "It would solve a lot of problems." She shared a smile with her father.

"Not all men are as bad as you make them out to be," Aidan murmured. He studied her as her gaze became distant again. "And not all men are what they appear."

Zylphia nodded absently and curled up further into herself on the settee.

CHAPTER TWENTY-NINE

Teddy sat in his third-floor study at the back of his parents' large house. A fire warmed the room and lent a gentle glow. One lamp was lit, next to his leather chair, and he stretched out his legs to rest his stockinged feet on the matching ottoman. His mother was at a function, while his father remained in New York City. Teddy studied the financial section of the newspaper, jotting down notes for investments for the following day. He heard a commotion two floors down, then silence.

After a few moments, he focused on the newspaper again, idly raising a glass of whiskey for a sip. He stiffened as he heard the doors on the hall open and shut, and turned toward his study door as it slammed open.

Zylphia stood there, panting and vibrating with fury, her ice-blue wool coat covered in a light sheen of moisture from the early April evening mist.

Teddy rose, waiving away the butler who reached forward to extract Zylphia from his master's private sanctuary. "Leave us," he commanded the butler, who nodded and shut the door with a loud *click*. "Zee?" He walked toward her. "Are you all right? Has something happened?"

"How could you, Teddy?" Zylphia asked as she slapped him across his cheek.

His head reared to one side, and he stumbled back a step, bumping into the ottoman.

She advanced on him, ready to pounce. "How could you?"

He narrowed his eyes at her shrieklike wail. "I don't know of what you accuse me, Zee. Please calm down and explain why you've barged into my private study and attacked me."

"Don't act innocent. Don't act as though you didn't enjoy gossiping with your friends about poor, pathetic Zylphia. Raised among the gutter scum in the orphanage." She pounded on his chest with her fists, her hair falling from its pins with her erratic movement. "I trusted you!"

He gripped her hands, only releasing them when she struggled with such ferocity he feared she'd harm herself.

She collapsed to the ground, silent sobs heaving forth, her shoulders shaking. She bent over herself, her face burrowed into her knees.

He knelt beside her and ran a featherlight caress over her head, shoulders and back. "I never betrayed you." His whispered avowal failed to penetrate her sorrow as she sobbed.

He settled beside her, groaning slightly as he maneuvered her to settle between his legs. Rather than the expected fight and show of bravado, she curled into him, sobbing into his neck.

"What did they say, my darling girl?" He kissed the top of her head, her eyebrow and her temple, while running a soothing hand over her shoulder and back.

She rubbed her face into his shirt, soaking it with her tears. After a few minutes she calmed and spoke in a halting voice. "A few of the men learned I'd spent my youth in the orphanage. How it wasn't until later my father returned, when I changed my name from Maidstone to McLeod. They intimated I was like my mother, eager to trap a wealthy man any way I could." Her voice faltered. "They said any father as wealthy as mine who refused to provide a dowry was either ashamed or not my real father."

He groaned. "You know that's not true, Zee. You know your father's proud of all you do." He stroked a hand over her head, kissing it, imparting all possible comfort.

She shivered in his arms as the aftereffects of crying and rage faded.

When a few minutes had passed, and she grew calmer, he whispered, "What did they do to you?"

She shook her head, rubbing her cheeks against his shirt, her breaths coming out in stuttering exhalations. "They cornered me, propelled me into a back room." She tilted her head to meet his horrified gaze. "I was terrified. I didn't know what to do."

"What happened?" His voice emerged as an angry hiss.

"I kneed one of them and stomped on another's foot, as my cousin Richard taught me." She flushed as his eyes shone with pride.

"What did they call you?" He pushed her away enough so he could meet her gaze and rub her forehead and cheek with his thumb.

She turned her face into his palm and kissed it. "The daughter of a who—" She closed her eyes, shaking her head. "I can't say that word in any relation to my mother. It's not true! She's a good woman."

"You're right. It's not true. They're just men being cruel." He pulled her more tightly against him.

"They said it was my nature, and I shouldn't fight it. That I was a fraud, dressed in fine materials when I should be on their elbows in Scollay Square, passed from one to the other." She shivered. "How did they know?" Zylphia asked, shuddering a few more times against him.

"Not from me. I imagine one of them discovered a small kernel of your true story, and they extrapolated from there. Your reaction would only have been a confirmation for them."

"I don't know how to play by those rules. How to act as though I were emotionless with ice coursing through my veins." She rubbed her face once more against his shirt, sighing with relief and pleasure. She turned up her face, kissing the underside of his chin, evoking a quiver from him.

"Thank God you don't. That's not who you are or the woman I want." He kissed below her ear, earning a different sort of shudder.

"Teddy," she whispered.

"Was Owen one of the men?" he asked, his warm breath on her neck eliciting another tremor.

"Yes. Except for Owen, they were men I didn't know but were good friends of his. Owen took tremendous pleasure in causing me pain." She arched back to meet his gaze. "Why? I thought he was my friend."

"His father and your father recently had a disagreement about business. It cost Owen and his father quite a bit of money and embarrassed Owen, while earning your father a tidy fortune." He sighed. "I'm afraid the knowledge of you not having a dowry wasn't as much of a secret as you'd hoped. Owen found out, and I'd heard him complaining to friends in one of the gentlemen rooms at a recent function." He stroked a hand over her riotous hair before easing her away.

"Let's get you comfortable," he murmured. He caressed her shoulder for a minute before slipping his hand under the collar of her coat. He eased it off her shoulders, leaving it pooled around them on the floor. He watched her with a fierce intensity for any sign of resistance, but she smiled as she was freed from her outerwear and moved to be closer to him again.

"Why should he want to hurt me for it?" Zylphia quivered for a moment as she adjusted to the room temperature without her coat.

"To hurt you is to hurt your father. No matter what his friends said or he intimated, he knows how much your father loves you." Teddy tugged her back into his arms. He sighed with contentment as she curled into him. He stifled a moan when she kissed the underside of his jaw.

"Zee"—he kissed the side of her neck—"tell me to stop if I'm offending you." When she pressed closer and ran her hands over his back, he clasped her even more tightly to him. "I'm afraid Owen desired your father's influence and dowry. After the business actions of this week, he must have realized he'd have neither and lashed out."

"I never thought he'd act in such a way," Zylphia said on a sigh as she tilted her head to one side, allowing Teddy to kiss under her ear.

"For some, money and social prestige are of the utmost concern." He kissed her again along her neck, moving toward her collarbone.

"What is your priority?"

"Pleasing you." Teddy raised passion-filled eyes to her and brushed her hair away from her face. "Tell me what you want, love."

"To be with you," she whispered, leaning forward to kiss him softly, groaning in frustration when he eased away from her. She sighed with relief as he deftly unbuttoned the back of her dress. It gaped open, and he pushed it down her arms to her waist. He raised a large hand to cup her cheek. "Trust me?"

"Yes." Zylphia's breath hitched as he brushed his hand over her chest.

He kissed her, each subsequent kiss deeper than the previous. All the while he worked on the ties to her corset, easing it away as they kissed. He raised a palm, cupping her breast covered in light linen, and she gasped with pleasure. "Let me," he pleaded, lowering his head. He paused, waiting for her acquiescence. "Zee?" He looked up at her through his eyelashes, to see her head thrown back, a look of unbridled pleasure on her face.

She then focused on him, ran a hand over his face, tracing his lips. "Please," she whispered.

He groaned, moving forward to suckle and kiss her. She arched back and felt like she was falling, but, rather than tumble to the ground like she had the day she'd visited his private art gallery, Teddy eased her to the carpet, all the while kissing and caressing her.

He pushed aside her dress and corset, leaving her bared to his gaze. "Tell me that you don't want me. Tell me to stop," he said, bending forward to kiss her collarbone.

"Teddy," she moaned, curving up to meet his caresses. "Please. Don't stop."

He shucked his shirt, lowering his naked torso to hers, rubbing against her. "You know what this means."

"Yes. That I'm more like my mother than I thought." Zylphia ran her hands over his bare back, growling in frustration when she reached his pants. "Please, Teddy."

"We can never turn back from this, Zee," he whispered as he kissed her under her ear. He lifted up, shucking his pants. He moved over her, grasping her face between his palms, kissing her deeply. He swallowed her whimper of pain, then her cry of pleasure, gifting her with his gasps of ecstasy as he lost himself in the pleasure of being with her.

***

Teddy lay on his back with Zylphia curled in his arms. She stirred, and he held her more tightly to him. "No, love. There's no need for you to leave yet." He kissed the top of her forehead, unable to hide a contented smile.

She relaxed into his hold, her breathing deepening as though she were falling asleep. "Teddy?"

Her muffled exhalation tickled the hair on his chest. "Hmm?" He traced a lazy pattern on her shoulder, tangling his fingers in her long hair. When she didn't speak again, he continued to caress her back and hip. She groaned as she moved, and he winced. "I'm sorry I hurt you, love. I hope you know I'd never intentionally cause you pain." He kissed her head again. "It won't hurt like that again."

Zylphia reared up, nearly knocking her head into his. "I have to leave. I can't be found here like this. What would your parents think?"

Teddy sat up, stroking the silky skin of her shoulders to soothe her. "Zee, no one comes in here. This is my private study on the floor only I live on." He kissed her shoulder. "My mother would be shocked, but I'll talk her round."

"What do you mean?"

He gazed into Zylphia's luminous eyes. "My mother has always imagined I'd marry a daughter of a duke or some such nonsense. It will take a little effort to convince her that she must set aside those dreams and accept mine."

Zylphia lowered her eyes, becoming increasingly tense as he spoke. "I don't wish to come between you and your parents."

He huffed out a laugh at her whispered words. "You couldn't."

Zylphia sighed, her shoulders remaining rigid. She glanced around the room, her eyes widening with momentary pleasure as she saw the painting she'd given him. "I didn't think you'd kept it."

"Of course I kept it. I treasure it. As I treasure every memory I have of our time together."

Zylphia rocked back, distancing herself farther from him. She grasped her chemise and held it against her chest. "I know this was rash, and I should never have come. I'm sorry if I've given you the wrong impression about me. That I've proved your friends correct about my origins."

"Anyone who slanders you is no friend of mine," he growled. "Zee, what happened here between us was inevitable. It's been coming since the day I found you injured on the cliff walk last July."

"I don't believe that. I can't believe that." Her bright blue eyes shone even brighter as her skin paled. She pulled her hair forward, covering her chest with her disheveled locks.

"Why?" His soft voice, meant to soothe, inflamed her anxiety.

"Because I have free will. The ability to choose my destiny, and what I will and won't do."

He grinned at her, reaching forward to trace her furrowed eyebrow. "Of course you do. You executed it this evening when you pleaded with me to make love with you." He leaned forward, kissing her on her lips. He backed away with a confused frown when she failed to respond to his touch.

"I was overwhelmed with what was being said about me. About what I truly felt." She scooted away from Teddy, away from his soothing caresses.

"Are you saying you don't envision a future together?"

"You know I've never seen myself as a wife. A mother."

"Because you've never allowed yourself to imagine what could be. You're too focused on the hurts from your past to be able to look forward."

"I refuse to allow anyone to control what I want or do." Zylphia searched for her clothes, tugging her dress to her lap, blushing when she saw a singed stocking peeking out from the edge of the fireplace.

"You think so little of me that you believe I'd want to control you?" Teddy hissed, reaching for his pants and slipping them on. He rose, buttoning them deftly, staring down at her, covered in her heap of clothing.

She stood, holding her disheveled evening dress before her, shivering now that the fire had burned low and she was no longer in the warmth of his embrace. "It's always about what you want me to be. What you need me to be. What about what I want? What I need? Have you ever considered that?" She stomped her foot in agitation.

His irate countenance softened. "Here's what I know, Zylphia McLeod. You love to paint. You paint with an unbridled passion, as though you can't hold in what you are compelled to express. You are fiercely loyal to those you love, although you're reluctant to allow anyone to show you the love and loyalty you so freely give. You fight against injustice. You believe women have the same rights as men. And you are terrified of ever depending on another."

Zylphia's eyes filled with insistent tears. "That's not fair," she whispered.

"I love you, Zee. The woman strong enough to forgive her father for inadvertently abandoning her to be raised in an orphanage for more than half of her life. The woman passionate enough to withstand mistreatment from a drunken crowd in Washington, DC, as you proclaimed your beliefs. The woman brave enough to enter the vicious circle of polite society."

She looked away, hugging her clothes tighter to her chest. She took a deep breath, as though forestalling a sob.

"I'd never want you to be anything other than who you are, Zee." He reached forward to run a hand over her head, cringing when she recoiled from his touch. "I'd never want you to change for me."

She raised defiant, panicked eyes to his. He stepped forward, as though seeing her true emotions, but she remained guarded, her impenetrable wall around her. "I ca—don't love you, Teddy. I only wanted to know what all the fuss was about. It seemed as good a time as any other to find out."

He blanched, his hands fisted at his side. "I don't believe you."

"Then all your claims of knowing me were for naught. I don't love you." Her voice cracked. "I'll never love you. How could you ever believe I'd be content with a man who spends all his time tinkering away on meaningless projects, hidden away in a lab?" Her voice strengthened the more she spoke, and the determined defiance in her eyes masked her true emotions.

***

Teddy nodded, and nodded so many times he feared he would never stop. He turned away from her, placing a hand on the fireplace mantel, gripping it so tightly he thought he'd be able to tear off a piece of the marble. He heard the rustling of cloth, the silent mutterings and groans as she dressed herself without the aid of a maid.

He turned to watch her struggle with her long evening dress, unable to button up the back by herself. "Come here, Zee," he murmured. At her wary expression, he rasped, "I won't do anything more than button you up. You've made it abundantly clear I've been nothing more than an experiment to you over the past months."

He attempted to fasten the buttons without touching her but failed numerous times. Each time she shivered or gasped as his fingers brushed against her bare skin. "I, of all people, should have known you would never see me as anything more." He gripped her shoulders, kissing the back of her nape before turning her to face him. "No matter how you feel about me, or this evening, I will always be thankful you called." He sighed against her forehead, before releasing her.

Zylphia paled. "Teddy, you can't believe we will ever be any more to each other." She pointed around the room, at the chairs pushed away, the cushions on the ground that they'd rested on after their bout of passion. "This is all we'll ever have."

"How do I know you aren't speaking rashly, like you often do? That you aren't just lashing out, intending to cause pain, because you're afraid of what you feel?" He gripped her arms for a moment before trailing his hands down to hers, clasping them, lifting them to hold them in front of his heart. "Tell me plainly, so there is never any doubt. Will you marry me, Zylphia? Now or ten years from now? Will you be my wife?"

"No. No, I will not. I refuse you, Theodore Goff. Now and forever."

His eyes went dull, as though experiencing a soul-shattering grief, and he squeezed her hands once before releasing them. "Then good-bye, Miss McLeod. I wish you well. My butler will ensure that a car sees you home."

"Teddy—"

He held a hand up to her lips, silencing her. "There is no more to say. And I think from now on, should we meet, as distant acquaintances, I should always be Mr. Goff to you. For you will always be Miss McLeod to me. I'd never want to be perceived as impertinent in my attentions to you."

He bowed formally and moved toward the door, opening it for her. He dug his fingers into his pant leg when he heard her sniffle. He refused to watch her walk away from him forever, so he abruptly closed the door on her retreating form.

He collapsed onto the leather chair he'd occupied hours before and stared into the dying embers of the fire. Idly stroking a hand over his heart, he knew no elixir existed for this ache.

CHAPTER THIRTY

A gentle fire roared in the fireplace, and Zylphia flinched as the pieces of coal collapsed onto each other, sending sparks flying up the chute. Lights on low side tables were lit, although the overhead lights in the family parlor were off, giving the room a soft, intimate glow. Rich burgundy wallpaper lined the walls, with silver sconces on the walls. To one side of the room, two chairs surrounded a small table set with an unfinished game of chess atop.

"What's got you riled?" Delia asked as she passed Zylphia a cup of tea after dinner.

"Problems with one of your suitors?" Aidan asked with a wink to Delia. He sobered when he saw Zylphia flinch again. "I heard you attracted quite a bit of attention last night. I'm glad you are taking to society as you wished."

Zylphia paled, her teacup rattling on its saucer before she set it down. "I fear your informant was misinformed."

Delia leaned forward and patted Zylphia on the knee. "I was there last night, Zee. I saw the number of attentive men wanting to speak with you."

"Did you see the last bit? Where I had to knee one in the"—she waved her hand around rather than speak the word—"and stomp on another's foot?"

"Of course not. I heard laughter, as I always hear when you are about. You bring joy wherever you go."

"Mother, they were laughing at me, not with me." Zylphia blinked away tears. At her father's nod to tell him what had transpired, Zylphia spoke. "They found out I'd been raised in an orphanage. They realized I wasn't reunited with you, Father, until I was much older."

"And thus believed that you are a young woman of loose morals and it was acceptable to abuse you?" Aidan's eyes flashed.

Zylphia flushed, images of the evening before with Teddy flashing before her. "Yes." She took a deep breath and met her father's gaze. "They learned I'm not to have a dowry and extrapolated from that how you are ashamed of me. Or that I'm not truly your daughter."

Aidan shook his head and stood, his expression wild. "Idiots. If they had a modicum of the intelligence they are credited with, they'd realize I refuse to have happen to you what happened to Savannah." He began to pace, his agitation evident.

"Enough scandal has occurred in the past ten years that Sav's barely whispered about now," Zylphia said. "Instead they believe that you've been duped into believing I'm your daughter. Some even expressed their sympathy for you."

Aidan's eyes glowed with a fierce love as he stopped before his daughter. "Tell me who said such things, and I will destroy them. They have no right to disparage you or to make you doubt, for one second …"

Zylphia rushed to reassure him. "I didn't, Father. I was angry and frightened but never doubtful. As a loyal friend said to me recently, I only need look in a mirror to know I'm your daughter."

"I do not want you to doubt my love for you, Zee," Aidan said, kneeling beside her. "If my not dowering you until after you're married is proving a problem, please tell me. I believed it would keep you safe from the fortune hunters."

Zylphia sniffled at the boundless love she saw in her father's eyes. "As I have no immediate desire to marry, it also aids in determining who is interested in me rather than forming an alliance with you."

Aidan nodded his agreement and smiled as he ran a hand over her head before he frowned. "You didn't come home immediately after last night's gathering." He raised an eyebrow.

"I thought I'd been betrayed by a friend. I confronted him, only belatedly realizing he never betrayed me." Zylphia looked down at her shaking hands. The realization that Teddy was no longer her friend was only beginning to register.

"Would this be Theodore Goff?" Delia shared a worried glance with Aidan.

"Yes. I'd told him of my past a few months ago, and I thought he'd told his friends. But he hadn't."

Aidan let out a sigh of frustration, rising to take his seat again. "Why are you so devastated, Zee? Those men are obviously buffoons and beneath your consideration. I wouldn't waste one moment's worth of worry over them."

Zylphia rose, wandering to the fireplace. "If you can believe it, Mr. Goff asked me to marry him last night."

"Oh, Zee," Delia murmured. She shared a long glance with Aidan when Zylphia remained silent, staring at the flames.

"And? How did you answer the man?" Aidan demanded.

"How would you expect? I don't want to marry. At least not yet. I want to dedicate myself to the movement, not be tied down to a husband or babies." Zylphia's voice shattered as though fighting a sob. "Besides, could you see me married to him?"

Aidan took a deep breath, and Delia clasped his hand. He gave it a quick pat before strumming his fingers on his knee. "What more could you want than a man dedicated to you and family? A man who's intelligent and isn't afraid of the fact you're equally as intelligent? A man who isn't threatened by your brilliance as an artist? A man who's only ever had eyes for you since he saw you? What more could you want?"

"He's dull. All he does all day is tinker with his experiments and read! He doesn't like to go out, dance ..."

"You think a man interested in the likes of Scollay Square will make you a better husband?"

"Father, please." Zylphia swiped at her cheeks, her grip on the fireplace mantle tightening. Her mind flashed back to Teddy the night before doing just this, and she shook her head, freeing herself of the memory.

Aidan rose and strode toward her. He gripped her shoulders and turned her to face him, taking her chin between his fingers so she had to meet his gaze. "Being afraid of love, of losing that love, doesn't mean you don't feel it. You never know when you'll be fortunate enough to find love, Zee. If you turn away from it out of fear of disappointment or of what might come, you lose out on the absolute joy to be experienced today. For today is all that matters and all that we've been promised."

"I don't want him to realize those men were right or to disappoint his parents in his choice of me," Zylphia whispered, as the tears flowed. She looked toward her mother as her mother choked back a sob. "And for him to regret his choice but be unable to undo it because he's married me."

"You have to trust him, Zylphia," her father said. "Trust that he knows his mind and heart. Just as he will have to learn to trust you after this disappointment. I imagine your refusal devastated him."

"I'm not sure I love him," Zylphia whispered, brushing away a tear.

"Imagine your life without him in it. Never speaking with him again. How do you feel?"

Tears coursed down her cheeks. "Like I can't breathe."

Aidan's expression softened as he pulled her into his arms for a gentle embrace. "When you envision the friend you want to discuss your day with, who is it?"

"Teddy." Her voice emerged as a croak.

"Then there's your answer. You can run from it all you want, Zee. But you already know the truth." Aidan held her as she sobbed in his arms.

"I hope you were kind in your refusal so that there is some hope for you, when you meet him again," Delia murmured.

"I don't know what to do." Zylphia pushed away from her father, rubbing at her cheeks. "I was cruel last night. I spoke to intentionally hurt him."

"Then you must make him understand that you feel differently now. Or rather that you are now willing to acknowledge how you truly feel." Delia held out her hand to Zylphia, who walked toward her. She sat next to her mother and burrowed into her mother's shoulder.

"The next time you see him, ensure he understands how you feel. I'm certain he will forgive you." Aidan watched his wife and daughter on the settee, a warm glow in his eyes. "I don't know how any man could deny either of you."

***

Zylphia sat in Sophronia's front sitting room, decorated in shades of pale blue verging on gray. She drummed her fingers on the satin settee, its aquamarine color almost a match for Sophie's eyes and clashing with the more somber tone of the room. She faced the door when she heard the approach of Sophie's cane.

"*Hmph*," Sophie grumbled as she entered the room. "I knew I shouldn't take my daughter's advice and use her decorator. He made this room look like a mortuary."

"Clarissa always told me how soothing this room was to her."

"Yes, when it was a nice bright yellow. Now it's a mixed-up medley of blues and grays, and it's always darker than it should be even during the brightest part of the day." She collapsed onto her chair, keeping a firm hand on her walking stick. "But what's done is done. No use throwing good money at something as ridiculous as furnishings."

"You should be comfortable, Sophie."

"If you think, for one moment, I'm not comfortable in my lovely little mansion on the Hill, you are quite mistaken." She cackled. "I'm fine. Stop fretting over me." She stared pointedly at Zylphia. "Now I'd like to believe you're in a lather over the recent developments with regard to the cause. The news I've received from Washington and Alice are quite disturbing. I had hoped that President Wilson was a more progressive man. However, I fear it will be some time before he voices his support for universal suffrage."

"I'm surprised you've succeeded in hiding your correspondence with Alice from the leaders of NAWSA." Zylphia raised an amused eyebrow.

"I may not inform my colleagues, Carrie or Anna, that I remain on friendly terms with Alice, but I refuse to alienate a woman determined to earn the vote for women. She may be considered radical and unconventional, but I'm hopeful she will prod those unwilling to act from their inertia."

"I would think you'd favor more conventional tactics."

"Conventional tactics have produced limited results. They've obtained us the vote in nine states. Alice's dream of a constitutional amendment may seem radical, but I believe it is the only way to ensure all women have access to full enfranchisement." She frowned. "I refuse to go to my grave, like Elizabeth and

Susan, clinging to the dream of casting a vote. I demand that I'm allowed to vote before you throw dirt on my casket!"

Zylphia frowned at the mention of Sophie in a casket. "I fear this will take longer than we had envisioned after the triumph of last year's march."

"If you call *triumph* being mauled and harassed by a horde of drunken men with little police oversight and a congressional unwillingness to find wrongdoing, then you are truly an optimist." Sophie gripped the handle of her cane. "We need to ensure that men see the value of women voting. That they see the advantage of women possessing the full rights of citizenship. I fear that the actions of Alice's group, with her banner-waving and chalk-writing on boardwalks will only alienate men. They'll see us as no better than hooligans. But I'm afraid I don't know what else to do to raise awareness of our cause."

"If we are respectful and law-abiding, I don't see as they can turn against us." Zylphia took a sip of water.

"Oh, you'd be surprised what they'll do to ensure we don't succeed. What they'll say. They've already bandied about that the young suffragists are a horde of free-willed women with loose morals."

Zylphia blushed involuntarily, earning an intense stare from Sophie. "I'm sure that's an exaggeration. The women who are part of this movement are upstanding members of society."

"Quite a few espouse the notions from the Village in New York City. It's rumored they live in communes." Sophie raised her eyebrows, and her eyes twinkled with mischief.

"Sophie! I can't believe you listen to such gossip." Zylphia fanned herself as she flushed.

"Well, I'm afraid it's more than gossip. And, from what I've experienced, what begins in New York City tends to spread."

"You make it sound like the plague."

Sophie cackled. "Whether I like it or not—and I truthfully couldn't imagine a granddaughter of mine espousing such a life, even though I like to think of myself as a free-thinking woman—the world is changing." She stared pointedly at Zylphia. "And you need to embrace it. Not continually fight against it. You'll only become disillusioned and bitter, and I can't imagine my Clarissa's cousin in such a state."

Zylphia dropped her head in her hands, tears running down her cheeks.

"Zylphia? I meant to challenge you, not cause you such distress." Sophie heaved herself to her feet and moved to sit next to Zylphia on the settee.

"Forgive me. I don't know why I'm crying." She swiped at her cheeks, smiling her thanks as she accepted a handkerchief from Sophie.

"Has that Goff boy upset you?" Sophie's mouth turned down in disgust. "I thought him more sensible than that."

"He did, yes, but it is my own stupidity that's brought me such grief." She took a calming breath, raising confused eyes to Sophie. "I fear I've ruined everything. Forever."

"Said like the young. Always so dramatic." She tapped Zylphia's hand, either in encouragement or impatience. "Tell me what happened."

"After I was insulted at a gathering last week, I went to Teddy's to confront him. I thought he'd told his friends about my past, even though he'd promised he wouldn't. He assured me he didn't, and then, after a while, he asked me to marry him."

"I'm assuming something momentous happened during the *after a while* portion of the evening," Sophie said drily. At Zylphia's blush, Sophie *harrumph*ed and nodded her encouragement for Zylphia to continue.

"He thought it meant we'd marry."

"Why should you be upset he'd think that? I'd think you'd be disturbed if he didn't feel that way."

Zylphia shook her head, tears falling.

"You're not making any sense, darling girl."

"I know. He told me how he wanted us to be together, and all I felt was panic. Panic that my life was no longer my own. Panic that he'd now control me in some way."

Sophronia stroked a hand over Zylphia's hair, soothing her. "I'd feel more panic if he bedded you and pushed you out the door, with no thought to your future or your happiness." She smiled ruefully. "Which goes to show I'm an old-fashioned woman at heart, no matter how much I like to consider myself a radical."

Zylphia whispered, "I hurt him, Sophie. Intentionally. I told him that I would never want to marry him. That I'd never love him. How he was boring and a fool to believe I'd ever consider him worthy of marrying me."

"Oh, Zee," Sophie breathed, paling. "I've never met a young woman with such a rash tongue."

"I know. He even attempted to determine if it was my fear speaking or what I truly felt, and I lashed out even more. I felt cornered, and I was terrified."

Sophie gripped her hand. "Did he in any way force you to intimacy?"

"No!" Zylphia rushed beet red. "No. I knew it wasn't proper, but I acted in such a manner, regardless of propriety. It was"—her gaze became distant as she remembered soft caresses, gentle murmurs and an overwhelming passion from that evening—"wonderful."

"Good," Sophie said with a resolute tap to Zylphia's hand. "That's as it should be."

Zylphia took a deep breath as a pair of tears tracked down her cheeks. "He asked me to marry him. Now or ten years from now. He said he'd wait for me."

"He sounds like a man who cares deeply for you. What are you afraid of?"

"I know he'll realize his good fortune that I turned him down. I couldn't bear to be there when he realized he was trapped with me. I couldn't do that to him." She looked at Sophie with pleading eyes, as though begging her to understand.

Sophie smiled with tenderness. "Darling, he's as much a social misfit as you are. He's only accepted in society because he's such a brilliant financier."

"What?" Zylphia gaped at Sophie. "He tinkers all day with meaningless experiments."

"It's how he clears his head to figure out what stocks to support or what schemes to back. And I wouldn't discount his experiments. I'm sure one of them will alter our lives someday. As is, he's one of the preeminent financial men of the time."

"How can this be? Why does no one speak of it? And why would he be here rather than in New York City?"

"Because he's taciturn at worst and sullen at best when in society. He's only appeared remotely approaching conventional norms of behavior when near you. He had planned to move to New York City after last summer, but then changed his plans." She shared a meaningful look with Zylphia.

"You're wrong, Sophie," Zylphia argued as her mind whirled with snippets of conversations. "His father is the genius."

Sophie scowled. "His father allows his son to be mocked, while basking in his brilliance. Every morning Teddy's assistant sends a telegraph with the approved stock trades to Teddy's father, who executes them, accepting the credit."

"How do you know this?"

"I heard him advising Owen Hubbard in Newport, and I commented that it seemed unlikely an absentminded scientist would have much to offer by way of business acumen." Sophie smiled as she remembered that interaction. "When I pressed Teddy on a few stock picks I was likely to execute, he became haughty, as only the upper-class British can, before losing his polished veneer. He was appalled at my ineptitude, as he called it, and offered to help me with my portfolio."

"Did he?"

"Yes, quite successfully. He prevented me from investing in a horrible scheme that would have cost me a large portion of my fortune. Instead I doubled it."

"You mean, Teddy did."

Sophie shrugged her shoulders in agreement.

Zylphia leaned against the settee, her gaze distant. "Why did you never tell me about this aspect of Teddy? Why did you allow me to believe him a scientist who tinkered away his time each day?"

Sophronia sighed. "You needed to discover it yourself. For, if I had told you and then you had appeared interested, he would have thought you were only after his fortune." Sophie raised an eyebrow. "Which is quite considerable. He's saved his family in England from almost certain insolvency."

Zylphia shuddered. "When I think of all the cruel things I've said to him and how many times he's told me that I didn't truly know him ..." She closed her eyes in defeated resignation. "He listed all the things he loved about me that night. Things that only someone who knew me well would know. And I'd never taken the time to learn more about him."

Sophronia squinted as she studied Zylphia. "If you truly don't want to marry him and truly don't care for him, I don't see how that should bother you."

"I don't feel the indifference and scorn I expressed that evening." She closed her eyes and took a deep breath. "I fear I love him."

"It's nothing to fear. It's something to be cherished and embraced." Sophie's smile became broader as she watched Zylphia accepting her feelings. "I'd tell that young man how you feel, rather than this old woman."

"I can't barge into his laboratory today, telling him I lied. He'd think I was a deranged woman who can't make up her mind."

"You have to do something to inform him that your sentiments are different than those you expressed." Sophie's gaze became distant.

"Thank you, Sophie."

"What will you do if there is a child?" Sophie raised an eyebrow as Zylphia blushed.

"There won't be." She shared a meaningful glance with Sophie. "You can imagine my relief when my monthly came a few days ago."

"A lucky break," Sophie said.

"Yes. Besides, I'd hate for him to think I only wanted him because there'd been consequences from that night."

"Whether or not you're with his child, there are consequences, dearest. To your spirit. To his." Sophie watched Zylphia with intense sincerity for a moment. "Don't make him wait too long before you contact him."

***

Zylphia danced with Mr. Wheeler, her dance card half full for the first time in a month. "I'm surprised to see you anywhere near Miss Tyler." Zylphia smiled her apology as she tripped over his toes. He grimaced but tried to hide it with a chuckle.

"She and I have never agreed on anything. She's a deviant woman who refuses to embrace social norms for women. I attempt, in my small capacity as an old family friend, to enlighten her as to the errors she is making in her behavior."

Zylphia stifled a laugh. "I can't imagine Miss Tyler appreciating such counsel."

He smiled with grim humor. "She doesn't." He studied Zylphia. "You were able to throw off the mantle of the suffragist twaddle. I'd think you'd be able to help Parthena be successful with the same."

Zylphia flushed and then laughed. "It seems I fooled you all. I've never ceased in my beliefs for women. I simply decided to not be as strident in my expression of my beliefs to see if I could sway others to my way of thinking."

"I imagine you weren't all that successful," Mr. Wheeler said as they danced.

"Not at all."

He closed his eyes for a moment, unable to withhold a deep laugh. "I wish I could have seen Mr. Hubbard's reaction when he realized you were as radical as ever."

Zylphia's eyes flashed. "I, too, wish you'd been present."

Mr. Wheeler sobered immediately. "Did he harm you in any way, Miss McLeod?"

"No, but it was a singularly unpleasant scene."

He twirled with her one last time as the waltz ended. "I'm sure you'll come to realize your good fortune. It was a pleasure, Miss McLeod." He walked her to the side of the ballroom, lifted her hand for a kiss and then nodded before turning to disappear in the dense crowd.

Zylphia stood alone on the side of the room, swaying slightly to the music. She looked for a passing tray of drinks and sighed with frustration to see the servants were on the opposite side.

"Why the heavy sigh, Miss McLeod?"

Zylphia closed her eyes at the deep voice, breathing in sandalwood and a faint hint of peppermint. "Teddy," she whispered. A firm hand at her back dissuaded her from turning to face him.

"Don't call me that."

She reached a hand down, brushing at the side of her rose-colored overskirt. "How are you?"

He stiffened as her hand brushed against his leg. His dropped from her back to clasp her hand, transforming from a grip of chastisement to a caress in a moment. "Zee ..." He sighed, his breath sounding closer to her ear.

She swayed—to an onlooker as though she were reacting to the music—but, rather than from side to side, she moved backward nearly into Teddy's embrace before moving forward again. She repeated the movement a half-dozen times before she realized what she was doing and swayed side to side. "I've missed you."

He squeezed her hand once before releasing it. "I hope you are finding enjoyment in tonight's entertainment. You seem to bask in the attention from your previous dance partners."

She froze. "I like to dance."

"You appear to enjoy dancing attendance on the most eligible men present."

She shivered at the rancor she heard in his voice. "Why are you here?"

"I know I promised to never approach you."

"No, you didn't." She smiled and nodded at an acquaintance across the room while she clenched and unclenched her fingers hidden in her skirts.

"I did to myself."

She stifled a gasp, as though suffering bodily harm.

"Forgive me if my bluntness has hurt you, but there is one thing I must know."

She nodded, portraying some enjoyment in an engaging conversation. All the while she blinked furiously to forestall tears from falling.

"Were there any consequences?" he breathed into her ear.

Zylphia choked back a sob. "So honorable. The only reason you could force yourself to reenter society and deign to speak with me in over a month. The only reason why you could no longer avoid my letters. Has it given you pleasure to return them to me, unopened? Do you sit in your study, envisioning what I feel each time I receive my sealed letters you refuse to read?"

"There's very little left for us to say. I've no need of you or your letters."

Zylphia flinched at his cold words. She moved to the side to turn and meet his eyes. She battled despair as she met his cold gaze, devoid of all its customary affection. "No. No, there were no consequences," she whispered.

"I can't imagine my refusal to read your letters caused you any true disappointment, Miss McLeod." His pursed lips relaxed although the desolation in his gray eyes remained. "I bid you a pleasant evening."

She reached forward, gripping his hand a moment, laughing as though he'd just told her a joke. "Don't leave, Teddy. These events are horrid without you. There's so much I want to—"

His eyes flashed with a deep hurt before kindling with anger, and he cut her off. "This is how it must be, Miss McLeod. You don't want me as anything other than a momentary diversion, and I can't be what you need."

Zylphia paled as words similar to what she'd said to him were repeated to her. "Teddy, please. Listen to me." Her voice wavered as she spoke. "You won't read my letters, and I have to explain—"

"Why would I be interested in anything you have to say? You were quite eloquent last we met." His eyes chilled as he stood stiffly next to her. "My only consolation is that your incessant letters will cease with your travel to Montana." At her startled gaze, his smile appeared a mixture of triumph and sorrow. "Yes, even a lab rat can learn some gossip."

"Teddy, please, you must understand ..."

"Good evening, Miss McLeod." His eyes roamed over her, as though memorizing her, before he took a small step backward.

She nodded, blinking rapidly to prevent her tears from falling, as he gave a perfunctory bow and slipped along the periphery of the crowd, disappearing from sight.

***

Zylphia stood on the promenade overlooking the Charles River, a warm May breeze hinting at summer ruffling her hair and jacket. She leaned forward, resting the top portion of her body against the metal railing. The scene from last night with Teddy played through her mind, but each time she edited it so that he was forced to listen to her. After a month of waiting, of hoping to see him, of a growing anger as each letter was returned unopened, a restless purpose filled her. Determined to remain inactive no longer, she turned for home on nearby Marlborough Street, with a plan forming. "If he refuses my letters, I'll invade his lab," she muttered to herself, the thought putting a small spring in her step for the first time since she had last left Teddy's private study.

She arrived home, smiling at the eager welcome of their butler, Jimmy. She stopped at the small mound of mail on the front hallstand, picking up a few pieces addressed to her. She came to an abrupt halt when she saw Teddy's distinctive, brusque handwriting.

After ascending the stairs, she entered her studio, closing the door behind her. She curled onto the red velvet chaise and ripped open the letter.

May 17, 1914
Miss McLeod,

Please forgive me for causing you any further distress by writing. I realize now, after your blunt refusal to envision a future with me and knowing that no consequences came from our foolish behavior, that I must move on. That any hope I held for you was a fantasy I had built from my own imaginings.

I fear you might feel uncomfortable, worrying we might pass each other on the street or meet at a ball at a mutual friend's house. I would like to alleviate such a concern. Although I had planned to remain in Boston, working on my inventions, my grandfather is ill. By the time you read this, I will have sailed for England, with no plans to return until at least the fall.

I know you envision an independent life. One where you are free to determine what you want, moment by moment. Where you decide who and what you need. My hope is that you do not come to realize how lonely such a life can be.

I loved you. I love you still.

Theodore Goff

She reread the letter over and over, tears coursing down her cheeks. She traced the words telling her how he loved her, only stopping when she feared she'd smudge them. After carefully folding the letter, she rose, placing it in her keepsake rosewood box on a bookshelf corner. She returned to the chaise longue, curling on her side as she succumbed to tears.

CHAPTER THIRTY-ONE

"**Z**ee!"

Zylphia swiveled, dropped her bag, turning to where she heard her name. She raised a hand, then bent to lift her bag again and rushed toward the crowd on the platform. "Jeremy," she said, leaning into his embrace. "I can't believe I'm finally here."

"How was your journey?" he asked, taking her day bag before leading her toward the side of the railway station. He spoke with a porter for a moment, and then moved toward a horse and wagon. "I imagine you don't mind stretching your legs after days on the train. If we wait a few minutes, they'll bring out your trunks." He nodded to the young woman trailing after Zee, and shared a rueful smile with Zylphia.

"You wouldn't expect my father to allow me to travel alone?" She rolled her eyes. "She's intended to be my maid, but I'll find something else of use for her to do here." She smiled as Jeremy laughed.

Zylphia arched her back as she stretched out her body, long cramped by her travels. She looked at the distant mountains and hills, shimmering a golden green as the recent heat burned off the spring's moisture. "It's beautiful here."

"Yes, in its way," Jeremy said. "It's much smaller than what you're used to in Boston."

"How far away is Butte?" Zylphia asked.

Jeremy pointed toward a canyon in the direction she'd just arrived from. "About one hundred miles that way. I'm sure you passed through it on your way here."

"I fell asleep for a good portion of the latter part of my journey and missed a few of the stops." Zylphia smiled at the porter as he emerged with her two trunks and her maid's trunk. After Jeremy and the porter loaded the trunks, Jeremy helped Zylphia and her maid climb into the horse-drawn wagon, and they began the short journey to his house.

"I thought you'd have an automobile by now," Zylphia teased.

"We do, but it's always breaking down or getting stuck in the muddied roads after a rain or the snowmelt. A horse is reliable." Jeremy nodded to his left and a large brick building spanning half a city block. "That there's the Merc. Anything you need, you can buy at the Merc, or they'll find a way to have it shipped here for you."

The wagon clattered over a bridge, and they crossed into a newer section of town. Jeremy turned left, then right, easing the wagon to a halt behind a large house with a wide wraparound porch, multiple gables and a large turret. "Who gets the turret room?" Zylphia asked.

Jeremy laughed. "Melly. She says it makes her feel like a princess."

"I can see why. What a glorious house." Zylphia accepted his help from the wagon and followed him inside. Her maid trailed behind her.

A shriek heralded their arrival, and a girl on the cusp of womanhood threw herself in Zylphia's arms. "Zee! You're finally here!" she proclaimed.

"Melly," Zylphia murmured as she held her cousin close. "You've grown so much since I last saw you."

"Come. I can't wait to show you our house." She grabbed Zylphia's hand, intent on towing her from room to room. She stilled her movement at her father's clearing of his throat.

"Let me see your mother first, and then I'd love a tour," Zylphia soothed, running a hand over her blond curls. She looked behind her and smiled her welcome to her young companion, inviting her silently to join them.

Melly dragged Zylphia into an informal sitting room, filled with potted plants and comfortable furniture.

"Zee," Savannah exclaimed, rising to hug her. "I'm thankful you've arrived safe and sound." She noted the woman hovering in the doorway. "I beg your pardon. I'm Savannah McLeod, Zylphia's cousin." She reached her hand out to shake the young woman's hand.

The woman bobbed a quick curtsy as she shook Savannah's hand. "Pleased to meet you, ma'am. I'm Charlotte, Lottie, McGivens."

Zylphia shared a long look with Savannah and turned away to roam the room. "My companion for my journey out here."

"I'm to be a maid to Miss Zylphia," Lottie said.

Savannah smothered a laugh as she beheld Zylphia's disgruntled look. "I see. Why don't you ask Jeremy to show you to a room so you can rest from your travels?" Lottie backed from the room, giving another half curtsy as she left. Savannah bit back a chuckle as Zylphia collapsed into a comfortable, tufted chair across from her. "Why must she curtsy me?"

"She thinks it's proper to curtsy everyone." Zylphia sighed and reached a hand out to Savannah. "Thank you for welcoming her."

Savannah shrugged. "Please forgive me for not traveling to the station. Rissa and I had work to do this morning, canvassing for the vote, and we lost track of time."

"How are Rissa and Gabe?" Zylphia asked, absently noting Jeremy passing by the sitting room door with one of her trunks.

"Much better. Clarissa is ecstatic you are joining us here to help us earn the right to vote." Savannah beamed at her.

"It was Sophie's idea."

"Most outrageous ideas are Sophie's," Jeremy said, poking his head into the room.

"I wouldn't call having your cousin visit us in Montana as outrageous," Savannah protested.

"No, but, if I know anything about that woman, there's more to this story than we've been told." He winked at them before moving toward the back door for her second trunk.

"I'm afraid I won't be here long, Sav. I was advised I had to travel to Butte to discuss my role with the women leading the campaign."

"Never fear, Rissa and I will travel with you. Rissa likes any excuse she can find to travel to Butte to see her brother Patrick. Besides, I'd like a few new clothes. We'll have fun." Savannah smiled. "Besides, there's no chance I'm letting them convince you to canvass in another part of the state. You must work with Rissa and me here in Missoula and the valley."

Zylphia sighed her agreement. "Thank goodness. I was afraid all Sophie's planning would be for nothing, and I'd be relegated to the backwaters of the state."

"Well, I'm sure we'll visit some rather rural areas, but we'll be together." Savannah's expression became determined. "I promised your father in a recent letter that you would always be with family while here."

"My father is very protective," Zylphia grumbled.

"He might be protective, but he's earned that right. You're his only daughter, and you're precious to him."

"I was shocked when he forced poor Charlotte to leave Boston and travel with me," Zylphia said.

"I'm sure it was better to travel with her than alone," Savannah said.

"Then you'd be wrong. From the minute the train departed Minneapolis, all she discussed was the possibility of an Indian raid and how we'd survive, and what would we do if they attacked a group of unarmed women." She speared Savannah with a glare as Savannah giggled. "As though that could possibly occur in 1914!"

"It appears she has an overactive imagination," Savannah murmured.

"And no sense of current affairs," Zylphia said, her glower transforming into giggles. "Oh, it was awful. I think I feigned sleep for a thousand miles so as not to listen to her."

Savannah smiled as she caught Melinda hiding in the doorway. "Come here, Melly. You should be a part of this discussion as you will most likely travel with us."

"Will I?" Melinda asked, unable to hide her glee.

"Yes, school's about to end, and I think it's important you realize what women, citizens of this country, must do to obtain their proposed objectives."

A door opened and slammed shut, with heels clicking rapidly on the wooden floors. "Zee!" Clarissa exclaimed, rushing forward to clasp her cousin in an exuberant hug. "You're finally here."

"Sit, Rissa," Savannah said. "Zee needs to travel to Butte."

"Oh, that's wonderful. I haven't seen Patrick in too long." She frowned as she beheld Zylphia. "You're not working with the others, Zee. You'll be assigned to Sav and me."

Zylphia laughed. "I know. I feel badly for whatever group would dare to deny the two of you what you wanted."

***

Three days later Zylphia found herself on another train, this one heading east toward Butte. Lottie had remained in Missoula to help Araminta with her duties. Upon their arrival, the women checked into their rooms at the Finlen but decided to postpone their meeting with the leaders of the women's suffrage committee for another day. "Let's explore," Rissa said.

"What could we possibly find here?" Zylphia asked, glancing out a window at the smokestacks spewing ash into the sky and the mountains barren of vegetation.

"You haven't been to Hennessy's," Savannah said with glee. She grabbed her purse, tilted her hat at a jaunty angle and grabbed Zylphia's arm. "We have the right to one afternoon of shopping before spending the next months going door-to-door, convincing the males of this state that we are worthy of the right to vote."

They walked down Broadway to Main Street before turning up the hill. Zylphia glanced around with avid interest. "They're dressed as well here as in Boston," she whispered to Clarissa, who walked arm in arm with her.

Clarissa nodded with a broad smile, paused outside the large glass doors on the corner of Granite Street, waiting for Savannah and Melinda to catch up to them. They entered the front doors, the floor sparkling from the prism glass over the doors, lit by the afternoon sun.

Zylphia stopped, glancing around the large store.

"Everything you could ever imagine wanting is here," Savannah said as she led them to the second floor and the dress department.

They sat in comfortable chairs, perusing the latest women's fashion plates before Savannah decided on a teal dress for her. Clarissa chose a sky-blue dress with matching jacket. Zylphia demurred, her trunks filled to bursting with clothes from Boston. They then descended to the accessories department to purchase gloves, hats and handkerchiefs to match their new dresses.

"Come. I'm exhausted from all this shopping," Clarissa said.

They departed to a nearby café that advertised booths for ladies. They settled in for a cup of tea.

"Don't eat much, if anything. We're meeting Patrick for dinner tonight, and they like to serve large portions in Butte."

"I never realized you had another brother," Zylphia said as she sipped her tea.

"He left home precipitously around the time Gabriel left Boston." Clarissa shared a long look with Savannah.

"I imagine that was quite difficult for you," Zylphia murmured, frowning at the unspoken undercurrents.

"It was. I thought he had died, since we never heard from him after that. However, he's alive and well, and, even if we can't—yet—convince him to move to Missoula, I couldn't be more delighted he's returned to us," Clarissa said.

"As am I," Savannah murmured. "He's my cousin too."

"And my brother!" Melly said with glee before frowning. "Although he doesn't like me much."

"He likes you just fine," Clarissa said on a rush. "I think he's simply adjusting to being part of a large family again after so many years of estrangement."

As Savannah stroked an arm down Melinda's arm to soothe her, Zylphia adroitly changed the subject. "Could you tell me a little more about the people we'll meet with tomorrow?"

"I'm not certain who you'll see. I doubt Miss Rankin will be here," Clarissa said. "She's the head of the committee and of the movement for women to obtain the vote. We've yet to meet her, although she's from Missoula. She's always away canvassing."

"We read about her in the paper frequently," Savannah said, raising her eyebrows.

"She encourages all of us to travel to each homestead, each farm, to speak with the women and the men about the reasons for voting for enfranchisement," Clarissa said before taking a sip of tea. "That's raised quite a furor among some of the women in Missoula, who'd rather not expend such energy." She shared an amused glance with Savannah as she thought about the meddling sisters in Missoula.

"That must take a tremendous amount of time in a state so large," Zylphia said. "I can't imagine such an endeavor."

"Well, if we're successful, it will be because of actions like the ones Miss Rankin has encouraged us to take. It's shown the residents of Montana that all are important, not just the ones in the big cities like Butte."

"I'd like to meet her," Zylphia said. "I'm sure she'd have ideas for the Massachusetts campaign."

"Whether you meet her or not, you'll learn plenty," Savannah said with a wry smile.

***

Clarissa sat at the reserved table at one of the best restaurants in Butte, tapping her fingers in agitation. "He told me that he'd come," she said in a low voice to Savannah, Zylphia and Melinda. Her frown lifted as Patrick burst through the doors, but her frown reappeared when she saw a woman on his arm. "I didn't realize he'd bring her."

Patrick scanned the room until it settled on them in the corner, and he smiled. He slipped past the waiters, guiding Fiona as they neared the tabled toward the rear of the restaurant.

Clarissa rose, pulling him close for a quick embrace. "It's wonderful to see you," she whispered into his ear. He gave her a squeeze before releasing her.

Savannah and Melinda did the same, Melinda throwing herself into his arms and wrapping her arms around his waist.

He chuckled, caressing her golden curls a moment before kissing her on her head and releasing her. "Hi, Sav, Melly," he murmured. "You look wonderful."

Savannah beamed at him and included Fiona in her smile. "Thanks, we've had a fun afternoon shopping at Hennessy's." Savannah looked to Fiona. "I'm Savannah. This is my daughter Melinda, and Clarissa is Patrick's sister." Savannah nodded to Clarissa, a teasing smile on her face. "The black-haired beauty is Zylphia, our cousin from Boston."

Fiona met their curious gazes but did not smile. "I'm Fiona O'Leary. I'm a friend of Patrick's."

"You're more than that if what I hear is true," Clarissa muttered, earning a glare from Savannah.

Melinda, oblivious to the tension between the adults, tugged on Patrick's hand and dragged him into a chair next to her. "Mama bought a new dress today, as did Rissa."

"Did you get one too?" Patrick asked, his gaze taking in Melly's evolving features, less girllike and more like a young woman every day. He brushed a golden curl away from her cheek. He smiled up at Fiona as she sat between Savannah and Zylphia.

"No, I have plenty of clothes. And I can buy whatever I need at the Merc. That's what Papa tells me, and he's always right."

Patrick laughed. "Yes, your father is always right." He turned his focus to the remaining member at their table. "I beg your pardon. I'm Patrick." He held out his hand.

Zylphia smiled. "I'm Zylphia, but everyone calls me Zee. I'm Aidan and Delia's daughter."

"Of course you are," he said with a broad smile. "You look just like a McLeod."

Zylphia ran a self-conscious hand over her raven hair. "That's what everyone says."

He nodded to Fiona. "All of the McLeods, who include Clarissa's and Savannah's husbands, have black hair and either green or blue eyes."

"What part of Scotland is your family from?" Fiona asked.

"I was always told we were from Ireland, but I could be wrong," Zylphia said with a shrug.

"You're from Ireland, Miss O'Leary?" Savannah asked.

"I am. From Kerry originally." She attempted a small smile as she pleated the tablecloth over and over.

"Well, we're glad you moved to Butte to meet our Patrick," Savannah said. She reached out a hand to clasp Miss O'Leary's and met her startled gaze. As the conversation continued around them, she began a quiet discussion with her. "I can't tell you how delighted I was to receive your letter, asking me for my aid. I wish I'd had the courage to do the same."

Fiona met her gaze and whispered, "I'm so ashamed. I never meant to harm your family."

"The only way you'll harm our family is if you treat Patrick false." Savannah shared a long look with her. "Henry would have found a way to enrage his cousins with or without your help. Just thinking about him angers them. Besides, we're a notorious-enough group that he didn't need to do much detective work to discover hurtful facts about us."

"You talk about your notoriety as though it brings you pride." Fiona watched Savannah with bemused wonder.

"It's either that or hide away in shame, and I refuse to do that. When you get to know Rissa, she's the last person who will ever retreat from another person's opinion about her or her life." She saw Fiona look around the table—Zylphia laughing at Clarissa, Melinda teasing a smile from Patrick—and squeezed Fiona's hand. "We're really not a scary bunch, but we are outspoken and fiercely tight-knit and protective of each other."

Fiona nodded as she met Savannah's gaze. "I want in."

Savannah threw back her head as she laughed. "You'll fit in just fine."

"Fiona," Clarissa asked from the other side of the round table, "how have you been feeling?"

"Fine, thank you." She stared pointedly at Melinda, who beamed at her.

"When's your baby coming? I can't wait to meet it!" She bounced in her chair in her exuberance, reminding everyone she was more of a child than a young woman.

"Oh, I imagine your little cousin will be a Christmas present," Zylphia said as Fiona appeared struck dumb at the casual conversation.

"Yea! I can't wait to meet her. I don't want a boy cousin. They're not much fun to play with."

"Just because Billy didn't understand the fine art of a tea party doesn't mean he isn't fun to play with," Clarissa protested with a laugh. "If I remember correctly, you enjoy your romps in the woods with him the most because he's not afraid of getting dirty."

Melinda looked toward the ceiling as though deep in thought. "I guess either one would be fine."

Patrick chortled out a laugh. "Well, that's a good thing because those are your two options, and you don't have a choice." He held up a hand as she opened her mouth. "No more questions. You're overwhelming Fee."

Melly slumped into her chair, and the adults around the table chuckled.

He looked over to Fiona and shared a long look with her, earning a small smile from her.

Clarissa watched the interaction, relaxing for the first time into her chair since she'd seen Fiona enter the restaurant with him. "Fiona, it's lovely to finally meet you," Clarissa said.

"If you are able to spend a few days here in Butte, we hope you will witness our wedding," Patrick said with a toast of the champagne that had just been poured for them.

"It's final then?" Clarissa asked, reaching forward to grip his arm and then outstretching a hand toward Fiona for one of hers. At Patrick's nod, she squeezed their hands once in support before releasing them. "Thank God."

"I received word today. I'm no longer a Flaherty," Fiona said.

"You never were a Flaherty," Patrick said. "And soon you'll be a Sullivan." Then addressing the others, he said, "We plan to marry the day after tomorrow."

"Excellent. We'll simply change our tickets and stay for another day," Clarissa said, sharing a quick look with Savannah.

As they ate their meals, Clarissa glanced around the restaurant. "Patrick, there seems to be a nervous energy in the city right now. It's not how I remember Butte."

Patrick sighed, his fingers strumming alongside his beer glass. "You're observant to detect it." He lowered his voice, and they leaned forward to hear him.

"The miners are on edge. You remember last year when I told you about the card system?"

They nodded, but he glanced at Zylphia and knew she wouldn't understand. "There's been a card system in place for over a year among the miners. It ensures that they are members of the union and is supposed to help the mine owners know they are getting capable miners. However, some believe it unfairly favors the Irish, to keep other nationalities from getting good work and to unjustly label miners as Socialists.

"Last year, five hundred Finns were forced from their jobs due to the card system. A large number of miners protested because the union didn't strike for their unjustly fired members. So, two weeks ago, a group of men refused to show their cards at the Black Rock and Speculator mines." He shook his head at Clarissa's unasked question. "Not any of the Company's mines. A small act of defiance but it may be just the beginning."

"So you think something more will happen?" Savannah asked.

"Well, the next day was the disturbance at the annual miners' parade. Generally a day where the miners march, showing unity and their pride in what they do. Instead there was a near brawl and violence. Then, that evening, men broke into the Miners' Union Hall, stole the safe and all the records."

"What would that accomplish?" Zylphia asked.

"If the union and mine owners don't know who's paid union dues, then the cards are worthless," Patrick said. "The union plans a meeting tomorrow night at the miners' hall to calm everyone. Even officials from out of state are coming to calm the members of their largest union." Patrick shook his head as he considered what was going on in Butte.

"What will happen to the miners if they have no union?" Clarissa whispered.

Patrick glanced around the room and raised his shoulders in a shrug.

She reached forward and clasped his hand. "Stay safe. Please, Patrick."

"I'm not a miner, Rissa. This has nothing to do with me."

"But you work for the Company. You could still be harmed in some way." She squeezed his hand once before releasing it.

"How do you know so much about the miners?" Zylphia asked. "From what I understand of businessmen, they pay little attention to the men working under them."

"Well, those with any sense treat their workers well. Like Ford and his eight-hour day and $5-per-day pledge for his workers." Patrick took a bite of his steak. He lowered his voice further. "I have a friend who's a miner. He keeps me informed when he's in Butte."

"Not something your Company appreciates?" Clarissa asked with a wry smile. Patrick shook his head.

"They should," Zylphia argued. "They should be relieved someone knows what's going on so that things aren't such a surprise to them."

"Those in charge at the company aren't that intelligent." Fiona's eyes blazed with impassioned anger.

"As Fee said, that's not the nature of things here," Patrick said.

***

The following morning, the McLeod women walked into the suffrage committee headquarters and waited their turn to speak with the secretary. They looked past her at the rows of desks bustling with women typing or discussing strategy. A large map of Montana hung on a far wall, with stick pins of differing colors highlighting the cities and towns.

"How may I help you?" the secretary asked when she was free.

"I am Savannah McLeod. These are my cousins Clarissa and Zylphia McLeod, and this is my daughter, Melinda McLeod. We've traveled from Missoula to meet with Miss O'Reilly" She shared a wink with Melinda as the secretary's eyes widened slightly.

"Of course. If you will wait a moment." She rose and moved toward the back and entered a small office area.

"Who's Miss O'Reilly?" Zylphia whispered as they waited.

"One of the leaders who works closely with Miss Rankin," Savannah whispered.

The secretary returned a few moments later and motioned for them to follow her.

Miss O'Reilly sat behind a desk covered in newspaper clippings. She smiled weakly as they entered the room and frowned when she realized she only had two chairs. "I beg your pardon. I don't have enough seats."

"It's fine," Savannah and Clarissa said at the same time. Zylphia motioned for them to sit, and she stood behind them with Melinda.

"I'm thankful you were able to travel here to us. Miss Zylphia McLeod's arrival was heralded by numerous letters from our counterparts in Massachusetts. I've honestly never seen the like before." She raised an eyebrow as she watched them over her wire-framed glasses. Her fingers were smudged with newspaper ink, as were her previously pristine shirt cuffs.

"That would be our friend Mrs. Sophronia Chickering's doing," Clarissa said as she swallowed a chuckle. "She's a firm believer in introductions."

Miss O'Reilly rifled through the papers on her desk before extracting one and tipping her head down to read it. "She wrote as though I should be preparing for the arrival of the pope himself." She grinned as she saw the women sitting across from her hiding their embarrassment. "*I expect her to be feted to the highest of your abilities. Never again will such a woman with such dedication to the cause present herself with no expectation of remittance of any kind.*" Miss O'Reilly raised an amused eyebrow. "It goes on for a good three pages."

"For the love of ..." Zylphia muttered.

"After reading your good friend's ramblings, I finally discerned that her main worry was that I would separate Miss Zylphia from the rest of you. I find I don't have the heart to write such a letter. Thus, I'm happy to report that Miss Zylphia should canvass with the McLeod women in Missoula and the Bitter Root Valley as we work toward success in November."

Zylphia sighed her relief and smiled her agreement.

"I have two other concerns we must discuss, since you are here," Miss O'Reilly said, picking up a pencil and doodling on a scrap piece of paper. "First, Mrs. McLeod—Mrs. Savannah McLeod," she clarified, "I wanted to assure you that everything has been prepared for your brother's tour through Montana. We of the committee were anxious when he needed to postpone a few weeks but are thankful he will arrive in early July for the concerts. All performance halls have been booked, and we have secured rooms for him."

Savannah nodded her agreement. "When he is in Missoula, he will stay with family. No need for a hotel room there."

Miss O'Reilly wrote herself a note. "Now for the more unpleasant business." She pinned Clarissa with an intense stare. "I've had complaints that you are not as welcoming as you should be to all who are interested in our work."

Clarissa tensed. "Have you had a letter from a Mrs. Vaughan or a Mrs. Bouchard?"

"I have. They claim you actively discourage women of a certain age from participating in the movement and that you believe this is a movement solely for the young."

Clarissa clamped her mouth shut after she sputtered. A few deep breaths later, she spoke. "First, I'm not that young anymore, so I think their argument is a weak one. Second, at our meeting in March, the two sisters spent the majority of the gathering pointing out reasons why they thought the campaign was doomed to fail and that we shouldn't get people's hopes up. They are against campaigning door to door."

Miss O'Reilly steepled her fingers as she considered what Clarissa had said. "I wondered if that wasn't closer to the truth. I've never had complaints about the organization in Missoula and the Bitter Root Valley until now. It struck me as odd." She nodded to Clarissa. "I must warn you. If I have further complaints, someone from central will have to come to investigate."

Clarissa nodded. "That's fine. I have—we have—nothing to hide."

***

That evening, Patrick slung his jacket over his arm rather than donning it as he moved to the shadowed side of the street. Heat emanated off the brick streets, and a faint breeze stirred to alleviate the oppressive warmth. As it was the night before his wedding, he wasn't supposed to see Fiona, and the women from his family had told him they were also expected to be too busy helping her prepare for the wedding to see him either. He thought he had walked without purpose but found himself proceeding up Main Street toward the Miners' Hall. He frowned upon noting the large crowd buffeting the front of the Hall.

"Patrick," Elias said as he approached the Hall, too. "What are you doing here?"

"I was wandering and ended up here." He pointed to the mob of men. "I know you're supposed to have a meeting, but I never imagined this sort of turnout."

"As you know, the new president of the Western Federation of Miners is visiting. I think they hope it will calm things after the events of the past few weeks." He bumped into Patrick as he was jostled by other miners moving toward the Hall.

"Do they know who stole the safe?"

Elias rolled his eyes. "Someone does, but they're not saying who. They made off with all the records and over one thousand dollars."

"I'd heard it was closer to fifteen hundred. A profitable night for someone."

"And now that there are no records, the union has no idea who's paid up, so that rustling system you boys are fond of won't work." Elias tried to hide a triumphant grin.

Patrick sobered and gripped his friend's shoulder. "Please tell me that you weren't involved."

"I wasn't, but I can't say I didn't agree with it." Elias freed himself from Patrick's grasp.

Patrick stiffened as a shot rang out from the second floor of the Miners' Hall. He and Elias dropped to their haunches and then moved away from the building as the masses of men entering the hall fled.

Elias spoke in rapid-fire Finnish to some men nearby and then turned to Patrick. "A few progressives want to liberate the Hall."

"What does that mean?" Patrick asked.

"Bare minimum is to free it of the BMU."

Patrick shook his head at the thought of Butte without the Butte Miners Union. He and Elias watched from across the street as a few men scurried up the hill. Patrick raised an amused eyebrow. "Seems an odd way to liberate a place." He clapped a hand on Elias's shoulder and steered him into a nearby bar for a drink. "So where've you been recently? I haven't seen you around." Patrick paid for their drinks, and they moved to a calmer part of the bar.

"I traveled to Idaho for a bit. Worked for a month in the mines there and then thought I'd come back. See if Butte was more open to the non-Irish." He shrugged his shoulders. "It's the same as always, although the past few weeks have been interesting."

"The progressives have been active," Patrick said.

A loud boom shook the bar, and Patrick reached out a hand to steady himself against the wall. "Was that ..."

"Dynamite," Elias said with glee. "Come on!" They moved outside with the men from the bar, remaining on the opposite side of the street as boom after boom was heard. The Hall shook, smoked and finally caved in on itself before crumbling and dissolving into a pile of rubble. Men across the street hooted and hollered with joy.

Patrick fanned the dust from his face with his hat, coughing. "Why do such a thing to your own union?"

"It's never been ours," Elias said. He winked at Patrick as he moved to the men across the street, slapping them on the back before slipping into the crowd and disappearing.

"A bunch of goddamn amateurs," muttered a man next to Patrick.

Patrick turned to him in confusion. "What do you mean?"

"Any decent miner coulda taken that place down with three or four sticks. From the sounds of it, took them over twenty. Waste of good dynamite, if you ask me." He cleared his throat and spat on the ground in disgust before returning to the bar and his drink.

Patrick bit back a smile. He finished his beer in two long sips, gave the glass to a man entering the bar and headed toward the Finlen at a brisk pace. He arrived at the hotel to find his family departing. "Rissa!"

She beamed as she saw him. "Patrick! We finished helping Fiona and have her settled for the night. Now the rest of us have decided to see a motion picture starring a man called Charlie Chaplin. Do you want to come?"

"No, and I don't think it's a good idea for you to go out tonight. The miners just blew up the Miners' Hall, and I'd hate for you to be harmed."

"They blew up the hall?" Zylphia asked, her eyes lit with interest as she edged toward the door.

Patrick reached out a long arm to grasp her shoulder. She frowned at his shake of his head. "It would be much safer for you to remain here," Patrick said. "The miners are angry, and a group of angry men together is dangerous for everyone."

"You could accompany us," Savannah said. "That way we'd have a gentleman to protect us."

"Sav, be serious," Patrick said.

"I am. We want to see this actor everyone is talking about, and this is our opportunity. Come with us," Savannah cajoled.

He sighed before nodding. "Fine, but we won't go toward Main Street. We'll head down toward Wyoming to Park and the cinema."

As they entered the theater, Melinda grabbed Patrick's arm and dragged him toward the concession stand. They bought a large bag of popcorn, Melinda hopping in delight.

"Are you sure you're almost fourteen?"

"Papa says I have plenty of time to act like a grown woman, but that I'll never have another chance to be a child." Melinda beamed up at him.

Patrick thought for a moment before grinning. "I find I must agree with him. He's smart, isn't he?"

"He's the smartest! Except for Uncle Aidan. He's brilliant," Melinda said, earning a laugh from Zylphia.

"He's no smarter than your father, Melly. He's just older," Zylphia said. They smiled as they turned to enter the cinema.

Patrick met Savannah's and then Clarissa's gazes. "How was Fiona today?"

"She's wonderful. And that is all we will tell you," Clarissa said with a laugh at Patrick's frustrated glower.

They took their seats and waited to see who Charlie Chaplin was and why he'd become popular.

CHAPTER THIRTY-TWO

Fiona woke the morning of her second wedding and rolled onto her side. She closed her eyes, battling the dream she'd had of her perfect wedding day. She then rolled onto her back, groaning as the motion nauseated her, and threw her forearm over her eyes, banishing her vision of a room filled with flowers, soft music playing, and family surrounding her. A tear trickled out, and she swiped at her cheeks as loud knocking sounded on her bedroom door.

Before Fiona could rise, Clarissa poked her head in. Her friendly smile faded as she saw Fiona's distress. "Fee," she whispered, entering the room and closing the door behind her. She moved toward the bed, perching on the side of it. When Fiona threw an arm over her face again, Clarissa gripped her other hand. "It will be all right."

"It will never be all right. I'm ruining a good man's life today, and I hate myself for being so desperate that I agreed to such a bargain." She stuttered out a breath. "I feel like my life has turned into one huge bargain."

"Do you care for my brother?" Clarissa whispered.

Fiona lowered her arm and frowned at her. "Of course I do. I'd never marry him if I didn't."

"He obviously cares for you." She met Fiona's gaze. "I know what it is to be terrified on my wedding night. You've chosen well, Fiona. If you tell him how you feel, he'll treat you kindly."

"I can't stand the thought of a man's touch."

"I didn't think I could either. But Gabriel changed everything." She smiled wistfully at Fiona. "I hope Patrick is the same for you."

"If I weren't pregnant ..." she said with a mutinous firming of her chin.

"But you are," Clarissa said. At Fiona's long sigh, Clarissa stroked a hand down her arm. "Come. Let's get you ready for your wedding."

***

Patrick entered the church and came to an abrupt halt. Standing near the nave were Jeremy, Gabriel and Colin. They wore their best suits and paced slightly as they awaited his arrival. He walked toward them with a broad smile and teased, "I'm the one who's supposed to be nervous."

Colin laughed and slapped him on his back. "Today's a big day, brother," he said. "We wouldn't miss being here with you."

Patrick clasped each of their hands, eventually hauling Colin into a bear hug. "Stand up with me?" he whispered.

Colin gave a small *whoop* and nodded. At the priest's clearing of his throat, Colin murmured an apology but couldn't hide his grin.

Patrick nodded to a pew a few rows back, where his nieces and nephew sat with Araminta and Lottie. "I can't believe you all came," he whispered.

"You're one of us and not getting rid of us anytime soon," Gabriel teased. He glanced down the aisle and nodded with his chin for Patrick's attention. The McLeod women arrived, moving to sit beside the children and Araminta. They beamed at Patrick as soft music played from the church's organ.

Patrick moved to await his bride, smiling at her sister and cousin as they preceded her. He beamed at Fiona, dressed in a simple light-blue dress she could wear again with a short veil over her face. He itched to lift the veil but contented himself with running his hand down her arm and clasping her hand.

When the priest intoned "man and wife," he turned her toward him and raised her veil. He frowned when he saw the tears in her eyes before bending to kiss her softly. He smiled when his family cheered, and he raised their clasped hands to kiss her hand as he turned with her to face them. As they walked down the aisle, his smile dimmed when she whispered, "Thank you."

***

Patrick stood with Colin and his brothers-in-law, watching his wife as she laughed with his female family members. "She's doing a good job keeping you at arm's length," Gabriel murmured. "Clarissa attempted the same."

"How did you convince her you were different from Cameron?" Patrick asked, taking a sip of the drink he held in his hand but failing to taste it.

"By showing her kindness and patience." Gabriel nodded to Jeremy. "He was the same with Sav. She was brutally beaten by her first husband, and he had to teach her to trust again." He shared a rueful smile with Patrick.

Patrick was approached by a miner friend, and Gabriel moved to stand near Jeremy. He stiffened as he saw Henry sidle into the small reception room where they celebrated the wedding lunch. He caught Jeremy's eye and nodded toward the door, but, by the time Jeremy looked in that direction, he didn't see anything. Jeremy searched the small crowd of well-wishers and froze.

Jeremy grabbed Gabriel by the arm, forcing him to approach the opposite side of the room at a measured pace. He muttered, "Discretion, Gabe." Gabriel gave a terse nod and slipped through the crowd sipping champagne and murmured his apology when he bumped into merrymakers, spilling their drinks on themselves.

They reached the opposite side of the room, but Henry had disappeared. Gabriel and Jeremy stood taller than most present, but they failed to see him.

"Where'd he go?" Gabriel asked.

Jeremy shook his head before noticing a small alcove off the side of the room. "There's a good hiding place. But, more important, where's Rissa?"

Gabriel nearly growled as he and Jeremy hastened toward the small alcove.

***

Clarissa stilled at the voice behind her, taunting her. She'd moved to the side of the room for a moment alone to capture the day's festivities in her mind without the distraction of conversation. Now she looked around the crowd, desperate for anyone to meet her panicked gaze. She shuddered as a hand grabbed her waist and tugged her backward into the small alcove. She spun her head to meet Henry's taunting gaze. When he attempted to pull her into a mockery of an embrace, she stomped on his foot, earning a grunt of pain even though his grip on her arm tightened.

"You believe he'll run over here and rescue you? That you're that valuable to him? He's across the room with his pathetic brother, oblivious to your distress."

"You lie," she said. "No matter where Gabriel is, he cares."

"Do you honestly believe this pathetic charade of a wedding will protect that whore from me? At any point, all I have to do is whistle, and she will do my bidding."

"She isn't a whore, nor is she some animal trained by a cruel master." Rissa pulled at her arm but remained tethered to him.

"You think not? I'm certain my months of training will come to bear on her wedding night. She won't be thinking of your dear brother when he touches her. Just as I'm sure you weren't thinking of your dear Gabriel when he touched you that night. Do you still dream of Cameron's touch?"

"You bastard," she hissed, slapping him across the face with her free hand.

He reached forward, gripping her by her hair, his actions hidden by a fake tree. She gave a muffled yell as he covered her mouth with his other hand. He yelped when she bit so hard on his palm that she drew blood.

He tugged on her hair, forcing her head up as he leaned over her, even though only a few inches taller than her. "You think your Gabriel is better than me? He's the same as any man. I'll let you in on a little secret, cousin. All men think like I do about women. All men wish they could treat women as I do. They simply lack the influence and fortune to do it with impunity."

When he tugged her farther into the alcove, she lifted her skirts, and he laughed. "Already eager for what I can offer you?"

"Yes," she whispered, granting herself more freedom by raising the hem of her skirts. Her answer pleased him, and he loosened his hold on her head. She wriggled in his grip, and, when he bent forward to kiss her, she kneed him in the groin with all her might. "That is what I think of your attentions."

When he groaned and collapsed to the floor, she kicked him in the stomach. "That is what I think of men like you." She kicked him again. "How dare you compare yourself to Gabriel?" She reared back to kick him a third time, unaware tears of anger coursed down her cheek. Strong arms gripped her from behind and pulled her away.

"It's all right, my darling," Gabriel whispered, tucking her into his arms. When she settled, he chuckled. "Ah, you were fierce, my love. I couldn't be more proud."

"I don't know what came over me."

"I do. The mere mention of him puts me in a rage. The sight of him makes me want to do physical harm to him." He held her as she shuddered. "Never forget. Everything he says is poison."

"I know. But I do worry how much he's harmed Patrick's relationship with Fiona."

Gabriel ran a hand down her head. "That's for them to straighten out, love." Gabriel looked over to see his brother speaking in low tones to a prostrate Henry.

***

Jeremy whispered to Henry, "Must be a hell of a thing to realize a slip of a woman can bring you so low. I would say it unmanned you, but you never really were a man, were you?" When Henry raised irate eyes to his, Jeremy grasped his arm in a punishing grip. "Stay away from the McLeods, the Sullivans, anyone who has to do with our family. If you don't, you'll come to realize a well-placed blow by Clarissa was the better part of the bargain." He slapped Henry on the shoulder and rose, nodding to Gabriel as he led Clarissa from the alcove to freshen up before rejoining the party.

***

Fiona lay underneath the covers, pulled to her chin, in the ornate room rented for them by Patrick's family at the Finlen Hotel. When Patrick entered, her wan smile failed to alleviate his concerned gaze. "I won't bother you tonight, Fee."

She sighed with relief as she collapsed against the pillows. She stiffened when he sat beside her on his side of the bed. She calmed her panicked thoughts and thought of conversation. "Did you enjoy the day?" At his nod, she bit her lip. "Your family has gone to too much trouble on our behalf."

"They like to meddle. They always have. Now that Sav has money, more money than she knows what to do with, she'll continue to be generous." He flushed as he failed to meet her gaze.

"What more has she done?" Fiona was unable to fight a smile at his discomfort.

"She's bought us a house here in Butte." He gripped her hand. "I think she'd have preferred to buy one in Missoula, but she understood you have family here. I also have work, and a means of supporting us. I refuse to live off of my cousin's charity as I re-establish myself as an architect."

Fiona sat up straight in bed, her concern about holding the covers to her chest forgotten. "She can't have. It's too much."

He sighed, falling backward on the bed until his head was pillowed on her lap.

After a moment of awkwardness, she ran her fingers through his hair and relaxed.

"Try telling that to her as she's handing you a deed to a house, fully furnished, with the option to change anything we don't like."

"What is it?" Fiona whispered, her hands massaging his head.

He tilted his head to give her better access, stifling a groan of pleasure as she rubbed at a knot at the top of his spine. "I was without family for so long, it seems unfathomable at times to have them all back again. For them to welcome me back."

"You're a good man, Patrick. Of course they'd welcome you back." She dug her fingers into a knot in his shoulders, and he groaned, rolling to his stomach and off her lap as she pushed him to the bed. She rose to her knees and continued her massage. Even when she finished, she stroked his back, upper arms and shoulders.

"My only regret about remaining here is that you might see Henry," Patrick said, turning his head to meet his wife's guarded expression. "I rarely interact with him now that I'm no longer one of his favored workers, but I hate that he could harm you in some way."

"He won't, Patrick." She ran a soothing hand over his upper back and he arched into her touch.

"You don't know that," he said, rolling onto his back and meeting her worried gaze. "There are many hours in the day when I'll be at work and you'll be home alone. I hate to think anything could happen to you."

She caressed her fingertips over his eyebrows, soothing away the furrows that had formed. "I hold no interest to him now."

"I pray you are correct." He kissed her fingers that had dropped toward his lips, frowning as she flinched from his display of affection. "I have no expectations tonight, Fee. It's enough for you to touch me of your own volition."

"I'm sorry, Patrick," she whispered.

He reached out and traced her cheek, brushing away a strand of hair. He sighed as her pleasure dimmed at his soft touch. "Someday, when I touch you, when you look at me, you won't think of him first. You'll only think of me." His hand fell to the coverlet, and he pushed himself up. "Enjoy your sleep, Fee." He kissed her on her forehead, rose and exited the bedroom for the sitting room.

CHAPTER THIRTY-THREE

The McLeods left the Missoula Opera House in early July, the strains of Lucas's music lilting in their ears. Clarissa beamed as she held Gabriel's hand for a moment, before grabbing Myrtle's and Geraldine's hands, spinning them as she hummed aloud. They giggled, and Clarissa shared a contented smile with Gabriel. They walked the short distance to the Florence Hotel, where a reception was to be held on the second floor. She listened to the exuberant proclamations about Lucas's talent as they walked, content in her silence.

Gabriel held Billy, already nodding asleep against his shoulder, and they entered the large reception room lit with electric light chandeliers. The room was cleared of its customary tables and chairs so that their group could move freely. A long table along the far wall held punch and snacks. Clarissa saw women standing to the side of the room, yellow sashes strung across their chests, waiting for the room to fill before they mingled and cajoled a few coins from those gathered here in support of the referendum.

Zylphia gripped Clarissa's hand. "I'd love for Lucas to meet my friend Parthena in Boston. She's a pianist also, although she'd argue she doesn't have nearly Lucas's talent."

"I'm sure he'd enjoy meeting her, too, sometime," she murmured, as they applauded his arrival with Savannah, Jeremy and Melinda.

He saw them and winked. Clarissa found a sofa for Geraldine and Myrtle, and they sat with Melinda who joined them. Araminta moved to stand near them, motioning for Clarissa to rejoin the crowd and Lucas.

Clarissa approached Lucas and gave him a hug and kiss. "It was an extraordinary concert, Lucas. Your new composition is stunning."

"I'm thankful I had it ready for this performance," he said with a nod to those around him. "I'm glad you enjoyed it." He smiled as Patrick and Colin thumped him on his back in congratulations before moving to speak with other members of the assembled crowd.

Clarissa wandered over to Gabriel and Jeremy, grimacing as she saw Lucas cornered by Mrs. Vaughan and Mrs. Bouchard. Mrs. Vaughan wore a bright teal dress accentuating her large backside and bosom, while Mrs. Bouchard wore a fuchsia dress, nearly as ill fitted as her sister's. Mrs. Vaughan's daughter, Veronica, stood silently by as her mother prattled away. Clarissa saw Lucas attempt to move on a few times, but Mrs. Vaughan gripped his arm, preventing his escape.

"Should we save him?" Jeremy asked, hiding his smile as he took a sip of the punch.

"I'm not facing those two harpies," Gabriel said as he chuckled. "Oh, God," he whispered, biting back a full-bodied laugh.

Clarissa glanced toward Lucas, seeing Colin now ensnared in the sisters' web. "This would be amusing if it weren't so tragic. Look at how miserable her daughter is," she murmured.

Mrs. Vaughan's daughter looked at the ground, refusing to meet Colin's gaze, a red flush on her neck and cheeks.

"I wonder that her mother can be so cruel," Savannah whispered, joining them.

"Well, her mother never has been the most insightful," Gabriel said, watching as Mrs. Vaughan latched on to Colin's arm as though her hand were a talon, preventing him from escaping their group.

He attempted to joke his way out of the awkward moment, but his shoulders and posture became increasingly tense the longer he stood with them. Finally he freed his arm, applying enough force that Mrs. Vaughan tottered on her heels and nearly fell over. He slapped Lucas on the back and led him away.

At Clarissa's giggle and Savannah's snicker, Colin glanced at them, shaking his head in frustration. Clarissa caught a flash of amusement in his eyes before he guided Lucas to speak to other members of Missoula society.

"Hester," Clarissa said as Miss Loken sidled past them. "How wonderful to see you. Were you able to attend the concert?"

"Yes, I was. Thank you for the ticket," she said, a soft blush highlighting her freckles. "It was wondrous."

"Lucas is very talented," Savannah said. "Before he was famous, he used to spend his evenings entertaining us."

"You're very fortunate," Hester said, smiling her thanks as Jeremy handed her a glass of punch.

"We are. We're even more fortunate he has decided to perform rather than work in his father's linen store." Jeremy nodded to Hester as he joined their group.

"Oh, his talents would have been wasted," Hester said.

"We haven't seen you in some time, Hester," Clarissa said. "Are you well?"

"Yes, the library keeps me busy." She flushed. "I'm sorry I haven't come by since that evening in October. I've wanted to apologize for my behavior, but, as the days and then months passed, I didn't know how."

"I wanted to ask you to forgive us for attacking your beliefs. You have as much right to believe what you do as anyone else," Clarissa said. "I'd like us to remain friends."

"Thank you," she whispered.

Clarissa excused herself to check on the children. Araminta smiled at Clarissa as she approached the children, now mostly asleep or in a dazed state on the sofa. With Clarissa's arrival, Araminta had a few moments for herself, and she moved away to speak with the women suffragists circling the room and for a glass of punch. Unfortunately she was cornered by Mrs. Vaughan at the punch bowl.

"I don't know why you are here with them," Mrs. Vaughan said in her quietest voice possible. However, she'd been hard of hearing for over a decade, and her voice emerged as a stifled bellow.

"I have as much right to be here as the next person," Araminta responded. She picked up her glass of punch and a cookie, her attempt to sidestep Mrs. Vaughan thwarted when Mrs. Bouchard moved to stand beside her sister, forming a near impenetrable wall of indignant large women.

"I don't know why we should expect better, with the company you keep," Mrs. Bouchard said.

"I keep excellent company. There are no better in this town than the McLeods and the Sullivans." Araminta lifted her chin, unable to hide her pride in her association with the two families.

"If you prefer to consort with women of loose morals who've never learned the acceptable role of a woman." Mrs. Vaughan glared at Savannah and Clarissa, who were laughing with Lucas as they sat with their children.

"If you mean, remaining at home, starching their husbands' shirts, taking care of their children, cooking in the kitchen, then I would have to agree with you," Araminta said with an arched eyebrow.

"They've brought you down their dishonorable path, and I'd think your parents would be ashamed of your conduct, Miss Araminta," Mrs. Bouchard said with a sniff of disdain.

"I know of no such misconduct, thus there has been no need to feel any shame." She stiffened her shoulders.

"Your licentious relationship with Mr. Sullivan is widely spoken of," Mrs. Vaughan said in her bellowing whisper, causing those nearby to stiffen as they listened in.

"I do not know to what you refer," Araminta whispered, paling as she realized she was the center of unwanted attention.

"The easy access to your body, outside of the bonds of matrimony, is the reason he's yet to make an offer for my beloved niece. Your selfishness, your inability to follow the moral dictates of society, just like those McLeod women, has denied a young woman of her dream of matrimony. How dare you be so selfish," Mrs. Bouchard hissed.

"You are mistaken." Araminta pushed past them, inadvertently spilling her punch on Mrs. Vaughan and smashing her pastry on Mrs. Bouchard. Araminta rushed from the room, ignoring the worried calls of Clarissa and Colin.

***

Colin returned to Savannah's house, leaving the party early, before the rest of the McLeod and Sullivan clan. He let himself in with a spare key, taking a few moments for his eyes to adjust to the shadows and darkness. He stopped, listening intently for any sound from Araminta. After a moment, he heard a quiet sob coming from the rear of the house. He walked down the long hallway, easing open the conservatory door. A lamp in the corner limned the room with faint light.

"Ari," he whispered.

Her head jerked up, her face blotchy and streaked with tears. She lay on a sofa, a pillow clutched to her chest. At his entrance, she sat up. "You shouldn't be here. You're just making the gossip worse."

"What gossip?" Colin asked. He reached forward, smudging away her tears. He frowned as they fell to the floor. "Why did you leave in such distress after speaking to the sisters?"

Araminta shook her head, sobs bursting forth. She bent her head forward, refusing to look at him.

"Why won't you face me?" He touched her shoulder, frowning when she flinched at his touch. "Ari, I'd never hurt you."

At her persistent sobs, he pulled her forward until she toppled off the sofa onto the floor next to him. He settled her so she leaned against him, and he encouraged her to nestle into him. "There's nothing that bad to merit all this crying. Especially if it has to do with those wretched sisters."

"They ... they said because of me you aren't marrying Veronica."

Colin snorted. "That's the fantasy they've spun for themselves. I'd never marry Veronica. Not if she were the last woman here."

"Are you sure?"

"Of course I am. What kind of simpleton would bind himself to a woman whose mother is such a malicious gossipmonger? Not to mention the mother comes with an equal busybody in the form of the mother's sister. It'd be like having two horrendous mothers-in-law."

He felt her shudder as her sobs slowly abated. "I'd never want to ..." Araminta whispered.

He waited, but she failed to speak anything further. "You'd never what, Ari?"

"Never want to keep you from being truly happy."

"Ari, what is this all about? It doesn't make any sense." He leaned away, taking her face between his palms and forcing her to meet his worried gaze.

"They said it was common knowledge you had no interest in marriage because I shared your bed. If I wasn't such a loosely moraled woman, like Savannah and Clarissa, you would be inclined to marry an upright woman."

"They think we ... That we've ..." Colin sputtered, a light flush on his cheeks.

"They made their proclamations so loudly that others heard. Soon, most in town will have suspicions about us." Araminta lowered her gaze.

"Let them. I could never care what they think. Those I love know the truth. As do we." He traced away a silver tear track. "I'm sorry my friendship has made you vulnerable to their spiteful attacks."

"No, please don't regret being my friend. I'd be lost without it," Araminta said on a rush.

Colin smiled. "As would I." He pulled her close, holding her in his arms. He sighed as she settled, holding her against his chest until he heard the sounds of the others arriving.

***

Savannah looped her arm through Lucas's as they walked toward her home across the river. Jeremy followed with a sleepy Melinda, fatigue silencing her habitually inquisitive nature. "You performed beautifully tonight."

"Thanks, Sav. I want to always play my best, but tonight, with all my family there, I wanted my performance to be even more special." He winked at her. "What's with Colin and the women of this town?"

Savannah chuckled. "Ever since he bought the forge and turned it into a roaring success"—she squeezed his arm as he chuckled at her weak pun—"he's had the interest of most of the families here in Missoula. Especially those intent in marrying off their daughters. However, he's never had much interest in them. Now it seems, they believe it's due to Minta."

"He seems taken by her. You can't fault their reasoning."

"I can, and I will because they are spiteful women. All they care about are themselves." She bit back any further harsh words. "Colin and Araminta have led the same dance for years. We should let them continue at their own pace."

Lucas turned to share an amused glance with Jeremy. "I'd want to push it along, one way or the other. Otherwise, they'll never come to a decision. He's too comfortable with her as his good friend and confidante. And she's not sure enough of herself as a member of your family and group."

Savannah swatted him on his arm. "You think you know so much." He shrugged his shoulders at her assessment and laughed as she swatted him again. "Someday you'll find a lady who leads you on a merry dance, and then you won't find Colin's predicament so humorous."

"That'll be a long time coming, sis," he teased. He stood beside her as she opened the door to her house and entered a darkened hallway.

"They should be here," she said. "Col? Minta?" She bustled down the hallway, pausing at the conservatory door to find Araminta in Colin's arms. "Sorry," she whispered. She backed up, bumping into Lucas.

Colin rolled his eyes and pointed to chairs in the room as he soothed Araminta into remaining in his arms. Savannah frowned as she saw Araminta settle into his embrace. When she moved to approach her, Colin shook his head, and she backed away, opting to perch on a nearby chair.

"Did you have an enjoyable evening?" Lucas asked Colin.

Colin speared him with a glare, unable to do anything else. "I enjoyed the musical aspect of the night. I could have done without the rest. Why those harpies remain intent on harming Ari is beyond me."

"*Ari*," Lucas murmured with an amused smile. He grinned more broadly as Colin's glare transformed into a glower. "They're spiteful old biddies," Lucas continued, "bitter their lives didn't turn out as they'd liked and without the confidence to act in such a manner as to provoke change in their own lives. I wouldn't give them a second's worth of thought."

"Easy to say when you don't live here," Araminta murmured.

Lucas leaned forward and spoke softly to Araminta. "If I had minded every negative review or word spoken about my music, I'd still be selling linen in my father's store. I would never have had the courage to break free. Don't let those with a limited view of the world prevent you from reaching for your dreams. Someone will always be there, wanting to hold you back. Look to those who nurture you, encourage you and understand you. Know your passion. Your joy." He met her eyes as she peeked out from Colin's embrace. "You're worth ten of them, Miss Araminta."

"Thank you, Mr. Russell."

"As long as you don't forget it," he said with a smile and a wink. "Now I, for one, am for bed." He rose, reaching out a hand for Savannah and tugging her along with him.

"Your cousin is nice," Araminta whispered. She moved to leave Colin's embrace but stilled when he murmured, "No, stay, love."

"Don't say such things to me," she breathed.

"Why?" He whispered the question in the nape of her hair, almost kissing her.

"Don't make me dream."

He unpinned her hair, running his hands through it. "When have I ever given you reason to doubt me?"

She pushed back, struggling until she was free of him. "Tonight," she choked out, rushing from the room.

Colin reached for her but failed to grasp her ankle as she limped past him. He collapsed onto his back, stared at the ceiling and heaved out a sigh.

CHAPTER THIRTY-FOUR

August 1914

Zylphia straightened her turquoise linen jacket and stood tall before approaching the door. Charlotte hovered on the nearby sidewalk. She rapped loudly, listening as heavy footsteps approached. Smiling with polite determination, she produced a pamphlet to hand to the man. He frowned for a moment, keeping his door ajar, preventing her from seeing more than the entranceway to his house.

"Sir, I'd like to discuss the referendum on November 3, 1914. It's to grant women the right to vote. May I come in to speak with you and your wife?"

"My wife's too busy to be bothered listening to you yammer on about something that will never affect her."

"Sir, I must disagree. Women should have the right to vote."

"Why? Give me one good reason why women should vote." His eyes narrowed as he looked her over from her hat with matching turquoise ribbon to her jacket to her brown skirt and ended at her polished black shoes.

"Why should you have the vote?" Zylphia asked, her voice hardening. "What did you do to earn the vote?"

"Nothing. I'm a—"

"*Man*. Exactly. Just as you did nothing to earn the vote, women should be granted the same distinction. Nor should I have to justify what I or women will do with their vote. Men don't explain how or why they're voting. They vote, using their rights."

"Why should my wife want the vote? She's got no need for it. I vote for her. I provide a good home. That's the way it's always been. That's good enough."

"Do you understand that 'good enough' isn't actually good enough? That women have the right to think for themselves and determine, themselves, who and what they believe would be best for them?"

"That's where you're wrong, miss. Women don't have the right. Not now and hopefully never. And come November 3, I'll vote so it stays that way."

Zylphia flushed as she stood taller, her polite smile fading. "What about your daughter? Don't you want her to have more opportunities as she grows up?"

"She's got more now than women have ever had. That's good enough."

"I wonder how you'd feel if all you or your son could manage was 'good enough,'" Zylphia snapped. "If you had to depend on the charity of others for your rights as laws were enacted that you had no ability to alter. If you had to wonder if the generosity of others would ensure that you would have the care you needed when you were in labor, hoping that those allowed to vote in your state had passed laws to protect you and your child."

"That wouldn't happen," he scoffed, although he seemed less certain as he listened to Zylphia.

"Imagine doing the one thing you'd always wanted to do—provide a good, healthy home for your family—and you couldn't because the food you served was tainted or spoiled due to lack of oversight."

The man cocked his head, listening intently.

"These are issues that are important to women. They are important to families. They are important to our society."

A spark of understanding appeared in his eyes as he nodded. "I hear what you're saying, miss, but I ain't convinced."

"I understand. Please, will you take one of these pamphlets? I encourage you to discuss this with your wife and daughters. Talk with your friends. I believe the more you discuss it, the more you'll realize the grave injustice that has been perpetrated against Montana's women, and the nation's women, for so long."

He nodded again, reaching with less reluctance for her pamphlet.

"I thank you for listening to me, sir, and I hope, come November 3, we can count on your vote." She stepped away from the door and moved to the next house.

***

"Zee, there's a package here from your mother," Savannah called out from the sitting room as Zylphia entered the front door. Charlotte close the door behind her and moved to the kitchen.

Zylphia unpinned her hat and took off her gloves before entering the sunny room. Only Savannah was present, and Zee collapsed onto a chair with a sigh of relief.

"Rough day?" Savannah poured her a glass of lemonade from the pitcher she had set in front of her.

"If I have to listen to one more man extoll the virtues of a home where the woman thinks and acts as the husband, I think I'll scream." She shared a sardonic smile with Savannah as she reached for her glass of lemonade.

"You know those aren't nearly as common now as they used to be. Most of the homes we visit are quite excited about the upcoming vote."

"*Excited* is being optimistic. I think they are curious, and some are cautiously hopeful. Those are the homes where the wife has the ability to influence her husband. Or thinks she does. For she has no idea how he'll vote when he's in the voting booth! It's so unfair we have to depend on a man's decision to determine if we'll be granted the right to vote."

"I agree, Zee, but there's nothing more we can do." She studied her. "Unless you've begun to think it's not a worthwhile endeavor and we should give up?"

Zylphia nearly growled at Savannah before laughing. "I know your game. Of course I think it's essential work. I simply find myself out of sorts today."

Savannah raised her eyebrows. "You've been out of sorts since you arrived."

"It's nothing."

"As you've said since you arrived. And yet I think it's something important or else you wouldn't be so easily upset." Savannah reached out her hand to touch Zylphia's knee. "What happened in Boston before you decided to travel here? For I can't imagine retreating to the wilds of Montana to help us garner votes for the upcoming election is the sole reason you journeyed all this way, even if this was Sophie's idea."

Zylphia's eyes filled with tears before she shook her head to clear them. "I acted a fool and now must live with what I did." She smiled with a false brightness. "Where is that package from my mother?" At Savannah's nod to a small parcel on a table near the door, Zylphia rose to retrieve it.

She sat again, ignoring Savannah's sigh of displeasure that Zee wouldn't share more of what happened before she left Boston. Upon opening the small package, she found it filled with letters. A small note from her mother lay on the top, but she barely scanned it before flipping through the envelopes.

Her hands shook, and she paled as she traced the writing on the outside of one of the envelopes. "Teddy," she whispered.

"Zee, are you all right?" Savannah asked.

"If you'll excuse me"—Zylphia rose, bumping the low table and nearly knocking over her glass of lemonade—"I have a few letters to read." She rushed from the room and raced up the stairs to her bedroom, slamming her door shut behind her. She held the envelopes, slightly weathered and all showing signs of travel. After flipping the lock on her door, she moved to her bed and carefully opened a letter.

My Darling Zee,
I knew it was too much to hope you'd write me after how I ignored you. However, although it might annoy you to receive letters from me, I'll persist in writing to you. I find, as I sit and wait for what comes next, you are all I think about. Our short time together was the most vivid time of my life ...

She set aside the letter, saving it for later, wanting to find the first letter he'd written her and read them in order. She found a faded postmark, compared it to the others and opened it.

My Darling Zee,
Do you know how much comfort it gives me just to write your name? How much more it would give me to say it? To whisper it into your ear as I held

you?

I have no right to say such things, but a man in battle begins to wish for the unattainable. I know by now you must hate me, and, for that, I am sorry. More sorry than I could ever express.

I don't know if you realized it, but I kept one of your letters, and I finally read it. I read your words of love and hope as I was shipping out to fight in the Great War. I've read them more times than you can imagine, and I carry your letter as though a talisman to get me through each day.

In what you'd call a manly fit of pique, I fulfilled my grandparents' wish for me and enlisted in the British Expeditionary Forces. I can't tell you more than to say I'm somewhere in France. Dreaming of Boston, of holding you in my arms in my study. I miss you, my darling girl. My impetuous, loving, passionate Zylphia, who was brave when I faltered. Please forgive me and give me hope when I have so little.

I love you, Zylphia. I always will.
Your Teddy

Zylphia bowed her head and sobbed. She held the letter to her chest while she curled into herself on her bed and shook with her tears. Soon she was curious what his other letters said, and she swiped at her face as she reached for them. A loud knocking on her door interrupted her. "Yes?"

"Zee, Rissa is here and would like to see you," Savannah said.

"I'll be down in a moment."

"Don't be too long," Savannah said.

Zylphia traced the unopened envelopes but decided to wait to read them, rather than rush in reading them now or make her cousins wait for her. She rose, rinsed her face with water from the ewer in her room and avoided looking at herself in the mirror.

She walked down the stairs at a more sedate pace than she had ascended them and reentered the sitting room.

"Zee, it's great to see you. Sav and I were just discussing the canvassing and upcoming ..." Clarissa's voice faltered as she turned to look at Zylphia. "What happened? Is your mother ill?"

"My mother?"

"Sav mentioned you had received letters in a package from your mother." Clarissa reached out a hand to tug Zylphia onto the settee next to her. When Zylphia sat down, Clarissa placed an arm around her shoulder, encouraging Zylphia to lean into her. After a moment of sitting with erect posture, Zylphia crumpled and burrowed into Clarissa's side as she cried.

Clarissa shared a long look with Savannah, who shook her head in confusion. Clarissa stroked Zylphia's head and shoulder, comforting her with her silence.

"I fell in love this past year," Zee whispered. "It wasn't wonderful like everyone says."

"Oh, Zee." Savannah sighed. "What happened?"

"He's a brilliant inventor and financier, but I was a coward. I didn't want to love or be loved, so I pu-pushed him away," she said as her tears flowed. As she accepted Savannah's handkerchief, she nodded her thanks. "He left, angry with me and the harsh words I'd said to him, to return to England." She raised terrified eyes to her cousins. "Now he's fighting in the Great War. What if he dies?" She sobbed in earnest now, and Savannah moved nearer to stroke her back as Clarissa held her close.

"Is there any way to write him? To let him know you were a fool to let him go?" Savannah asked in a gentle voice.

"I'd already tried that, but he ignored my letters last spring. He kept one and read it as he was going to fight. Now that he's in battle, he says all he can think of is me. I have letters upstairs from him."

"Write him, Zee," Clarissa urged. "Don't hold back telling him what's in your heart. If you forgive him for hurting you, as it appears he's forgiven you, tell him. Don't live with that sort of regret." She clasped Zylphia's tear-streaked cheeks between her hands and raised her head to meet her gaze. "Not when he's fighting in a war and ..."

"I know," Zylphia whispered. "Even without knowing he's fighting, I've tried to ignore reading about the battles occurring in France. Now I fear I'll become obsessed, imagining what could be happening to Teddy." She took another deep breath.

"It's all right, Zee. Go upstairs. Read your letters. Write him." Clarissa stroked a hand one last time over her head and gave her a gentle prod from the settee.

Zylphia stumbled once before she regained her balance and then hastened toward her room.

***

Zylphia sat at the small desk, tapping her pen in agitation on a piece of paper. She smiled wanly as she thought of her mother when she was annoyed and how she always tapped a pen. She took a deep breath and envisioned Teddy in her mind. In an instant she was writing.

My Darling Teddy,

Please forgive me for not writing you sooner. I did not receive your letters until today. I am in Montana, staying with my cousins, as I canvass for the vote for women in the upcoming election. I took your advice, Teddy darling, and, although my life has more purpose, it has still felt rather empty.

I miss you. I miss teasing you, laughing about something only you or I would understand. Sharing my paintings with you. Hearing about your inventions. I miss everything. What I wouldn't give to hear you whisper "Zee" in my ear as you held me close.

Keep my letter next to your heart, my love, for that is where you are for me. I love you, Teddy. It still scares me how much I feel for you, but I refuse to run away from my feelings again.

I dream of the day I can look in your eyes and tell you that I love you in person.

Your Zee

CHAPTER THIRTY-FIVE

September 1914

The car lumbered over a hill before making a slight turn. Zylphia gasped as she glanced out the window. "Oh my, look at those mountains."

"Mr. Pickens always said the Bitter Root Mountains were his favorite," Clarissa said as she stifled a groan when they hit a pothole. "They are majestic," Clarissa breathed.

"That there's the Como Peaks," their driver said helpfully. "We'll be in Darby in a matter of minutes."

"Do you know where the Carlins live?" Clarissa asked as she hissed at another jolt.

"You bet. Everyone knows Sebastian and his missus." He grinned at Clarissa, sitting beside him in the front seat. "He ensures his men have enough work but also time to hunt. Everybody likes Seb."

"He's a good man," Clarissa said. She glanced out the window as Darby came into view.

They passed a school on the edge of the town before the road dipped and curved, entering the main part of Darby, cutting through the heart of town. A few of the buildings, including a saloon and a bank, were constructed of redbrick, although the majority were wooden. Men in rough work clothes lingered on the boardwalks or loitered outside saloons, openly staring at the automobile as it trundled into town.

The driver turned left down a side street, taking them one block off the main thoroughfare and came to a lurching stop in front of a small two-story home painted in an evergreen color. A pair of rocking chairs sat on one side of the large front porch. Clarissa heaved open the passenger-side door and tumbled out, groaning with relief to be out of the car.

Zylphia and Savannah followed her, exiting the backseat, nearly crashing into her. They giggled as they waited for the driver to unload their luggage. "You'll come back the day after tomorrow to drive us to Hamilton?" Savannah asked.

"Yes, ma'am," he said as he lifted out their small traveling bags. "Enjoy your stay in Darby."

They each hefted their small bag and approached the front door. Clarissa raised her hand to knock when the front door swung open.

"Rissa!" Amelia squealed. She pushed open the screen door and launched herself into Clarissa's arms. They rocked for a moment before Amelia released her and grasped Savannah in a tight embrace.

"Oh, it's wonderful to see you both again." Her eyes lit on Zylphia. "I beg your pardon. I didn't mean to exclude you." She frowned as she examined Zylphia, noting her McLeod coloring. She raised an eyebrow to Clarissa and Savannah as she ushered them inside.

"This is Zylphia, Aidan's daughter," Savannah said. "She's come to help us canvass for the vote."

"How wonderful," Amelia said as she leaned forward and embraced Zylphia. "I'm delighted to finally meet you. Please, set down your cases and hang your hat and coats on the stand there." She pointed to a rack by the front door. "If you don't object, let's move to the kitchen."

Clarissa laughed. "As long as I'm not expected to cook." She looked to Zylphia to explain. "Amelia is a wonderful cook and taught me all I know. I was her first student and most likely her worst."

"Hush such nonsense," Amelia said as she led them through a comfortable living area with mismatched chairs and settees, a formal dining room with the table already set for the evening meal and into the kitchen. A scarred large wooden table sat in the middle of the big bright room. The wood stove emitted much-needed warmth on this cool early September afternoon. Amelia waved to them to sit at the table. "Please, make yourselves comfortable."

She moved toward the stove where a kettle of water sat warming and made a pot of tea. "How is the canvassing progressing?" she asked.

"It would be easier if my automobile hadn't broken down last week." Savannah shook her head in disgust. "We'll have to return in October for more canvassing as we can't travel to all the small towns and rural homes as planned without our own means of transport."

"Other than your travel problems, how is it going?" Amelia asked with a smile.

"Well, although it is hard at times to bite our tongues at some of the ridiculous things said to us …" Zylphia began with a roll of her eyes.

Amelia frowned with curiosity.

"For example, a man yesterday told me there would be no point to marriage if his wife could vote too, because she thinks as he does in all things and couldn't possible have a use for the vote. It would simply give two votes to the same candidate." Zylphia huffed out a sigh of disgust.

"How are they reacting to a group of eastern women advising them how to vote?" Amelia asked, biting her lip as she fought a smile.

"Fairly well," Clarissa said. "When I explain I've lived here for thirteen years and Sav for over eleven, that helps. I hate that, the moment I speak, I'm thought of as an outsider."

"Well, everyone in Montana is an outsider of sorts, so you shouldn't take it personally. It's more that they'd hate to think they're being told how to act or vote." Amelia grinned as she looked at Zylphia. "I imagine you could be too forward thinking for many."

"It's no different than what I've heard in Boston," Zylphia said as she shrugged her shoulders, either in resignation or agreement. "It's all the same. Men, and women, afraid of change."

"Well, as Sophie would say, the one constant we can rely on is change," Clarissa said.

"Could I join you tomorrow?" Amelia asked. "I know it's not much of a contribution, but I'd like to do something."

"That would be wonderful. It would also help if the locals see that one of their own is supportive," Savannah said as she took a sip of tea.

"And that you are our friend," Clarissa murmured. "Too many times when we've come into a town, we've been seen as radical outsiders from the big city of Missoula, and it's taken time we didn't have to convince people to listen to us."

Amelia nodded with enthusiasm at the thought of being part of the canvassing.

"Amelia, how are your children?" Savannah asked.

"Very well. I can't believe how quickly they are growing," she said as her eyes lit with a mother's pride.

"I can't believe you have seven children!" Clarissa said.

"Seven?" Zylphia asked. "I remember someone remarking that you had quite a few, but I never thought to ask how many."

"Yes, we've been quite blessed," Amelia said with a broad smile. "Thankfully Sebastian has a good job, and I'm able to add to our income by selling sandwiches to the workers."

"Where do you sell them?" Savannah asked.

"In a few of the local saloons."

Clarissa choked on her tea while Zylphia's eyes widened. "You've been in a saloon?" Clarissa gasped.

"Yes, numerous times."

"Why did you never mention this in one of your letters?"

Amelia attempted to bite back a smile and failed. She nodded to Clarissa. "I know how it would upset Gabriel, and I had no desire to provoke his concern."

"And Sebastian knows this?" Savannah asked, shaking her head in surprise.

"Yes. He's quite supportive," Amelia said as she laughed at her friends' dazed expressions. "It's not that scandalous."

"Yes, it is," Clarissa said as she shook her head at Amelia. "Tomorrow, are we expected to canvass in saloons?"

"Well, the majority of the men will congregate there," Amelia said. "And, if you are with me selling sandwiches, they'll be more apt to listen to you."

"Oh my," Savannah said as she sat back in her chair, shaking her head. "I'm not sure I could do that."

"I'll be happy to join you," Zylphia said. "It seems like quite the adventure." Her smile dimmed. "It would give me something interesting and exciting to write to Teddy."

Amelia nodded, sparing Zylphia any questions when the back door burst open.

"Mama!" a blond-haired girl said as she burst into the kitchen. "Guess what I …" She broke off, her eyes going round as she beheld the visitors. "Aunt Clarissa!" she shrieked as she ran around the table to fling herself in Clarissa's arms.

"Annie, darling," Clarissa said as she held her close and kissed her on the side of her head. "Oh, how you've grown." She shared a smile with Amelia. "I find it's the same with Geraldine. They keep growing no matter how much I want them to remain my little angels forever."

"How long can you stay?" Annie asked, bouncing around to give Savannah and Zylphia hugs. "Nice to meet you!" She said to Zylphia before returning to Clarissa's side to burrow into her. Annie sighed with contentment when Clarissa gave her a soft squeeze.

"I've missed you, Annie," Clarissa said before the girl raced away to wash her hands and help her mother.

Nicholas clomped into the room, wiping his boots on the rug outside before entering the kitchen. "They came," he said with a broad smile.

Clarissa, Savannah and Zylphia had stood at this point to hug the children as they trickled in from school.

"My, how you've grown, Nickie," Savannah said as she ruffled his russet-colored hair. "I can't believe you're almost seventeen."

He puffed out his chest with pride. "I've begun to help my father at the mill."

"As long as you continue with your studies and don't fall behind," Amelia said with a hint of a warning in her voice. "I don't mind you working at the mill, but you will complete your education." She set down a sliced loaf of warm cinnamon bread with butter, and the children fell on the snack as though they hadn't eaten in days.

While the children ate, Amelia introduced them to Zylphia. "You've met Nicholas and Annie. Mary is ten, Adam is nine," Amelia said, stroking a hand over their shoulders. "Then there's Shane who is seven, and David's six."

"I thought you had seven children," Zylphia asked, confused.

"John is away playing with a friend this afternoon. Come. Let me show you to your room," Amelia said. "I wish I had space for each of you to have your own room, but it's not possible."

"Amelia, we're thankful to have this time with you. We know what an inconvenience it is to have us here."

"Not at all," Amelia said with a wave of her hand. "It's our pleasure. We don't travel to Missoula nearly as often as I'd like. It's a major outing with all nine of us. Although I appreciate letters, it's never the same as seeing you." Her smile included all three women.

She walked down a long hallway and opened a door. "We fit a single bed in here along with the double that's usually here, but it is quite cramped."

"This is lovely," Savannah said as she moved toward the single bed that appeared to be a cot. "This will suit us just fine."

"I agree," Zylphia said as she inched her way toward the double bed. "I can't imagine needing anything more."

"Oh, stop it!" Amelia said with a laugh. "At least we'll be together, and that's all that matters."

A few hours later, Sebastian's deep voice resonated throughout the house as he called out, "I'm home!" The squeals of delight from the children as they raced toward him provoked smiles as Clarissa and Savannah rose to greet him.

"Sebastian," Clarissa said. "It's wonderful to see you."

"Clarissa," he said as he enfolded her in a hug. "It's been too long since we've seen you." He turned to Savannah and gave her a quick hug, and then nodded to Zylphia.

"Seb, this is Zylphia, although we call her Zee. Aidan's daughter," Clarissa said.

"Ah, that's why you have the look of a McLeod about you, although I detect a touch of Delia in you too," he said as he studied her. "Around the eyes. I met your mother a few years ago when they visited."

Zylphia smiled. "It's nice to meet you." He gripped her shoulder before turning to watch Amelia enter the room, his eyes lit with love and pride as he beheld her.

"How was your day?" Amelia asked, running a quick hand down one of his arms.

"Fine. The usual. No one was hurt, and we have a shipment ready to head out tomorrow on the train," he said as he tucked a strand of hair behind one of her ears. "Dinner smells delicious."

"It's a roast, and we'll eat in the dining room tonight."

"Then I'd better wash up," he said with a smile as he winked at their guests. He walked with a barely discernible limp.

When they sat for dinner, Clarissa turned to Sebastian. "Is there any chance you could be transferred back to run the mill in Missoula?"

"I could apply for one of the newer ones, like the one run by Mr. Polley, but I have no interest in leaving Darby. We have a good home here, and I like the men I work with. I run a good mill."

"I never doubted you did," Clarissa said, belatedly realizing her question could be construed as critical in some manner. "It's just I wish you lived closer."

"It's not that far," he said with a wry smile. "Although those final few miles in an automobile or carriage do seem to last an infernal distance, don't they?"

Savannah laughed. "I thought a rib would rattle loose today as we drove here from the station in Grantsdale. Our driver took great care to land in every pothole in the road!"

"I know my father loves his automobile and encourages me to ride in it as often as possible, but I always prefer to ride in a streetcar instead," Zylphia said.

"Well, you don't have that option here." Amelia laughed.

"At this point, walking doesn't seem half bad," Zylphia muttered.

"We should have planned better when we learned Sav's automobile was not available and decided to canvass while riding our bicycles throughout the valley," Clarissa said.

Amelia and Sebastian laughed at the thought.

Clarissa continued her argument. "Susan B. Anthony believed the bicycle would bring great freedom to women, and she was correct."

"Yes, but I can't imagine you bicycling all those miles, arriving disheveled and shrouded in dust, showing the citizens of each town that you were respectable women worthy of listening to. I think you've opted for the correct course of action," Sebastian said. He winked at Amelia as he pushed away his plate. "Who'll join Amelia as she makes her rounds through the saloons tomorrow?"

Clarissa tapped him on his arm. "I can't believe you condone such actions!"

"Of course I do. She's insistent in earning money for the family, and she could conceive of no other way. She can't teach because she's married." Sebastian watched Amelia as she tended to their youngest child, John.

"Besides, Rissa, the majority of those men understand she's my wife and know better than to cross her. She's not there in the evenings. She's there midday at the latest." Sebastian winked at Amelia.

"What are you saving money for?" Clarissa asked.

"Well, if the children wish to attend the university, I want them to have the opportunity. With seven children, I need to look at all options. Nicholas is almost of age to attend."

"He'd always have a place to stay in Missoula," Clarissa said as Savannah nodded.

"I can't bear the thought of him away from home, but I know he must leave at some point. Knowing he'd have the support of ... family would ease my mind."

"Simply let us know what you need, and we'll help in any way," Clarissa said.

"Seb, are you and Amelia traveling to Helena in a few weeks for the parade?" Savannah asked. "It's remarkable to have a woman's day and suffragist parade planned during the state fair in Helena this year."

"I was hoping Amelia, Annie and the younger children could travel to Missoula and make the journey with you," Sebastian said. "Nicholas and I will rough it while they are away." He winked at Nicholas.

"We plan on traveling to Helena on Tuesday to be settled before the parade on Friday," Savannah said. She smiled slyly as she watched Zylphia. "Anna Howard Shaw is coming to speak to those gathered on Friday after the parade."

Zylphia sighed with disgust, pushing the remnants of her meal around on her plate.

"What don't you like about her, Zee? I think she's a remarkable woman," Amelia said.

"If you like antiquated tactics destined to yield no result, then I'd recommend listening to what she has to say." Zylphia shook her head.

Amelia squinted as she studied Zylphia. "Do those from the East, who sent you out thinking you were a faithful member of NAWSA, realize you're really an ardent supporter of Alice Paul?"

Zylphia grinned. "No. Sophie thinks it best to keep them on their toes. She also thinks it best to understand what both groups are doing. She doesn't really care who has the more successful tactic, as long as she has the opportunity to vote before she dies."

Clarissa shivered. "Don't even mention that. Although I only receive her guidance through her weekly letters, I couldn't imagine life without Sophie."

"Well, last I saw her, she was feisty and reigning over her fiefdom with her usual vigor. I wouldn't be concerned," Zylphia said with a smile.

Sebastian frowned. "*Alice Paul.* Isn't she the one advocating that we vote against Democrats because Wilson is a Democrat and has failed to vocally support universal enfranchisement?"

Zylphia nodded.

"Seems a crackbrained policy to me, especially as many of those are your most ardent supporters."

"She wants to show the president that his intransigence will lead to instability in Congress and his party. That universal enfranchisement is a policy that must be supported and advocated for by the president."

Sebastian shook his head. "She didn't change his mind after the disgraceful way you were treated at that march in Washington, DC, so I doubt this will change his mind."

"Then we'll have to increase our tactics until he does," Zylphia retorted, her cheeks flushed and blue eyes flashing.

Sebastian watched her and shook his head. "If you don't look like Gabe when he's angered. Listen, Zee. Fight for universal suffrage. But don't turn to violence."

"I promise. I won't."

Sebastian studied her a moment before grinning. "Speaking of radical places, how is your brother faring in Butte under martial law?" he asked Clarissa, holding up the *Missoulian* and the editorial written by Joseph Dixon. A bold quote by Dixon proclaimed *There does not seem to be any reason but the desires of Amalgamated for martial law and the troops in Butte.*

"Patrick wrote me that, when the troops arrived, they thought they'd be feted with a heroes' welcome. Instead everyone watched them with distrust and anger. There's no need for them there, except to promote Amalgamated's agenda."

"That's the way of this state," Sebastian said. "Who do you think purchases the majority of my lumber?" He raised his hands as though in defeat. "There's little we can do to fight them."

"Write your politicians. Write articles in your newspapers," Zylphia argued.

Everyone around the table laughed, but Zylphia was perplexed.

"They have bribed every politician here and own every newspaper," Amelia explained. "There's no way for a resident of Montana to have freedom of knowledge as everything we read is filtered through them."

"How is such a thing possible? Why doesn't the federal government do something?" Zylphia asked.

"As long as Amalgamated produces the copper the country needs to continue America's rapid growth, they will allow Amalgamated to do what it pleases," Sebastian said. "Things are very different here, Zee."

"Why does your brother, Patrick, remain in Butte, rather than move to Missoula? I'd think he'd grasp at any reason to escape and live closer to you and Colin," Sebastian said.

Clarissa sighed. "He writes that Fiona has been advised that she should refrain from any travel and should remain in a familiar environment."

"I think Patrick is also determined to make his way for his family without depending on us," Savannah said. "He knows I'd be happy to help and able to help."

"You don't want to interfere with a man's sense of pride," Sebastian said.

Amelia rolled her eyes as Clarissa chuckled. Clarissa said, "I know. I wish he'd move to Missoula, but I'm content knowing where he is."

"And as long as Fiona remains healthy, that is what is important," Savannah said.

After a few moments of silence, Sebastian asked about Clarissa and Gabriel's children and the goings-on in Missoula, halting further discussion about state politics and Patrick's persistent presence in Butte.

***

The following morning Zylphia slipped from bed just before sunrise and donned a simple dress. She grabbed a small case from her bag and cracked open the bedroom door. A floorboard creaked as she walked down the hall toward the front door. She eased it open and walked in haste toward an open field she remembered passing when they drove into town to catch the sunrise.

When she arrived a few minutes later, the sky was just lightening to a robin's-egg blue, each moment changing and limning the mountains in a different hue. She breathed deeply, inhaling wood smoke and the elusive scent of the pine forest. She found a small boulder to perch on and watched as the mountains came into greater relief with the dawning day.

She pulled out her case and extracted a small sketch pad and a sharpened pencil. Her hand flew across the paper as she drew, capturing the mood and atmosphere of the morning with light strokes and deft shading. Intent on capturing the scene, she became lost to her surroundings.

A hand settled on her shoulder, and she flinched, nearly marring her drawing with a deep pencil scratch. She screeched and jumped up, spinning to face the person behind her. "Sebastian," she whispered, holding a hand to her heart as she caught her breath.

"I'm sorry to startle you, but you didn't answer when I called your name." He smiled his apology. "I hadn't realized you were an artist."

"I have a near daily compulsion to draw something," Zylphia admitted. When Sebastian nodded at her sketch pad, she handed it to him.

He began with the unfinished sketch from the morning before flipping through the previous days' work. "These are something," he said as he swayed to and fro in front of her.

Zylphia noted he always seemed to be in motion, even when standing still. "What do you plan to do with them?"

"If I have the opportunity, I hope to paint them. I think oil paintings." Zylphia nodded her thanks as she accepted the sketchpad. "They're to help me remember when I'm at my easel in Boston."

"I'd think you'd have an easel here to capture the moment as it's in front of you."

"It would be difficult to obtain what I need," Zylphia protested.

"Most anything you could imagine can be had from the Merc in Missoula. Just ask Gabe, and he'll help you." Sebastian watched her intently. "I'd be honored to hang one of your fine paintings in my house. I have a feeling you'll soon be as well-known as your cousin, Lucas."

"Oh, this is just a hobby," Zylphia said, her breath coming quickly.

"Well, I ain't no artist, but I'm smart enough to know this is art worth having in my house. You're talented, Zee. Don't waste it. Not even for this cause you espouse."

"It's essential for women to obtain the vote," Zylphia said with a flash of her irritation in her eyes.

"I'm not arguing against it. I'd love for my Amelia to be able to vote and have her say in her future. But this cause is a fleeting thing, Zee. Your art, now that's something to be nurtured for life." He smiled. "You're fortunate your father's wealthy enough you don't have to worry about such a mundane thing as money."

Zylphia blushed. "I know."

"Come. I'm sure by now they've all awakened and are worried about your absence. I always leave for work early, so Amelia will think nothing of my not being home."

"Did you follow me?" Zylphia walked next to Sebastian, thankful he walked at a slower pace than her male cousins.

"I heard someone leave. I glanced down the street to see you turn the corner. By the time I dressed, you had disappeared. It took me a little while to find you." He watched her with a worried gaze. "The men of this town are respectful, for the most part. But there are always drifters. You must take more care, Zee. I would hate for something to happen to you."

"Thank you," Zylphia whispered. "All I could think about was having a few moments alone to sketch. To lose myself in art."

"Well, you've become a bit too lost when you don't even hear a man of my size approaching."

"You move with the stealth of a cat!" Zylphia protested with a laugh.

"Even so, Zee, even so," Sebastian said.

"My father sent me west with a maid, but I can't stand having her hovering a step or two behind me all the time. She remained in Missoula to help Araminta care for the children." She shared a chagrined smile with Sebastian. They walked a few minutes in the quiet of the early morning.

"Can I ask you something that I don't want to worry Amelia about?" At his nod, she asked, "Do you worry about Nickie and the Great War?"

"Of course we do. She reads the newspaper reports every day with the hopes that the fighting will soon end. She has nightmares about her son being called to fight. He'll be eighteen soon and of perfect age." He looked at her. "You and your women want voters to shun the president and his party 'cause he won't support your cause. I have to say that his determination to keep us out of this war, and boys like Nickie safe, is reason enough for me to vote for him."

Zylphia frowned, nodding her understanding as she linked her arm through his and matched his stride toward his home.

"Zee!" Clarissa exclaimed when she walked in through the kitchen door with Sebastian. "We've been so worried. Amelia just sent Nicholas to the mill to fetch you, Sebastian."

"I'm sorry," Zylphia said, looking chagrined. "I woke with an overwhelming desire to sketch this morning. I didn't think I'd be missed, but I must have become lost in my drawing. Sebastian found me."

"I heard her leave and eventually found her," he said as he moved toward the sky-blue coffeepot and poured himself a cup. At Zylphia's nod, he poured her one too. "She was immersed in sketching the mountains."

"Oh, Zylphia!" Amelia exclaimed, gripping her in a tight hug as she burst into the kitchen. "You've had us frantic."

"I'm sorry," Zylphia said again as she was pushed into a chair and a plate of pancakes, eggs and bacon was set before her.

"There's my Amelia," Sebastian murmured as he leaned forward to kiss his wife on her forehead as she bustled past him. "Always assuming we'll need plenty of food, especially if there's a calamity of some sort." He grunted when she elbowed his side good-naturedly.

Nicholas burst into the kitchen, and groaned with frustration to find his father and Zylphia sitting down to breakfast. "Where were you?" he demanded, gasping from his dash to the mill and back.

"Thank you for your help, son," Sebastian said, running a quick hand over Nicholas's head as he sat next to his father. Seb pushed his full plate toward Nicholas, sharing his breakfast.

After breakfast, Clarissa and Savannah helped Amelia make sandwiches while Zylphia finished her sketch from the morning. When it was time to go, Zylphia took the basket offered to her, placing pamphlets next to the sandwiches.

They walked the short distance to the Sawmill Saloon, a two-story brick building in the central part of the town. Men called out greetings to Amelia, and one opened the door for them to pass.

"Not like you to have a companion, Mrs. Carlin."

"Miss McLeod is my friend from Missoula," Amelia said with a nod of thanks as she led the way into the saloon. She turned to Zee and whispered, "He always tries to sweet talk a free sandwich from me."

Zylphia turned around as the door was closing and thrust a pamphlet at him. "Thank you for your help," she said with a broad smile. He frowned when he realized he received something other than a sandwich but then tipped his hat at her. The wooden door slammed shut with a thwack behind her.

Zylphia looked around the saloon. To her left was a long wooden bar. Behind it was a mirrored wall of shelves filled with glasses. Men leaned against the bar or sat at small round tables. The wooden floorboards creaked in places and were scuffed from the multitude of booted men visiting the saloon. Bright light shone through the front and side windows, and the tin ceiling reflected it.

Amelia turned to Zylphia with an inquisitive smile. "What do you think, Zee?"

"It's not what I thought it would be," she whispered.

"A den of iniquity," Amelia giggled as she approached a group of men, joking with them and cajoling them into buying two of her sandwiches. She handed them each a pamphlet, urging them to vote for women in November. She moved from table to table, and Zylphia emerged from her trance and walked toward the other side of the saloon.

"Would you like to purchase a sandwich?" she asked a group of men deep in discussion.

One man tapped at an article in the newspaper and then scowled at her. "No, miss. We want one of Mrs. Carlin's," he said, turning his attention back to the paper.

"Excuse me, but I'm staying with her, and I'm helping her today. These are her sandwiches."

He nodded, and each man at the table bought a sandwich. As they searched their pockets for coins, she twisted her head around to read the newspaper headline. She absently handed them sandwiches with a pamphlet and placed their coins in her pocket. "May I borrow your paper for a moment?"

At the man's nod, she grabbed it and turned away, her eyes racing over the headline and its story. "Imagine," she breathed as she read about six hundred Paris taxi drivers ferrying over six thousand reserve troops from Paris to the frontline to help protect the city and prevent it from falling to the Germans. The article mentioned heavy losses for the British Expeditionary Force, and Zylphia took a deep breath as she fought panic.

"Zee?" Amelia asked, placing a gentle hand on her shoulder and glancing at the newspaper she held. "Oh, yes, the war. It's quite something to imagine all those taxi drivers, isn't it? The men have been talking of little else."

"Why?" Zee shook her head as she forced herself to imagine Teddy well and whole.

"If they hadn't acted as they had, Paris could have fallen. Can you imagine?" Amelia asked. "Their actions may have kept us from having to enter this war."

"We'll never join in," Zylphia said. "Too many are against it, including the president."

"I hope you're right." She traded her empty basket for Zee's full one and moved through the saloon.

Zylphia faced the men at the table she'd approached. "Thank you for lending me your paper," she said. She gifted them a weak smile before following Amelia onto the boardwalk.

"I have another stop. Do you still want to come along?" Amelia asked. At Zylphia's resolute nod, they walked toward another saloon, this one a single story with low ceilings and a darkened interior.

"This is what I thought a saloon looked like," Zee whispered, a miasma of smoke, unwashed bodies and stale beer permeating the air.

"I only have a few sandwiches to sell, and then we can leave," Amelia whispered.

Zylphia followed behind Amelia, smiling encouragingly as Amelia sold her sandwiches and handed out pamphlets.

When they emerged onto the boardwalk a few minutes later, Amelia paused, watching the men coming and going. "We need an event. Where you three could discuss the merits of women voting. It would be much more effective than handing out pamphlets one by one with sandwiches." She grabbed Zylphia's arm, tugging her along. "Come with me."

They walked along the main street of Darby, Amelia calling out hellos to most of the people she passed but not stopping. She turned left down a side street, and Zylphia heard the whirring of a saw.

"The mill's not far," Amelia said.

They made another few turns, and they were in a large yard filled with stacked logs yet to be sawn into lumber. Nearby a group of men loaded lumber onto railroad cars.

"I never imagined it would be such a big operation," Zylphia said, slowing her stride as she watched in fascination as the men worked in concerted effort.

Amelia kept her hand gripped around Zylphia's arm. "Lest you have an inclination to wander away," she said. She pulled Zylphia from any possibility of harm and toward a doorway.

Zylphia raised her hands to cover her ears at the piercingly shrill sound of the saw cutting wood.

"Amelia!" Sebastian yelled, emerging from his office. He led Zylphia and Amelia outside to the relative quiet of the yard, steering them to a safe area. "Has something happened?"

"No. I had an idea," Amelia said. She smiled as Sebastian pulled out the last unsold sandwich in her basket and ate it.

He nodded for her to continue, watching her with intent interest.

"Do you think you could spread the word that we're having a social tonight at the Hall? I'd like Zee, Rissa and Sav to have the chance to talk to more men, and that seemed a better way to go about it."

Sebastian nodded. "Sounds like a good idea. 'Bout seven?" At Amelia's nod, he leaned forward to kiss her on her cheek. "I'll spread the word and see you home tonight."

Amelia beamed at him and then spun, gripping Zylphia's arm as they left the mill yard.

"Does he always go along with what you say?" Zylphia asked.

"Not always but generally. He respects my opinion, as I do his. Sometimes we argue, but I hate fighting over things that are petty or senseless."

"Are you always this rational?"

"No, of course not. We have our fights. But, more often than not, we talk things through. We argue, but we never endeavor to hurt the other."

Zylphia flushed at Amelia's words.

"Why should that embarrass you, Zee?"

"Because I intentionally hurt the man I love. Out of fear." Zylphia shrugged her shoulders. "Makes me realize I'm not as mature as I like to consider myself."

"Or you've yet learned to trust yourself and others," Amelia said. "I know what it is to be afraid of the future. To wonder how I'd ever survive." At Zylphia's curious stare, she nodded back toward the mill. "Sebastian's my second husband. Liam—Nickie and Annie's father—died in the mines in Butte when they were very young. I never thought I'd love again."

"But you did."

"I did. You never know what's possible, Zee, unless you give yourself permission to fully experience life. To not worry what others are saying or if you are disappointing someone." She smiled at Zylphia. "It doesn't mean you have no concern for those around you. But I think we become so focused on what is expected of us and our vision of who we think we are that we lose sight of what we truly want. Who we truly are." She gripped Zylphia's hand. "Come. Let's go to the Hall and organize the gathering for tonight."

"I'm an artist," Zylphia blurted out. "It's the one thing in this world I love to do."

Amelia smiled and then teased her. "Good. Because when you're rich and famous, the painting Sebastian says you're gifting us will have even more value."

***

"Amelia, are you certain about this?" Clarissa asked as she ushered the McLeods into the Hall. Amelia and Clarissa carried boxes filled with cookies. Sebastian was at the saloon, obtaining a few kegs of beer and drumming up interest in the gathering, while Zylphia and Sav carried pies. Along with beer would be kegs containing apple cider.

"This is the perfect way for you to speak to the members of the community. Who doesn't like a gathering?" Amelia asked as she set up her treats on one of the tables. "Besides, when people learn Sebastian will play his fiddle, they'll come out to hear him and to dance."

"I'm not sure the women in charge of the committee would be pleased we're serving alcohol," Savannah muttered.

"Well, those temperance women aren't welcomed here," Amelia said. "If we didn't have beer, there wouldn't be much of a gathering. The men want to have a drink when they've finished a hard day's work."

Clarissa shared a worried look with Savannah and Zylphia but moved to work beside Amelia. "Have either of you thought about what we'll say?" she whispered.

"No," Savannah said, then giggled. "This could be an unmitigated disaster."

"I think we need to keep it short and to the point. The men coming here tonight will have worked a long day and won't be interested in listening to us go on and on," Zylphia said. She winked at young David as he purloined a cookie, then ran off to join his friends on the other side of the Hall.

"Zee, you're the calmest of us all. You should speak," Savannah said.

"I'm from Massachusetts and have the strongest accent. I haven't lived here for over a decade. They won't listen to me like they would you. Besides, you're the one who's best friends with Amelia and Sebastian," Zylphia argued, nodding at Clarissa. Zee pulled out a scrap of paper and handed it to Rissa. "Here's a list of things you might want to touch on but keep it brief."

Clarissa groaned. "Fine, I'll talk, but you'll all be up there with me."

Savannah and Zylphia grinned conspiratorially at each other.

Sebastian entered the Hall, smiling to many of those present and slapping the backs of most of the men. He asked a few to move the casks of beer outside into the Hall. Sebastian approached the women. "I'll introduce you. Most of the men know me, and it'll help when they realize I'm for this referendum to pass." He winked at Amelia who chatted with women near the long table. "Are we ready?" he asked them all.

Clarissa took a deep breath and nodded. "As ready as we'll ever be."

"Great." He rose onto a small stage, holding up his hands and motioning for those present to cease speaking. He smiled at a few ribald jokes and whistles, but the room's occupants quieted.

"Thanks for coming to the Hall tonight on such short notice. It's always a pleasure to have our friends, the McLeods, visit us from Missoula. This time they're here to promote the upcoming referendum granting women the right to vote. It's something I urge you to consider, and I can't wait for voting day so that my Amelia will have the right to vote, too." He smiled as a few of the men whistled and hooted. He then waved an arm in the women's direction, and Clarissa stepped slightly forward of Savannah and Zylphia.

"Mrs. McLeod, Miss McLeod and I would like to thank you for the warm hospitality you've shown us as we've walked through your beautiful town. Although you might not realize it, you have the opportunity to make history on November 3. For on that date, the men of Montana have the opportunity to enfranchise the women of this state.

"You will be joining the company of esteemed states such as Wyoming, Utah, Colorado, California and Washington. You will grant for women what no state east of the Mississippi has granted. As you know, those easterners like to say they are progressive, but their actions have proven otherwise."

The men laughed at that, hearing a hint of Massachusetts in her voice.

Clarissa smiled and laughed with them. "Now I know many of you may wonder what a woman would do with a vote. Well, she'll do much the same as you. Enter a booth and practice her rights as a member of this country. As a full citizen.

"Just as you do, she will determine what issues are important to her. She will listen to the candidates as they campaign, deciding the merits of their arguments. Just as you are concerned about safety at the mill, she may promote causes such as food safety or care of infants. Causes that affect her family's health." She continued on in that vein for a few more minutes. "Vote for women in November!" Clarissa raised her hand in triumph as she finished.

Clarissa blushed as the men hooted, hollered and whistled at the end of her speech. Savannah and Zylphia giggled and they moved off of the miniscule stage.

Sebastian pulled out his fiddle; others joined him with a banjo, guitar and another fiddle, and the music began. Before Clarissa had a chance to speak with Zylphia or Sav, she was grabbed by one of the men and spun into a lively dance. She shrieked, then laughed as she twirled around the dance floor in the arms of a tall lumberjack.

Clarissa looked to see Zee, Sav and Amelia dancing and laughing as they enjoyed the evening. They spent the entire evening dancing, barely taking a moment to rest. Clarissa felt her concerns about the upcoming election fade as she danced with a different man each time. Finally she held up a hand, out of breath and on the verge of falling over. "Enough," she gasped. "I need a glass of water and a break."

She glanced around the room to see Amelia standing near Sebastian, pausing from his fiddle playing. Savannah was approaching them, and Clarissa went to join them too. "I don't think I've ever danced as much as tonight," she said.

"It's glorious," Zylphia said before she laughed as she was again led onto the dance floor.

"There aren't many womenfolk here, and the men appreciate any chance they can find for dancing," Sebastian said.

"They appreciate any chance they can find for holding a woman in their arms," Amelia retorted, earning a snicker from Sebastian and stifled giggles from Savannah and Clarissa.

"I appreciate their welcoming us," Savannah said. She shook her head at a man who approached her. She smiled apologetically. "I'd think any woman who came here would be hard-pressed to remain single."

"Well, they can," Seb said. "A woman can choose what she wants. The men are respectful in that way, as long as they haven't had too much to drink. But, if she encourages him, she better know what she's doing." Sebastian winked at Clarissa as she smiled at him. "That cousin of yours should be careful."

"Oh, I think Zee can manage well enough," Clarissa said as she watched Zylphia flirting with one man after another, never encouraging one more than the next. Clarissa hadn't seen Zylphia this carefree and youthful since her arrival. "I must write Delia about tonight. She'd like knowing how much Zylphia enjoyed herself."

CHAPTER THIRTY-SIX

G abriel watched the peaceful procession down Main Street in Helena, sharing a relieved smile with Jeremy. "I'm thankful this is nothing like the one last year in Washington, DC."

Jeremy nodded. "I hated disappointing Sav and Rissa by refusing to march here, but I didn't want to be far from them, in case they needed us this time, too."

"I know Rissa understood," Gabriel said, battling a frown. "Besides, she's the one who gave us the choice of either marching at the rear or awaiting their arrival at the finish. She denied us the option of walking through the crowd as they marched to ensure they remained safe." He grunted as he hefted Billy over his head and onto his shoulders, hooking one leg on either shoulder, so Billy could see better.

"You can't blame her for wanting to believe that this parade would be peaceful," Jeremy said. He smiled as his brother bit back a growl of displeasure. "And I don't blame you for wanting to make sure no harm came to her or any of the marchers."

Gabriel and Jeremy waited for the marchers at the end of the parade. They waved the homemade flags their children had made for them, cheering loudly when they saw Clarissa, Melinda, Amelia and the collective assortment of their children. Gabriel beamed at Clarissa as she walked toward him, grasping her to him for a hug with one arm, the other on Billy's legs to keep him balanced. "Well done, love," he murmured into her ear.

"Thank you," she whispered, her eyes shining with pride and love. She ran a hand over his cheek as she backed away before smiling up at Billy. "Billy, darling, how are you?"

"I'm with Daddy. I'm his best boy," he said with pride as he squirmed in place.

"You are," Clarissa whispered, running a hand down his legs hanging off Gabriel's shoulders. They turned to watch as Zylphia, dressed in black, finish her march, the lone representative of Massachusetts.

"I hate that I had to wear black," she grumbled when she joined them.

"Well, until you get the vote, it's a powerful visual," Jeremy said, with a wink to his disgruntled cousin.

Amelia laughed. "I imagine, for an artist, it's rather disturbing to wear such stark clothes."

Zylphia smiled her agreement.

"Come. Aren't we supposed to continue to the auditorium to hear that lady speak?" Gabriel asked, grabbing Myrtle's hand. Billy chortled with glee as they walked, holding on to his father's broad shoulders as he rocked to and fro with each step. Clarissa walked arm in arm with Geraldine, while Savannah, Jeremy and Melinda walked in front of them. Amelia, Zylphia, and Amelia's children walked behind them.

"Yes, we're to hear Anna Howard Shaw," Zylphia grumbled. At Savannah's raised eyebrow, Zylphia sighed. "I know. I should be pleased to hear anyone from the National speak."

"Just because it isn't Alice ..." Clarissa murmured.

Zylphia nodded, still somewhat despondent. They entered the large reception hall, festooned with red, white and blue ribbons, plus a bright yellow banner strung along the podium.

They found seats in the middle of the crowd where they could all sit together as a group, taking up two rows of chairs. Zylphia sat between Clarissa and Savannah, and she whispered, "I'm certain you put me here to ensure I behaved."

Clarissa chuckled her agreement while Savannah merely grinned.

The speakers began. First Jeannette Rankin was introduced, to loud applause. She spoke for a few minutes on the day's successful march and the continued need for vigilance as the campaign entered its final month. She then introduced Dr. Anna Howard Shaw.

Zylphia squirmed in her chair as she listened to the speakers. She grunted her agreement as Dr. Shaw said, "They call us clinging vines, and they tell us to let the sturdy oaks take care of the politics. But I have noticed in the forests that each sturdy oak with a clinging vine is a little withered at the top."

Zylphia joined in the applause. She leaned over to whisper to Clarissa. "I wish I could hear her and the others argue. It must be something to behold."

"You'd never just observe, Zee. You'd jump right in and join them," Gabriel said with a fond smile to his cousin.

The children behaved throughout the speeches, the promise of wandering the fair and eating cotton candy an inducement to not fidget. Once the speeches were over, and Zylphia realized she'd be unsuccessful in speaking with Miss Rankin, they departed the hall and walked to the expositions at the fair.

Each child received a small portion of cotton candy. After they devoured it, turning their mouths pink, they wandered into the livestock barn. Gabriel grabbed Billy's arm as he attempted to scamper away and pet a steer. "No, Billy boy," Gabriel said with a laugh.

He hauled him up again, carrying him on his shoulders. He lowered him to pet a sheep but kept a tight hold on him. He shared an amused smile with Clarissa. He saw Melinda laugh as a sow pig came forward and stuck out her snout, intent to eat the lace at the hem of her skirts. She scampered away, shrieking with delight.

When the children tired, their group left the pavilion for the hotel. Clarissa leaned into Gabriel's arm a moment, Myrtle's hand in hers. "I can't believe it's already over and that we return home tomorrow."

"As Miss Rankin said, now's the time to buckle down and really focus on your canvassing," Gabriel said.

"It may mean I'm away from home quite a bit." Clarissa eyed Gabe for his response.

"I understand. I know how important this is for you. Jer, Col and I will survive. Hopefully Araminta and Charlotte will remain to help us. If not, we'll cook. I still remember how from the days before I met you."

"Thank you, darling," she whispered.

He kissed the side of her head. "I want you to know you've done everything possible for success. To never doubt that there was one more thing you could have done. Then, no matter what happens, you know you did what you could."

***

Patrick sipped a cup of coffee at the kitchen table before he headed to work. He smiled at Fiona as he read a letter from Colin. He chuckled. "Only Colin would have problems with a woman he's known for over ten years."

"What do you mean?" Fiona asked, coming to sit across from him, her pregnancy showing with a slight curve of her belly behind the apron she wore over her housedress.

"Somehow he offended Araminta, and she'll no longer speak with him. He says that she threatened to stop cleaning his house altogether if he keeps pestering her about what he did wrong." Patrick sighed. "I always thought they would end up together."

"They might yet," Fiona said. "Although pestering her isn't any way to show a woman he cares."

Patrick shrugged his agreement as he thought about his brother's predicament. He reached across the table and gripped Fiona's hand, considering it a success when she didn't flinch or fight his touch. "Something doesn't seem right, but I'm sure it will straighten itself out."

He released her hand and rose, carrying his dishes to the sink. "Clarissa, Sav and Zee marched in the women's parade at the State Fair a few days ago. They seemed excited to hear one of the leaders of the national movement speak."

"I wish we could have gone," Fiona whispered. She placed a hand over her lower belly. "I know the doctor advised me I shouldn't travel and must rest, but I hate missing any chance to spend more time with your family. I would like to know your sister better."

"You'll have plenty of time to become acquainted with Rissa. Once you have the baby, they'll be here all the time, offering more advice than you could imagine." He shared a rueful smile with her. "At least that's what she threatens."

When Fee remained silent, he squeezed her shoulder. "Besides, with how tense things are at work right now, I couldn't ask for any time away."

She lifted the newspaper, a sensational headline about the upcoming trial of Butte's mayor and sheriff along the top, proclaiming both officials had colluded to destroy the Miners' Hall. "Do you believe this?"

"It's nonsense. Anyone who was near the Miners' Hall that night knew that the mayor and sheriff had nothing to do with its destruction. However, Amalgamated hates that those two are Socialists, so the Company will do anything in their power to rid them of their presence, and power, here. They can't stand that the mayor's the only official in Butte to have been freely elected by the populace twice, even with all the money the Company spent to prevent his reelection." He sat again, drumming his fingers on the tabletop. "I never realized one company could wield so much power."

"They're like the British, running everything," Fiona said, her gaze wistful.

Patrick recognized that look. She was thinking of her homeland, Ireland.

"The Company wanted to ensure they ruled supreme," Fiona continued, "so they had the governor declare martial law here. They had no reason to remove the mayor, so they invented a law!" Fiona pursed her lips. "Makes me wish there was something to do to protest them."

Patrick gripped her hand, staring at her fiercely. He battled a mixture of fear for her safety and relief that she felt safe enough with him to want to act out against the tyranny they lived under. "You know as well as I do what living under martial law means. Don't say or do anything inflammatory. Please, Fee." When she remained defiant, he whispered, "People are disappearing, Fee. Not many but enough. I hear things at work, and I couldn't bear it if anything happened to you."

She nodded, her shoulders stooping. "I won't. I promise. I just hate that there's nothing we can do."

"I know. But I'm sure they'll leave soon. There's no reason for them to stay as we aren't a riotous group."

"I hate that you still work there, with him," she said, refusing to say his name.

He nodded "I'm working as much as I can on my portfolio and hopefully someone will take a chance on me soon as an architect. I have to be able to provide for you and the baby, Fee." He caressed her hand on the table. "And I refuse to live entirely off my family's charity by moving to Missoula without work. It was hard enough accepting this house from Sav."

She sighed. "You know I understand. I just wish I could escape this place sometimes."

He leaned forward and stroked her cheek. "No matter where we live, you'll have to find a way to make peace with the memories."

She met his somber gaze, blinking once to acknowledge her agreement.

He leaned forward and gave her a kiss as he rose to leave for work. "Remember, don't let anyone in but your sister or cousin."

She nodded her agreement. "You know as well as I that Henry isn't interested in me any longer."

"I don't," Patrick said, gripping her shoulder. "I fear he's merely biding his time. I need to know you'll stay safe here, Fee. You and the baby." He kissed her forehead again. "I'll stop by the library on my way home and pick up more books for you."

She reached out a hand, caressing a hand down his arm. "Thank you, Patrick."

***

A few days later Zylphia sat, sipping a cup of coffee at Clarissa's kitchen table in Missoula, and watched Araminta expertly roll out a pie crust. "I should really learn how to make a pie from you."

"It's not that hard," Araminta said as she lifted the crust into a pie plate and crimped the edges of the crust. "I could teach you in a few hours." She frowned when she saw Zylphia's distracted nod of agreement.

Clarissa entered the kitchen, smiling when she saw them together. "Zee, Minta's busy making more pies, and I need to be with the children this afternoon. I promised I'd play with them in the park. Would you do me a favor and bring one of the pies that Minta's already baked to Mr. Pickens?" Clarissa moved toward the cooling pies and picked up the heaviest one. "This looks delicious."

"I'd think you'd give the smaller one to a single man," Zylphia said.

"Mr. A.J. always has friends over. And he'd rather eat pie than anything else. So I ensure he has a pie at least once a week. These are his favorite. Apple with plenty of sugar and spice." She placed the pie in a small basket with a lid and pushed it across the table toward Zylphia.

"I could use some time outside," Zylphia said as she gripped the handle of the basket with one hand, her hat with the other and exited the kitchen door. She smiled at Clarissa as she shut the door behind her and turned down the small path beside the house. The dahlias at either side were in full bloom.

She looped the basket through one arm, lifting her face to the warmth of the late-afternoon sun for a moment before obscuring her face with her hat. She walked the short distance to Mr. Pickens's home, smiling at the few people she recognized.

She knocked on his door and leaned forward, listening for his distinctive shuffling gate as he approached the door. She heard guffaws, chairs moving and numerous voices speaking while she waited for him to answer her knock.

"Oh, it's you, ZeeZee." He beamed his toothless grin, waving her inside.

She reached out a hand, grabbing him as he teetered to one side to prevent him from falling to the floor.

"I'm not as steady on my feet today," he said with his accordionlike laugh. He used his cane but also gripped other pieces of furniture in the room as he walked, needing support on both sides for each step. "The Wandering Wastrels were just leaving," he said as she noted his friends sitting in his haphazard assortment of chairs.

"Hello, Mr. Amos, Mr. Goudy," Zylphia said with a nod. She placed her basket on a table in the kitchen area but refrained from extracting the pie.

"That smells like a fresh baked apple pie with plenty of spice," Mr. Goudy said as he raised his nose to sniff the air.

"Yer like a bloodhound, *Gouty*." A.J. collapsed onto the comfortable wooden chair Gabriel had made him years ago, topped with a cushion provided by Rissa. "I ain't sharin' my pie with the likes of ye this week. Not after ye bled me at poker."

"I'd say it's your own fault for playing with two card sharks," Zylphia said as she settled on a vacant chair between Mr. Pickens and Mr. Amos.

"Don't ye be takin' their side," he said, his eyes filled with mischief and glee.

"Ah, we should be going," Mr. Amos said as he tapped A.J. on his shoulder. "See you at our regular time at Gabriel's tomorrow."

Mr. Pickens tapped his cane on the floor in agreement. "Don't let those winnin's go to yer gizzard. I plan on winnin' 'em back next time!" He smiled as his friends closed the door behind them. "I haven't seen ye in too long, my ZeeZee."

Zylphia smiled at his nickname for her.

"It's as though ye've been avoidin' this ol' buzzard."

She flushed and looked away from his penetrating gaze.

"Ah, I see I'm right. What's happened to cause ye to lose yer youthful blush?" When she rose to extract the pie from its basket and remained silent, A.J. squinted at her. "I bet it has to do with a young man." He thumped his cane. "A senseless clod, if ye've lost yer bloom over 'im."

Zylphia set down the pie with a *thunk*, causing A.J. to grimace. "Don't damage my pie just 'cause yer out 'o sorts, ZeeZee."

"Would you like a piece, Mr. A.J.?" She was already cutting into the pie, ready with a plate and a fork for Mr. A. J.

"I've never been so simple-minded as to turn down a piece o' pie. 'Specially one made by Minta." He sighed with contentment when he held his piece and sniffed all the spices. "She always makes mine extra spicy an' sweet." He speared Zylphia with an intense stare. "Now, while I'm eatin' my pie, you sit an' tell me what's got yer gander up."

Zylphia sat next to him again, her eyes filling with tears. "I didn't come to Montana solely to fight for women's votes."

When she paused a long time, A.J. grunted. "No, ye were runnin' away. Somethin' the ladies of yer family like to do. Ye lot have yet to learn it's best to remain an' face what's comin'."

Zylphia glared at him. "For the record, I'm Gabriel's cousin, not Clarissa's or Savannah's."

"Coulda fooled me by how ye act," he said around a mouthful of pie. He waved his fork at her as though directing her to get on with her story.

"I pushed away the man I love, and he traveled to England to be with his ill grandfather. I never had the opportunity to tell him that I'd been a fool. That what I'd said was said in fear."

A.J. tapped his fork against his half-empty plate. "He must've been one mad young man to flee from ye." He squinted at her. "Or ye've yet to learn to control yer temper an' mouth."

"My mother always said my rash words would come back to haunt me." She gasped as she swallowed a sob. "They have."

"So ye love the man. Tell him."

Zylphia bent over and wept. She spoke through her tears, swiping at her cheeks. "He's fighting in the war. We've begun to write each other again, now that he's fighting. He's in danger, and there's nothing I can do."

Mr. A.J. reached out a shaky hand to stroke her head. "Ah, it's like that then? Has he come to his senses, now he's afeared he'll meet his maker?"

Zylphia nodded and sniffled.

"Have ye written him? Told him ye forgive him?" He watched her with worried eyes. "For ye must, even if yer still angry with 'im. Ye don't want that regret should somethin' happen."

"I have. I've written him that I love him and want to be with him." She bit her trembling lip as she fought tears. "But I'm so angry."

"At what, ZeeZee?" He reached out a gnarled hand, patting her head and cheek in an awkward yet comforting caress.

"I wrote him, more times than I can count, when we were both still in Boston. I begged him in those letters to give me a chance to explain. And he never read any of them." She firmed her jaw as she flushed with anger as her words came out stilted. "If he'd simply read one letter—*one*—before leaving, he would be safe in Boston. Not in some field fighting in France."

"We all make mistakes. Ye must forgive him." Mr. A.J. patted her hand on the table. "An' yerself. For if ye hadn't pushed him away, ye wouldn't have needed a letter."

"It's all my fault if he dies," Zylphia whispered.

"That's *prepostosense*."

Zylphia shook her head as she thought through his word. *"Preposterous?"* At his nod, she frowned. *"Nonsense?"*

"Exactly," he beamed. "You're getting better an' better at understandin' my way o' talkin'." He sobered. "And it is *prepostosense.*" He waved his hand around to indicate the two words. "Ye've nothin' to do with causin' a war. An' ye have nothin' to do with forcin' that man to join the army."

"He says it was a matter of honor," she whispered.

"As it always is during a time o' war," Mr. A.J. said, his gaze distant. "Write yer young man and dream o' him. But he won't come back the same

CHAPTER THIRTY-SEVEN

October 2, 1914

My Darling Zee,

You will never know what joy your letter has brought me. I live, each moment, knowing that the next I might be separated from you forever, and that has truly taught me to fear. In truth, it's no different than when I lived in Boston, for, at any moment, some tragedy could have befallen us. I think seing man's ability to craft such destruction in war has made me more aware of our fleeting time together.

And it is time I want with you, Zee. I want to hold you. Just hold you. To be warmed by you. To breathe in the soft scent of jasmine in your hair. To kiss your paint-stained fingers and know you'd had as good a day creating art as I'd had at my inventions. To know that there's nowhere you'd rather be than with me.

Your letter is next to my heart, as it's been since I opened it. I no longer need to read it, having memorized it weeks ago. I miss you, Zee. More than you'll ever comprehend.

Your Teddy

***

"Have you had any news from Teddy?" Clarissa asked as they walked along the streets of Hamilton.

She, Savannah and Zylphia had traveled throughout the Bitter Root Valley during the past few weeks to champion the upcoming vote for women. They paused for a moment on a corner of Main Street, as Zylphia scrawled "Votes for Women! Vote Yes November 3!" in chalk on the wooden boardwalk.

Clarissa smiled at a man who frowned and appeared on the verge of spitting a large wad of chewing tobacco next to Zylphia. He continued to frown but refrained from any expectorations and walked on down the boardwalk.

"The last letter I received," Zylphia said with a slight huff as Clarissa helped heave her upright, "was a few days ago. He seemed to be doing all right, although, reading between the blackout lines, he was a bit dispirited."

"Why?" Savannah asked as she handed out a pamphlet to an inquisitive woman walking with her husband and son. Savannah stopped to speak with them for a few minutes before rejoining her group.

By now they were used to interrupted conversations and continued as though Savannah had just asked her question.

"I'm not certain, but I think they'd hoped to make more progress. From what everyone had said, this would be a short conflict, but Teddy's letters give me the impression he doesn't think so."

"He would know better than anything we're reading in the papers here," Clarissa said as they approached their hotel. They trudged up the stairs, entering their rooms to collapse onto their cotlike beds.

"I'd think with a fortune like yours we'd be able to afford more comfortable accommodations," Clarissa groused, her foot nudging Savannah's.

Savannah let out a breathy sigh. "I'm so tired I could sleep on a block of cement. Who would have thought traveling around canvassing for votes would be this exhausting?"

"I wish someone would bring us our supper," Zylphia moaned as she stretched out on her bed.

Clarissa laughed. "Only we would think of such a thing! Oh, but it feels good to relax for a few moments."

All three women groaned at an insistent tapping on their door. After a moment Zylphia moaned and rose. "I know. I'm the youngest and closest. But you two owe me." She wrenched open the door and attempted a sweet smile for the young man. "Thank you kindly," she said as she closed the door.

Clarissa leaned on one elbow while Savannah peered from her prostrate position on her bed. "Well?"

"A telegram for you." Zylphia held it out to Clarissa.

Any lassitude disappeared with those words. Clarissa sat upright, while Savannah rolled onto her side, her head propped on her hand, as Clarissa ripped open the telegram. After she read it, her lips moved as though trying to speak, and she became flushed and then pale.

"Rissa?" Savannah was at her side in an instant. She gripped the telegram, easing it from her cousin's tight grip. "Read it," she commanded Zylphia as she took Clarissa in her arms. "Whatever it is, Rissa, it'll be all right." She looked up questioningly to Zylphia.

"Mr. Pickens is dying." Her eyes filled with tears. "Gabriel says to hurry."

Savannah held a shaking Clarissa to her as Savannah nodded to Zylphia. "Right. We must leave. Zee, go to the garage. Agree to pay whatever you must, but make sure they fix the car now."

"I'll be back soon," Zylphia said as she squeezed Clarissa's shoulder and then raced from the room. They could hear Zylphia's boot heels as they clattered down the stairs.

Clarissa shook as she curled into Savannah's embrace. "I know it's ridiculous to be this upset. He's an old man who's been sickly for years."

"He's as a grandfather to you. You love him," Savannah soothed. "There's nothing silly about it."

"He's helped me through every major, and minor"—Clarissa half laughed—"crisis I've had since I arrived here in Montana. I don't know how I'll go on without him."

"You know we'll all help you through this."

Clarissa pushed herself away, rising and throwing her traveling case on the bed. "I know you will, but some griefs are so deep." She paused as a sob struck. She turned away for a moment before approaching her things in a small chest of drawers, placing those few items inside her bag. Savannah rose and hastily packed for herself and Zylphia, working in a companionable silence.

When they'd packed their bags, they sat, staring at each other. "How long do you think it will take to fix the car?" Clarissa asked.

"I don't know." Savannah's expression darkened. "I hope they have the part they needed."

"I can't spend another night here. He could die before morning. He can't die before I see him again." Clarissa's voice emerged in a near pant, as though on the verge of hyperventilating from her agitation.

Zylphia returned, breathless, a few moments later. "The automobile is out front. They'd just finished with it at the garage. I paid the hotel bill downstairs as well, so we're ready. It will be dark soon, and it's a long drive, but we have plenty of fuel."

"Thank God you purchased the automobile this spring," Clarissa said to Savannah as they grabbed their bags and rushed down the stairs.

"Thank goodness they fixed it today," Savannah said.

They nodded to the man working the front desk and bustled out the front door to their car. They heaved their bags to one side of the backseat, and then Zylphia climbed in the free space there. Savannah settled in to drive, while Clarissa paused, glancing at the mountains Mr. A.J. so loved for a moment. A canyon with tall granite peaks glinted in the late-evening sun.

"Mr. Pickens loved these mountains," Clarissa murmured. She shook her head to clear it from her reverie and heaved herself into the car, slamming the door shut behind her.

Savannah eased the car into motion, beginning their journey to Missoula.

During the long car ride, little was spoken. Clarissa's thoughts were flooded with memories of Mr. Pickens. His impatience mixed with caring when she acted foolishly. His glee as he told a story about the olden days. His joy and sorrow when he spoke of his late wife, Bessie. Clarissa broke the tense silence. "I don't know what I'll do without him."

Savannah nodded her agreement. "I know, Rissa. He's important to all of us, but to you most of all."

Savannah had barely parked the car before Clarissa leapt from it and raced into her house. She banged the door open, startling Gabriel who stood at the fireplace. He spun to face her before moving toward her in a few strides to pull her into a tight embrace.

"No," Clarissa gasped. "Don't tell me that I'm too late."

"You're not, love," he whispered against her ear. "I needed to hold you." He backed away a step, and she noticed his eyes were tear-brightened. "He's upstairs. When I realized how ill he was, I couldn't fathom him all alone in his rooms. He agreed to come here, and Araminta's been sitting with him the past half hour. We've been taking turns." He rubbed at his eyes. "I should've known he was more ill than he was letting on, but I didn't. Otherwise he never would have agreed to leave his home."

Clarissa stroked a hand over Gabriel's stubbled cheeks before racing upstairs. She peeked into her bedroom to see her children altogether in the one large bed, sound asleep. She moved to Billy's room, to find Mr. A.J. in Billy's bed. She placed a hand on Araminta's shoulder as she sat on a chair by his bed. She nodded and rose, leaving silently.

"Mr. A.J.," Clarissa whispered as she fell to her knees by his bed.

"None of this, Missy." He coughed a rattling noise. "Ye knew I couldn't live forever." He raised a shaky hand, his skin splotched with purple age spots and thinned by the passage of time. Gnarled fingers reached out to trace away her tears, his fingertips nearly as downy soft as a baby's newborn skin.

"I—" Her voice broke before she could say anything further.

"I know, Missy. I love ye too. Ye were the granddaughter I never had. I gave thanks every day after ye walked into that depository all those years ago. I just wish my Bessie coulda met ye."

"Mr. A.J." Clarissa bit back a sob. "You were the grandfather I'd always wanted to have. Kind, funny and yet giving me a kick in the skirts when I needed one."

"Darn straight." His breathing became incrementally more labored. "I always knew when my Missy was troubled. And when ye were overthinkin' a problem." He speared her with eyes still lit with a fine intelligence born of a life well lived.

"Ye and that man o' yers are gonna have to find a way to yer own solutions now, Missy."

She sniffled out a giggle. "I'll have to imagine to myself what you'd say to me and then do it."

"Shouldn't be too hard," he gasped out.

"No, you always recommended less fighting and more time spent canoodling."

"Darn straight," he whispered, his voice failing.

She held on to his hand as his eyes fluttered close. "Mr. A.J."

"Don't fret, Missy. I'll always be with ye," he breathed out. He gripped her hand and closed his eyes. His chest continued to rise and fall, although he didn't speak with her further.

She lowered her head to the bed and cried, only calming when she felt warmth at her back. "Gabe?"

"I'm here, love," he murmured, kissing her nape. "I needed to be here too." He placed his hand over hers, holding Mr. A.J.'s, and together they kept a silent vigil by his bedside. Eventually she leaned into Gabriel, crying silent tears against his collar as Mr. Pickens's breathing became increasingly labored.

She shuddered as she realized his time was nearing and reached forward to stroke a hand over Mr. A.J.'s forehead, his cheeks. She whispered, "I love you, Mr. A.J.," and then, with one last deep exhalation, he was gone.

"No, no, no," she moaned against the edge of the bed, her body shaking with her sobs.

"Clarissa, love," Gabriel said, his voice as tentative as the hand he stroked over her shoulders and back.

She continued bent over the bed as though alone with her grief, and he stiffened, moving to leave her alone. She reached back, gripping his thigh. "No, Gabriel. No." She spun and flung herself into his chest. "Hold me. Help me to bear this pain."

He settled on the floor, pulling her onto his lap, cradling her. He whispered endearments, stroked his hands over her back and through her hair until it hung in disorderly strands down her back, and he shivered with relief as she clung to him like a burr.

Only as she settled did Clarissa realize that Gabriel's cheeks were wet. She traced her fingertips over his face and met his reddened eyes. "Darling?"

"I loved him too," he said in a grief-ladened voice. "He always knew what to say to ensure I'd find my way back to you."

"Oh, my darling." She leaned forward to kiss his cheeks, brushing the hair off his forehead before resting her forehead against his chest.

"And I realized, as I held you just now, this is what we missed by not mourning Rory together. And I'm sorrier than I can say." His voice emerged roughened from his attempt to quell his tears.

Clarissa sighed, stuttering out her agreement. After a moment she shuddered and choked back a sob. "I hate the thought of telling the children in the morning."

"I do too." He kissed her forehead. "For now we need to tell those awaiting us downstairs." He stood, reaching a hand down to help her to her feet.

She leaned against him for a moment before she turned to pull the covers over Mr. Pickens. He appeared to have fallen asleep.

After a deep breath, she turned, grasped Gabriel's hand and moved with him to the hallway and then downstairs. When they entered the living room, they found Araminta asleep, curled in an armchair, and Zylphia and Savannah huddled together on the sofa. Gabriel walked toward the fireplace, and his quiet movement was enough to wake them.

Zylphia sat bolt up while Araminta tilted her head, her sleepy eyes immediately focusing on Gabriel and then Clarissa. Savannah yawned and stretched, her gaze alert after her short sleep. Zylphia reached out a hand to Clarissa and tugged her down between her and Savannah. "Rissa?"

Tears ran down her cheeks, and Zylphia pulled her into her arms while Savannah stroked her back. "I'm so sorry," they both whispered.

"You were in time," Araminta soothed. "He was waiting for you."

"I am so thankful for that. I don't know what I'll do without him," Clarissa whispered, swiping at her tears. "He was …"

"An ornery old goat who loved to meddle," Gabriel said with deep affection in his voice. "Somehow he always said or did the right thing to help those he cared about."

"I didn't know him long, but he was very supportive," Zylphia said.

"I'll miss how he spoke. Melly loved figuring out his words and then using them when she talked," Savannah said. She tapped Zee on a knee. "Come. We should head home for the night."

Araminta rose with them, and the three women left after exchanging long hugs with Clarissa. She stood, swaying in place for a moment, lost in her memories. She started when Gabriel touched her shoulder before leaning into his chest. He laid his cheek on her head, his hands lazily tracing her back.

"Thank you for the telegram."

"I imagine it terrified you," Gabriel murmured. "You've always hated them. Ever since you received the one about your father's death."

"It did. But I couldn't have missed being here," Clarissa whispered, leaning farther into him.

His arms tightened around her, accepting her sorrow. "Cry, love," he urged. He held her through her tears, eventually leading her upstairs, to their daughter's bedroom. He laid her on the small bed and rested with her until she fell into a deep slumber. When she was asleep, he eased away from her and tiptoed to Billy's room.

He sat with Mr. Pickens through the long night. "I haven't kept vigil since my good friend Liam died in Butte. I'd hoped not to need to do so for some time again." He swiped away a tear and pulled out his handkerchief to rub at his nose.

"I'll miss you, Old Man. You had a way of helping me see the truth, even when I didn't want to. You eased my Clarissa's torment, more times than I can count." He stared at the lifeless form on his son's bed, unable to quell the tears that poured from his eyes.

"You were faithful, honest and knew what was important in life. Family. Friends. Forging memories together. Thank you for enriching our lives," Gabriel whispered.

He continued to speak, on and off, for the rest of the night. He recalled his wedding night, when A.J. had chivareed him with a group of local men. Gabe recounted the stories he'd heard, of A.J.'s travels to Montana from St. Louis, of the night he'd met Mark Twain, of the time he'd been trapped in a tree by an irate moose. Gabe remembered A.J.'s deep and abiding love for his wife, Bessie.

Finally the room lightened with the dawning of a new day. He yawned, groaning with appreciation as Clarissa crept in and massaged his shoulders.

"Have you been here all night?" she whispered.

"Yes. I thought someone should keep vigil until dawn," Gabriel said. He raised a hand, gripping hers loosely placed on his shoulder.

"Thank you, darling," Clarissa whispered, wrapping her arms around his chest and hugging him from behind.

Jeremy eased into the room, carrying cups of coffee. "I made some downstairs before coming up," he said, handing one to each of them. "I know you prefer tea, but I think a day like today calls for coffee." He looked to the bed, closing his eyes for a moment as though in prayer. "I'll miss him," he whispered.

He pushed on Gabriel's shoulder, urging him to rise. "You've kept vigil all night. You'll need to sleep some, wash up. I'll remain."

"Thanks, Jer," Gabriel said as he rose.

Jeremy sat, his hands folded in front of him as his gaze became distant, filled with sorrow. "I'm sorry for what you must do. Your children will be devastated. Melly was heartbroken this morning."

Gabriel gripped his brother's shoulder a moment before leaving the room.

***

Clarissa and Gabriel walked toward the new library, which had been funded by Mr. Andrew Carnegie. The two-story building sat a block off Broadway. Pillars framed the front door, while redbrick gleamed in the sunlight.

"I would think a day like today should be gray and gloomy," Clarissa muttered.

Gabriel grunted his agreement, patting her hand looped through his elbow. He opened the door for her, and she entered, moving to the right to the main part of the library. The assistance desk was there, and Hester sat behind it. As it was early in the day, few patrons had arrived.

"Hester," Clarissa said in a low voice. "I ... You might want to close the library today."

Hester looked up from a book she was reading and frowned. "The library only closes on Sundays, holidays or when natural disaster strikes."

"Yes, I know, but something's happened." Clarissa fought tears. "Mr. A.J. has died."

Hester stilled, her book falling closed as her body froze. "You must be mistaken. I saw him, not a few days ago, and he was fine."

"He put on a good show, ma'am, but he was ailing," Gabriel said. "I finally realized how sick he was yesterday and had him move to my house. He passed last night."

A strangled noise, like a stifled sob, sounded in her throat, and she turned away. "I beg your pardon."

Clarissa moved toward her, uncertain how to reach her as she sat behind a large wooden desk, and she didn't know how it opened. Gabriel grunted, hefting her and sliding her across the top so that she could slither to the ground on Hester's side of the desk. "Hester." Clarissa placed her hand on Hester's trembling shoulder.

She turned to Clarissa with tears coursing down her cheeks. "He was my only friend here."

"That's not true," Clarissa said as she pulled Hester into her arms. Clarissa shared a worried glance with Gabriel as Hester sobbed in her arms. He moved to the library door and flipped the sign to Closed. He turned the key in the lock so that bold patrons wouldn't be able to barge in unwelcomed.

"I was only invited to your gatherings because he asked me," she stuttered. "I'm sorry. He's died, and all I'm doing is thinking about myself."

"We'll still be your friends, Hester," Clarissa soothed. "The wake will be tonight and then the burial tomorrow. We wanted you to know to be able to attend."

"Thank you," she said as she nodded toward her and Gabriel. "I know you didn't have to come to tell me. You could have let me read it in the evening newspaper."

"You were his friend," Clarissa whispered. She gripped Hester's shoulder before she moved to climb over the desk again.

Hester saw Clarissa's intentions and unhooked a hidden latch, lifting the top of the desk so it swung open, allowing Clarissa to walk out.

"We'll see you tonight, Hester," Gabriel said. Clarissa slipped her arm through his as they departed.

***

Clarissa sat in a sort of dazed stupor in the living room as the wake occurred around her. Mr. Pickens was in a casket in the dining room. The food disappeared in the kitchen as fast as it was brought by concerned neighbors and friends. Kegs were in the backyard, and mourners traipsed through her house in incessant waves. Everyone in Missoula knew old A.J. and wanted to come and pay their respects.

Clarissa lifted her head at the sound of a fiddle, its tune mournful. Plaintive. She glanced around. She only knew one person who could play like that. "Seb," she whispered. She rose, looking for him. She pushed her way past mourners, nodding her thanks as those she passed expressed their condolences. She made it to the backyard to find Sebastian, standing to one side playing the fiddle.

She glanced around. "Amelia!"

Amelia turned at Clarissa's yell. She rushed toward Clarissa, and they rocked to and fro as they embraced.

"I had no idea you were coming," Clarissa whispered, swiping away tears as they stood apart.

"Gabriel sent us a telegram. When I showed it to Sebastian, he insisted we travel here for it. Mr. A.J. was always very good to us." Her eyes filled. "I'll miss him."

Clarissa gripped her arm, and they walked arm in arm to the rear part of the garden. Sebastian took a break from playing, and he enfolded Clarissa in his arms. "Rissa, I'm so sorry," he whispered before backing away and reaching for Amelia.

"Thank you for traveling all this way."

"We needed to be here," Sebastian said.

"Of course you'll stay with us."

"Thank you," Amelia said with a relieved smile.

"The children might be on pallets on the floor, but there's plenty of room." Clarissa smiled at Gabriel as he joined the group. "Seb, Amelia and the children are staying with us tonight."

"Wonderful," he said, raising her hand to kiss her knuckles. "I heard the fiddle and knew it had to be you." He sobered as he looked at Amelia and Sebastian. "The more family we have around us, the more we'll be able to bear what comes." He squeezed Clarissa's arm before moving away to speak with those who'd come to pay their respects.

***

Gabriel stood next to Colin, Sebastian and Jeremy. They rose as one, moving toward the casket and hefted it onto their shoulders to walk down the aisle of the church and to the nearby graveyard. Clarissa followed, Billy in her arms, leading the mourners behind her.

Billy sniffled, burying his face in her neck.

"It's all right, darling," Clarissa whispered. "He had a good long life."

"Don't leave me, Mama," he murmured.

Her hands tightened on him at his words, and she held him closer to her. "I don't plan to, my little man." He sighed, and she knew he wouldn't let go of her until they were away from the cemetery.

When they arrived, the men lowered the casket into the ground, and the mourners placed handfuls of dirt on top of it. Clarissa said a silent prayer of thanksgiving for all Mr. Pickens had been to her before she backed away into Gabriel's strong arms. He placed his arms around her, enfolding her and Billy in his strength. Myrtle and Geraldine came to stand in front of them, and Clarissa and Gabriel each placed one hand on a daughter's shoulder, linking them all.

"Mr. A.J. would be pleased, Rissa."

She nodded as tears streamed down her face, the priest intoning a final prayer.

CHAPTER THIRTY-EIGHT

"I hate that there's nothing more we can do," Clarissa groused. She settled against the back of her chair, a pillow clutched to her chest. A warm fire lit the hearth in Savannah's living room, while a cold November wind rattled the windows.

"There *is* nothing more to do," Savannah argued. "If there *was* something more to do, I think I'd die from exhaustion."

Zylphia snickered at her joke. She leaned against the settee, one foot curled up underneath her. "I never knew a state could be so large. And we only traversed the western part of it. If I never ride in an automobile again, I'll be content." She arched her back as though remembering the agony of the hundreds of miles they'd spent in the automobile while canvassing.

"I hate that, come tomorrow, the men decide while we once again wait to learn of our fate. It's so unfair," Clarissa said.

"Rissa, you knew this day was coming. And I'm thankful it's finally upon us. I couldn't imagine knocking on any more doors," Zylphia said.

"Just wait until next year. You have another state to conquer," Savannah teased. She rested her feet on an ottoman.

"Oh, don't remind me!" Zylphia flung herself backward against the settee, her laughter ringing out in the room.

"Any word from Teddy, Zee?" Clarissa asked.

"Nothing more than he misses me and is thankful for my letters. He writes a lot about what we did when we were together and how he dreams of a time when we are reunited. I think he's realized he can't say anything of substance or it will be blackened out." Her gaze became distant.

"Well, with that dreamy look in your eyes, whatever he said pleased you," Sav teased.

Zylphia flushed. "He'd asked me for a sketch of Montana. I sent him one of the mountains. I also sent him one of me."

"I'm sure he will be delighted to receive both of them," Clarissa said. "Although I would think it would have been easier to have your photograph taken."

"I realized as I labored over it that I was being a fool. However, I needed to send him my drawings." She blushed again. "He always encouraged my art."

"I've never met the man, but, the more you talk about him, the more I like him," Savannah said. "A man who encourages you to embrace the best parts of you is a man to love."

"They said this war would be over by Christmas. What if it isn't?" Zylphia asked.

"Then you'll face it, just like you've faced everything else," Clarissa said.

***

A few days later Zylphia entered Savannah's living room with a letter from her mother in her hand. She settled on the settee, ripped open the letter, glancing at her mother's friendly salutation before stilling. She read and reread one sentence over and over, but it failed to make sense.

At that moment, Savannah, Clarissa, Araminta and Melinda burst into the room, waving newspapers over their heads.

"It's as we suspected!" Clarissa said with a *whoop* of joy. Although still recovering from her recent loss, she was beaming. "We won!" She grabbed Zylphia and pulled her into an impromptu dance, twirling her around. Clarissa stopped abruptly when she realized she was spinning Zylphia like a rag doll.

"Zee?" Savannah asked, touching her with a gentle caress on her arm. "Aren't you happy all our hard work paid off and we won the vote for women here in Montana?"

"Of course I am," Zylphia said with a forced smile. She blinked rapidly as tears threatened. "Delighted," she gasped out as she burst into tears.

Araminta picked up the fallen letter near the settee and handed it to Clarissa. "May I read this?" Clarissa asked. Zylphia fell against her cousin as she sobbed, and Clarissa handed the letter over to Savannah to read, so Clarissa could hold Zylphia tight.

"Oh, no," Savannah murmured, raising worried blue eyes to meet Clarissa's.

"Teddy?" At Savannah's nod, Clarissa rasped, "Is he ..."

"No, he's missing. According to Delia, he's been missing for over a week." She took a deep breath. "The longer a soldier is missing, the more likely he's ..."

"Dead," Zylphia cried, her sobs intensifying.

At that moment Jeremy walked in, a beaming smile on his face. "Congratulations, my enfranchised women of Montana!" He picked up Savannah and twirled her around, frowning when she squirmed to be put down.

"Now's not the time, Jeremy." She stroked a hand over his arm to temper her harsh tone. "Zee's young man is missing in the war."

He sobered instantly and, after giving Savannah a soft squeeze, moved toward Zylphia. "Zee?" He stroked the back of her head and eased her from Clarissa's arms into his own. He held her tight as she clung to him. "*Shhh*, ... darling. Making yourself sick won't help you or Teddy."

"I can't ... I can't." She shook her head.

"I know what it's like, fearing for those I love who'd gone missing," he whispered into her ear. "I know how it tears you apart, the not knowing." He eased her away, a deep sorrow and torment rarely seen in his eyes. "If there's one thing he needs, even though he's miles away, is for you to always believe he's alive. That he'll come home to you. Until you receive the news telling you otherwise, be strong, darling Zee."

"I don't ... I don't know how," she cried burrowing into his shoulder again.

His strong, callused hand stroked over her head to impart some form of comfort. "You do, Zee. I know you do." He sighed as he kissed her head. "It's all right to cry with us now. To cry with us during the upcoming days. But always keep that hope in your heart. That he'll come back to you."

"I couldn't live without it," she whispered.

"There's my Zee. Already stronger than you knew." He held her, rocking her gently side to side as she sniffled and shook in his arms. He didn't release her until she loosened her hold on him.

"Thank you," she whispered first to Jeremy and then more loudly to all of them in the room. "I'm sorry to have ruined the celebration of what we've all been working toward."

"There's nothing more important than you than family," Savannah said as she blinked tears from her eyes. She held an arm around Melinda's waist, and Melinda turned her face into the crook of Savannah's shoulder.

"We'll help you be strong, Zee," Clarissa said.

Zylphia looked around at her extended family, realizing that Florence had been correct. Zylphia wasn't meant to journey through life alone, without the support of those who loved her. She said a prayer for Teddy, gave thanks for all she had, for her family and their welcoming embraces. For now, she planned to remain busy, celebrating the victory earned by and for Montana women. Soon, she'd travel home to Boston to her mother and father and Sophie and her friends, and begin the fight for the vote in Massachusetts ... as she kept hope in her heart and awaited further news about Teddy.

AUTHOR'S NOTES

Thank you for reading *Tenacious Love*. Never fear, dear reader, I'm already busy at work on the fifth book in the series. I hope you will continue to join me on their journey.

Would you like to know more about behind the scenes, insider scoop of my writing process? Would you like to receive special bonuses not available to everyone? Would you like to know first when my next book is available? You can sign up for my new release e-mail list, where you'll be the first to know of updates and special giveaways at http://www.ramonaflightner.com/newsletter/

Like my Facebook page for frequent updates: http://facebook.com/authorramonaflightner

Reviews help other readers find books. I appreciate all reviews. Please consider reviewing on the retailer you purchased the book, at Goodreads or both.

Most people learn about books by recommendations from their friends. Please, share *Tenaciuos Love* with a friend!

HISTORICAL NOTES

As you can imagine, there is a lot of research required for each novel. In *Tenacious*, I took the liberty of altering a few things so that my characters would be present during events.

For example:
--During the march in Washington, DC, Alice Paul and Lucy Burns did arrive in cars and help clear the way for some of the women marchers. However, it was for the women at the front of the parade.

--I know of speeches and events at Marble House in Newport in the summer of 1914, but Zylphia was there in 1913. Alva Vanderbilt Belmont was an ardent supporter of the suffrage movement, thus there most likely was some sort of function there in 1913.

--The Miner's Union Hall was blown up in June 1914 in Butte, over 20 sticks of dynamite was used and wasn't successfully destroyed until the middle of the night/ morning.

As you can see, these and other subtle changes, allowed the McLeods and Sullivans to be involved in all of the important events of the times!